PRA...

"Touching...surprisingly poignant.. builds to an emotional crescendo...The book becomes so engrossing that it's tough to see it end."
—*The Washington Post*

"A beautiful, witty story that rings with heartbreak, hope and laughter...Kring's brilliance lies in her powerful reversals and revelations, taking readers and characters on a dramatic, emotional roller coaster."
—*Publishers Weekly* (starred review)

"Sandra Kring weaves an intricate and heartwarming tale of family, lo... ...iscent of ... ...a laugh, ...friends, ...*Review*

...of fam... ...ers the ...*Book* st

...vestern ...unpre- —*Salon*

...inning ...laugh- ...*Times* ...ginners

ALSO BY SANDRA KRING

Carry Me Home
The Book of Bright Ideas
Thank You for All Things

How High
the Moon

How High
the Moon

A Novel

Sandra Kring

BANTAM BOOKS TRADE PAPERBACKS ❧ NEW YORK

A Bantam Books Trade Paperback Original

Copyright © 2010 by Sandra Kring

Published in the United States by Bantam Books,
an imprint of The Random House Publishing Group,
a division of Random House, Inc., New York.

BANTAM BOOKS and the rooster colophon are
registered trademarks of Random House, Inc.

LIBRARY OF CONGRESS CATALOGING-IN-PUBLICATION DATA
Kring, Sandra.
How high the moon: a novel / Sandra Kring.
p. cm.
ISBN 978-0-385-34121-9
1. Female friendship—Fiction.   2. Actresses—Fiction.   3. Wisconsin—Fiction.
I. Title.
PS3611.R545H69   2010   813'.6—dc22   2009052878

Printed in the United States of America

www.bantamdell.com

2 4 6 8 9 7 5 3 1

Book design by Diane Hobbing

For Brenda Larson ... and everyone else who has stood before a bathroom mirror, singing into the end of a hairbrush like a rock star

How High
the Moon

PROLOGUE

I lost my first tooth when I was six years old. Well, *lost* isn't exactly the right word, since it's not like it just plopped into my chicken noodle soup out of the blue, or fell out when I sneezed. In truth, it got yanked out of my head by Teddy, who didn't know what to do with a wobbly baby tooth that hurt when you bit down, so he asked some guy at work.

It took Teddy three songs on the radio to finally get the string wrapped around my tooth, but when he slammed the door—more like a shut than a slam—the string slipped right off. After a lot of howling by me, and pleading by Teddy, he pinched the tooth between his fingers and yanked.

I screamed bloody murder and whacked his arm so hard that my tooth went pinging across the room. So while I bawled and bled into my hand, Teddy scooted around the floor on his knees, smoothing his hands over the linoleum to find it, because I was wailing that I wanted it back. When he found it, I popped it into my mouth like I was Mr. Potato Head and my tooth was a part you could take off and put back on, take off and put back on.

Teddy took me by the hand and led me to the couch, where he sat me down beside him and tucked me under his arm. "I shouldn't have pulled it like that, Teaspoon," he said. "I'm sorry. I should know by now that there's some things in life that just hurt too much when you're forced to let go of them before you're ready."

"What things?" I asked Teddy as I sniffled, because I wanted to know what else somebody might try yanking from my head.

"Well, I guess a lot of things. Hope...love...childhood..."

"And teeth." I said, careful to keep my yanked tooth tucked up against my cheek. "You forgot teeth."

At bedtime Teddy tried to convince me to put my tooth under my pillow for the Tooth Fairy. I shook my head no, so Teddy said I didn't have to until I was ready, but that I couldn't keep it in my mouth while I slept because I might choke on it. So I hid it in a sock in my drawer in case the Tooth Fairy heard I'd lost it and decided to come snooping. I put it back in my mouth when I woke up, but after a few days, when the tooth started graying and feeling dry, like it wasn't a part of me anymore, I put it under my pillow and the Tooth Fairy left me enough money to buy a Mars Bar.

For a lot of days after I lost that tooth, I couldn't stop rubbing my tongue over the hole where it had been. I asked Teddy when I'd stop doing that because it had started getting on my nerves, and he said, "When you're used to having it gone."

I don't know why the words Teddy said that day stuck in my head like gum on hair, since most things Teddy said—or anybody else, for that matter—went right in one ear and out the other, but they did. I'm thinking about them now, as I walk toward home with Teddy, the neighborhood so quiet that I can hear the clicking of my shoes on the sidewalk while we move out from under one streetlight beam and into another, my mind rubbing over the last few months like a tongue over the hole where a baby tooth should be.

CHAPTER ONE

I was sitting at my desk, second seat back in the row by the window, staring outside watching jump ropes twirl and kids chase one another across the playground. The sounds of thumping red rubber balls and excited voices floating in through the rectangle screens were nothing but a big fat tease, though, because I couldn't go out for recess. *Again.* I had to sit at my stupid desk and twiddle my thumbs while Mrs. Carlton, my fifth-grade teacher, corrected papers and ignored me, even though I was baking like a potato in the sun.

I was supposed to be working on my English assignment, but I hadn't gotten farther than writing the date—May 13, 1955—at the top of my paper. I knew that was about all the farther I'd get, too, because I was supposed to write about Moby-Dick, and I didn't even know who the guy was. I wasn't really listening when Mrs. Carlton read us a chapter after recess for about a bajillion days in a row. I could see the book cover in my head, though, and it had a big fish on it, so I was thinking Moby-Dick might be that guy who got swallowed by a whale and became a rib bone in the story that Miss Tuckle, the Sunday school teacher, told us. But I wasn't sure because I wasn't exactly listening then, either.

"Isabella…your paper…," Mrs. Carlton said, and I turned away from the window.

"I can't concentrate with all that yelling and laughing going on outside," I told her.

"Try," she said, without looking up.

"Plus," I added, "I'm about melting to death. These windows are working like a magnifying glass. I'm not kidding. It's so hot on my arm that I think I might start on fire. That can happen, you know. Jack Jackson started a grass fire in his backyard using a magnifying glass, and Johnny, his big brother, had to put it out with a blanket. I have very dry skin, Mrs. Carlton."

She looked up at me and sighed, her lips painted big and red like Lucille Ball's, and said, "Then take a seat over there." She pointed to the first desk on the other side of the room. The one closest to the door.

Me and my big mouth!

I didn't have a thing to do but hum and think about how hungry I was. After recess we still had to have math and reading class before it was lunchtime.

I thought about the ice cream we were going to have for dessert, and the next thing I knew, my mind was scooting off to the drugstore to remember the best strawberry sundae I ever had.

I guess you could say that I got that sundae because of Ma. All because one night while I was still in kindergarten, she came and sat on my bed, the stink of smoke and booze from The Dusty Rose still clinging to her auburn curls, and she said, "I gotta go, kid. I've got dreams to chase." Then she walked out. Just like that. Leaving nothing behind but me, a sinkful of dirty dishes, a pair of elbow-length gloves still in their box, and Teddy, her boyfriend of a year, bawling on the arms of his ratty work shirt.

After Ma left, Teddy tried to help me stop missing her so badly. He was sweet as sugar at first, hugging me when I cried and playing with me when I was lonely. But when a few days went by and I still wasn't eating more than a sick mouse, he got downright bossy.

"Teaspoon, I know you miss your Ma. I do, too," Teddy said. "But you've got to start eating again, even if you don't have an appetite." He put a plate of scrambled eggs and a cup of milk in front of me and told me I *had* to get them down. "If you don't, you're going to make yourself sick."

I didn't know people could *make* themselves sick by not eating, but I sure was glad to hear it! When we were living above the bar in Peoria, Ma left me with a lady down the hall, and on the third day I got so sick that I puked on her quilt *and* her cat. She somehow got ahold of Ma and told her to come get me. So when Teddy told me I would get sick if I didn't eat, I decided that it was a good plan. I slid my plate away and crossed my arms, and said I wasn't going to eat for nothing. Teddy swayed on his feet a bit, then he planted his boots on the floor and cleared his throat and said, "Isabella Marlene, if you don't eat, I'm going to have to punish you."

Maybe it was Teddy's scrambled-egg-soft voice, or the way he couldn't set his chin when he gave an order because he didn't really have one to set in the first place, but whatever it was, his warning didn't scare me. It only grated on my nerves like a skeeto bite itch. So I crossed my arms and I said, "I hope I do get sick, because then you'll have to call my ma and she'll come and get me."

Teddy's squished-back chin quivered a little, and he put his hand on the top of my head. "Teaspoon, your Ma wouldn't even know it if you got good and sick, because I don't know where she is to tell her." He looked down at me, and there was water in his eyes. "It's just you and me now," he said. "Teaspoon and Teddy. And I'm not going to let you get sick."

My arm came up to hide my eyes when he said that, because I started crying and I didn't want Teddy to see. He hugged me to his leg and stroked my dark curls. And when my tears turned to hiccups, he took me to the drugstore and bought us both a strawberry sundae for supper. While we were there, somebody popped a quarter into the jukebox and played Teresa Brewer's "Music! Music! Music!" and just like that my toes got light enough to tap (even if all they could tap was air, since my legs were dangling off the bar stool), and I started singing along with that snappy tune:

All I want is having you, and music, music, music! Teddy didn't even tell me to stop singing because I was in public and had a mouthful. He just put another coin in the jukebox and asked me what else I wanted to hear. Course, I knew that that would be the last time Teddy'd ever let me sing at the table or with food in my mouth without harping, and so far, I was right.

"Isabella. Stop daydreaming and get to your paper," Mrs. Carlton said, not in a very friendly tone, either, and the memory of that sundae melted right off my tongue.

I picked up my pencil and poked the lead between my two front teeth as I tried to think about what to write, wishing I hadn't thought about strawberry sundaes because it made me start thinking about how sad I was when Ma left. I didn't like thinking about that, so instead I tried to think about how pretty she was. How good she could sing. How nice she smelled. I didn't have much luck, though, because the truth of the matter was, by the time I was eight years old most of the pictures of her I had in my head had dried like spilled milk nobody sopped up, and they flaked away. I had six stupid miniature plastic baby dolls to thank for that.

I got those dumb things and that little pink crib to put them in at Ben Franklin, and all I did in the days right before Ma left was sit on the floor and play with those dolls. I should have been looking at Ma instead, because after she was gone for about a year or so, when I tried to see her all I saw were those dolls—naked and pink like newborn hamsters, two blue dots for eyes painted crooked on their faces, seams running along their sides.

Sure, sometimes I tried to talk to her when her bath was done and she was sitting under that helmet drying her rollers and paging through movie magazines, but she couldn't hear me with that hair dryer whizzing in her ears, so I just went back to playing, bouncing those dolls in the plops of water Ma dropped on the floor when she stepped out of the tub because those were their mud puddles.

I let everyone believe that I still remembered Ma well—how she looked, the sound of her voice, the way her skin smelled—but the truth of the matter was, I wasn't sure I remembered her right anymore at all, because when I thought of her, her face looked suspiciously like Glinda's, the good witch from *The Wizard of Oz*. And when I thought of her singing voice, it sounded an awful lot like Teresa Brewer's. Even when I thought I was remembering her smell, I'm not sure if it was *her* smell I was remembering, or the perfume of Mrs. Fry's peonies in summer.

It didn't matter, though, I told myself. One day soon I was going to be watching a movie at the Starlight Theater and Ma was going to come on that screen and I'd take one look at her face and remember her as though I'd never forgotten her. And then I'd know that she'd be coming home to Teddy and me soon, because the way I saw it, chasing your dream was like winning a race at the last day of school picnic, and once you crossed the finish line the winner, there wasn't nothing more to do but pick a prize out of the basket and head home.

And wouldn't it be a happy day when Ma came back! For me, *and* for Teddy, who I knew missed not only *her* but his Oldsmobile, too.

Teddy didn't have the money to buy another car after Ma drove away in his, and it was too far for him to walk to work come winter and would cost him too much to take Ralph's taxi every day. So he had to quit his job with the Soo Line Railroad to take one closer to home. At the meatpacking plant over on the south side of town, Mill Town Meats, though most folks called it The Hanging Hoof. Every morning until I was eight and could get around by myself, Teddy got me out of bed, fixed me an egg, and walked me across the street to the Jacksons' to get sat on—babysat by Mrs. Jackson, or sat on by Jack for real, if he was in a scrappy mood—then Teddy hiked to work. When his shift was done, he'd pick me up, fix me some supper—usually eggs and fried potatoes, because after seeing all that blood at work, the last thing Teddy wanted was to see more of it sizzling in his fry pan—then he'd sit on the sofa and mourn the loss of the lady he loved more than electricity.

I was upset when Teddy had to stop working for the Soo Line after Ma left—upset because I thought he was the conductor, and whenever a train rattled through town while he was gone, I was sure it was Teddy blowing that whistle. Promising me that he was at work, and that he hadn't run off to chase his dream of becoming an electric man. Jack Jackson set me straight on that one, though. Telling me right in front of his brothers and sisters—all six of them with J names and heads shaped like lightbulbs—that Teddy wasn't nothing but a Soo Line shit shoveler. "It's true!" Jack yelled when I called him a liar. "Teddy doesn't do nothing but scrape the shit out of the cattle cars once they're delivered to The Hanging Hoof."

I never did tell Teddy that I knew he was a shit shoveler and not a conductor, which was probably for the best, him always wanting to look so respectable and all. Not that it mattered, because soon after, Teddy stopped being a shit shoveler and took a job at The Hanging Hoof, probably butchering cows, judging by the blood on his clothes, even though that seemed impossible since Teddy wouldn't even kill a spider. Not even if it was big as a fifty-cent piece and I was standing on a chair screaming at him to lambast the creepy bugger. Instead he got a plastic cup and an envelope and he trapped the spider under the cup, then slipped the envelope under it for a cover and carried him outside. If Teddy did kill cows at The Hanging Hoof, I told myself, then it had to be one of those *contradictions*. I didn't know for sure if I was using that word right, though, because when we had it on our spelling list and Mrs. Carlton asked for a sentence using the word, I raised my hand because I thought I had a good one: *Teddy Favors is a cow-killing, spider-saving contradiction*. But Mrs. Carlton called on Jolene Jackson instead.

It was the same week we had *affliction* on our spelling list and I raised my hand for that word, too, planning on saying: *People who sing while peeing on the toilet probably have an affliction,* but she didn't call on me that time, either. Which is probably a good thing, come to think of it, because we weren't supposed to say *pee* in school. Only *restroom.* And I didn't think that *People who sing while restrooming on the toilet probably have an affliction* was a real sentence, because it didn't sound right to me.

I looked at the desk at the front of the room. "Mrs. Carlton?" I said. "Is *People who sing while restrooming on the toilet probably have an affliction* a proper sentence?"

Mrs. Carlton looked up from her work and frowned. "Isabella, what does *that* have to do with Moby-Dick?"

I shrugged. "I was just wondering."

She sighed and told me to get busy, then she went back to grading papers.

I was singing a chorus of "Maybellene" under my breath and looking at the long poster of alphabet letters strung above the chalkboard when Miss Simon appeared in the doorway, papers in one hand while she knocked with the other, even though the door was already open.

She rapped three times but still Mrs. Carlton didn't look up, so I told her that Miss Simon was there. "Oh, I'm sorry, Debra," she said. "I heard tapping, but thought it was..." She glanced over at me, then looked back at Miss Simon, who gave her an understanding smile. "Anyway, do come in."

Miss Simon didn't look surprised to see me sitting there, but then she wouldn't have been. When I was in her room, I spent a lot of time inside during recess, too.

They talked in hushed voices as Mrs. Carlton looked over the paper Miss Simon handed her, and I stopped singing so I could catch a word here and there. "What an ingenious program, Debra," she said in an excited voice.

"Mrs. Gaylor suggested it to our girls' club as this year's summer community project," Miss Simon explained. "She's going to help us with it."

"Well, it's a wonderful idea," Mrs. Carlton said. "I can think of a few girls who could benefit from this program." They both looked at me and dropped their voices to whispers.

After Miss Simon left, Mrs. Carlton slipped all of the papers—except one—into her wire basket. She brought that one over to my desk and handed it to me. It had the words SUNSHINE SISTERS drawn across the top of the mimeographed page like it was supposed to be Bible-fancy. "What's this?" I asked.

"It's a new summer program, one I'm hoping you'll be interested in. I think you'd get a lot out of it."

I skimmed the page, then looked up and tried not to get distracted by her skinny stretched-out earthworm lips, lipsticked out of the lines to make them look fat. I wondered when she started painting them like that.

"Oh. I get it," I said after I skimmed the paper some more. "It's a program where older *good* girls try to help younger *bad* girls learn to act like respectable young ladies."

Mrs. Carlton leaned her butt against the desk across the aisle from me. "I wouldn't exactly say that, but it does sound like a wonderful program. They match a grade school student with a high school girl with similar interests, and you spend time together."

I sat the paper down. "To do what? Schoolwork? Because if that's it, then I'm not much interested." The way my hands fell when I folded my arms over the desk, my right hand ended up cupping my left elbow, where the skin was gray and dry and scratchy. I poked my elbow out toward her. "See this, Mrs. Carlton? How my elbows are cracked and gray like little volcanoes? Teddy harped on me all winter about these things, saying that no respectable young lady would run around with elbows that look like this.

"Teddy said this as if there is one thing respectable about me in the first place. Or him, for that matter. We're poor white trash,

Mrs. Carlton, both of us. And like I once overheard Mrs. Gaylor say at the post office: There's nothing short of reincarnation that can change poor white trash into something respectable.

"I don't think Teddy believes there's such a thing as a hopeless case, though, because he still tries to make me better. Always telling me to wash up good before school, because hand-me-down dresses or not, I should have enough pride in myself to scrub the gray scales from my elbows, put my messy curls back in barrettes so people can see my eyes, and look like a little lady. He harps on me to curb my temper, because little ladies shouldn't fight like barroom drunks, and he reminds me to stop singing at 'inappropriate' times. His harping about that doesn't do much good, either, because I can't help singing and humming. Even when I'm sitting on the toilet. You ever hear of anyone doing that, Mrs. Carlton?" I shook my head. "I don't know. This singing all the time is like an affliction, or something."

"You call your father Teddy?" Mrs. Carlton asked.

"Oh, Teddy's not my dad," I said.

"Oh, yes, that's right. Mr. Favors is your uncle."

"My *uncle*? Nah. He's just the boyfriend Ma left me with."

The minute those words got out, I thought, *Shucks! I hope I didn't say something I wasn't supposed to!* "He's real respectable, though, even if he's dirt-poor," I added quickly. "He taught me to stop swearing...can you believe it? I can't. You remember when you were on playground duty last year, how many times you had to send me in for cussing? Anyway, Teddy is as good as Jesus. I'm not kidding. Okay, maybe the only affliction Teddy's gotten out of me so far is cussing, but he never gives up. Course, he should know he's out of luck changing me on all counts, because the fact of the matter is, no matter how many times I scrub my elbows to bleeding, they still look like this. And no matter how many recesses you make me spend inside for being naughty, you know like I do that the next time you let me loose on the playground, somebody—probably one of the Jacksons—is gonna say or do something to make me mad and I'm going to scream at them or slug them, or both. Then I'm going to end up right back in here baking like a potato while you do your papers. Not because I want to be bad—I don't—but it's like it's in my blood and I can't get it out.

"I don't know what's wrong with me, Mrs. Carlton, but frankly, I think it might be a situation like with old Mrs. Fry's dog. He's so mean that he has to be kept tied all the time, and she has to toss his food to him and scoot his water dish to where he can reach it with a stick. That's how mean he is! Jack Jackson says the only thing that's gonna calm that mutt down is a lead pill between the eyes, but Mrs. Fry won't have him put out of his misery. It's probably just bad breeding. That's what Teddy says is wrong with Poochie, anyway. And if that's the case with me, then you can bet I got that bit of bad blood from my dad's side. But I'm getting off the topic now, aren't I? Sorry about that. And sorry to seem ungrateful about this program you and Miss Simon think is so swell, but frankly, Mrs. Carlton, I don't think no high school do-gooder is going to be able to clean these things out of my blood, do you? Well, not that I even want my affliction for singing fixed, because I love music more than anything."

Mrs. Carlton's eyes got soft, like maybe I wasn't getting on her nerves so bad anymore, even though I was still babbling. She slipped sidesaddle onto the seat of the desk she was resting against, and her voice sagged, too, when she said, "Oh, Isabella. You don't have bad—"

I interrupted her. "Mrs. Carlton, I sure do wish you'd call me Teaspoon. Every time you say 'Isabella,' I've got to think about who you're talking to, because nobody calls me by that name but you teachers. I swear, when you yell at me during class and I don't shut up, it ain't so much that I don't hear you, it's that I don't know you're talking to me."

"Well, Isabella. A teacher—"

"You know how I got the name Teaspoon?" I asked, because I was sure if she knew, she'd appreciate the name a bit more and maybe start using it. Mrs. Carlton started to say something, but I thought she was just planning to tell me that she didn't know, so I continued.

"Well, before my ma and I came here to Mill Town, we lived in Peoria, Illinois, and downstairs there was this tavern. Every Tuesday night, this old guy would come in to dig the coins out of the back of the jukebox and to change up a few of the forty-fives. The first time we were down there, after he got done with his work, he got a few tunes going, and 'After Midnight' by Patsy Cline came on. I knew that song because my ma sang it sometimes, so I started singing along.

"I wasn't more than four years old, so I don't remember the whole incident, but my ma sure did. And she'd tell the story every time someone asked about my name. She'd tell them how that whole place got quiet when I started singing, people turning around on their stools to look at me, their eyes bugging out of their heads. And when the song ended, the whole crowd exploded with clapping. Well, except the old jukebox man, who was staring at me like he just got gobsmacked.

"When the applause ended, he just stood there shaking his head, and finally he said, 'Now you tell me how a lil' bitty baby like that—who don't look like she got more than a teaspoon of breath in her whole body—can belt out a tune like that!' Everybody laughed, and from that day on, my name was Teaspoon. And every night we went down there, they'd sit me on the bar, or a stool, and they'd have me sing. Gave me chips and soda pop for doing it, too. And money. I'd put the nickels and dimes or quarters into my pocket and Ma would shake them out each night after I changed into my pajamas."

Mrs. Carlton's out-of-the-lines clown mouth smiled a bit.

"Okay, so maybe I did just turn ten last week," I said, "but let's face it, I'm still way small for my age, so the name still fits. That bracelet you have on your wrist there? I'll bet I could slip it clear up my arm to my shoulder, and if I let it go, it would slip right back down and bounce across the floor. It stinks to be this little, because I get treated like a baby all the time, but I guess I shouldn't mind because skinny, small girls grow up to have nice figures, while girls who are just-right and filled out by the age of twelve usually grow up to be fat ladies. Anyway, I really do wish you'd call me Teaspoon. *Isabella* is just too fancy of a name for someone like me, don't you think? When I grow up and fill out and become a glamorous singer, then *Isabella Marlene* is going to fit me like an elbow-length glove, but for now, Teaspoon will do."

"Isabella," Mrs. Carlton said, putting her hand up like Mrs. Fry did when she was trying to get Poochie to stop grabbing at her reaching stick. "Can you pause a minute and take a breath? I'd really like to talk to you about this program before the bell rings—"

"Sure," I told her, and I clamped my lips tight so no more words could get out.

She started talking about the story we just had in our *Weekly Reader*. The one about ducklings who didn't know they were ducks because the first thing they saw after they hatched was a ball, or a human being, and how this made them grow up to believe *they* were a ball or a person, too. I fidgeted in my chair while I wondered why on earth she was talking about ducklings, when she said that what she wanted to talk about was that Sunshine Sisters program.

About the time I started being suspicious that Mrs. Carlton had the same affliction as me and her mind had wandered off like a puppy with no leash, I got it, because she brought up how girls need role models, just like ducklings, so they can learn how to be ladies. "You lack feminine influence, Isabella," she said.

I was trying hard to be a good listener and not interrupt her, but she was wrong on that count, so what could I do but butt in?

"Well, things aren't always how they look, Mrs. Carlton. Here. Take my hair for example and I'll show you how it works." I used my pointy fingers to bring her gaze to the bottom row of my curls, hovering about an inch or so below my ears. "It looks like I got short hair, doesn't it? Well, watch this." I grabbed clumps of curls on both sides of my head and tugged them straight so that they touched below my shoulders. "See? I don't have short hair at all." I let go of the clumps so they could bing back into place.

"Yep, that's how things are in life now and then, so you can't always believe your eyes. Like you looking at me living alone with Teddy and assuming that I don't have anybody to teach me about being a girl. It might look that way, but it ain't so. I have feminine influence. I have the Taxi Stand Ladies, for starters. They're the ones who gave me that bit of smarts about skinny girls growing up to have nice figures. Do you know the Taxi Stand Ladies, Mrs. Carlton?"

"The Taxi Stand Ladies?"

"Yeah, that's what *I* call them anyway. They're the two ladies who stand on the corner of Fifth and Washington, right across the street from The Pop Shop, where the mailbox is—or inside the store at the window if it's raining or there's a razor wind blowing. Right where people on my side of town wait if they want a lift in Ralph's taxi. But the Taxi Stand Ladies have only been in town a couple of weeks so maybe you don't know them yet, even if you know The Pop Shop. Or maybe you just don't get to my side of town. A lot of fancy folks don't, and you strike me as kind of fancy with that nice bracelet and all.

"Anyway, I call them the Taxi Stand Ladies because all afternoon and night, they wait there on the corner for Ralph to come along so they can take a spin. Then after a bit of time, they come back and stand there until Ralph makes his way back to the corner again, some gentleman or other in the front seat.

"By the way, the Taxi Stand Ladies go by nicknames, too, which proves that you don't have to be a baby to have one. They call themselves Walking Doll and The Kenosha Kid."

Mrs. Carlton made a funny sound in her throat, like maybe she had a hair stuck on the back of her tongue or something, so I asked her if she was all right. She nodded, so I continued.

"Anyway, I got the Taxi Stand Ladies, and I got old Mrs. Fry, too. She's my neighbor lady. The one with the mean dog. She fixes me and Teddy's clothes when they get a tear, and sends us over baked stuff now and then. Teddy helps her out, too. Last week Ralph came and brought her a great-grandson she didn't even know she had. Imagine that! He came with a note pinned to his jacket, written by Mrs. Fry's daughter in Texas, saying that the boy was sent to her by *her* son, who lived in Chicago and was getting sent to the clink for doing something bad, though Mrs. Fry's daughter didn't say what. She only said that with her rheumatoid paining her feet and hands so bad, she didn't have it in her to chase after a kid. Old Mrs. Fry doesn't have the rheumatoid, but frankly, I don't see what difference it would make, since from what I see that kid never moves anyway—well, except for his hands—so why would anyone have to chase after him? Anyway, Charlie got sent from Chicago to Texas to Mill Town. Sort of like a homing pigeon that doesn't know his directions. Charlie Fry is the new kid that's always sitting on the brick ledge on the edge of the playground at recess like a Humpty Dumpty, if you're wondering who he is. He's only eight years old, but he's as tall as me. A whole lot fatter, though.

"But I'm veering off the trail again, when I only meant to tell you that Mrs. Fry gives me pointers on how to be a little lady. Yep, that's what she does. She tells me not to thump my feet so hard when I walk indoors, and not to stuff whole cookies in my mouth. And she reminds me to keep my knees together when I sit in dresses. Things like that. By the way, I passed along that bit of smarts about keeping your knees together when you sit to the Taxi Stand Ladies, since apparently they never heard that one before."

Mrs. Carlton looked shaky as she tugged the paper out from under my arms and took it to her desk, where she scribbled something at the bottom with a red pen. I sang a bit more of that Chuck

Berry song, because it had a lot of zip, the toes of my water-stained canvas shoes tapping the floor so I could keep good time.

"I got good timing, don't I?" I said to Mrs. Carlton when I forgot the rest of the words because the song was new and I'd only heard it a couple of times. "That's because I work on my timing with my radio. It was Teddy's radio and he used to keep it on the kitchen counter and listen to it quiet when he was cooking or doing dishes. But I suppose he saw that I liked it even more than him, the way when it was on I always came in and sang with it, so he gave it to me to keep in my bedroom. Anyway, I sing along with the tunes it's playing, then right in the middle of a verse or a chorus, I turn the sound down all the way and keep singing. Then here and there, while I'm still singing, I crank the sound back up to see if I'm in the right place. Sure is a good trick to learn timing, Mrs. Carlton. I'm so good at it now that I can start singing at the beginning of a song and even if I don't turn the sound back on until the very last line, I'm smack-dab on the same word they're singing. Timing is very important if you're going to be a singing sensation," I told her.

"Do you sing, Mrs. Carlton?"

"I sing in the church choir," she said as she capped her pen, then brought the paper back to me.

"Well you should sing more often than on Sundays," I told her. "Singing makes you feel happy. And you could probably use a little happy right about now, if it's true what Mrs. Delaney said. That your husband is running around with Betty Rains."

Mrs. Carlton looked like she had a whole fur ball clogging the back of her throat after I said that, and she turned away.

"Uh-oh. I probably shouldn't have said that, so I do apologize. That's another affliction I have, Mrs. Carlton—if you hadn't noticed already. I say things I probably shouldn't. But just for the record, that Betty Rains isn't nearly as pretty as you. She must have filled out at about the age of seven, judging by the size of her, don't you think?"

The bell in the hall rang then, and the two teachers on playground duty blew their whistles. "You may return to your seat now, Isabella," Mrs. Carlton said.

I folded and stuffed the paper she gave me into my desk, which was already so full that I had to lean on the lid to get it closed. Then I tapped my toes and watched the clock and waited for the school day to end.

CHAPTER TWO

When the last bell for the day rang, I leapt out of my seat like I had ants in my pants, but I didn't even get out the door before Mrs. Carlton stopped me.

"Isabella? Do you have the paper on the Sunshine Sisters program that I gave you?"

"Yeah," I said, even though I didn't think I did. Mrs. Carlton asked me to show it to her.

I dug around in my jacket pocket and screwed up my face to look all surprised when I didn't find it.

"Go get it," she said, and I marched back to my desk with a big sigh. Once I found it, I held it up so she could see, and she said, "Be sure and give it to Mr. Favors tonight, okay? I put a note on the bottom asking him to call me."

"Oh. We don't have a telephone, Mrs. Carlton."

"Well, does your neighbor lady have one he might use?" she asked.

"Mrs. Fry can't afford a phone, either. That's why her daughter sent Charlie up with a note pinned to him; because she couldn't call her to tell her he was coming. Course, you'd think she would have sent a letter. Her daughter bought her a television set last year. I'll bet she wished she'd have bought her a phone instead, when it was time to ship Charlie off."

"Well, where does Mr. Favors go when he *has* to use a phone?"

"To the pay phone outside the drugstore," I said without thinking.

"Good, ask him to call me from there tonight, please."

I didn't want to put myself in a pickle, because I didn't want no part of that do-gooder program, so I had to think fast. "Well, he works long, long shifts, Mrs. Carlton, so it's late and he's all in when he gets home. He ain't gonna want to walk all the way to the drugstore after walking two miles home from work."

"Won't want to, Isabella. "Not *ain't gonna.* Does he work on weekends?"

"He works on Saturdays. He gets an extra twenty cents an hour when he works them, so..." I stopped right there and didn't tell her that he has Mondays off so he can work those Saturdays and stay under forty hours, because then she'd be wanting him to come in for a meeting.

"Well, maybe he can call me from work on Monday while he's on break," she said, shuffling papers around on her desk.

"Oh, there ain't no phones where he works. Only dead cows."

Mrs. Carlton sighed. "It's *aren't any.*" She looked up with squinted eyes. Most of her lipstick had worn off her real lips, so that the red rimming them looked like an outline that some kindergartner forgot to color in. "Give the note to Mr. Favors. If he doesn't call me back, I'll just drop by to see him one evening next week."

"Well, he's not home much," I lied.

Mrs. Carlton took a deep breath, and one of her eyelids twitched. "Isabella, I'm trying to be patient here, but the school year is almost over and you are in serious jeopardy of failing fifth grade. I know you're a bright child and could pick up what you missed in no time if you applied yourself, but as things are, I only see trouble ahead for you in sixth grade. It's been a long time since parent–teacher conferences and I think Mr. Favors and I need to regroup and put our heads together to figure out what would be best for you. This program may be grasping at straws, but at least it's something. I'd rather not hold you back, Isabella, but I need some assurance that you'll not be doomed to failure next year if I pass you."

Her words felt like a yank on my hair and a punch in the stomach at the same time. A flunky? *Me?* Sure she'd harped at me lots all year to turn in my work, but she didn't tell me I might flunk if I didn't! Holy cow. She flunked me and she could just as well write DUMB HEAD across my forehead, because that's what everyone was going to call me. "I promise I'll work hard over the weekend and turn in all my late papers by Monday. Please. I'll do anything. I don't want to be no flunky!"

"I hope you mean that," Mrs. Carlton said, and I crossed my heart to show her—and me—that I meant business.

"We need to use all the resources we have available to us, Isabella. Do you understand?"

"Gotcha," I said, and she told me that the proper reply was *Yes, ma'am. Thank you,* so I said that instead. Then I hightailed it out of there.

By the time I got outside, the playground was empty but for a few lost school papers and smashed candy wrappers, so I had to walk by myself. I sang a few bars of a made-up song, but I never cared much for singing outside on breezy days, the wind yanking your voice off to who knows where. Nope. I liked singing in the bathroom when Teddy's dirty clothes heap didn't ruin the echo, or into a fan (especially if I was singing country), or best yet, in the basement where the echo was good, which I only did once, though, because that place has more spiders than The Hanging Hoof has dead cows. Nope, I didn't care much for singing in the wind, so I stopped singing and just hummed as I watched my shoes take turns playing peekaboo from under the hem of my dress and thought about Teddy's fixation with being respectable.

Teddy's desire to be an upstanding person seemed to be in his blood the way being naughty was in mine, because he talked about it the way other men talked about cars or baseball. "As long as you got your pride, you still have something," Teddy always said. It didn't matter to him that he had to wash his work clothes in the tub every other day because he didn't have but two pairs of work pants and two shirts, and the motor on the wringer washer was deader than a T-bone steak. Clothes that were a bloody mess by the end of each workday, so he couldn't just hang them up for another day after he got home, the way I did my dresses on days when I didn't slop my lunch. So every night, he had to stand over the tub and rub the legs and arms of those clothes until the rinse water turned clear, then run them out to the clothesline hanging between two trees in the warm seasons, and over the heat register inside if it was winter. And if his clothes got even one little tear in them, he raced that shirt or pair of pants over to Mrs. Fry's for patching, as if the shirt itself was doing the bleeding and Mrs. Fry was the doctor. That way he could walk to work clean, with his head held high.

Every night after Ma left, his shoulders and head wanted to sag so low that it looked pitifully hard for him to lift them, but he perked them before he left the house each morning to walk me across the street, and he kept them held high until the door shut behind us each night. And when we took a walk so Teddy could run errands, it didn't matter if Marion Delaney and Marge Perkins watched us pass from where they gossiped over the fence splitting their yards, pity in their eyes. Or if Frank Miller gave him that nasty smirk as he was opening the door to his Lincoln Continental to head to the savings and loan where he worked as a loan officer (which I guess is sort of like being a policeman of the bank's money, but I'm not sure), or to Miller's Sales and Service, the place on the other side of town where he sold cars so expensive that Teddy couldn't even buy one of the used ones. A smirk that said, *Couldn't keep her, huh, Big Guy?* which is what Mr. Miller called

Teddy every payday when he made his deposit, even if Teddy stood only five foot four.

Sure, Teddy's hand might have gripped mine a little harder, and his step might have picked up a bit until we passed them, but still he kept his shoulders back, and his chin (what little he had of one) held high.

Teddy never did see me slipping my free arm behind my back to flip those people the bird, which is what Jack Jackson called holding up your middle finger when you wanted to cuss somebody *really* bad but weren't allowed to swear anymore. Teddy would have gone ape had he seen me, for sure. Especially about me flipping the bird to Mrs. Delaney and Mrs. Perkins, who he claimed meant well. I guess Teddy didn't know what one of the old regulars back in Peoria knew: that sometimes the only difference between pity and scorn is which side of the coin is facing up.

Poor Teddy. Maybe things would have been different for him if he'd used that money he was saving up to go to electricity school like he wanted to. He spent his whole twenties and part of his thirties living with his crippled ma, trying to clean up the mess she made of her finances so she wouldn't lose her house. Tucking what little he could of his paychecks away so that after she was gone he could get a respectable trade and make a good wage. But the very week after the Lord took his ma home (which is what Mrs. Fry said you call it when somebody croaks), Ma and me rode in on the Greyhound, stopping in this town that sits like a pimple on Milwaukee's butt-end, because she didn't have enough cash to get us the last fifteen miles to Milwaukee.

Teddy could tell Ma was in trouble the minute he saw her digging in the bottom of her purse and trying to count out enough change to order us a plate of french fries in the restaurant we'd stumbled into. So he hurried to her rescue and asked her point-blank if we'd like to join him at the table where he was having coffee. Ma took him up on his offer to buy us supper, calling him her knight in shining armor.

After we ate, Teddy called for a taxicab and Ralph came to bring us to the house Teddy's ma left him, which had the same white paint peeling like a sunburn even then, and a porch with no walls that leaned to one side like it needed a cane. Teddy's Oldsmobile was in the shop getting a new tranny so he couldn't take us the rest of the way. And giving Ma fare wouldn't have mattered, since we'd rode in on the last Greyhound that Mill Town would see until morning. That night, after Teddy tucked me into his dead ma's bed, him and Ma stayed up half the night talking and she told him her whole pitiful story. About the mean man she left down south while I was still in diapers when she couldn't take it no more, and how her own family—her ma, her dad, her grown-up brothers, and even her married sister—wouldn't take her in because she'd made her bed, and she should sleep in it. Just like they had to do theirs— even though she was only sixteen when she made that bed, she said.

After Ma spilled out her story and tears, she told Teddy how all she wanted in this life was to be a piano bar singer, even if she needed more practice on her pianoing skills to get hired in a place worth her salt. "I want to be a somebody, for just once in my life," Teddy recounted her saying. And then Ma sang for him, right there at the table, her fingertips pitter-pattering over the Formica as if it was ivory.

Ma and Teddy didn't marry because Ma thought marriage was nothing but a ball and chain, but they became like man and wife anyway. (Teddy didn't tell me that part. I just figured it out, based on the fact that they slept in the same bed, doing the "Juicy Jitterbug," which is what the Jackson boys called it when a ma and a dad banged around in bed at night, and I sure heard a lot of banging around back then.) And after we'd been with Teddy for a month, he dipped into his electricity school savings and bought Ma the fine upright piano that sits jewel-shiny in our living room, so she could practice her playing and get a job at The Dusty Rose. A piano I wouldn't touch, so that it would stay pristine for her. He bought her fine dresses, too. Silky ones that showed the tops of her balloons and clung to her hips like lotion. Fancy high heels with pretty rounded toes, too, and matching handbags.

Course, Teddy could have saved the money that piano cost him, because by the time Ma got a job as a piano singer at The Dusty Rose, her and I had seen the inside of the Starlight Theater on Bloom Avenue, and the rest is history, as they say.

I was so busy thinking that I forget to watch my feet, *and* where I was going, so I didn't realize that I was crossing the road without looking until I heard tires screech and the honk of a horn. "Watch where you're going, kid!" some high school boy yelled. I wanted to flip him off, but I didn't because I saw that I was already on the corner of Fourth and Washington, and Mrs. Fry was coming out of her door with a pitcher of water for Poochie.

"Hello, Mrs. Fry," I called. She grabbed her reaching stick that was leaning up against the slate siding. "How was school today, dear?" she asked.

"Fine," I said, because if I told her it stunk because I had to stay in at recess and that I might become a flunky, she'd have gone tattling to Teddy. "Say hello to Teddy for me," she said, then she disappeared around the side of her house, her support stockings the color of bandages rolled just under her knees, her slippers flapping at her heels. I heard Poochie snarling at her as I zipped up my front steps.

The gold lid of the mailbox tacked alongside the front door was open and shoved with envelopes and junk papers. I didn't empty it out, though, because Teddy didn't allow me to get the mail. He was afraid I'd lose something important, like I guess I did once when I was little. I stepped over an IGA flyer lying on the porch, and went into the house to grab my jump rope and marble bag. Then I raced across the street to find some Jacksons to play with.

* * *

I swear, sometimes I didn't know why I even bothered being friends with any of the Jackson kids! Well, yes I did. They were the only kids on my block, but for a fat baby named Heloise, whose mother, Jack Jackson said, was a whore because she was a mom but not married, and now that timid, lazy new kid, Charlie Fry.

Jolene had to go first, and she picked "Apples, Pears, Peaches, and Plums" for her jump rope rhyme. I don't know what she was thinking, picking that one, since Mrs. Fry could probably jump faster than her. Right after you say, "Tell me when your birthday comes," you have to jump peppers until you get to your birthday month. Jolene's birthday was in May, but she didn't even get past March when her feet tangled like hair in a tornado. "You're out!" I shouted. "I'm next."

Jolene, who had more freckles than she had regular skin, put her hands on her hips. "You were turning too fast. That's why I tripped. It's still my turn."

"Stupid!" I yelled. "That's a pepper-jumping rhyme. If you can't jump fast, why'd you pick it?"

"Who you calling stupid? You're the one who's probably going to flunk fifth grade, not me! And I can too jump fast, but you were turning high-waters."

"I was not! The rope was scraping the sidewalk the whole time! And who says I'm gonna flunk?"

Jennifer, like her sister, was plastered in freckles. She had thin blond hair that when braided wasn't any thicker than three cooked spaghetti noodles twined together. And every time she got scared she'd tuck a braid into her mouth and chew on it, because her spine was as noodley as her hair. "Jennifer? Was I turning high-waters? *Was I?*"

Jennifer shrugged, that skinny braid stuck sideways in her mouth like a dog's bone. "Fine then. Have your way. Jumping rope is for babies anyway." I yanked my jump rope out of Jolene's hand and went into the backyard to see what Joey was up to.

Joey was my favorite Jackson. He was eleven years old, a tad on the hotheaded side like Jack, but he always played fair.

Joey was playing sword fighting with his brothers. "Want to play marbles, Joey?" I asked.

"Why don't you go play with the girls," James said. "We're busy."

Jack, whom I liked even less than school, was on one knee, winding the handle of his homemade cardboard sword with electric tape so it would stop flopping. He looked up and eyed my marble bag. "You got your steelies with you?" he asked. I knew he wanted to know because the week before, he lost all three of his steelies to James.

"A couple of them," I said, even though I only had one on me. Jack tossed his sword down. "I'm in," he said.

We always played marbles underneath the clothesline. On the patch of bare ground that Mrs. Jackson rubbed free of grass with her feet, her having so many kids that she had to wash even more often than Teddy.

Jack didn't hardly have the circle cut into the dirt before Joey and James were running back with their marble bags.

All four of us agreed that we were playing keepsies, and that we had to put one of our most favorite marbles in the pot. And sure enough, when Jack won my favorite cat's-eye—the eye twirled with cobalt-blue like the sky at the Starlight Theater—he scooped that marble up along with the scuffed, milk-colored plain marbles I didn't care if I lost. But when it was my turn and I flicked my shooter and it clicked against his favorite agate, he changed the rules the second his aggie even looked like it was leaving the circle.

"You can't do that!" I yelled. "We already called keepsies!" Joey wasn't noodley like his sister, so I turned to him. "Tell him to give me my winnings!" I said. Joey stood up for me, saying I'd won that aggie fair and square, but Jack didn't care. He said he wasn't giving up his favorite aggie to a girl, and he gave me a shove that toppled me over. That got me ear-pulsing mad and I hauled back and slugged him. In one second Jack had me flat down, his legs straddling me so I couldn't get up, and he was whacking me, James egging him on. I couldn't reach high enough to pull his hair, but I managed to get a few scratches on his arms before someone shouted, "Hey!"

Jack stopped swinging, and twisted his trunk around to see who was yelling. I lifted my head the best I could with a thirteen-year-old sitting on me, and saw Johnny Jackson striding across the yard, his car keys swinging from his hand. He marched over to us and lifted Jack in the air, dropping him on the ground.

"You, shit head," he said. "You don't whale on girls."

"Like hell!" Jack spat. "She's as nasty as a boy, and she looks like one, too. She hits me, I'm gonna hit her back!"

"That's right!" James said. "She slugged Jack first. She was trying to steal his aggie, saying that—" James didn't get the chance to finish, because Johnny cuffed them both, one hand for each head. "Ouch!" Jack yelled when Johnny's car keys caught him on the temple, which according to Mrs. Fry could kill a person, which in this case wouldn't have been so bad.

I always did think that Johnny was the best looking of all the Jackson boys, him being the one with the least lightbulby-shaped head. Still, I hadn't noticed until that very moment just how much he looked like James Dean, the dreamy movie star I saw in *East of Eden* at the Starlight. Johnny had the same long legs, and the same hair with waves rising on top. That is, when he didn't have it slicked oil-shiny because he was heading out to drag race on River Road and wanted to be noticed by the girls. Then he combed it sideways from the temples to the very back, the sides meeting in the middle to make one of those little tails called a Duck's Ass. Johnny's eyes had those little pouches underneath like James's had, too, like he needed to go to bed, but Johnny's eyes were a little closer together.

"Only sissies fight with girls," Johnny said. Then he turned to head to the house. Jack smirked his lips like that Teddy-insulting Mr. Miller always smirked his, and he said to me, "Maybe you should go look for your ma so she can teach you how to be a girl. It might keep you from getting your face punched in, tomboy."

I pretended I didn't hear him. Or James, when he added, "No wonder her ma ran off. I'd run off, too, if I had a kid like her."

I hadn't cried in front of anybody but Teddy since I was six years old, and I wasn't about to break that record. So I just swallowed hard and snatched my marble bag off the grass like they weren't even saying mean things about me. That's when Johnny turned around.

"You little bastards," he said to James and Jack as he hurried back to where we were standing. The boys ducked, like they were going to get their temples smashed in good this time, but Johnny didn't hit them. Instead, he ripped their marble bags out of their hands. "Hey, what are you doing, asshole?" Jack shouted.

Johnny handed me their bags. "Here. Take what you want. Compensation. Might help the little sissies learn how to be gentlemen."

I knew I could take every single marble in their bags if I wanted to, but I didn't. I only took my blue cat's-eye back from Jack's bag, then I walked away.

CHAPTER THREE

There was nothing to do in the morning since I couldn't play with the Jackson kids until I stopped hating them (well, except my make-up schoolwork, but it *was* only Saturday, which meant I had plenty of time)—so I grabbed a dime from my Sunday school offering stash to take to The Pop Shop for an Orange Crush.

When I jumped off my porch steps, I saw Charlie Fry sitting on his, his elbows propped on his round knees, his hands holding up his peach-fat cheeks. Just looking at him sitting there like Humpty Dumpty in front of that house that smelled like old people and musty newspapers made me feel sort of sorry for him. So I went over to the Frys' steps and invited him along. "I'm getting an Orange Crush. I'll give you a few swigs," I said.

While he was thinking it over, I looked down at his head. Mrs. Fry had cut his reddish blond hair with clippers because it was girlie-long and caked with enough dirt to fill a sandbox. Mrs. Fry told Teddy that she used to clip her husband's hair, too, but I decided that it must have been so long ago that she forgot how, because Charlie's hair looked like a lawn mowed by a blind man. The narrow paths were wobbled this way, then that, and his scalp was gouged and dotted with red scabs in the baldest patches. He looked up at me with a face so freckled that he could've been mistaken for a Jackson if his head wasn't rubber-ball round. "So you want to go, or what?"

Charlie looked nervous, like I was scaring him just by asking. "I don't bite," I told him. "Not anymore."

Charlie stood up, which I took to mean a yes, so I called through the screen to Mrs. Fry that Charlie was walking down the street with me to The Pop Shop, and that we'd be right back. Then off we went, Jolene Jackson taunting me because I was walking with a little fat boy. I didn't turn around to see who was heckling along with her. I just flipped them off behind my back.

"So your dad is a jailbird, huh?" I said, just to make conversation.

"Yeah."

"I met a jailbird once. Back in Peoria. He stole a car, I guess. Did your dad steal a car?"

"I dunno," Charlie said.

"So how come you're not living with your ma then?" I asked.

"She lives in heaven now," Charlie said.

He was waddling slow, like a penguin on ice, so I slowed my pace a bit.

"I'm sorry to hear that," I said, which was not only the respectable thing to say, but the truth. "What happened to her?"

Charlie put his right hand against the fat folds inside his elbow, held his first two fingers in a V, then stuck his thumb through it. I didn't get it at first, but then I realized he was giving himself a polio vaccine, but in the wrong place.

"She died from getting a *shot*?"

"Yeah."

"Holy smackers!" I said. "I didn't know a vaccine could kill you. I got one. See?" I pulled my arm out of my jacket and yanked the neck of my shirt down over my shoulder so he could see the white puckered scar.

I put my arm back in my sleeve. "I don't know anybody living in heaven. Well, except for Esther Morgan. She was a kid who lived right there on the corner," I said, pointing to the green house across the street. "She was the color of chocolate and wore short pigtails that looked like S.O.S pads stuck to the sides of her head.

"I didn't know her because it happened right after my ma and I moved in with Teddy. I was five years old then, and I think she was about ten or so. She got hit by a car. Right there at the intersection. I didn't see it, but I heard the tires screech and I saw her twisted-up bike afterward.

"Once I saw a dog get hit by a car. Not hit dead, but close to it, and the howl he let out when his back bent in a way it shouldn't have almost made me puke. Still, that mutt's howl wasn't nothing compared with the one that came out of Mrs. Morgan's mouth when she ran out on that street after she heard the tire screeches. Teddy ran out to see what happened, but he made me stay inside.

"I didn't know Mr. and Mrs. Morgan, but Teddy did, so he brought them a sorry card and signed his name and mine and Ma's. I went along with him when he brought it over and I brought them a picture that I colored from my Sunday school lesson book. It was a picture of Jesus sitting on a rock, probably in heaven if they have rocks there, and lots of kids, playing happy all around Him. I colored one of the little girls with my brown crayon so they'd know which one was Esther. If they ever have a picture of ladies in heaven sitting around Jesus in our lesson book, I'll color it for you." Charlie didn't say anything, so I told him that the proper response to my offer was, *Thank you, I'd like that.*

"Anyway, the Morgans moved away, but their son, Uriah, stayed here. He lives on the south side now. He's an usher and a cleaner over at the Starlight. He lets me sneak inside to catch a matinee now and then. I guess because his ma liked my picture so much that she framed it and hung it in her kitchen. Anyway, Uriah Morgan—I call him Mr. Morgan now, because he turned into a man since then—is really nice to let me see movies for free."

I could see the Taxi Stand Ladies up ahead, and I pointed them out to Charlie.

They both had long blue-black hair, pulled back at the sides and swaying halfway down their backs. The rest of what they had didn't look the same, though, with Walking Doll having blue eyes instead of brown, and a round face, while The Kenosha Kid's face was fish-skinny. Close up, you could see how they were different, but from even a block away it was hard to tell them apart since they were about the same tall and had the same-sized hips and balloons, and wore each other's clothes so often that I don't think they even knew whose clothes were whose anymore, though sometimes they thought they did and argued about it.

Charlie and I got closer, and I could see that it was Kenosha Kid who was wearing the pretty kimono-style red silk dress, one arm resting on the big mailbox bolted to the sidewalk, her other hand on her hip. Walking Doll was wearing the silky black that hung a tad off her shoulders, like the neckline was too big and in need of Mrs. Fry's sewing machine. She was swinging the foot of her dancer-tight leg over the edge of the curb as she watched traffic go by.

"Whoa," The Kenosha Kid said when we reached them. "Looks like somebody got in a catfight. You okay?"

I only remembered my bruise when she touched my right cheek and it was sore. I'd had to fib, telling Teddy that I tripped and whacked my cheek so he wouldn't get miffed that I was fighting again.

Walking Doll stopped dipping her foot and looked up. "I hope you left whoever it was bleeding."

"No, but I got my marble back," I told her.

"Way to be," Walking Doll said.

The Kenosha Kid looked at Charlie. "You're not the one who roughed up Teaspoon, are you?" she said with a bit of tease in her voice, probably because she could tell that even though Charlie and me were the same height, I could have outrun him in a heartbeat if I couldn't hit hard enough to flatten him.

I rolled my eyes. "She was just funning you, Charlie," I said when he tucked his head like he was a turtle and his shirt was his shell.

"This is Charlie. Mrs. Fry's great-grandson," I explained. "He thought you were serious. Anyway, he's living with Mrs. Fry now because his dad is in the clink and his ma is in heaven."

Walking Doll and The Kenosha Kid exchanged glances, then started fussing over Charlie. Patting him and cooing at him like he was just the cutest thing on earth, even if he was way fat and had scabs on his head.

"Do I look like a boy?" I asked when the fussing slowed down.

The Kenosha Kid laughed. "Well, you don't have these yet," she said, giving her pointy balloons and her little hips a pat, "but you've got the face of an angel. And I don't mean Michael, either."

"Did someone call you a boy?" Walking Doll asked, her head snapping up.

I nodded.

"Who?"

"Jack Jackson."

The Kenosha Kid laughed, "We've been called worse. Probably even by him."

Walking Doll's face got tight with mad. "The kid who gave you the bruise?"

"Yeah."

Walking Doll, who was more hotheaded than me and Joey Jackson put together, looked so mad I was expecting steam to blow out of her ears like on the cartoons. "That limp-dicked little bastard!" she said. She put her hand on my shoulder. "Listen, kid. Anybody tries to cut you down, you stand up for yourself. You hear? You're just as good as anybody, no matter who they are. And don't you ever let a boy rough you up. You'll never be as strong as one, but you don't have to be. You've got a tongue, and honey, there ain't no lash that cuts deeper than the tongue. *If* you know how to use it. Got it?" I nodded.

"And you," she said to Charlie. "Don't you grow up to be one of those mean bastards who roughs up women, you hear?" Charlie nodded his head hard and his fingers started do-si-doeing.

I blinked up at Walking Doll, but the sun was so bright behind her I could barely make out her face. "I know I don't look like a lady yet, but do I look like a boy now? I don't want to look like a boy."

"Hell, no!" The Kenosha Kid said, "Here, we'll show you how much of a girl you are." She pulled a black pencil from her purse and told me to close my pretty baby *blues*. The Taxi Stand Ladies always called my eyes my "baby blues" and every time they said it, I smiled because it was like they were saying that I had music in my eyes.

The Kenosha Kid stretched my right eyelid so she could draw on it, leaving my left eye free to watch Walking Doll. "You got your mole on the wrong side today," I told her.

"Now, how do you know that?" Walking Doll said. "You got your eyes closed."

"I only got one shut," I said. "Your mole is always on the right side. Right here." I tapped my cheek on the right side where her Marilyn-Monroe-drawed mole usually sat.

"Yeah, well I'm changing it up a bit," she said as The Kenosha Kid let go of my lid. I opened both eyes as she dropped the pencil back into her purse and took out a small red, rectangle container. She slid the lid back with her fingernail. Inside, there was a little square that looked packed with pencil lead shavings, only darker, and packed tight. She spit on the lead part, then rubbed a little brush across it and told me to close my eyes partway. I did like she told me, and after a couple more spits and swishes, my spitty-wet eyelids felt almost too heavy to lift. "Don't blink too hard until it dries," she warned.

Then right there, with folks walking by and gawking, The Kenosha Kid rubbed my cheeks with a sponge, swiping creamy pink over my cheeks, and painted my lips, staying in the lines.

"Take a look," she said, shoving her flipped-open compact in front of my face.

Wow, I couldn't believe it. Any bit of boy I had in me (along with the bruise I got from one) was painted over and I looked as pretty as a Taxi Stand Lady. "Holy cow!" I said.

The Kenosha Kid grinned. "You were a bit older, you'd be giving us a run for our money. *Now* let's see that little bastard call you a boy."

"Hey, you forgot my mole," I said, and The Kenosha Kid took her eyebrow pencil out and twisted the tip above the right side of my lip. Just then, Brenda Bloom and two other girls came walking by. All three of them were wearing poodle skirts, and pink anklets peeked out the tops of their saddle shoes. Brenda walked two steps behind the other girls, her hands clasped behind her back, her head down.

Brenda Bloom was the eighteen-year-old daughter of Gloria Bloom, the owner of the Starlight Theater (and a whole lot of other places in town). Brenda was going to graduate from high school in two weeks, same as Johnny Jackson, though he'd just turned nineteen.

Every time I ran into Mrs. Bloom at the butcher shop where Teddy sometimes sent me for hot dogs or sausage (because they didn't bleed in the pan), ladies were always swarming her, asking her questions about Brenda. Mainly if her and her boyfriend, Leonard Gaylor, the rich lawyer's son, were going to get married right after Brenda graduated, or if they are going to wait until Leonard graduated from the university in Madison where he was studying so he could be a lawyer like his dad. Those ladies always gushed on and on about what a fine job Mrs. Bloom did raising that girl on her own—Mr. Bloom being the *late* Mr. Bloom (another word for dead people—like they left the house to run to the store and were just a little late getting back) when Brenda was just two years old, probably because he was older than the hills when she was born, which is what I'd heard.

Even when Mrs. Bloom was nowhere around, they still talked about Brenda like she was a star plucked from the silver screen. They gushed on and on about her beauty and her fine piano-playing and singing skills. Yep, everybody loved Brenda Bloom and spoke highly of her.

Well, except the Taxi Stand Ladies, judging by the way Walking

Doll glared at her, and The Kenosha Kid said "Well, la te da" in a nasty voice as Brenda and her friends passed.

Brenda glanced up, just for a second, but she didn't glare back at the Taxi Stand Ladies. Instead, she looked at me.

I'd never seen Brenda Bloom up close before, but when I did, I knew why she'd been crowned the Sweetheart of Mill Town. She was the prettiest girl I'd ever seen, with big blue-green eyes and curly lashes that touched her eyebrows. Her skin was as creamy as French vanilla, and her lips and cheeks look like they've been dabbed with strawberry juice. She was prettier than either one of the Taxi Stand Ladies.

"Oh my gosh," one of Brenda's friends said. "That little girl is wearing makeup!" Brenda grinned and a dimple sank in her right cheek. Her teeth were so tight together you couldn't even squeeze the ace of spades between them. I wanted front teeth like hers someday, not ones with a space between them so big you could stick the whole tip of a pencil between them without snapping the lead. Teddy promised me that mine would move together when I grew some more, just like his did, but I couldn't count on that because Teddy still had a little gap between his front teeth, whether he knew it or not. Course, he hadn't grown much, either.

"What you looking at, Prissy Bitch?" Walking Doll hissed, and Brenda lowered her head again and kept walking, while her friend whispered, "I told you we shouldn't walk down this way."

I watched Brenda as she passed, her golden ponytail and the hem of her skirt swaying as she glided by. She still had her hands clasped behind her back, and they weren't even twitching like she *wanted* to flip off the Taxi Stand Ladies.

After they were gone, Walking Doll opened her purse and started rummaging around. I dipped my head over her purse. "What you digging for?" I asked, thinking maybe she'd forgotten to put something on my face.

"A couple of dimes. For you and your friend," she said. "So you can get a soda pop."

"Oh, Charlie's not my friend. He's my neighbor."

I uncurled my fist and showed her the dime I already had. "That's what we were gonna buy. Soda pop. We were gonna share."

She pulled one dime out, like that's all she could find, and put it in my hand. "Well, here. Now you can each get one. Go on now," she said as Ralph's taxi rounded the corner.

Charlie and me got two Orange Crushes from the vending machine butted up against The Pop Shop, and man oh man, did it taste good, all fruity and cold and fizzly on my tongue. I took a long swig and was about to wipe my mouth with the back of my hand like I always did, but stopped myself. "Did I just smear my lipstick from the bottle?" I asked Charlie. He shook his head.

"Hey, we should walk over to the theater and see what's playing," I said. Charlie glanced toward the direction of our houses, like he thought we should head back there instead, but then he followed me.

"The Starlight Theater," I began, as we headed over toward Bloom Avenue, Mill Town's main street. "Now, there's a place with more magic than Houdini! It doesn't look like much from the outside, but inside? Oh man! The walls were made to look like a castle, and there's tall pillars with gold trim—probably *real* gold, too—clinging to them. And balcony boxes with red drapes. It has eleven hundred seats, wood ones with red velvet butt and back cushions.

"With all that splendor alone, the Starlight Theater would be special enough, but those fancy things aren't nothing compared with the ceiling. I'll tell you, Charlie, not even God Himself ever created a night sky as grand as the one in there."

My stomach rumbled and I started thinking about the candy they sold at the Starlight, and how me and Charlie should have shared one pop, then bought candy with the other dime. I suppose it was thinking about candy, and walking with Charlie, that had me suddenly singing the Good & Plenty jingle about Choo Choo Charlie. Whatever it was, it made Charlie perk right up. "You like music, or just Good and Plenty?" I asked.

"Both," he said. "But music best."

"Me, too. Do you sing?" I was hoping he'd say yes, because I needed someone to practice singing harmony with. But he said no. Shucks.

When we reached the Starlight, there was a movie poster in the NOW PLAYING slot, with two cartoon dogs sitting at a restaurant table slurping spaghetti noodles from one plate. "Hot dog, Charlie! Look at that!"

Charlie looked up, his empty pop bottle dangling from his pudgy hand. "Walt Dizzies's Lady and the Tamp...Tramp"—leading me to believe that he did even less schoolwork than me.

"Wow, Charlie," I said, "we gotta see this one!"

I shouted to a man walking down the street, "Hey mister, you got the time?" He scooted his jacket sleeve up to look at his watch and said, "Twelve fifty-seven."

"That's grown-ups for you, Charlie," I said. "Always giving the time like that so you have to count up to the next tens, then picture the face of a clock to know what time it *really* is." Which is exactly what I had to do. I grabbed Charlie's arm. "Come on!" I told him. "Fast! Mr. Morgan comes around one o'clock."

When we got to the alley, there was no sign of Mr. Morgan, but I knew it didn't take us more than three minutes to cut between the theater and the dress shop, even if Charlie was running at about the same speed as Jolene Jackson jumped peppers.

I drained the last few drops of Orange Crush from my bottle and gave it a toss up into the dumpster, scattering the flies. I told Charlie to do the same. He couldn't throw any better than he could read, though, so his bottle clanked against the metal side and crashed to the pavement. "I ain't feeling so good," he said, like he was trying to blame his toss on something besides his wimpy arm. "Must be from the pop."

"Well, you guzzled it like a pig," I told him as I sat down on one of the empty crates sitting beside the metal door that only Mr. Morgan and the delivery guys used. I turned another one on end so Charlie could sit down, too. "It's just from the fizz," I told him. "Burp and you'll feel better." Charlie didn't know how to make himself burp, so I showed him how to swallow air and burp it back up. "Joey Jackson showed me that trick. He knows how to do all sorts of cool things." I burped a big one. Charlie laughed, so I did it again, my loudest ever, and he laughed all the harder.

Charlie's burps were about the size of a pimple, which made me laugh until I snorted, and pretty soon we were doing nothing but burping and cracking each other up. That's when Mr. Morgan swung around the corner and started down the alley. "There he is," I told Charlie. "Come on!"

Mr. Morgan's eyes got buggy when he got up close enough to see me good. "What you got on your face there, Teaspoon?" he asked. I explained as quickly as I could, because I wanted to get to the important question. Mr. Morgan didn't let me, though. Not until he told me that respectable little girls didn't paint their faces. I reminded him that I wasn't respectable anyway. Mr. Morgan looked at Charlie then, wincing, like he thought maybe the orange on Charlie's lips might be lipstick, so I set him straight on that one.

Mr. Morgan didn't look too happy when I asked him if me and Charlie could sneak in to see the Disney cartoon. And I knew why. He told me once that I couldn't tell a soul that he let me in for free, because if Mrs. Bloom ever found out, he'd get the ax.

"It's okay, Mr. Morgan," I said. "Charlie's the only person I've ever, ever told. Cross my heart. But Charlie's not going to tell a soul because he doesn't talk. I'm not kidding. You can't get a word out of him for nothing. Watch . . ." I turned to Charlie. "Say something, Charlie."

"What do you want me to say?" Charlie asked, like he didn't have a brain in his round, scabby head. I jabbed him in the gut with my volcano-cracked elbow, and he grunted.

"Mr. Morgan," I said, "Charlie's dad is in jail, and his ma is in heaven. Now he's living with Mrs. Fry, his great-grandma. And although she's real nice, it can't be much fun living with an old lady who doesn't do nothing but sew and knit and turn channels on her TV looking for a love story.

"Look at him once, Mr. Morgan. Ain't he the most pathetic thing you ever saw in your life, with his head all gouged up like that and not a friend in the world but me, and I'm not even his friend? This is a good movie for kids, not like that *East of Eden* or *Giant* you said you'd never have let me watch if you'd seen them first. Charlie's never going to get to see a movie at the Starlight unless he gets snuck in, same as me. Ain't that a shame? And he's only eight years old, so he's got to wait four whole years before he's old enough to get in without an adult. Who knows if he'll even be here by then. His dad could get springed from the clink and come get him, or his grandma might get cured of her rheumatoid and ask for him back...you never know. I've only got to wait two more years, though, so if it's that you don't want to let *two* kids in for free because you think that's doubling the chances of getting the ax, then let Charlie go in my place and I'll wait for him out here."

Charlie looked horrified when I said that, like he thought I meant it, even though the truth of the matter was, if Mr. Morgan was only going to let one of us inside, then it was going to be me.

Mr. Morgan sighed. "Just this one time," he said. "And you two be quiet in there, or I'll have your hides—right after Mrs. Bloom has mine." Then he slipped inside to see if the coast was clear.

The second Mr. Morgan disappeared, Charlie turned to me. "I don't feel good again," he said. And for sure, he didn't look good. His face was as pale as popcorn despite of the spatters of butter-colored freckles. I told him to burp again and he'd feel better, but did he listen?

"What if we get caught?" Charlie said. "Then all three of us are gonna be in big trouble."

"Nobody is even in the building yet, Charlie, and we'll be watching from the catwalk. Nobody goes up there but for Mr. Morgan when a light needs changing. I've been doing this forever and I've never gotten caught. I don't plan to, either."

"But we told Grandma G that we were just walking down the street. We said we'd be right back."

"She won't even know how long you've been gone," I said. "She's always asking Teddy for the right time because that grandfather clock of hers keeps losing it. According to that old thing, it will probably look like we've only been gone for ten minutes."

Luckily, Charlie didn't have time to think up more reasons why he should be a worrywart, because Mr. Morgan opened the door. He didn't say anything. He just poked his head out, looked up and down the alley, then nodded when he saw that the coast was clear.

Charlie almost fell over when he got inside because the place was midnight-dark and there was a stack of candy boxes lined up just inside the door. I steadied him while Mr. Morgan clicked a switch to give us at least enough light to see where we were going.

Once Charlie's eyes adjusted, his Orange Crush mouth opened and his eyes were sparkling so bright they would have made mine water if I'd had a cold and they were dripping to begin with. I gave him the *shush* sign, even though who would have blamed him if he'd shouted out *Wow!* at the top of his lungs, right then and there.

"Look up there, Charlie," I whispered, pointing to the sky above the top edges of the castle and stretching high above our heads. The ceiling was forty-five feet high. Cobalt-blue, and dark even when lit with thousands of twinkling lightbulb stars.

The door that would lead us up to the catwalk was across from the lobby. Not the front lobby, with its dangling chandelier as big as a Volkswagen Beetle, but the lobby where the bathrooms and two concession stands were lined up. That meant that we didn't have a wall to hide us, and had to crouch down between the first and second rows of seats and wait while Mr. Morgan hurried up the stairs. When he got to the top of the third tier of seats and slipped inside the projector room, I grabbed Charlie's arm and ran him fast past rows of seats, showing him how to crawl on hands and feet like a monkey over the swirly carpet.

Up, up, up the steps we went, past the balcony seats that sat behind a wrought-iron guardrail, getting to our feet only when we reached what Mr. Morgan called the nosebleed seats.

The door was open when we got there, and we slipped inside. "Crouch down, Charlie," I said, "so if anybody comes into the theater, they don't spot us through the windows." The windows in the projector room had no glass, because the projector gave off far more heat than the sun coming through a row of school windows and if the room was closed up, Mr. Zimmerman, the tall skinny guy who ran the projector, would have cooked like a french fry.

Mr. Morgan unlocked the attic door and was about to scoot us up when Charlie moved to the front window and hooked his fingers on the ledge. I went to stand by Charlie and together we peeked out into the dimly lit theater. "This place was built way back in 1928 by some big film company," I told Charlie. "But they sold it to some other theater outfit, who messed with it and almost ruined it. So Mrs. Bloom bought it after her rich husband croaked, and she fixed it up just how it was when it was first built.

"See those gold light things hanging along the walls? Mr. Morgan said they're the originals. Mrs. Bloom found them in the basement and had them shined up like new and hung back up.

"She brought back the old ways, too. And at every movie, the show starts with the emcee, Randolph Carter, wearing one of those tuxedo suits, stepping onto the stage under a spotlight with a microphone in his hand, announcing what we're about to see. The crowd claps, and then that red velvet curtain with the gold tasseled fringe at the wavy bottom rises up so we can see the screen."

I looked at Charlie to see if he was impressed. He was, so to dazzle him a little more, I told him, "This place cost a whopping six hundred thousand dollars when it was built back in '28. That's five zeros, if you don't know, which is a whole lot."

Mr. Morgan checked his watch, gave a little sigh, then leaned over and whispered, "Watch this, Charlie." I grinned because I knew what was coming, and I couldn't wait to see Charlie's face when it happened.

Mr. Morgan opened the door to the electricity room—the one I figured would make Teddy as happy as electricity school itself if he saw it, with all those switches and fuse boxes—and stepped inside. There was a flick of a switch and light spilled out of the three giant domes over the balcony seats. Charlie uttered an "Ooooo," and I grinned, because I knew the magic was just beginning. Another click woke up the lights at the floorboards, and their beams raced up walls the color of beach sand.

And then it happened. Mr. Morgan flicked the switch and brought the cobalt sky to life. "Wowwwwww," Charlie whispered, his head tipped back. His mouth stayed open but no sound could even get out when Mr. Morgan flipped another switch and lit the stars.

"Ain't that something, Charlie?" I said in a hush. "Mr. Morgan doesn't know how many stars are in that sky, but there's got to be a billion."

"There's gotta be," Charlie whispered back.

We stood there quiet for a few seconds, watching the stars twinkle. Me thinking about how nobody in their right mind could blame Ma for wanting to give up her piano bar playing and becoming a movie star once she saw the inside of the Starlight.

I pointed at the blue behind the top of the castle walls. "Look there, Charlie. Don't those treetops look real? They aren't though. They're just painted ones."

Suddenly you could hear the faint giggles of girls in the distance, and Mr. Morgan opened the attic door in a rush, then pulled us to it by our jackets. "You tell Charlie the rules," he whispered as he gave our backs a shove.

"Ow," Charlie said when the heavy metal door shut behind us with a click, probably clipping his heels. And then, "Uh-oh," when he found himself standing with his toes and nose butted up against the black metal steps that went straight up like a ladder. "What's this?"

"It's the steps to the attic," I said, my voice hushed as I grabbed the railing and climbed up a couple of rungs. "Hurry now, or we'll get caught." I went up a few more steps then cranked my head around to see if Charlie was following.

He wasn't.

I motioned him up, but Charlie just stood there. He looked scared. Scared enough to turn and start pounding on the door for someone to let him out. I backed down the steps and hissed in his ear, "You gotta come up, Charlie. Mr. Zimmerman could come into the projector room any minute now, and he'll hear us if we're standing here. Come on!"

When I reached the top of the stairs, the attic was wool-blanket hot. I waited a second to let my eyes adjust, because the only light up there was the pale glow coming from where the spotlights poked through the floor, then I turned and looked down.

"I don't like high things," Charlie said from where his feet were frozen, halfway up.

"It'll be okay," I said in a hushed voice. "Just hang on to the guardrails. It's not like this the whole way."

Charlie hung on for dear life as he climbed the rest of the steps.

If Tinkerbell had looked from the ceiling, she would have seen a flower-shaped catwalk, the path to the flower's center straight like a stem, and six walkways sprouted out like petals. At the end of each of the three top petals, underneath, where the ceiling was the lowest, there sat a round, empty hole about the size of a tetherball, serving no purpose that I could see but for letting a kid watch a movie if they lay flat on the catwalk and turned their heads sideways to get the right angle. Mr. Morgan said the catwalk was set up like that so a guy could go down any one of the paths to change a burned lightbulb or to reach the wiring if there was an electric problem. I loved the shape of the catwalk, and wanted to run down the length of its stem and out onto each petal. But Charlie? Well...

When he got to the top of the stairs, he stopped and looked up at the bunches of cables that stretched across the ceiling and the vents big enough that we could have run through them standing upright without bumping our heads and he froze all over again. I could tell that he didn't care for the way the ceiling was tall only in the middle—like a tent with a pole holding it up—and the way it slanted down so far in every direction that anybody over the age of five would have to duck or downright crawl unless they wanted to scrape their heads on the ceiling when they reached the circular ends of each petal.

"Just look at the catwalk, Charlie," I said when I saw how he was weaving. "See? Nice and flat. No more steep steps. And look, the floor is only two feet below us. Course, we can't walk on it, or... or...they'll hear our footsteps. So hang on to the guardrail and stay over on this side so there's no chance of falling off the edge, because if you fall, you can bet they'd hear the thud."

I just made up that last part because I knew Charlie would have croaked on the spot if I'd told him the truth—that the reason the catwalk was there in the first place was because when Mr. Morgan or an electric man came up to fix something, they wouldn't have to step on the floor, which was really the theater ceiling. If they did, they'd plunge right through and fall forty-five feet down, smashing right onto the red velvet theater seats and splattering like bugs.

The top petal was my favorite hole to watch from, because it was dead-center in front of the screen. I led Charlie there and tugged his jacket to get him to sit down. I pointed to the hole. "That's where we look to see the movie."

Charlie sat in a tight ball. "When's the movie starting?" he asked, his pale gray eyes bouncing all over the place.

"Soon," I said, even though it would have been more accurate to say, *Not anytime soon.*

When I sat here by myself, waiting that hour or so for the workers to get in and make the popcorn, and Mrs. Feingold to open the ticket booth so people could buy their tickets and refreshments and take their seats, I always kept busy by thinking up good things. Things like the opening credits coming on and the words, STARRING CATTY MARLENE appearing across the screen. Then Ma driving home from Hollywood in Teddy's car, because the second she found her dream, she realized that she missed me and Teddy until it hurt. I'd imagine her bringing home lots of movie-star money, and paying Teddy back so he could go to electricity school, and her and me spending our afternoons at the Starlight, sitting in the first row, sipping soda pops from waxy paper cups and dipping our hands into a red-and-white-striped box of buttered popcorn.

But there was no chance to think up good things like that with Charlie up there. He was sitting with his feet pinned under his butt, fidgeting as though he was afraid that if he didn't hold his feet down, they'd go banging around on the floor. He leaned over to look down every couple of seconds, though, while his nervous hands picked at his clothes and the scabs on his head. I offered him a half of the piece of Wrigley's Spearmint I found in the back pocket of my jeans, but he didn't want any. He had me so riled up that by the time the movie started, *I* was more glad than he was.

It sure was a good movie, though, with those dogs cute as can be—one respectable, one not—falling madly in love. Even Charlie forgot about being scared long enough to giggle behind his hand at the funny parts as we lay on the catwalk, the metal diamond-shaped floor working like cookie cutters against our bellies, the tops of our heads touching and our faces cocked sideways. Every now and then, when the beam from Mr. Morgan's flashlight waved below because somebody was talking too loud, or putting their feet on the seat in front of them, or throwing popcorn, I'd look down at the heads below us to see if I recognized anybody.

When the movie ended, the kids clapped, and everybody started leaving. Man, oh man, were they loud. Messy, too. When Mr.

Morgan turned up the lights, the theater looked like a dump, with the seats and carpet polka-dotted with popcorn, and tipped-over paper cups and empty candy boxes strung all over the place.

Charlie stood up, like he was going to leave right along with the crowd, so I had to pull him back down. "Can't go down yet, Charlie. Mr. Zimmerman has to rewind the movie to the reel it came on, and Mrs. Feingold has to count up the ticket money. The concession stand people have to clean their area and restock candy, too. Mr. Morgan will get busy cleaning while the others do their work, because he can't open the door until the coast is clear."

I don't know. Maybe it was having Charlie swiping at his sweaty face every couple of seconds, twisting his shirt and picking at his head, jumpy as a spooked alley cat, that made time seem to stretch on forever. "Mr. Morgan should have comed for us by now, shouldn't he?" Charlie asked for the millionth time. Only this time I was thinking the same thing.

I peered down and saw the floor and seats spiffy-clean, the lights even dimmed. "Come on," I told Charlie. "We'll stick our ears to the door. Maybe Mr. Zimmerman's just being extra pokey today."

Charlie got that I-might-pee-my-pants look at the ladder, so I put my pointy finger against my lips, then turned around and went down, showing Charlie how it's done. He followed me, but probably only because he didn't want to be up there alone.

At the bottom of the stairs, I turned and leaned my ear against the heavy metal door, listening for the whir of the projector as it rewound the film, the thudding of footsteps—anything. But there wasn't a speck of sound coming from behind that door.

I turned back to Charlie. He was wobbling like a bumblebee in a windstorm as his feet felt for the next step, all while trying to spin his chubby self around to face me. And then it happened: Charlie fell, rolling into me like a bowling ball.

We rammed against the door with a loud thump. "Charlie, get off me!" I said as I shoved, probably too loud, but man, that kid was heavy.

The door opened then, and there she was, Brenda Bloom herself.

Before any of us could utter anything but a gasp, Mr. Morgan bursted into the projector room, dressed in his fancy black-and-white tuxedo. He cringed like his fingers just got pinched.

"Busted!" I said. Charlie just started to cry.

CHAPTER FOUR

"*What were you kids* doing up in the attic?" Brenda asked. When we didn't say anything, she turned to Mr. Morgan as if she expected him to tell her what was going on. I didn't want the good Mr. Morgan to get fired, him having a dead little sister and a moved-away mom and dad—he already had enough bad luck in his life as it was without losing his job, too, so I had to think of something quick.

"He doesn't have anything to do with us sneaking in to see the movie," I said, making my voice sound smooth as soap poured on a finger to help a too-small ring slip off. "We were in the alley when the candy truck came. The delivery guy left the door propped open while he went for more boxes, and we slipped inside when he wasn't looking." As proud of myself as I was for coming up with that fib, it bothered me to think that I might be getting the delivery guy in trouble. What if he'd had a down-on-your-luck life like Mr. Morgan?

Brenda folded her arms, one foot pointed out to the side like a ballerina's. "If you were sneaking in to watch the movie, what were you doing up on the catwalk?"

"Well, it's not like we could *hide* by sitting in the theater. Mr. Morgan is the one who rips the tickets in half, and he's got a memory like Dumbo's mama. He would have known we never handed him a ticket."

"And did the delivery man open the attic door for you too, so you could get up there to hide?" Brenda's lips weren't smiling, but I swear there was a bit of a grin in her eyes.

"No, but Mr. Morgan went up there to change a bulb or something, and we snuck in after him. He was over on that end by the stage, so we went down a different path to the very end where it's good and dark, and we lay down flat until he left. So there."

"Sneaking in without buying a ticket is a form of stealing, you know. I could call the police if I wanted to."

I knew Charlie was whimpering because he was afraid of getting sent to jail, which didn't exactly make sense to me. You'd have thought he would have wanted to get sent to the clink since his dad was there.

"Look, it ain't our fault that you snobby folks make the rules so that kids like me and Charlie can't get in. I don't have a ma to bring me to the movies, and neither does Charlie. All he's got is a great-grandma, and all I've got is my ma's boyfriend. Neither one of them has money to take a kid to the movies. And besides, not like you Blooms need our lousy twenty cents anyway."

I wanted to stay grouchy, but when I looked out at the empty theater, the red curtain still open, the stars still lit, my mad turned to sad because I knew that Mr. Morgan was never going to let me in again. I looked at Brenda. "Maybe sneaking in without buying a ticket is a little like stealing, like you said, and maybe we shouldn't have done it, but I had my reasons."

"And those would be...?" Brenda asked. That grin was still sparking behind her eyes, only by then it was getting on my nerves.

"None of your beeswax," I said.

"Then maybe you can give your reasons to the police. I'm sure they'll think it's *their* business," she said. Charlie slipped his sweaty hand into mine but I shook it away.

Brenda turned, like maybe she was going to go off to call the cops, so I shouted, "Okay! So maybe it *is* your beeswax."

Brenda turned around.

"I snuck in because I love this place. Probably even more than you do. And because I wanted Charlie here to see it. Look at this sad-sack, with a ma in heaven and a dad in the clink. I thought it would cheer him up."

Brenda's eyes got soft, foggy looking, like the eyes of a leading lady when she's in love, or the eyes of a regular lady when she looks at a newborn baby. Only she wasn't looking at Charlie with that face. She was looking at me.

"Well, before you start thinking I'm some kind of do-gooder, you should know that I snuck in for my sake, too. See, my ma went off to become an actress—probably to Hollywood—so I like to check in at the theater now and then, thinking maybe I'll catch one of her films."

Brenda smirked. Like she thought I was fibbing about that last part. "So, your mom is a cartoon dog?" she said, and boy, was that smart-alecky comment enough to make me want to take up swearing again.

Mrs. Bloom walked into the Starlight at that very moment, her hair bright gold under the dome light, one section of seats from us, her voice rising up to us through the empty windows that kept Mr. Zimmerman from roasting. Glen Perkins was with her, dressed in the green jumpsuit he always had on when he stopped in at The Pop Shop to pick up a pack of Camels. The one that had PERKINS CONSTRUCTION stitched over his back. Mrs. Bloom was pointing down toward the stage and yakking, though we couldn't hear what she was saying. Then suddenly she swooped around so she could point at something at the back of the theater. That's when she looked up and saw us in the projector room.

It was too late for me and Charlie to duck. Brenda gave a sigh and Charlie swallowed so hard that if he'd let that gulp of air come back up, you can bet he'd have burped loud enough to put Joey Jackson's best one to shame.

Mrs. Bloom said something to Mr. Perkins. He nodded and headed down toward the screen, while Mrs. Bloom marched between a row of seats to get to the stairs leading to the projector room.

"Brenda?" she said when she stepped inside—like her name itself was a whole question.

Boy, that Mrs. Bloom sure was decked out! Big, sparkling rings glowed from her fingers, and more jewels dangled from her ears and swirled around her neck. So much gold and so many gems, it was almost enough to blind a person in such bright light.

Her face screwed up like *her* stomach was full of pop fizz when she looked at Charlie and me. She winced as she checked out Charlie's head full of bald patches and red knicks, then his patched knees. After she took in Charlie's dirty sneakers with the hole in one toe, her gaze zoomed right over to my feet and started crawling up my legs, which made me look down, too. I hadn't paid any attention when I bounced out of bed and grabbed clothes from the drawer Teddy put my playtime clothes in, and now I was a bit sorry about that because I wasn't looking so good in my mismatched ratty pants and stained shirt. My jacket zipper was broken because Mrs. Fry still hadn't found one that size to yank from her bag of rescued zippers, so I pulled it shut to hide my stain. Mrs. Bloom's head lifted and her eyebrows crawled right up to hide under her bangs when she got to my face. "This child is wearing makeup!" she said.

Mrs. Bloom turned to Mr. Morgan and asked him who we were and why we were there. Poor Mr. Morgan looked too scared to move, so I started talking. "I'm Isabella Marlene, but you can call me Teaspoon. Everybody does. Well, everybody except my teachers. And this here is Charlie Fry. We..."

Brenda got that your-name-is-ringing-a-bell look, and even though I was staring up at Mrs. Bloom, I saw her stretch a little taller, even though she was still squeezing her hands like she was wringing out wet laundry. "She's...she's my new Sunshine Sister," she blurted. And didn't *that* just figure, Brenda Bloom being a part of that do-gooder program, her being so perfect and all.

"I was just showing her and her little friend around the theater," Brenda added.

"Actually, he's my neighbor," I corrected, but I went along with her fib about me being her Little Sister in that dumb program.

"I thought Mrs. Gaylor said you were planning to pair with Veronica Hanson, the little girl who lost her mother a couple of years ago?" Mrs. Bloom said.

"Veronica Hanson? Oh, I know her!" I said. "She's in my grade, but she's in a different classroom. She lives with her new stepmom and her dentist daddy. And while she ain't exactly heading for a walk down the Sweetheart of Mill Town runway, she sure doesn't seem like a big enough mess to be a Sunshine Sister to me. She gets good grades and keeps her hair combed and everything. It just goes to show, though, things aren't always how they look."

"Well, I was, but..." Brenda looked at her mother, her perfect pearlies biting at her lip. She looked over at Charlie and me, then gave her ma one of those just-a-minute signals with her finger. She opened the door and asked Charlie and me to follow her. "And you," Mrs. Bloom said to Mr. Morgan while we were walking out, "if you're done with your work, you can leave. I don't pay you to stand around and eavesdrop."

Brenda led us to two seats up against the wall opposite the projector room. "Don't go anywhere," she said, like she was a mind reader and could tell that I was already thinking that the second she turned around, me and Charlie should make like a banana and split.

We were about to, too, until we got to the aisle and I realized that we could hear Mrs. Bloom and Brenda's voices coming through the glassless window in front of the projector. Sure enough, they were talking about me!

"I know, Mother... but... then we had our meeting where Miss Simon gave us a bio on each Little Sister, and afterward, she took me aside and personally asked if I'd pair up with Isabella. Her teacher is considering holding her back in fifth grade for another year, and says she's in desperate need of a good mentor."

"Well, I just spoke to Mrs. Gaylor and she said—"

"I know. I know. I haven't gotten the chance to tell Mrs. Gaylor about the request yet, because she was gone by the time Miss Simon and I got done talking. I'm sure she'll agree to switch things around once I tell her that Mrs. Carlton and Miss Simon both said that they couldn't think of a girl better suited to be Isabella's big sister than me, because I've been raised to perfection and would have so much to teach her."

"She said that?" Mrs. Bloom asked, her voice as proud as if she'd just won an Oscar Award.

Man oh man, I said in my head. Teachers! What snitches, telling the Sweetheart of Mill Town that I might become a flunky! Why, I'd bet my last Sunday school dime that Mrs. Carlton and Miss Simon told her that I have a couple of drops of bad blood in me, too.

"Well," Mrs. Bloom said. "You'll certainly have your work cut out for you, judging by the looks of her." Mrs. Bloom gave one of those now-what-was-I-doing groans, then she said, "I need to get back to Glen, and you need to show Raggedy Ann and Andy out. Don't forget to close out Mrs. Feingold's till."

I tugged Charlie back toward the seats Brenda assigned us, but I couldn't get us sitting by the time Mrs. Bloom came out and started down the stairs, walking like a bossy queen. My teeth were still gritted as Brenda led us down and to the door that opened into the alley.

She held the door as we stepped out. "See you Monday for our getting-acquainted meeting, Little Sister," she said with a smirk.

I spun around so fast that I almost made myself dizzy. "Whoa!" I said. "Look, I don't know why those two busybodies went and asked you to be my Sunshine Sister. But I never said I'd be part of that do-gooder program."

Brenda wasn't just kind of smiling then—she was outright laughing. This made me so mad that I marched right up to her, standing on tiptoes so I was almost, almost looking her square in the face. "Listen, Miss Goody Two-shoes. I don't care if Miss Simon, or Mrs. Carlton—or the good Mother Mary herself, for that matter—asked you to be my sister in that dumb program, I'm not going to have my whole summer ruined. Got it?"

Brenda's smile fizzled. Then she said slowly, "I think you're about to learn that in this life, what we want to do is often the opposite of what we get to do."

You'd think that a kid you risked jail time for so he could see a movie at the Starlight Theater would have been grateful enough to at least walk home alongside of you so you had someone to belly-ache to—but oh no, not Charlie. He just took off ahead of me, waddle-hopping down the street faster than I would have guessed he could go, like he couldn't get back to that old, smelly house fast enough. "It's not like you're going to get a spanking or something," I shouted. "Mrs. Fry won't even hit Poochie with her stick when he's trying to chew her leg off, so she sure ain't gonna hit you!" Still Charlie didn't slow down, and I wasn't going to bother catching up to him if he wasn't going to be a good listener anyway.

Mrs. Fry was pacing in front her steps when Charlie reached the yard. I was still half a block away, but I could see how upset she was. She had her old-lady hankie out and she was holding it against her bony chest as if her heart was about to explode and she had to be ready to catch the mess.

She grabbed Charlie and hugged him, then gave him a little I'm-mad shake. Mrs. Fry's voice was as small as she was, so I couldn't hear what she was saying as she guided him inside, but I could tell he was in for a good ear chewing.

A couple of hours later, I was in the bathroom wearing Ma's elbow-length gloves tucked up to my armpits and singing into my hairbrush microphone, admiring my black, curled-to-crusty eyelashes, when Teddy came home. I didn't hear him come in because there weren't any clothes in the bathroom and the echo was real good; I only knew he was there when I saw him in the mirror, his face fit-to-be-tied cranky. "Teaspoon, you come out here right now. Mrs. Fry just told me what you..."

Teddy stopped. "What on earth do you have on your face?" He stepped into the bathroom and spun me around, staring hard at my Taxi Stand Lady makeup. "Who did that to you?" he asked, as if I was wearing a gob of spit instead of pretty cosmetics.

I didn't tell him, but Teddy was a good guesser. "Didn't I tell you that I don't want you talking to those two?" he asked, vibrating like the wringer washer right before it croaked.

"Why?" I shouted.

"Because I said so," Teddy almost yelled. "Now scrub that junk off your face and come into the living room. I want to talk to you."

But it wasn't just because he said so. He couldn't fool me. He didn't want me talking to the Taxi Stand Ladies because he was afraid if I did, I'd take up cussing all over again. I was sure of it, because right after those two came to town, before I even knew their names, Teddy and I walked down to The Pop Shop so he could get the Sunday paper to do his crossword puzzle. Ralph was parked up alongside of them, and Walking Doll was chewing him up one side and down the other about something, cussing like a sailor. They stopped arguing when they saw us, and Teddy stared right into Walking Doll's face—probably trying to figure out if her Marilyn Monroe mole was real or fake—and then he gripped my hand tighter and yanked me across the street to the store fast, even though there was a car coming. Teddy sure did hate cussing, but I didn't think it was very nice of him to not say hi back, or give a thank you after Walking Doll called to him to stop by anytime—which I thought was right neighborly of them.

As soon as we got across the street, while Teddy had his hand on the smudged door of The Pop Shop, but before he opened it, he turned to me and said, "I don't want you anywhere near those women. You cross in front of the Jacksons' house and come down this side of the street. You hear?"

"I heard. I ain't deaf," I said.

Teddy made me wash until my eyes stung and my skin looked like it was rubbed raw with pickled beet juice, then he made me sit on the couch while he chewed me out for sneaking into the theater, dragging Charlie along, and making poor Mrs. Fry worry herself to the brink of death.

While he blabbed on and on, the snappy melody of a song they played in *Lady and the Tramp* came back to me and I started singing it. It was one of those songs with no words, so I just sang la-la-la where there should have been some.

I expected Teddy to tire himself out from his ranting like he usually did, but this time, right in the middle of his outburst, he stopped. Just like that. And when I looked up, he wasn't even standing over me anymore, but sitting in his chair, even though his work clothes were cow-bloody. His arms were lying in his lap, limp as the empty sleeves of a wet work shirt.

I stopped la-laing. "What's the matter, Teddy?" I asked.

Teddy stared straight ahead and sighed.

"Teddy? What is it?"

"I don't know what to do anymore, Teaspoon," he said. His chin was tucked in so far that you couldn't even tell he had one, and his voice was raspy, like he had tonsillitis.

"What do you mean?" I asked, my chest feeling like Charlie was sitting on me all over again.

He clicked his tongue against his teeth, making that little sucking sound, then he sighed big. "Since your ma left, I've done my best, Teaspoon. But I fear my best isn't good enough. What do I know about raising a child, much less one teetering on the edge of womanhood. You run like a stray, you fight like a barroom drunk, and you don't do your schoolwork."

"But I don't cuss anymore," I reminded him. "That says something, doesn't it, Teddy?"

"...and now you've added breaking into theaters to your behaviors," he said, not even giving me one ounce of much-deserved praise for keeping a clean tongue.

"Oh, I didn't just add that, Teddy. I've been sneaking into the Starlight for a couple of years now." Boy, did I hate it when my mouth worked so quick I didn't have time to catch the words before they came out.

"And to top it off," Teddy said. "Mrs. Fry ran into Miss Tuckle today, and she told Mrs. Fry that you haven't been to Sunday school in weeks, even though every Sunday I give you a dime for the offering plate, and off you go."

I might have been scared as Charlie when Teddy brought up yet another one of my bad deeds, but I wasn't about to let him see that.

"Well, I guess you could say that I did get a little sidetracked on my way to church the last few Sundays, but I still got those dimes you gave me," I lied. "And I'll see that Jesus gets them when I go back tomorrow." I thought for a second, and chewed my lip. "Hey, Teddy. Mrs. Fry didn't blab about me and Charlie sneaking into the Starlight right in front of Miss Tuckle, did she?"

Teddy's eyes scrunched. "If we are doing things we wouldn't want our Sunday school teacher to know about, then maybe we shouldn't be doing them in the first place. Don't you think?"

Teddy stared straight ahead, then sighed again. "I've tried everything I can think of, but . . . well, I just don't know what to do anymore."

I could feel my heart thumping in my throat when I heard those words, and tears smarted my already stinging eyes. "What are you saying, Teddy? You gonna pack me up with a note pinned to me and ship me off to one of my mom's mean brothers or sisters who will make me stay in bed all day? You aren't going to do *that*, are you, Teddy?"

Then suddenly I was bawling like a Jackson girl, and I ran off to my room to dig around on the floor until I found that Sunshine Sisters paper. I uncrumpled it and ran it back to where Teddy was still sitting, staring at nothing.

"Look at this, Teddy," I said. I shoved the paper in front of his face. "It's a new program to help kids like me learn to be more respectable. This program is why I snuck into the Starlight. Really. Not to see a movie, but to ask Brenda Bloom to be my Sunshine Sister.

"Okay . . . okay . . . so maybe that part isn't exactly true," I said. "I did sneak in to watch the movie, but something good came out of it anyway, because Brenda Bloom told me she's going to be my Sunshine Sister.

"I know I've got a lot of afflictions, Teddy," I said as he looked over the mimeographed page, "but I don't know what to do about them any more than you do. It's not like I'm trying to be bad. Mrs. Carlton seems to think that the trouble is I don't have enough 'feminine influence.' She thinks this program might help. And like she says, we've gotta use every resource we've got. Heck, Teddy. You know as well as I do, that there ain't a girl more respectable in this whole town than Brenda Bloom, so maybe she's just the influence I need. You'll see, Teddy. It'll work. I'll make it work. With Brenda's help, I'll turn myself into a girl you can be proud of. Just don't send me away. Please."

Teddy looked up at me with water-shiny eyes. He reached out and took my hand, giving it a squeeze and a slow shake. "Aw, Tea-spoon," he said in his most Jesusy-gentle voice. "I'd never send you away. You know that."

But I didn't know that. So I promised myself, right then and there, that no matter how much I hated the thought of being part of that do-gooder program, I was going to do it. And I'd do my school make-up work by Monday, and stop fighting no matter how much those Jackson kids got on my nerves. I was going back to Sunday school, too. Even if that meant having to figure out how to put back the offering money that I'd been pocketing for penny candy and soda pop.

I gave Teddy my word and wanted to spit-shake on it, but Teddy shook his head. "All I want is a promise in deeds," he said. Then he told me that he thought *he* needed an ice cream sundae for supper, and off we went.

CHAPTER FIVE

Yep, I was going to do better. That's what I told myself when Charlie and I set out for Sunday school the next morning, both of us scrubbed clean, Charlie wearing a button-up shirt that I think must have belonged to his grandpa because it was gray and smelled like mothballs. And even if it was long enough to fit him like a dress, the buttons were stretched tight around his big belly like it was too small.

It was Teddy's idea that Charlie go to Sunday school with me. Mrs. Fry—who used to go to church when Teddy still had a car and could bring her there and pick her up, but who had to get her church from the radio on Sunday mornings after Teddy's car was gone—thought it was a wonderful idea. Charlie didn't look so sure, which kind of surprised me. He didn't know diddly about God or Jesus, but you'd think he'd want to know the people his ma lived with. I tried to fill him in as we headed down the street.

"So, first there was God. Got that? And He made everything you can see. The sky, the earth, the stars, even wood ticks—though I don't know why He'd have bothered with that one. Anyway, He made the whole kit 'n' caboodle. And in just seven days, too."

"Wha'd He make them out of?" Charlie asked as he looked up at the sky, his steps slowing until he was almost standing still.

"These," I said, and I swallowed two gulps of air and burped.

"Gases. But probably like the ones we learned about in science class, not the burping kind.

"I know for sure what He made the first lady, Eve, from, though. The rib from the first guy He made. Adam. I don't know how He did that, but He's sort of like a magician you could say. He didn't make them clothes though, I can tell you that much. So they had to wear leaves. Their Garden of Eden must have been in the jungle, because those leaves were big. No trees around here have leaves big enough to cover up a lady's balloons or a guy's wee-er." Charlie laughed again like I'd burped.

"Anyway, the garden had apple trees in it and He told them not to eat the apples. I don't know why. Maybe a witch poisoned them or something. But a snake told Adam to eat one—or was it Eve? Anyway, one way or another, that apple got ate, and now because of it, we all have afflictions and have to suffer, which is not exactly fair. Like when Mrs. Carlton made the whole class stay in at recess because somebody stuck a wad of chewed-up Bazooka on her chair. It made no sense, punishing us for what one kid did, just because she didn't know who did it. It wasn't like we all took turns chewing that wad of gum. But I suppose she figured that if God Himself could punish people for generations because Adam ate an apple he wasn't supposed to, then she should be able to make a bunch of kids stay in at recess because one person stuck gum on her seat. Not that it mattered much to me, since I had to stay in that day anyway.

"You walk too slow, Charlie. Pick up the pace or we'll be late." I tapped my plastic purse against my thigh in a rhythm, then sang a bit of "Jesus Loves Me" before I remembered that I was educating Charlie about God and Jesus.

"So anyway, after about a bajillion years, all those descendants—which is what you'd call Adam and Eve's kids and their kids and so on—got so naughty that God had to send His only begot son, Jesus, down to earth to straighten them out."

"What's a begot son?"

"One He got, I guess. Anyway, that's where things get a little confusing. Jesus is God's son, but He had a dad named Joe, too. But I suppose people can have two dads. I think a kid in my class does."

"Grandma G has a picture of Jesus above her dresser," Charlie said. "He has nails in Him."

"Yeah, that's because some bad people nailed Him to a cross and killed Him. But don't worry, Charlie. God lifted Him back up to heaven and He's okay now. Just like your ma."

I kicked a rock on the sidewalk, then hurried to catch up to it before it stopped rolling. I kicked it again. "Take a turn, Charlie," I told him, "and don't let it stop rolling before you do." Charlie waddled to the rock and gave it a kick. He kicked it hard enough that I had to run to catch up to it.

"I don't know if we're supposed to have a favorite," I said as we ran and kicked, "but I sure do. I love Jesus best. He's not as strict as God. He doesn't care how much of a mess you are, He loves you anyway." Then I sang Charlie a verse of "Jesus Loves the Little Children" as we played down the sidewalk. I even added a chorus of my own, just for Charlie and me: "...Fat or skinny, good or bad, Jesus loves you like a dad, Jesus loves the little children of the world." After I got done with that one, I slipped right into "This Little Light of Mine," which was my all-time favorite Sunday school song.

Just singing that song and remembering that Jesus loves us even if we have afflictions made me happy. Happy, because I knew I was making Jesus as happy as I made Teddy when he saw me in my best dress that morning, damp curls plastered to my head with barrettes, the plastic purse he let me pick out from Ben Franklin on my last birthday dangling from my hand. "See, Teddy?" I'd said. "I'm showing you in deeds." He gave me a hug then and said, "That you are, Teaspoon. That you are." My whole insides felt good then, because I knew I had made a guy as good as Jesus Himself happy.

I couldn't show Teddy the money I had in my purse, because I didn't want him to know that I'd spent my offering money in the first place. Too bad, because he probably would have been impressed, knowing that I sold my jump rope and my marbles in order to get the money back.

Well, not that I got all of the money I owed Jesus back. I was still fifteen cents short, but it wasn't my fault those Jackson kids were such tightwads.

"You don't happen to have an extra fifteen cents on you, do you, Charlie?" I asked as I shoved him out of the way so I could kick the rock twice in a row, even though it was his turn.

"No," he said. "I only got a nickel...and it was my turn."

We were coming to the corner, and I had to be quick on my feet and kick the rock with the inside of my foot so it would turn down Lincoln Street. I kicked so hard that it skipped past the house on the corner and landed in front of the one next to it. The one with a lawn filled with tables heaped with junk. "Hey, Charlie, look. A sale! Come on, let's see what they got."

I skipped past the stacks of yellowed tablecloths, stretched-out clothes, and shoes with more scuffs than Charlie's head, looking for a table with something good on it. Jigsaw puzzles maybe, or a new board game that Teddy and me could play after supper, in case we ever got sick of Scrabble.

I didn't see anything in the way of toys other than some matted-looking stuffed animals, but as I was circling the table, my foot bumped into something hard. I lifted up the end of the plastic tablecloth and bent over to see what was tucked underneath. Good thing I did, too, or I would have missed the best thing anyone could ever hope to find at a yard sale—a scooter, apple red!

"Holy cats, Charlie, look at this," I said as I pulled it out, but Charlie hadn't even reached the table yet.

"Hey, lady," I said to the woman behind a card table that was empty but for a cigar box, a tablet, and a pen. She was a bit on the bowlegged side, so her legs looked like two bananas in her yellow pants. "How much for this scooter?"

She stopped to say hello to some ladies just coming into the yard before making her way over to where I was standing, the scooter tipped upside down as I spun the wheels to make sure they were in good working condition. The red paint was chipped here and there, but the wheels spun like tops.

"Oh, fifty cents."

I picked up my plastic purse from the ground beside the scooter. "I only have twenty-five...maybe thirty," I added, thinking of Charlie's nickel. "Will you take that?"

"I'm sorry," the lady said. "The stuff at this table belongs to my sister, and she ran for change. She said fifty cents, so I can't say differently." Then she wandered away toward the group of ladies hovering over a table of bedding.

"Man, Charlie," I said when he reached me. "Look at this. I've always wanted a scooter." I stepped on it and shoved off. "It even works good in the grass."

"Honey, don't play with the toys if you don't intend to buy them," the lady called across the yard, even though the toys were played with already.

"Are we gonna be late for Sunday school?" Charlie asked. "I don't like getting to places late. Then everyone stares at you."

I propped the scooter against the table edge, then told Charlie, "Don't let anybody buy this, okay?"

I went over to the banana-legged lady, who was unfolding a quilt so an old lady with a hair on her chin as long as my pinkie could see the pattern. "Excuse me, ma'am," I said. "I don't mean to interrupt, but if I don't, we're going to be late for Sunday school. That scooter over there? Do you think I could make a down payment on it, and you could hold it for me until after I get out of my class and can run home and get you the other quarter?"

The lady sighed. "Well, I don't know...like I said..."

"I'll come back. Promise! In an hour and ten minutes, tops."

"Okay. I'll hold it for you. But if my sister gets back before you and someone wants it, she'll probably sell it. I'll give you your quarter back if that happens. That's the best I can do."

I dug the change out of my purse and dropped the two dimes

and one nickel into her hand, then went and shoved the scooter so far under the table that even one of Snow White's Seven Dwarfs would have had to bend over to spot it.

The Jesus-bells chimed down the street, so we had to get a move on. I grabbed Charlie by his grandpa shirt and hurried him along.

"Did you just give that lady your Sunday school money?"

Boy, that Charlie! He hardly ever talked, and then when he finally did open his yap, all that came out of it was something you didn't want to hear.

"Stop blabbing and run, Charlie. We're late and everyone's going to stare at us."

Course, they would have stared anyway, since I was bringing in a new kid. Not that I minded the stares. I wasn't shy that way, which was a good thing because I was going to get gawked at plenty when I got famous. But Charlie minded. He turned tomato-red and tried to turtle-tuck his head into his collar—like *that* was going to happen, with the collar so tight that it was a miracle his eyes weren't popping out of his head—when the kids sitting around the scuffed table looked up. Who could blame them for staring at Charlie, though?

"Sorry we're late," I said to Miss Tuckle, who paused from handing out her lesson plan to look up.

"Oh, you brought a friend," she said, smiling. "How nice."

"He's not my friend. He's my neighbor. His name is Charlie Fry."

Susie Miller—as uppity as her dad, *the* Mr. Miller from the First National, the one who was always calling Teddy "Big Guy"—stifled a snicker. I knew she'd be laughing out loud at Charlie if Miss Tuckle wasn't standing right next to her, so I glared at Susie until she wiped that smirk off her face. Maybe Charlie was only my neighbor, but I didn't want anybody picking on him, his mom being an angel and his dad being in jail and all.

"Well, welcome, Charlie," Miss Tuckle said. She asked a couple of kids to scoot their chairs closer together, then pulled an extra chair to the table for him.

Sunday school was the same as always: Miss Tuckle smiling for thirty minutes straight, Susie Miller almost throwing her arm out of its socket as she begged to read in my place once I reminded Miss Tuckle again that I couldn't read because I needed glasses and we still didn't have the money to buy them. Of course the minute I said this, Charlie looked at me like he was trying to figure out if I was *really* half blind. But it's not like I could tell Charlie the truth—that I could see like a hawk, but didn't like reading out loud in Sunday school because the story always had those Bibley names in it that were fancier than mine, and when I fumbled on one of them, Susie always snickered.

Too bad I didn't have the chance to warn Charlie so he could have claimed to be half blind, too, because when it was his turn to read, boy, did he make a mess out of things. His paragraph didn't even have any fancy names or those weird Bible words like *thy* and *thou,* either. Just simple words that even a first grader would know. Miss Tuckle had to help Charlie so much that she might as well have read it herself, so when Charlie was done reading, and Robert, the kid who smelled like a barn, was taking his turn, I leaned over to Charlie and said, "*That's* why I pretend I'm blind as a bat."

I tried to listen to the lesson, but it wasn't easy. Not when I had to figure out how I was going to get another quarter. I decided that maybe a loan from the Taxi Stand Ladies might be my best bet. Those ladies always seemed to have money, though I didn't know how, since they didn't have jobs, best I could tell. Course, they would have had more than the bit of money they did if Pop, the roly-poly guy who owned The Pop Shop, would stop swiping it.

Pop was Ralph's brother and they were both uncles to The Kenosha Kid. But Pop wasn't a very nice uncle, because whenever Walking Doll or The Kenosha Kid went into his store to get a pack of Pall Malls or a bottle of Coca-Cola, and lay down a couple of bucks, even when what they were buying was way under one dollar, Pop just rolled the money up and stuffed it in his pocket without giving them any money back. Neither of them ladies ever asked for their change, either, but once when I followed them back out on the sidewalk, Walking Doll called Pop a "thieving bastard."

At least Ralph wasn't lousy to the Taxi Stand Ladies, because I'd never seen him ask for a dime after taking them for one of their many daily spins. No jobs and a thieving uncle or not, those girls always seemed to have a bit of cash on them. And they liked me, too. So providing that the banana-legged lady's sister moved as slow as Charlie, I'd have it made in the shade.

When ten-till came, Susie got the box of broken crayons out so we could color the picture at the end of our lesson plan. While we colored, Miss Tuckle led the "God Is Good" prayer so we could thank God for our bounty of Kool-Aid. Then Susie got down the "offering plate," as Miss Tuckle called it, even though it was nothing but an empty Folgers coffee can. Susie begged to carry it around to collect the offering like she did every Sunday. "That won't be necessary," Miss Tuckle said, like *she* did every Sunday, then she added, "But thank you for volunteering, Susie. Children, please put your offering in and pass the plate to your neighbor."

When it was almost my turn, I opened my purse and dug around like my offering was on the bottom and I was scooping it up.

Susie made sure everyone saw her fifty-cent piece before she dumped it in, then she handed Charlie the can, instructing him—like Mrs. Fry buzzed off his ears along with his scalp so he couldn't hear Miss Tuckle's instructions—and as soon as he dropped his nickel in, she yanked the can out of his hand and reached it around him toward me. I glared at her. "I think Charlie can pass a can without your help," I said.

I pulled my hand out of my purse, keeping it balled into a fist like it was holding my tithing, and buried it deep in the can. When my knuckles touched the cool bottom, I swirled my fingertips to jingle the money already in it, to make the noise of "my" coins dropping in. Boy, it wasn't easy, feeling those coins cool against my fingers—including Susie's fifty-cent piece—knowing that I could easily lift out enough to pay for the rest of my scooter and save my-self a whole bunch of time. But I couldn't steal from Jesus, even if He'd forgive me as long as I was sorry enough afterward. Borrow-ing money from Him when I wasn't coming to Sunday school any-way was one thing, but swiping money out of the offering plate was another.

I felt Miss Tuckle watching me as I passed the can to Robert, and I hoped that she didn't know I had fake-tithed.

My stomach felt a little weird when Miss Tuckle took the can from Robert. I told myself I'd do better. Promised even. Next week, I told myself, I'd pay Jesus back every penny I borrowed. Even if I had to sell my plastic purse to Jolene to do it. Yep, that's what I'd do.

"Miss Tuckle?" I said, as I tossed a crayon back into the empty ice cream pail, my picture finished. "Didn't we have a story about Moby-Dick in one of our lesson plans?"

Miss Tuckle was dabbing up a mess from a tipped-over Styro-foam cup. "Moby-Dick?" she asked as she dropped the soggy pur-pled napkin into the trash can.

"That's not a Bible story!" Susie said.

"True," Miss Tuckle said. "That's a novel by Herman Melville. Maybe you're thinking about the story of Jonah and the whale?"

"Probably," I said, because didn't that just figure.

Miss Tuckle started telling the story of Jonah, which wasn't going to help me a bit, but I was polite and waited for her to stop before I asked her how to spell the last name of that Herman guy.

Miss Tuckle thanked us all for coming, especially Charlie, so everybody stared at him all over again. "Have a good week, chil-dren, and God bless."

The air outside felt like a fever after sitting in that cool, musty basement. Charlie and I waggled through the men and ladies who'd just finished church and were coming down the steps after shaking the good reverend's hand. Every time I saw the church folks, I thought of how respectable they looked in their suits and hats and nice dresses, and every time, I thought about how Teddy had the same church-look and how he should be standing with them. But maybe things weren't like they looked at church, either. And maybe Pop was right when he told a customer that church was for sinners. It sure would have explained why Teddy didn't go (though it didn't explain why Pop didn't go), because I doubted that Teddy had sinned a day in his life—well, except for if "Thou shalt not kill" meant cows, too.

"Come on, Charlie, let's hurry. I want to make sure no one bought my scooter."

We were halfway across the church parking lot when Miss Tuckle called my name. I stopped and turned, my Jesus picture flapping in my hand as I waited for her to reach me.

Folks in town called Miss Tuckle an old maid because she didn't have a husband (never even had a boyfriend) even though she was thirty-two years old. Everybody thought that was a shame since she was real nice, even if she wasn't much of a looker, with the only bumps she had above her waist coming from her shoulder blades, which poked out extra chicken-wing-sharp because she was a sloucher. Still, her face wasn't all that homely, and she *was* nice. Nice enough that I didn't want her to know what I'd done and be mad at me. Or worse yet, to tattle if she ever ran into Mrs. Fry again.

"Charlie?" she said when she reached us, her non-Christmas lips smiling. "Could you give us a minute?" Charlie nodded, then just stood there, so Miss Tuckle took my arm and walked me away from Charlie and the sinners.

"I have something for you, Isabella," she said. She reached out and took my hand, then put a quarter into it and curled my fingers around it. "For the offering plate next Sunday," she said in a quiet voice filled with so much pity that if she wasn't my Sunday school teacher or I didn't like her, I would have been tempted to give her both of my birds. She gave me a proud smile and walked away, her wide skirt rustling in the breeze like angel wings.

"What did she give you?" Charlie asked, probably because he

thought it was a piece of candy. I didn't answer him. I just ran across the parking lot as fast as I could, hoping that I wasn't getting the stomach flu or something, because my belly sure wasn't feeling good.

When we got back to the yard sale, I saw my scooter waiting for me under the card table right where I'd left it. The banana-legged lady had another lady standing next to her with the same bowed legs, so I figured she must be the sister. I sprinted toward their yard like a jackrabbit, that quarter Miss Tuckle gave me burning in my hand like a potato baked to hell-hot.

CHAPTER SIX

It sure is amazing how badly you want to do good after you've done something bad. Teddy came home from work that night, and for whatever reason, he came in through the back door, not the front, so he saw my new scooter leaning up against the side of the house. I didn't lie, I told him the money to buy it came from selling my toys. I just didn't tell him that the money should have gone to Jesus instead. Sure, I felt guilty after I said it, and that guilt gnawed at me all through supper, right through our nightly game of Scrabble (so that I was even *glad* when I lost). Stayed with me through school the next day, too, so that when school let out and I had to go to the first meeting of the Sunshine Sisters, I didn't even say *crap* on the inside.

Miss Simon was waiting in the cafeteria, looking smart in a fancy suit with what I knew from listening to the Jackson girls was a pencil skirt, the fabric probably tweed. She stood with her hands folded in front of her while two teenage helpers took the shoulders of us little kids and put us up against the wall like crooks in a lineup.

I stood with my arms tucked behind me, the bricks cool against my butt, doing what all the other Little Sisters were doing—

looking at the Big Sisters (though I was humming a little and I don't think anybody else was doing that). Boy, those Big Sisters sure were a clean, respectable bunch, with their clothes pretty and matching and their hair all shiny and held back in ponytails or with ribbon headbands. I couldn't say the same about the rest of us. Me especially.

At least once every season, Mrs. Jackson came out on the steps when I was in their yard and handed me a bag or two of hand-me-downs. I'd bring them home and Teddy would have me bring them to Mrs. Fry, who tugged each item over my head, then made me stand still while she poked straight pins up and down and around the seams so she could "fit them right," even if when she got done, they didn't.

Not that I cared one way or another. That is, until I realized that the Big Sisters were watching us, just like we were watching them, and I looked down. Man, how could I not have noticed until then that the hem of my red, white, and blue plaid dress was down past my knees on one side, and up above them on the other? Or that Jo-lene's old supposed-to-be-white-but-now-gray sweater was stretched like taffy? I turned in the toes of Jennifer's scuffed brown shoes and sank closer to the wall.

Back when I was still with my ma, I had long hair halfway down my back—my waist if I stretched it out—but I wanted short hair like hers. So I got ahold of the scissors one morning while she slept, and I cut it short (but for a few clumps of curls I couldn't reach in the back). When I was done, I sat sidesaddle on the edge of the bathroom sink and sang into the mirror, thinking I looked as glamorous as Donna Reed. But when Ma woke up and saw me, it was plain she didn't think I looked nice. "Oh, all your pretty curls. Look at them. Just look at them," she kept saying as she fished my curls out of the sink and swept more off the floor.

The next time I looked in the mirror, I didn't think I looked beautiful anymore. I thought I looked ugly. That's how it is when you borrow somebody else's eyes, I guess. And that's how it was when I noticed that the Big Sisters were gawking at us with pity-faces or wrinkled noses as they whispered to each other. Some of them looking like they were trying to decide which one of us might have scabies or fleas or some other dreadful health affliction that might be catchy.

Once we were all in place, Miss Simon clapped her hands to make everybody shut up, then introduced Mrs. Gaylor, who was an older lady, dressed to the nines but walking like her girdle was crushing her. Mrs. Gaylor yammered on and on about the importance of girls having positive role models and all that other hooey I already heard from Mrs. Carlton, then wound down her big blab with a promise that we'd all have a fun, "rewarding" summer filled with "wonderful surprises." I almost got excited about that part. Until I remembered that Teddy once told me that he had a nice surprise for me, and it turned out to be nothing but milk toast.

Some of the older girls didn't bother hiding their horrification (which I decided, if it wasn't a real word, should be) when they saw what Little Sister they were stuck with. Like Tina, who got Mindy Brewer, a bucktoothed girl with a snarl at the back of her head the size of France. Tina cringed like she suddenly smelled dog poop when Mindy stepped forward after her name was called. Just like the Big Sister with curly hair like mine did when she got stuck with Alice Limpkins, the girl who was a flunky—twice over—and *did* have flea bites on her legs in fourth grade.

Lots of those older girls looked upset when their Little Sister stepped away from the wall to join them—but not Brenda Bloom. She only smiled when she called out my name, like she didn't even notice that I was afflicted. When she put her hand on my shoulder to lead me to a table, I heard one of the Little Sisters behind me say, "That lucky!" And I almost did feel lucky, too. Because Brenda was the prettiest—and probably the nicest—best girl of the bunch of best girls, so getting paired with her was sort of like drawing the best gift under the tree in the classroom Christmas gift exchange.

When we got to the table—Brenda and I on one end, and some

other poor loser like me and a big girl with poufy hair and a shiny necklace sitting across from us—Brenda started paging through her packet for the GETTING ACQUAINTED paper. "I didn't think you'd show up," she said as she dug.

"Yeah, well I have my reasons," I said.

Brenda pulled a page out of her folder. "Care to share?"

"Nope," I said as I gawked around the room.

One thing I noticed right off was that the big Goody Two-shoes girls sat straight, like they had an invisible rope to the ceiling running right through them that came out the tops of their heads. I couldn't say the same for us afflicted kids, though. The girl sitting to my left was drooped over, her hand holding up her head like it was too heavy to stay up on its own, which it might have been, since she did have a noggin the size of a standard pumpkin, and me, sitting on one leg, my free leg bouncing. When I noticed, though, I put both my feet flat on the floor and sat up straight.

"Isabella," Brenda said, looking down at the paper. "I'm going to read a list of activities, and when I mention one you like, you tell me, okay? This is how we'll find out what interests we have in common."

Brenda sounded like a schoolteacher as she read the list filled with things like badminton and tennis. Things I never even did once, so how would I know if I liked doing them or not? And then she read things that weren't even "activities" but just plain work, like cooking and sewing. Things I *knew* I didn't like.

When the list Brenda was reading got so long I couldn't listen anymore, I got on my knees and leaned over the table so I could see just how much longer it was going to take. Sure enough, the activities under the pen tip Brenda was using to keep her place was Santa-list long. "How about I save you the trouble of reading that whole thing," I said, "and just tell you what I like doing. Okay?

"I like riding my new scooter—well, it's not actually new, but it's new to me—and playing marbles and jumping rope and jacks. Scrabble, too, but only with Teddy because he doesn't mind if I dance around and sing while he takes his turn. Those are the things I *like*. But the things I *love* are singing and movies. I sing all the time, and most of the time I don't even know I'm doing it. Did I hum or sing since we sat down? I'll bet I did." Brenda nodded and smiled. "Yep. Figures. It's an affliction I've got, but one I hope I don't have to fix in order to become respectable."

"You have a very pretty voice," Brenda said.

"Oh, I was probably just mumbling or humming. That's what I do when I don't know I'm doing it. I'm still hearing what's going on around me when I do that, but when I sing for real, I really belt it out. Jennifer Jackson—she's not here, even though she should be because she has the affliction of being noodley—told me once that when I sing, she can feel it shake right down in her tummy, and that I give her goose bumps. It's a very good sign if you give somebody goose pimples when you sing, you know."

Brenda smiled again, which made me wonder if she wasn't making fun of me in her head, like I did sometimes when kids said something so dumb that I thought it was funny, but I didn't want to laugh out loud and make them feel bad. "I've no doubt that you do," Brenda said. "And by the way, I like those same things."

Brenda twirled the tail of a pink scarf she had tied around her ponytail as she scanned the rest of the page. "And the last question. What do you hope to get out of this program?"

"Well, I've been thinking about that," I told her.

"Good," Brenda said.

"I hope to learn how to behave so I don't have to be a flunky, and so that Teddy doesn't throw my butt on the Greyhound bus. Is *butt* a swear word, do you know? I hope not, because I gave up swearing. Anyway, I hope you can teach me how to be better and do better so I can become more respectable. Past that, all I'm looking for is money."

"Money?" Brenda said, her eyes going Bette-Davis-big.

"Yeah. But not a handout, because Teddy says there's no pride in handouts. I'm not looking for a loan, either, because, well, you could say that's what got me in trouble in the first place.

"I can't explain why I need the money, but trust me, if you really want to help me be a better person, what you can give me is a job. I don't care what. I'd work real cheap, as long as I can make thirty-five cents. That's what I really need most right now. Well, that, and probably a lesson or two on keeping my yap shut when I should."

"Isabella—" she said, and I stopped her.

"Look, if we're supposed to be like real Sunshine Sisters—whatever that's supposed to mean, but I'm guessing all *sunny* with each other—then you're going to have to call me Teaspoon."

"Okay, Teaspoon. But this isn't a work program. It's a mentorship program."

"Wow," I said. "That's a pretty fancy word. I like learning new fancy words. You never know when you're going to have to read one of them out loud, or when you can use one to score big in Scrabble. In school this year, Mrs. Carlton let us choose from the regular spelling lists in our book, or the Spelling Challenge lists she made up herself. Those are the hard ones, and that's the lists I chose. I learned *affliction,* and *contradiction* not long ago, but *mentorship*? Hmm. Don't think we've had that one yet."

"Well," Brenda said. "A mentor is someone who guides you by giving you advice. Someone usually older and more experienced than you. *Mentorship* is a word to describe the relationship itself."

"Wow, you're smart. But I suppose you'd have to be or you wouldn't be the Sweetheart of Mill Town." Brenda looked down and cleared her throat a little, even though it was hard to believe that a girl like her ever got gunk in her throat.

"Meeting location...," she read. "Would you like to meet at the Starlight?"

"You're kidding me, right? That's my favorite place in the whole world! Of course I'd like to meet there."

"Good. We'll have our first meeting the Monday after school lets out. May twenty-third."

"*After* school lets out?" I almost yelled. "You mean I have to wait until school lets out?"

"Yes, that's when the program officially begins. Most of us girls have too much going on until then, with graduation." I groaned, and Brenda added, "But I'm glad to see you're eager to get started. You've had quite a change of heart since the last time I saw you."

"Oh, I didn't have a change of heart," I told her, only because the night before I promised Jesus and Teddy I'd try to stop being such a fibber-face. "It's just that I got myself into a bit of trouble, and I need a job and thirty-five cents to bail me out. Pronto."

I sure wished Brenda would stop grinning like I was Lucille-and-Ethel-funny. I wasn't trying to be.

Brenda grabbed her purse from the back of her chair and took out a wallet made of shoe leather, not plastic like mine. When I saw her take a quarter and a dime out, I stopped her. "Hey, didn't I just say that I can't take handouts?"

"It's not a handout," she said. "It's an advance."

"An advance?"

"Yes." She put the money on the table in front of me. "An early payment for a job you're going to do. I give you thirty-five cents in advance, and when we meet, you can stock candy for me at the Starlight to work it off. How's that?"

"Well, if it's not a handout, then I guess I can take it." I scarfed up the coins and shoved them in my purse, and whew, just whew!

Mrs. Pines, the cafeteria lady—the one who doesn't care if juice from your canned corn leaks into your mashed potatoes—walked around with a tray while we were all settling on private meeting times, and she put a Dixie cup of apple juice and a flower-shaped sugar cookie sitting on a napkin in front of each girl. We were ordered by bossy Mrs. Gaylor not to touch them, though, until everyone was served, even though our after-school bellies were grumbling. Since we had to wait, and Brenda and me had our business taken care of, I decided to make good use of the rest of the time I was stuck there, and I asked Brenda if she'd like to tell me a little story while we waited.

"You like being told stories?" Brenda asked.

"Only if the story is the story of Moby-Dick," I said. And

wouldn't you know it? Brenda knew that story and told it to me. Well, at least enough of the story for me to fill one page in my notebook if I printed big enough.

When the last table was served, I thought we would be able to gobble up our snack and get out of there, but no dice. We had to wait until Mrs. Gaylor gave us a talk on how to eat in public—like we'd never done *that* before!—and while she yammered, everyone had to watch Brenda demonstrate what Mrs. Gaylor was saying.

It was all a bunch of twaddle, if you asked me, taking such little bites that a mouse would have starved to death before that cookie was gone. And putting our napkins on our laps to catch crumbs, even though when we picked it up to dab our mouths now and then—as Mrs. Gaylor said we were supposed to—every crumb we caught was going to get dumped on our laps or on the floor anyway.

By the time Mrs. Gaylor's lesson and Brenda's demonstration were over, our apple juice was warm as pee, and my belly was so hungry that I didn't care who didn't approve, I broke the cookie in half and shoved a whole half into my mouth. Brenda didn't yell at me, though. In fact, she looked like she wanted to laugh, same way Charlie laughed when I burped.

I thought we could leave right after we ate, but no dice again. We couldn't go until the Big Sisters stood up and recited something that was supposed to be the "code" of the Sunshine Sisters that we were all supposed to memorize. It was about being well behaved so that we could be proud of ourselves, and our families and our community could be proud of us, too. Something like that, anyway.

"Would you like me to jot the day and time of our first meeting down for you so you don't forget?" Brenda asked when our meeting was over for real.

"No. I can remember anything that I make into a little song." I tossed the time and date into a little ditty and sang it back to Brenda. "See? That's how I remember important things."

✳   ✳   ✳

Humpty-Dumpty Charlie was waiting for me on the brick ledge where he still spent his recesses, my scooter propped against the bricks. "Thanks for watching my scooter. Did you take it for a spin?" Charlie shook his head. "Why not? I told you you could." But he didn't answer.

I handed Charlie my schoolbooks so I could use both hands to steer and off we went, Charlie walking so slow that I had to ride in circles around him or I would have tipped over.

"Why do you have to go to those meetings, anyway?" Charlie asked.

"Because I've got afflictions and no ma in my house," I told him.

"I don't have a ma, but I don't have to go."

"That's because you're a boy. This is just for girls."

"Do I got afflictions?" Charlie asked.

"You've got plenty of them," I told him, and poor Charlie grinned like having them was something to be proud of.

CHAPTER SEVEN

In one week's time, I made good with Mrs. Carlton *and* with Jesus. I turned in my make-up work, including my paper on Moby-Dick. Okay, so maybe the most words I had on one blue line was six, as Mrs. Carlton pointed out, but it was enough to get me promoted to sixth grade. And I put the quarter Miss Tuckle gave me in the offering plate (holding it out first so that Miss Tuckle and Susie Miller could see me doing it), and left the other dime I owed Him on the altar upstairs, holding it out first so He'd see me doing it and know that we were squared up.

That week I had another Sunshine Sister meeting with Brenda, too. Charlie tagged along, just to wait outside and keep an eye on my scooter for me.

Boy, that Starlight! It didn't matter how eager I was to learn how to be respectable, I forgot about everything but how much I loved that place the second I stepped inside.

Brenda led the way to the first concession stand while I followed behind her like a Charlie, my head gawking all over. "Ain't this place something, Brenda? I'll bet every time you step in here, you feel like somebody stole your breath all over again. That sure is how I feel."

Brenda looked up for a second, like she was thinking on what I said and checking out the place at the same time, and then she said, "It *is* a cool place, isn't it? I suppose sometimes I forget to really look at it because I'm so used to it."

"I don't think I'd *ever* get so used to the Starlight that I couldn't see the magic in it anymore," I said. And Brenda said that, somehow, she believed that was true.

The Starlight didn't have matinees every week, and they weren't going to have one this weekend. In fact, after the show that night, they weren't going to have any shows for a long time, because they were converting the theater to one that showed movies some times, and live shows other times. "Wow, Brenda," I said when she told me. "You mean with real first-class acts?"

"Yes," Brenda said. "That's what we're hoping for." Then Brenda explained how they were going to rip out some seats in the front row and build a big stage for the acts, and an orchestra pit for the musicians. Mrs. Bloom had bought the old furniture store next to the Starlight, so that when the live bands came, they'd have dressing rooms and a big room for dancers to warm up in. Wouldn't you know it! I finally get an "in" to see some movies legal, and they were closing for what might be the whole summer. Still, Brenda and I needed to make the concession stand ready for the seven o'clock show that night.

I thought it would be a good idea to line the candy up according to how good they tasted. Like start with the Jujubes and the Good & Plenty on the best end, the candy bars in the middle, Big Hunk leading the way, and then the Milk Duds and Boston Baked Beans on the other end, because if you asked me, they were both duds. Brenda said that while that was a good idea, it would mess up the workers, who were used to the order the candy was in already and would be grabbing the wrong things when it got busy before the movie and at intermission, so I had to keep the same lineup.

While I sat on my knees putting candy away, Brenda opened a box filled with striped popcorn boxes, flat as envelopes. I got to my feet and picked one up. "I didn't know these things came flat and you had to put them together. Look at that, they got tabs on them, just like paper dolls. Where does this one go?"

We talked about the movies we liked best as we made boxes. Brenda saw way more than me, so she mentioned ones I never saw, but highest on her list was *The Wild One*. "I heard about that movie. And I saw Mrs. Delaney and Mrs. Perkins gawking at Marlon Brando like he was as gorgeous as James Dean. Pop yells at me if I page through the magazines, even if I'm careful not to wrinkle the pages, but he didn't yell at them.

"Holy cow, is James Dean dreamy or what? I'll bet you're in love with James Dean, too. Well, maybe not, because you're in love with Leonard Gaylor, and I don't think people can be in love with two people at one time, can they? To folks here in Mill Town, you and Leonard Gaylor are as famous of a couple as Gregory Peck and Audrey Hepburn, Kirk Douglas and Lana Turner, Marilyn Monroe and Marlon Brando all rolled into one—which must mean that he's every bit as movie-star handsome as you are movie-star pretty. They talk highly about Leonard all the time," I said. "Him having been the number one smartest person in his whole high school class, just like you, and the most valuable person on the basketball team, the debate team, and about every other team there is." Brenda dropped her popcorn box and I picked it up because I was closer to the floor.

"Oh, I like Marlon Brando," she said.

And I said, "He's okay, but he's not as dreamy as James Dean."

That reminded me. "Hey," I said, "do you remember last Christmas when you guys had a free matinee for kids and a Santa afterward who gave out free goodybags? Popcorn, peanuts in their shells, and that hard candy that looks like frozen ribbons? I didn't get to go to that movie because you had to go with an adult, like always, and Teddy was working. My neighbors went, though. Jack—the meanest of the bunch—was first in line, and as soon as he got his goodybag, he slipped back in line behind his sister so he could con two bags out of Santa. I was at their house waiting for Jennifer and Jolene when they got back from the picture show, and when they were all bragging about getting those free bags, dumb Jack, who's never been able to keep his yap shut, unzipped his coat and took that second bag out so he could brag about how he'd gotten two and I didn't even get one. His big brother Johnny came in the kitchen then and grabbed his cheater bag. He pulled a handful of popcorn out of it and said 'Thanks, little brother,' and Jack cussed, like he does when his ma isn't around.

"I ended up getting a bag of candy anyway that day, because Johnny pulled a candy cane out and while he was snapping the hook part off with his teeth, he looked over at me and said, 'You get a bag, too?' And I said no. So he handed me the whole bag. 'Compliments of Jack, the little thief,' he said. Anyway, that was a real nice stash you Blooms gave away. And I'll bet the movie was real good, too."

Brenda frowned. "Well, this year I'll see to it that you get your own bag, and that you get to see the movie."

"That would be swell, Brenda. Can I sit in the front row, smack-dab in the middle?" I asked, knowing it would get Jack's goat, since he makes Mrs. Jackson get to the theater practically the day before so he can get that seat.

And Brenda said, "You can sit anywhere you want."

I fit the popcorn box I'd just put together into our stack of boxes that was growing as tall as the Eiffel Tower. "I'm gonna get up here so I can reach the stack easier," I said, then hoisted myself up on the counter and started swaying my legs like a *metronome*, which is what our music teacher said that gadget is called that helps you keep time if you don't practice with the radio. While I hummed and made boxes I answered a whole lot of Brenda's questions about my ma, and Teddy, and school. But the whole time I was answering Brenda, I was thinking about how nice Johnny Jackson had always been to me, and how I wanted to marry him when I grew up. Course, I couldn't get married for a long time, and in the meantime, I knew, I'd have to put up with Johnny having his share of girlfriends whether I liked it or not. Because like I heard Mrs. Delaney say to the butcher's wife when she was complaining about how much grief her teenage son was giving her, "Well, Mary. Young men need to sow their wild oats before they settle down," which I decided was another way of saying that they needed to have lots of girlfriends and drink lots of beer and drive their cars fast before they could get married, because that's what Johnny was doing. And sometimes he sowed two or three oats in the same week. I knew this for a fact, because Mrs. Jackson was always yelling at Johnny about necking with some girl over at Bugsy's Car Hop, or sometimes right in their driveway, where anybody could see. And once while Mrs. Jackson was outside, Johnny brought a girl through the front door and took her right up to his bedroom, and we saw them. Well, not Mrs. or Mr. Jackson, but the rest of us.

Me and Jennifer and Jolene were coming out of their room and saw her brothers outside Johnny's door, looking through a crack, their cheeks all red and puffed out from trying not to make noise. Course, then we had to see what was going on, too, so Jolene shoved the boys out of the way. Jack would have slugged her good and shoved her back, but he knew she'd scream bloody murder and Mrs. Jackson would hear all the way in the backyard where she was hanging laundry. So we squirmed our way to the crack and there they were, Johnny and some girl lying face-to-face on his bed, kissing movie-star hard. I thought they were playing a game where the object was to try to shove each other off the bed without using their hands, because they had their hands up each other's shirts and were only pushing with their hips. I decided they'd been playing it for a long time, too, because they were breathing real hard, like they just ran ten laps around a track. About the time the bed started squeaking, though, Joey whispered, "Holy crap, they're gonna do the Juicy Jitterbug." We didn't get to see that part, though, because Johnny heard us and threw a shoe at the door to make us scatter.

Mrs. Jackson found out about it, too, and she screamed at Johnny, "Look what you're teaching these kids! I'm going to tell your father!" And as Johnny was grabbing his keys off the counter and heading out the door, he said, "First you'd have to find him," which didn't make any sense since Mr. Jackson was sitting right in front of the TV where he always was when he wasn't at work.

Back when I saw Johnny and that girl "petting"—which is what Joey said couples do before they do the Juicy Jitterbug—it only made me giggle behind my hand. But thinking about it while I made popcorn boxes made my insides get all tingly. Like when your foot wakes up after it falls asleep because you've been sitting on it too long. Something like that, only better. I blinked a couple of times, then said, "Hey Brenda, do my eyes look all goofy?"

She leaned over and examined my face. "No. Why?"

"I don't know," I said, even though I did. "I was just wondering."

I thought for about two seconds, then said, "Brenda, as my Sunshine Sister, you're supposed to teach me stuff I don't know because you're older and know more, right?"

"Yes," she said.

"Well, can I ask you anything at all?"

"I have a feeling you will," Brenda said.

I wasn't sure what that meant so I ignored it. "What does it feel like to be in love?"

"Are you in love?" she asked, and I think she wanted to smile again but didn't, which was a good thing.

"Maybe. But I'm not sure. That's why I'm asking. You know how in the movies, the leading lady's eyes get that foggy look, like they might melt, when she's in love? Well, that's why I asked if my eyes looked weird, because if they did, then it might help me figure out if I'm in love or not."

"You have beautiful blue eyes," Brenda said. "Kind of a mix between a deep turquoise and navy." She said this like I'd asked her what color my eyes were, which I hadn't.

Brenda was standing close to where I was sitting, so I leaned forward. So far forward that I almost tipped off the counter. I looked hard into her eyes. Nice as they were, they looked pretty normal to me. Brenda looked away and got busy turning our giant stack of made boxes into two shorter ones.

"That's just in the movies, Teaspoon," she said. "They use special lighting to give eyes that soft look."

"Oh," I said. "Figures. Well, what about the weird tingling you get inside your belly...well, lower, too, I guess...when a boy you like looks at you or you remember him giving you a goodybag, or whacking his brothers for you? Does that mean you're in love?"

"Could be," Brenda said with a grin, then she got busy saying how we should only put together about ten more boxes, since extras would just be in the way after that night's show. "You can fill up the straw dispensers next if you'd like. I'll show you how."

But I had one more question. "Brenda," I said. "If you get a boyfriend, do you have to let him rub your balloons?"

"Balloons?" Brenda asked.

I patted my chest where my balloons were going to grow. "Yeah, these."

Brenda's lips bunched and her cheeks puffed out, because she was trying to hold some giggles inside. Then her eyes got that teasy kind of sparkle in them and she said, "Why are you asking? You afraid they'll pop?" There was no locking her giggles in then. She laughed until her face turned popcorn-box-red and she was hanging on to the counter to hold herself up.

"It wasn't that funny, wise guy," I snapped.

"I'm sorry. I'm sorry," she finally said, as she dabbed at her eyes. "I shouldn't have said that. In fact, we shouldn't be saying any of this. Mrs. Gaylor wouldn't exactly find any of these appropriate topics for Sunshine Sisters to discuss, so let's change the subject."

"Okay," I said. "But too bad, because I really want to know. I'll ask the Taxi Stand Ladies."

"The Taxi Stand Ladies?" Brenda asked, and I reminded her that she'd met them. When I got done refreshing her memory, Brenda bunched her lips all over again, like maybe Mrs. Gaylor wouldn't think the Taxi Stand Ladies were an appropriate topic for Sunshine Sisters to discuss, either, which had me wondering what *was* an appropriate topic for us to discuss? Then I thought of something that might be.

"Hey, Brenda. I noticed that you talk real respectable, using words like *appropriate* and stuff, and not saying *ain't* and *gonna*, like I do. You think you could help me learn to talk more respectable? Teddy sure would be happy if you did, and probably my next teacher, too. It drove Mrs. Carlton up the wall when I used those words. She'd get this little twitch on her face, right here," I said, pointing to the spot right under my eye, above the bumpiest part of my cheekbone. "Anyway, maybe you could catch me when I use them and correct me."

Brenda winced. "I think there's enough *correcting* going on in this place," she said. "How about if you just listen and catch yourself when you're using them."

One of the first things I learned as a Sunshine Sister was that respectable people act different around different people. Take Mrs. Bloom, for instance. Whenever I ran into her around town, there she was, walking ironing-board-straight, her feet gliding her along, her head moving side-to-side like a beauty queen going down the runway. She didn't say *Darlinggggggg* when she met up with another fancy lady, like they did in the old movies they played on Channel 12 on Sunday afternoons, but every single word she said sounded like she was saying it as she talked about Brenda this, Brenda that. But when she was talking to Brenda and nobody else was around but me, there wasn't any *darlinggggggg* in her voice at all.

I was still sitting on the counter, four metal straw dispensers lined up beside me, putting straws into the first one like Brenda showed me, when Mrs. Bloom came in, her purse and a First National Bank bag dangling from her arm. Her face looked like Mrs.

Jackson's when she came through the kitchen lugging a basket of laundry and stopped to peek at a pot of something cooking on the stove, *while* she yelled at Jack and Joey for roughhousing. Yep, that's just how Mrs. Bloom looked—only her hair was fixed a whole lot nicer.

Mrs. Bloom gave Brenda a quick peck on the cheek, right in the middle of a sentence about "securing a band director," and she didn't even wait for Brenda to say anything back before she was telling her that they had a lot of details to go over. I think she was about to say what those details where, but instead, she stopped and blinked. "Brenda, why are *you* stocking the concession stand? This should have been done by the crew before they left last night."

"Well, Melissa is having her graduation party tomorrow, a week late because her grandparents couldn't come last week, and Cindy—"

Mrs. Bloom didn't let her finish. "Honey, I've told you a hundred times, you are here in the capacity of a co-manager now. You're to orchestrate the operation, not to operate it yourself. Employees always have an excuse, but when it comes to work, there are none. You're too softhearted for your own good. Delegate, Brenda. Delegate."

"*Delegate?* Hmmm, that's a new one," I said. "What does that word mean, Mrs. Bloom?"

Mrs. Bloom blinked at me like I'd just appeared on the counter like magic. "Excuse me?" she said.

"Oh, I just like learning a new fancy word now and then," I said. "You never know when you're going to have to read them or get the right letter tiles."

Mrs. Bloom looked confused, like she didn't know if she wanted to answer me or to yell at me—or maybe she just didn't remember who I was, because Brenda quickly reminded her that I was her Sunshine Sister. "Farm out tasks…assign them to others…," Mrs. Bloom said, waving her hand, her words short and sharp, like high heels on a wood floor.

"Oh," I said. "How do you spell it?"

"D-e-l-e-g-a-t-e," Brenda said quickly, then I shut up so I could run the word around a few laps in my head so I wouldn't forget it.

Mrs. Bloom looked down at the opened, half-put-away candy cartons. "What are those doing on the floor?"

"Oh, I did that, Mrs. Bloom. I forgot I was doing the candy." I gave my mouth a quick pop with my hand. "I'll put them away as soon as I have these dispensers filled."

"Well, pick up the boxes until then. Food doesn't belong on the floor...and butts don't belong on the counter. Get down, please."

"Did you just swear at me?" I asked.

"Of course I didn't!" Mrs. Bloom said, which proved right then and there that *butt* wasn't a cussword. Then she gave Brenda a look that meant, *Make this kid respectable already, will ya?*

Mrs. Bloom dug in the First National bag, taking out rows of coins and clunking them on the counter. "Perkins and his crew will be here to get started in about an hour. I'm fit to be tied that Glen himself won't be working on this job—something about expanding his operation down south. If I could find someone on this late notice, I'd do it. Sure, he assured me that this Mel character is the best man for the job, claiming he made a stage or two in New York City and that he's run crews before, but who knows. Anyway, you'll have to let them in, Brenda, because I have to get over to the town hall for a meeting this morning about those two..." She glanced over at me and stopped talking right in the middle of her sentence, like she was about to say a cussword in front of me or something. "Glen said he'd personally check on the crew from time to time. If he doesn't, Brenda, then I want you to call him and complain. We're under such a time crunch already, we can't run the risk of something needing to be redone because it wasn't done right in the first place. After the town meeting, I have to get out to the site. They're erecting the screen today."

"*Mrs. Bloom delegated the job of calling Perkins Construction to Brenda,*" I said out loud, happy because I was sure I was using the word right.

Mrs. Bloom looked at me, her penciled eyebrows bunching. She picked up a roll of dimes and cracked it against the side of the money drawer, breaking it open like an egg. "Young lady," she said. "We are having a little meeting here. Do you mind?"

"Oh. That's what me and Brenda are having, too. A meeting. And no, I don't mind." I jiggled the dispenser to get the straws to stack nice and flat so I could squeeze more in, then looked up. Mrs. Bloom was still staring at me like she couldn't believe her eyes. I wasn't sure why, and would have asked, but Brenda was shooting me shut-your-trap looks, so I didn't.

Mrs. Bloom tore at a band of paper that wouldn't let go of some dimes, and when her picking didn't free them, Brenda reached over and took them from her to finish the job. "Oh, I know I'm being a bear these days, Brenda," Mrs. Bloom said, "but I'm a nervous wreck. I had coffee this morning with Mrs. Devon and Mrs. Rhine, and both of them were pumping me for details. What could I do but tell them that I'm saving them like a delicious surprise? And this project and all the headache that's given me..." She turned to Brenda, her eyes pleading like a kitty's when it wants milk. "I don't know what to do. The gala is Labor Day weekend and I don't have a theme, an opening act, or even a stage to put them on if I did. And I'm trying to set up a new business. I'm overwrought."

"Gala?" I said, when my ears perked to another new word.

"A big party. In this case, a live show on the new stage," Brenda said in almost a whisper, spelling it out for me, then adding a "shhhhh" as the last word of her sentence.

And I would have shushed up, too, except that I had a question. "Wow, you mean, like the big show Bing Crosby put on in that movie *White Christmas*? You mean like that?"

Brenda nodded and tapped my leg to hush me. "Sorry," I whispered back, my eyes still on Mrs. Bloom, who looked ready to cry even as she divvied up stacks of what had to be enough dollar bills to send Teddy to electricity school.

"Every day that passes lessens our chances of getting one of the better acts. Yet I have so much to do in regard to the drive-in that I can hardly think straight. I should have just let Mildred's nephew put one up in the first place, rather than outbidding him for that land."

Wow, those Blooms were a wealth of good surprises! "A drive-in theater? Mill Town is getting a drive-in theater? The Jacksons went to one last year when they visited their grandma. Joey said they watched the whole movie from the roof of their car. Well, he did anyway. Jack and James spent their time on the roof watching teenagers neck. Must have been true, too, because when I asked James what show they watched, he didn't even know the name of it."

"Brenda!" Mrs. Bloom said, as if Brenda was the one talking. A phone rang from somewhere just then, and Mrs. Bloom nodded toward the stacks of bills wrapped with rubber bands—I think because she thought one of my afflictions might have been stealing—then she hurried off to a small room I didn't know existed, alongside the second concession stand.

While she was gone, her voice nothing but a mumble behind a closed door, Brenda leaned over and whispered that I should just work quietly and not interrupt while her mother was there.

"Because she's upset today?" I asked.

"Yes."

"Oh," I said, putting the box I just made onto the stack Brenda had moved over by the popcorn maker. "Brenda? You have the Starlight, why do you need a drive-in?"

"Because they're the rage, and we have to stay competitive. Also, because the Starlight will be closed while we renovate."

"Oh, so your ma is afraid that if she doesn't put one up, people will just drive over to Milwaukee and stop coming to the Starlight? If so, she shouldn't worry. The Jackson kids came home from that drive-in with more mosquito bites than freckles. Who'd want to go to a movie and get all bit up like that?"

I stuck my head into the empty and burn-stained popcorn maker, pulling on the handle and making the big round pan tip sideways, which I imagined was how they got the popcorn out. "Well, someone who wants to neck, I suppose. Or someone who wants to watch people neck. But folks who just want to see a good movie, they'll come to the Starlight."

"Are you done with the straw dispensers?" Brenda asked.

"No, I got one left," I said, and Brenda suggested I finish up because our time together was almost over.

I opened a new box of straws and pulled out a handful. "Boy, this gala sure sounds special. Brenda, do you think you and me could have a meeting that night so I could see it? I've never seen anyone famous before—well, except my ma, but I don't think she's famous yet. I wonder who your ma will get? Probably anyone she wants if she sticks a picture of the Starlight inside her invitation. Who wouldn't come here?"

Brenda smiled, then said, "Well, it's not exactly that simple. The bigger entertainers mostly stick to the big venues—um, places, v-e-n-u-e-s—and they cost a fortune. Their schedules are set for months in advance, too."

"Wow, that *V* is worth four points."

I grabbed another handful of straws and patted them in the last dispenser. "Well, when I'm a rich and famous singer, I'll come sing here anytime you ask me to, Brenda. Even if you only give me one week's notice and I'm booked in New York City. I'll just call New York then and say, 'Sorry Lou, no can do,' and I'll come to the Starlight instead."

Mrs. Bloom wasn't on the phone long, and when she got back she told Brenda that it was Mrs. Miller on the phone. "She wanted to make sure I was joining their cause. Mrs. Miller, Mrs. Gaylor, Mrs. Delaney, my bridge club…every one of them are in a complete tizzy over those two…" She looked over at me and shut her trap again, then said, "Which, if you ask me, is sort of like worrying about what the rats at the dump are doing. I wouldn't bother, but I'm hoping to rope a few of them into coming to our gala organizational meeting this afternoon. Now, where was I?"

I didn't mean to stare, but it sure was interesting the way Mrs. Bloom's whole hairdo—sprayed stiff and Bakelite-hard—moved like a wig loose on the scalp when she scratched her head. Not one curl wiggled.

"Speaking of meetings. Is there coffee in the conference room for the organizational meeting this afternoon? Check on that and have Uriah pick some up before he comes in today if not."

"What about the bakery?"

"Yes, please," Mrs. Bloom said, then she kissed Brenda's cheek. "You're a dear, Brenda. I don't know what I'd do without you. I know this is overwhelming to you, too, all the responsibility I'm giving you, but you're a woman now, and you'll soon be a wife. These are all skills that will help you learn how to juggle your social responsibilities with your obligations at home."

Mrs. Bloom put small stacks of bills into the till, picked up the rest, and turned around. I leaned to the side so I could see what she was doing when she crouched down. "Is that a safe?" I asked. Mrs. Bloom turned the black dial knob first this way, then that, and the door popped right open. "Wow," I said. "I can't wait to tell Teddy that you've got a real safe in here."

Mrs. Bloom's wiggy head snapped up, her eyes almost as big as Brenda's, and I could tell what she was thinking. "Oh, don't worry, Mrs. Bloom. Teddy's not a bank robber or a crook. He's real respectable. He doesn't even need to go to church, he's so good. And if he was a little girl instead of a man, he wouldn't even need to be a Sunshine Sister. I just want to tell him because he likes to watch a western at Mrs. Fry's now and then. They have a lot of safes in those shows, so he might find it interesting."

Mrs. Bloom shoved the rest of the money into the safe, shut it fast, gave the knob a few more twirls, shut the cupboard, then stood up. She was staring at me as she straightened her jacket down over the belt of her skirt, and her mouth was puckered lemon-sucking sour. "Miss...Miss..."

"Isabella Marlene," Brenda reminded her.

"But you can call me Teaspoon," I told her.

Mrs. Bloom blinked hard. "Miss Marlene. I do happen to know that Mrs. Gaylor issued you girls a Sunshine Sisters code—which you should have memorized by now—that says that a Sunshine Sister should strive to be well mannered at all times. Well mannered, so she can be a good reflection on her family, her community, and the Sunshine Sisters' organization. Part of having good manners is not butting into other people's conversations or their business. Do you understand?"

"Yes . . . I mean, I don't have that code stuff memorized yet, but I know what *well mannered* means. It's the same as being respectable, ain't it? If it is, then good thing, because that's exactly what Brenda is gonna teach me."

"Teach her to use proper grammar while you're at it," Mrs. Bloom said, and I piped up, "Yep, I already told Brenda that I want to learn that, too."

"Young lady!" Mrs. Bloom shouted. "Did you not hear one word I just said?"

"I heard you," I said, rubbing my finger over my bottom lip like I could erase the words that spilled out, because suddenly I was feeling like a flunky, even if my report card said I wasn't.

Mrs. Bloom slammed the till shut and turned to Brenda. "Like I told you, you have your work cut out for you. Now, if you can only get her to be quiet long enough for us to finish our business so I can get to that ridiculous town meeting on time . . ."

"I'll be quiet," I said to Mrs. Bloom. Mainly so she'd hurry and go away because she was making my hands want to fidget like Charlie's. She rolled her eyes and shook her head, then took a pen and a little notepad thing out of her purse and handed them to Brenda.

So while Mrs. Bloom *delegated* to Brenda, I picked up the box of candy and pretended not to listen. "Oh, and don't forget your hair appointment on Saturday. I set it for two o'clock. We're expected at the Gaylors' at seven, but you and Leonard have your photo shoot at four."

"Okay," Brenda said.

Mrs. Bloom stopped yakking for a minute and bunched her lips in that way that sometimes makes people cry happy tears. "My baby. Almost engaged. I'm so proud of you, honey," she said.

"You're gonna get engaged?" I asked.

"Saturday," Brenda said, quietly and fast.

I stuck a fistful of straws into the last dispenser and shut the lid. It wouldn't lock into place, though, so I had to jam on it a little. When that didn't do the trick, I bent over so I could see what the problem was. While I eyed the latch Mrs. Bloom gave a quick, huffy sigh, "Okay, now where were we?" And they slipped right into all that business talk again.

"Hmmm," I said when I couldn't see a reason the lid wouldn't shut. I decided it just needed a harder shove, so I started pounding on it with my fist.

I didn't notice that I was making so much racket until Mrs. Bloom said I was, and Brenda's hand came down over my fist. "Teaspoon, I'll get that. Why don't you walk up and down the aisles and make sure there's no litter under the seats. Would you do that for me?"

"Sure thing, though I bet there's not gonna be, because that's Mr. Morgan's job and he's real fussy."

I wasn't but a handful of seats into the aisle, bending to look under each one and finding nothing, when I heard my voice boomerang back at me like it was coming from a speaker. I looked up and saw that I was standing underneath one of those big domes, the light spilling down on me. I hummed a little louder. Wow, that sure did sound nice! I glanced over at the counter to see if I was being too loud, but I must not have been because Mrs. Bloom wasn't glaring at me. She was leaned over the counter staring at something with Brenda.

So I tested the sound out a little more, singing a few *do, re, mi, fa*s, like we learned in music class, instead of just humming. Oh man, did that sound professional! Next thing I knew, I was singing the first song that popped into my head, one I had been bananas for when it first came out—"How High the Moon."

I sounded like I was using a real microphone, I swear! Even the snap of my fingers sounded as loud as two drumsticks banging together. So how could I help belting out the tune? Especially when I got to the part that always felt like I was singing it to my ma:

> *The darkest night would shine*
> *If you would come to me soon...*

I sang it snappy and loud, so that my voice filled the whole Starlight, sending those notes to every corner of the castle walls and sprinkling them over the balcony seats where I could see people sitting in my play-mind. I sang every verse, my fingers snapping, my body swaying like dance. When I got to the end and my voice rose with each *ah, ah, ah,* I lifted my chin and spread out my arms, shooting my voice clear up to the stars, which were lit (at least in my mind), and I didn't stop on that last *ah,* until every teaspoon of air I had in me was poured out.

When I got done with my fourth bow (because the crowd was still cheering), it took me a second to remember where I was. And when I did, I was scared to look over at the concession stand for fear that Mrs. Bloom would be fit to be tied, because Lord knows with that much echo going on, they probably heard me clear over at The Hanging Hoof. I tucked my head into my shoulders like a Charlie and looked over at the Blooms, ready to apologize.

Now, I can't say for sure, because I don't have my own recollection of what that old jukebox man's face looked like when he heard me sing for the first time, but I'll bet that gobsmacked look my ma claimed he was wearing was the same look Mrs. Bloom and Brenda had on their faces. There they stood, edged near the aisle, their eyes and mouths hanging open like doors on a safe someone forgot to close.

Mrs. Bloom turned to Brenda, suddenly as excited as if she'd won the jackpot at bingo, and she all but shouted, "That's it! Les Paul and Mary Ford—'How High the Moon'! I can't believe I didn't think of this before. You know how I love that song, Brenda. And what a perfect theme!" Mrs. Bloom was grinning like a cartoon cat, and Brenda was bouncing, her dimple deep as the Grand Canyon.

"Oh, I've seen the *The Les Paul and Mary Ford at Home Show*!" I shouted as I ran back to them. "And I still hear that song on the radio, and 'Via Con Dios,' and 'Tiger Rag.' They play lots of their hits!"

When I reached them, Mrs. Bloom tossed her arms around me and gave me a hug. It was as quick as a blink, but it was a hug. And she said, "You're a lifesaver, you know that?"

She turned to Brenda. "We'll call the show *How High the Moon,* and we'll get Les Paul and Mary Ford to perform it. Imagine the crowd we'll draw. We'll fill every seat in this place."

"Well, Mother...I don't know. They're huge. I'm not so sure we could get them..."

"Of course we can," Mrs. Bloom said. "Les grew up in Waukesha. He's practically homegrown. He'll feel some obligation to return to his roots."

"And Teaspoon?" Brenda asked. "I still have goose pimples, hearing her sing." Brenda held out her arm to show her ma.

Mrs. Bloom tapped her chin as she thought for a second, then she said, "We'll bring in the whole Sunshine Sisters crew. Nancy Gaylor will think it's a fabulous idea!" She put her lips together and cocked her eyes up toward the ceiling. "We'll have the girls sing something snappy, exciting...," she said. "Maybe 'There's No Business Like Show Business'—a whole medley of Irving Berlin songs. We'll have Jay choreograph dance steps...put you girls in matching dresses—"

"No...wait, wait!" I yelled. "I got it! How about that song Rosemary Clooney and Vera-Ellen sang in *White Christmas*? 'Sisters'! You know, because we're Sunshine Sisters!" I sang the chorus so she'd know which song I meant, and Mrs. Bloom got so excited at my idea, she almost hugged me twice. Almost. "Oh, what a wonderful idea!"

"Yeah, and oh, oh, I know! We could get dresses just like the ones they wore in the movie. You know those blue ones, with the lace? And those blue feather fans they had. We could get those, too!"

Mrs. Bloom turned to Brenda, "Tulle, weren't they?"

"Yes," Brenda said. "With lace on the bodice—a sash around the waist."

"Yes, I think you're right," Mrs. Bloom said.

"I have a picture of Rosemary Clooney and Vera-Ellen wearing them in one of my old magazines. I'm sure I do," Brenda said.

"Perfect! Dig it up and get the picture to Mrs. Campbell and her daughter immediately. They can sew the dresses."

"The sisters can come out in pairs. You and Isabella first, of course," Mrs. Bloom said to Brenda. "And we'll keep the two of you center-stage. I'm sure that's exactly where Mrs. Gaylor would want her future daughter-in-law to stand."

I went jumping-bean nuts when Mrs. Bloom said that. On stage. Me and Brenda. Dead-center in the Starlight Theater. The idea was enough to give me the vapors! Okay, I didn't really know what the vapors were. Just that they made olden-day ladies keel over for a bit if they had a shock, and a shock sure was what I was having.

Mrs. Bloom paced in little circles, "Okay. Paul and Ford. Who else? Someone either on their way down or on their way up because Lord knows, Paul and Ford will cost a fortune."

"We'll figure it out later, Ma," Brenda said. "You've got your town meeting."

Mrs. Bloom checked her watch quickly, frowned, then picked up her purse and the First National bag. "Yes, I've got to run. Brenda, listen for Perkins. And get on the phone and see if you can locate Les Paul's agent."

"How?" Brenda asked, suddenly looking as noodley as Jennifer Jackson. Mrs. Bloom rattled off a list of names of people who might know how to find the agent's name, but I was too excited to hear them or care.

"I gotta go tell Teddy!" I shouted. I started running down the aisle, the carpet soft under my feet so that even if I was going fast, all you could hear was dull thumps. I got halfway to the side doors, then stopped. "Oh! Brenda? Is our Sunshine meeting over now?"

"Yes. Go!" she called with a laugh. "See you Wednesday."

I took two steps, then stopped again. "I didn't put the rest of the candy away."

"I'll do it," Brenda said.

"Okay, thanks! Bye! And bye, Mrs. Bloom. Thank you!"

Teddy never sat down until after the supper dishes were done and it was time for Scrabble, so I whizzed through the living room to get to the kitchen, thinking I'd find him there, then did a quick zip through the rest of the rooms where he might be cleaning or fixing something. When I didn't find him in the kitchen or the bedrooms or the pantry, I headed back through the living room, thinking maybe he was at Mrs. Fry's. I got halfway through the living room again before I realized that he *was* in there. Sitting in the black chair with silver threads that were frayed here and there, envelopes lined up on his leg, a bill and envelope in his hand. His eyes were staring at nothing, even though I'd shouted his name through the whole house.

Yelling my fool head off or not, Teddy didn't seem to notice I was there until I was standing right next to his chair, tapping his arm. I startled him, and he got up so fast that the mail on his lap zoomed to the floor like paper airplanes. "Teddy! Teddy! You're never gonna guess what just happened!" I was bouncing so hard that my voiced bounced right with me.

Teddy looked down at the mail in his hand, like he didn't know what to do with it, so he shoved it in his pocket. "Something good, I'll bet," he said.

I was sure that Teddy didn't have something good just happen to him, because he didn't look happy. But then he always sank a bit when he opened his bills. And plenty of times he got downright rattled, the skin above his eyebrows staying puckered until payday, even when he was smiling. It's just the way Teddy was about money worries.

Quickly, I told Teddy what just happened, hoping it would make him feel better. "I was auditioning and I didn't even know it. But I must have did a good job, because now I'm going to sing on the live stage at the Starlight with the Sunshine Sisters. The same stage that Les Paul and Mary Ford are going to sing on. Can you believe it, Teddy? Can you? And me and Brenda are going to be pairs and stand dead-center."

"That's fantastic, honey," Teddy said, the bunched skin above his eyebrows not budging when he smiled.

"Oh, Teddy, just think. My debut! I didn't think *that* would happen until I was at least fourteen. I wish I could tell Ma. She'd be real proud of me, wouldn't she, Teddy?" Teddy sucked his bottom lip into his mouth and grabbed me, hugging me so tight that I had to wiggle free so I could tell him the rest.

CHAPTER EIGHT

It's weird how when you get a song in your head, you can't get it out. I must have sang "How High the Moon" a hundred times over the next five days, and when I woke up Sunday, it was the first song that popped out of my mouth. I was still singing it, too, when Charlie and me got to Sunday school.

Susie twisted in her chair and looked at us when we got downstairs—probably because she heard me singing, though I was keeping it soft because I was in the holy house of Jesus. "Miss Tuckle, Teaspoon brought a scooter inside," Susie said.

"Well, I'm not going to leave it out there for some thief to steal," I said as I propped it up against the wall out of the way.

Susie groaned so big she could have hurt herself. "You're afraid somebody's going to steal it in a *churchyard*?"

"Are you kidding me?" I said to Susie. "This place is crawling with sinners."

Miss Tuckle said she guessed it was okay that I brought it in, but that I should push it away from the door so nobody would trip on it. Then we got down to Sunday school business.

"I don't think Teaspoon listened to the lesson at all," Susie Miller said to Miss Tuckle as we colored our pictures. "How could she? She sang all the way through it."

"You *are* treating us with more songs than usual," Miss Tuckle said.

"I suppose I am," I said. "But I can't help it. You see…" And I told my news, right there at the Sunday school table. Robert and the boys didn't care, but I could tell that Susie and the other girls did. Especially when Miss Tuckle clapped her hands together and told me what wonderful news it was. "It sure is," I said. "Imagine, I'm going to go down in history as one of the performers at the Starlight Theater's first live show. Right along with Les Paul and Mary Ford.

"Did you see them on *Ed Sullivan*, Miss Tuckle? It was a long time ago, but I remember it. Boy, were they good! That Mr. Paul made a machine so that Mary can sing harmony with herself ten times over if she wants to. Teddy explained it to me, because I couldn't figure out how they found so many backup singers who sounded exactly like her. Anyway, it was my idea that they be the leading act." I looked up and saw Jesus staring down at me from the picture hanging over the Kool-Aid table, and added, "Well, it wasn't like I said, *Hey, how about we call it* How High the Moon, *and have Paul and Ford come perform the song for the big act,* but I'm the one they can thank for the whole idea."

Susie turned to Wanda, the quiet girl sitting next to her, and said, "See, told you so. She wasn't listening." She turned back to me. "The lesson was about being humble, Teaspoon, which is *not* what you're being." I stuck my tongue out of my mouth, pretending like I was licking the Kool-Aid off my bottom lip since Miss Tuckle was standing right there, but Susie knew what I was really doing.

Before we left Sunday school, Miss Tuckle congratulated me again, and said something I didn't catch, but that Charlie did and mentioned as we made our way across the parking lot. "She did say it," Charlie insisted. "She looked right at us before we went out the door and said, 'and I'll see you two at supper tonight.' "

"Well, that's about the craziest thing I ever heard!" I said. "You and me aren't even having supper together, much less with Miss Tuckle."

"Well, that's what she said," Charlie insisted.

Soon as we got back home, I followed Charlie into his house so I could get the scoop. Mrs. Fry was standing at the sink scrubbing potatoes and rapping on the window to get Poochie to stop barking, which wasn't gonna happen.

"Hello, Mrs. Fry," I said, loud enough so she could hear me, since she didn't even hear us come in, even though Charlie had slammed the door.

"Oh, hello there, children," she said when she saw me beside her.

I picked up a wrinkly brown potato that smelled like basement and had more eyes on it than the three of us combined, and twirled it around in my hand. "This sure is a lot of potatoes you're cleaning. Probably way more than even Charlie could eat." That was what you called trying to pump somebody for information, which is what Walking Doll said you should do when you want to know something but don't want to look like a snoop. Something Mrs. Fry already accused me of being on more than one occasion.

"Well," she said, "I ran into somebody from church yesterday, and I invited her over for a meal. I always liked April Tuckle, and I never get to see her now that I can't get to church. So I decided that you and Teddy should come over, too."

It was a good thing Mrs. Fry was almost as blind as she was deaf, or she would have seen me and Charlie exchange horrification-faces at the news. Because really, what kid except a do-gooder would want to have to behave for their Sunday school teacher through a whole meal?

Mrs. Fry told Charlie he had to help her, so I got out of there before she put me to work, too.

Later that day, me and Charlie sat Humpty-Dumpty on the steps in our church clothes while Miss Tuckle and Teddy helped Mrs. Fry set the dining room table. "Boy, this stinks, don't it, Charlie? I still don't see why she went and invited Miss Tuckle. Probably just to torture us."

"No," Charlie said. "She invited her so that she could get to be Mr. Favors's girlfriend."

"What?" I yelled so loud that for a second, the voices inside the house stopped. I leaned close enough to Charlie that I could see the dried soap caked in front of his ears. "How do you know that?"

"Because Grandma G told me. She said, 'Teddy is too good of a man to spend his life alone. April Tuckle would be perfect for him.'"

I suppose I should have seen that coming, the way that Mrs. Fry was always gushing every time Teddy mowed her lawn or shoveled her walk, or lugged heavy stuff out to her garage, saying how Teddy'd make some girl a wonderful husband one day. Mrs. Fry, old as God as she might be, admitted that she loved nothing better than a good love story with a happy ending. That's why every afternoon, day after day, she glued her old eyes to her television set when *Guiding Light* came on, waiting for the happy ending that never came, as far as I could see.

I stood up, my hands on my hips. "Teddy isn't spending his life alone, he's got me. And he's got a girlfriend already, too. My ma! They even slept in the same bed, doing the Juicy Jitterbug. If that don't make Ma his girlfriend, then I don't know what does."

I must have been shouting, because Teddy was on the steps in two seconds flat, his face red as the pinstripes on his shirt. He clamped his hand on my shoulder and steered me clear over to our yard, where he lectured me about not saying things to make others feel uncomfortable, and to never talk about that "Juicy Jitterbug thing" again . . . and where on earth had I heard such an expression in the first place, anyway?

"From the Jackson kids," I spouted, because anytime I got a chance to rat on those tattletales, I was going to use it. "But so what, Teddy? What I said was true, and you know it!"

"Lower your voice, Teaspoon," Teddy half warned, half begged.

"Well, I don't see why Mrs. Fry is sticking her nose into other people's business like she is. She warned me about not being a busybody before, and now she's doing it herself."

"Teaspoon, please. Mrs. Fry means well. And Miss Tuckle seems uncomfortable as it is, now that it's obvious what Mrs. Fry's intentions are, so let's not make her more so. Come on now. Let's go back and be cordial and enjoy our supper, okay? It's just a meal. That's all."

I huffed, but let Teddy drag me back to the Frys' yard, though I refused to go inside until the food was on the table and I had to.

It was pure torture, sitting there and eating those wrinkly potatoes that tasted like musty basement, too, even if the beef roast was good, all smothered in onions and garlic, while Mrs. Fry did everything she could to make Miss Tuckle brag about herself, when it was obvious that she didn't have anything to brag about.

Charlie didn't help matters, either, sitting there with his hair slapped down over his scabs with some oily-looking gunk, so afraid of saying anything for fear that he'd say something wrong in front of his Sunday school teacher. Like what? She was going to tell God if he did? Wasn't like God couldn't hear it for Himself. I tried to make eye contact with Charlie plenty of times so I had an audience when I rolled them, but he wouldn't even look up at me.

Mrs. Fry was so busy trying to get Miss Tuckle to tell Teddy about her job as a courtroom stenographer (whatever that was), she didn't even notice that her bread pudding had been in the oven too long. I noticed, because when I went into the kitchen to grab the napkins like Mrs. Fry asked me to, that bread pudding smelled ready to blow up. I didn't say anything, though. I just carried the napkins back to the dining room table and sat down, hoping dessert would burn so we could go home.

After a while, Miss Tuckle sniffed the air a couple of times, then leaned back on her chair so she could see into the kitchen. I guess that's when she spotted the smoke curling out of the oven door and Mrs. Fry realized that dessert was burnt toast. Teddy leapt to his feet, Mrs. Fry right behind him, and me watching from the kitchen doorway.

Okay, so maybe I felt a little bad when Teddy pulled the bread pudding out of the oven and Mrs. Fry looked ready to cry when she saw the top, black and smoking like just-spread asphalt. "It's ruined," Mrs. Fry said as she waved her white dishtowel like an I-give-up flag.

Miss Tuckle, a whole head taller than Teddy or Mrs. Fry, leaned over their shoulders. "Maybe the middle isn't so bad?" she said as she choked on the smoke. They were practically the first words Miss Tuckle said the whole time (though she giggled a lot), which had me thinking that fancy ladies aren't the only ones who acted different in public than they did at other times, because Miss Tuckle sure didn't have any trouble flapping her gums at Sunday school.

Teddy hurried to open the kitchen windows, then turned to me and asked if there was any pineapple upside-down cake left (which was a polite way of asking if Charlie had polished it off when we came back from Sunday school). "I think there's a piece or two left. Not much," I said, even though there was at least half of a pan last time I looked.

"We could cut the pieces small," Miss Tuckle said with a giggle. Teddy laughed like that was Jack-Benny-funny and invited everyone to our house for cake, even though I offered to go get it.

So there she was, Miss Tuckle, sitting at my kitchen table, the three grown-ups laughing about how none of us noticed that bread pudding burning because we were all having such a good time, while Teddy put the cake in the oven to get the syrup warm and gooey again. Charlie, who was supposed to be on my side, didn't even give me a glance when I knocked my knee against his every time the grown-ups said something dumb. All because he was too busy dabbing his fat finger at the drips of sugary syrup and few cake crumbs left on his plate.

Teddy noticed what Charlie was doing and said, "There's one more piece left, Charlie. I think it has your name on it."

Charlie stood up and leaned over the table to take a look. "Geez, Charlie," I said. "It doesn't *really* have your name on it. It's not like it's your birthday or something." Charlie turned to look back at me *while* reaching for the pan, and knocked over the milk pitcher. Down to the table it clunked, glugging milk right onto my lap.

Teddy jumped up to get me a dishtowel, and although I dabbed until I stopped dripping, my dress was sticking to my legs like wet Band-Aids. So I had to go to my room to change.

I shut my door and decided I was going to take my own sweet time getting back out there. I stripped off my wet dress and dropped it on the floor, then sat on my bed in my undershirt and undies, humming a little of "How High the Moon" to kill time.

Humming or not, I could still hear them in the kitchen, Miss Tuckle giggling like she wasn't even a Sunday school teacher, and Mrs. Fry yapping about how pretty she was when she smiled, even if her face was still the same plain-Jane homely then, only with more pink gums showing. Teddy was doing his share of laughing, too, even though he hadn't laughed since he got that bad bill. Not even when I gave him my good news.

I tuned them out and sang some more "How High the Moon," instead of just humming it. I guess they heard, because the next thing I knew, Teddy was telling them about me singing at the Starlight for the big gala. I went back to humming then, so I could hear Mrs. Fry ooooo and ahhhh since it was the first time she'd heard the news.

They didn't do that long, though, before Mrs. Fry was talking about how good her daughter said Charlie could play the piano. Then Miss Tuckle was gushing about Charlie instead. "I play, but not well"—*no kidding!*—"so I admire anyone with a natural musical talent," she said. "I see you have a piano, Teddy. Do you play?" My ears perked up like Poochie's when that nosy mentioned my ma's piano.

I wanted that piano saved pristine for Ma. And Teddy knew it.

I was still in my undershirt and underwear, my legs damp from their milk bath, when I went to the door and leaned up against it. Deciding right then and there that if Miss Tuckle thought she was touching Ma's piano, she had another thing coming!

But Miss Tuckle wasn't thinking about playing Ma's piano. She was thinking about having Charlie play it.

Charlie was talking so mumble-mouthed that I couldn't hear what he said, but I heard Mrs. Fry say, "Go on. Play us something, Charlie."

Having your old neighbor lady and your Sunday school teacher and your fat, scabby-headed neighbor who wasn't even your friend turn on you was one thing, but having the guy raising you say, "Go ahead, Charlie," well, that was the last straw! I grabbed the first dress I could reach in my closet and yanked it down so hard that the hanger banged me on the forehead. Charlie was hitting the middle-C key. I recognized the sound as soon as he struck it. And suddenly I could see her. Ma. Sitting right next to me, her limp nightgown outlining her lap as she showed me that very key, and then the chord that went with it.

I punched my arms through the armholes of my dress, and didn't even bother pulling the skirt part down over my damp legs before I shot out of my room and screamed, "What do you think you're doing, Charlie Fry? Get your hands off that piano!"

Teddy leapt to his feet. "Teaspoon!"

Charlie backed up, his brows cringing away from eyes that looked ready to jump out of his head.

I didn't care that Charlie started crying, any more than I cared if my shout startled Mrs. Fry. I didn't even care that my Sunday school teacher was staring at me like I picked up a case of rabies while in my room. I stomped across the floor, my fists bunched, and was about to haul off and slug Charlie when Teddy grabbed my arm. "Enough," he said.

I was so hot under the collar that I wanted to cuss really bad. "That's Ma's piano! We're saving it pristine for her. You know that, Teddy. Why'd you let him touch it?"

Charlie ran out the door, leaving it hanging open, and Mrs. Fry struggled to her feet so she could go after him. "Teaspoon," Teddy said. "Calm down."

"You calm down!" I screamed, even though Teddy was always calm as dead.

"I said enough, Teaspoon, and I meant it." He glanced over at Miss Tuckle, his face red with anger, or embarrassment, or who cared what.

"Teaspoon. Since when did you become so insensitive to other people's feelings?" Teddy let go of my arm and hurried to the window to gawk over at the Frys. "He didn't mean any harm."

"Well, he caused some," I said.

Teddy was so upset that he was moving in place, his hands on his hips. "Teaspoon...Miss Tuckle, Charlie, Mrs. Fry...they don't know how you feel about your ma's piano, but what Mrs. Fry *does* know—"

"But *you* know, Teddy!"

"As I was saying...what Mrs. Fry *does* know is how Charlie feels about music. That boy's known how to play the piano since he was four years old. His dad taught him. And he has a gift for playing. But he's not had a piano to play since he left his father's home eighteen months ago. Did you know those things about Charlie? Do you *really* want to keep his music from him, when we have a perfectly good piano sitting idle here?"

And then Teddy did what I guessed he'd do—what he always did when things got serious and he thought I was looking at things wrong. He tapped his hand over his heart and said, "Give it some thought," like a person's brains were there.

My face was stinging like Teddy'd smacked it when I ran out of the house, grabbed my scooter, and headed down the street. I didn't know where I was going. Just anywhere but home!

The wheels bumped in rhythm and my cheeks jiggled as I rode my scooter down the sidewalk, making it go faster than I knew it could.

Sure, I saw Walking Doll on the corner. Heard her call my name, too. But I wasn't planning on stopping because I didn't want to talk to anybody.

Walking Doll wanted to talk to me, though. So when I got up close to where she was standing, she called out, "Whoa, stop!" and jumped out like a wise guy, sticking herself right in my path.

"Ow! Damn it to hell, that hurt, Teaspoon!" she hollered when I slammed into her.

"It's your fault!" I said, while Walking Doll lifted The Kenosha Kid's black dress with the too-big neckline and rubbed her thigh and knee. "Why'd you jump out in front of me like that? Couldn't you see how fast I was going?"

Even though she was still ouching, she started laughing at the same time. "Wow, somebody's sure spitting nails tonight. Some boy go whaling on you again?"

"No. But my mad *is* about a boy."

"Aren't you a little young to be having man troubles?"

"Stop teasing me!" I shrieked.

I suppose Walking Doll saw that my eyes wanted to cry, because she stopped grinning. "Sorry, kiddo. What happened?" she asked, still rubbing her leg.

"That fat little kid, Charlie? He tried banging on my ma's piano. And Teddy got huffy with me when I got ticked about it. I got out of there before he could finish lecturing me about poor Charlie this, and poor Charlie that, because his ma's in heaven and his dad's in the clink—like *that's* the issue! That piano is my ma's and I don't want anybody touching it but her."

Walking Doll sat down on the curb, patting a spot beside her like it was her couch. "Come on," she said.

I didn't have enough energy to keep scootering, so I propped my scooter up against the mailbox and sat down. I almost wished Mrs. Fry would come walking by just then, pushing that little cart of hers that she took to the grocery store, so she could see me and Walking Doll sitting with our knees apart. It would serve her right!

"That piano is my ma's. My *ma's*! Charlie didn't have no business banging on it, and Teddy knows it."

"Can Charlie play the piano, or was he really banging on it?" she asked.

I looked at her like she'd lost her marbles. "I don't know. What's *that* got to do with it? The point is, it's my ma's and I want it saved pristine for her." I wrapped my arms around my knees and ground my eyes against them so no tears could leak out.

"Do you remember your ma playing it?" Walking Doll asked.

"Course I remember. When she was practicing her pianoing skills to get a job at The Dusty Rose. Most times she'd just keep playing the same song, starting over every time she hit a sour note. But sometimes she played just for fun, mistakes and all, and we'd sing together.

"Teddy lets me keep the radio in my bedroom and play it when I want, except for when it's bedtime. I play it loud when he's not home, but even with the dial on number ten, that radio can't fill up the house with music the way Ma and me could."

Walking Doll smiled. "Your whole face lit up when you remembered that," she said.

"She was going to teach me to play. She started to, but she left before I got past 'Every Good'... that's E and G in case you don't have any pianoing skills."

Walking Doll picked up a rock and rolled it in her hand. "My ma used to bake bread," she said. "To this day, whenever I smell homemade bread or taste it, I think of her. It's like a slice of memory."

"I didn't even know you had a ma," I said.

Walking Doll started scraping the rock against the sidewalk, cutting short, white lines into the cement. "Course I had a ma," she said. "What do you think, a stork dropped me here on this street corner?"

"Well, how would I know? You never told me you had a ma. But I suppose it's my fault that I didn't know that, even if you never said it."

"Now, why would that be your fault?"

"I don't know. Ask Teddy. He's the know-it-all," I said.

Walking Doll stopped scraping the sidewalk and looked at me. "Don't slug me for saying this, okay? But I'm thinking of you now...not Charlie...not your ma. Maybe if that kid really can play, you two could fill the house with music again. Just like you and your ma used to. It might work on you just like a slice of homemade bread works on me, and remind you of those times when your ma was with you, so you don't forget them."

"But I want the piano saved pristine. Ma ain't gonna wanna come back for some old beat-up piano."

"So that's what you think? That the only reason your ma would have to come back is to get a shiny, like-new piano? You're enough for her to come back to, kid. You're like the sun, even when you're grumpy, and if that's not enough for her, well then..."

She didn't finish that sentence, but added, "It at least might help you keep your memories of her pristine, you know?"

Walking Doll didn't give me time to hit her—not that I would have—she got up and brushed off the butt of her dress. "Damn, but it's quiet tonight," she said. She put her hand on the rubber handle of my scooter, leaning against it like she was suddenly too tired to hold herself up. "Where'd you get this thing, anyway?" she asked.

"At a yard sale."

"Nice," she said. Then she stared down the quiet street and sighed. I thought of telling her about the Sunshine Sisters and the gala, but I wanted to save that good news for a happier time. So instead, I asked her if she wanted to take a ride on my scooter.

She laughed like I was kidding, as she rocked it back and forth a bit. "Why not?" I said. "It's a whole lot funner than riding in Ralph's taxicab."

"What the hell," Walking Doll said. She kicked off her high heels and put her left foot on the scooter. "Now what do I do?"

"Nothing. Just push with your other foot and steer." She asked me to keep an eye on her purse, which was stuffed under the mailbox like it always was when she didn't feel like holding it, and off she went, past the shops, laughing and shouting "Wheeeeeeeee" like she was on a carnival ride.

"Oh my God," she yelled from down the street, her long hair waving in the breeze like clean laundry. "This is so fun!"

When she got back to the corner, she didn't stop. She circled around me, the front wheels coming close to falling off the curb, then she headed back down the street, whooping it up all over again. She was having so much fun that I ended up laughing, too, even if I didn't want to.

Walking Doll still had half of a block to go to get back to the corner when Ralph's taxi pulled up and The Kenosha Kid slipped out of the backseat, tugging down Walking Doll's red dress so her undies wouldn't show. There was a guy I didn't know sitting in the front seat beside Ralph, but The Kenosha Kid didn't say good-bye to either of them.

"Your lipstick's smeared," I told her as she slammed the door, but she didn't answer because she was staring down the street after Walking Doll. "What in the hell is she doing?" she said, a grin spreading across her face. "Jesus, like a little kid."

And Walking Doll did look more like a kid than a lady as she wheeled her way back to us, her head lolled sideways because she was laughing so hard, her cheeks bright pink as she jumped off. Just then, Mr. Miller's Lincoln Continental reached the stop sign. Walking Doll stopped giggling, but she put a smile on her face as she poked her hip out to the side and ran her hand down it. Mr. Miller watched her without turning his head all the way.

After his car passed, we could see that he was gawking in his rearview mirror. "I don't like Mr. Miller," I said. "He sounds mean when he talks to Teddy, even when he's smiling. His girl, Susie, is mean like him, too. Though she doesn't even try to sound nice." I said this like I'd forgotten that Teddy was a Benedict Arnold.

"Oh, he's a bastard all right," Walking Doll said, her voice quiet and low like a growl.

I looked up at her. "Then why'd you smile at him?" I asked. She didn't answer. She just kept staring down the street with narrowed eyes, watching Mr. Miller's Lincoln disappear. Walking Doll didn't look like a kid no more.

The last of the day's sun dipped down behind the tin roof of Pop's store, so that the glare that was usually there on sunny days was gone. "You better go home now, kid. It's getting dark, and we've got things to do."

I was half of a block from home when I saw Teddy on the sidewalk, coming from the Frys' house and going to ours, holding a bundle wrapped in tinfoil like it was a baby. (That was Teddy for you. So good that he wouldn't walk on the grass, even if it was yellowing from a lack of rain.)

Across the street, Jolene and Jennifer were sitting on their steps when I pulled into my yard, the white toes of their new shoes glow-in-the-dark bright. "Hey, Teaspoon," Jolene called, "want to come over and see our new saddle shoes?" I pretended I couldn't hear them over the shouting match Jack and James were having in their yard, and scootered around my house to sit on the back steps.

I should have known that Poochie would start snarling the second I got back there. Poochie was like that. Even when he caught a glimpse of people on the sidewalk, he went nuts. Snarling and biting at the air like he thought they were going to come into his yard and pull out his vocal cords, even though I'll bet not one person in the whole neighborhood would have stepped into that yard to do that, even they wanted to. I wanted to yell at Poochie to stop getting his fur in a bundle, but I didn't want Teddy to hear me. Not that yelling would have done any more good than Mrs. Fry's twisted knuckles giving him a warning rap against the kitchen window, which is exactly what she was doing.

Teddy must have gotten suspicious that I was in the backyard when he heard Poochie carrying on, though, because a few seconds later the doorknob jiggled and Teddy poked his head out.

I pressed myself flat against the corner of the house, siding scraping like sandpaper against my back as I hid in the dark shadow coming from the bush. Teddy opened the door and stepped out. Standing on the steps and cocking his pointy head this way and that, being nosier than I ever was. "Teaspoon?" he called.

Poochie's barks gobbled up my name the second time he called it.

Teddy stood there for a bit, looked over at Poochie, and went back inside.

"You girls seen Teaspoon?" I heard him call from the front door a few seconds later. And then the sound of Jolene Jackson's voice, screechy as a finger rubbing against wet glass. "She went around the back of your house a few minutes ago." I made a mental note to punch her twice as hard the next time we fought.

Teddy came out the back door again, his hands hanging limp, then finding their way into his pockets. "Why didn't you answer me when I called?" he asked, even though I don't think he knew exactly where I was. When I didn't answer, he sat down.

"I know you're mad at me, Teaspoon," he said, talking to me like I was sitting beside him. "And I can't say that I blame you. I know how it looked, me sitting right there, letting Charlie touch your ma's piano."

I wanted to stay hidden, but when my mad came out, so did I. I stepped into the glow made by the Frys' porch light. "Why'd you do it, Teddy?" I didn't want to cry, but I could feel that my eyes were going to make tears anyway.

"Well, Teaspoon," Teddy said with a sigh. "Because I looked at Charlie. That's why. Haven't you ever noticed the way that boy looks at your ma's piano when he comes over? Like he's starving to death for the sounds only that piano can make."

"Charlie don't look like he's starving for anything to me," I said.

"Teaspoon," Teddy warned. "You know what I'm talking about. Tonight when Mrs. Fry suggested he play, Charlie's eyes lit up. I could see his fingers twitching."

"His fingers *always* twitch," I reminded Teddy. I crossed my arms.

"Teaspoon, you're lucky. Your gift is in your voice, and you can open that gift anytime you want. But imagine if it wasn't. If you needed an instrument to make music happen. And it was taken from you."

"Well, I wouldn't go stealing his ma's vocal cords if mine got taken away, that's for sure."

"Come on now," Teddy said. "Hurt and upset as you are, you know that's silly."

I wanted to smart-mouth Teddy some more, but I couldn't because I had a lump the size of a fist in my throat.

"Teaspoon, Charlie won't wreck that piano by playing it. He'll help it stay in tune."

"He'll get gunk all over it, Teddy. You've seen Charlie's hands. They're as grubby as my elbows—always smeared with dried jelly, dirt, or head scabs . . . who knows what else."

"Then ask him to wash before he plays." Teddy sighed. "Teaspoon, you know what it feels like to miss a mother, now don't you? But at least you can have hope that you'll see yours again. Charlie won't be reunited with his dad until he's a grown man, and he'll never see his mother again. That's pretty sad, now, isn't it?"

"Boy, Teddy. You might not be a sinner, but maybe you *do* need to start going to church if you don't know that Charlie *will* see his ma again. In heaven."

Teddy stood up. "Okay. If you don't want Charlie touching your ma's piano, I won't make you change your mind. What I will ask you to do, though, is to give it some thought. Living with regrets over what we did, or didn't do, is a heavy burden to carry, Teaspoon. Now come on inside. It's late."

I went straight to my room and flopped on my bed. Through my shut door, I could hear water sloshing in the tub as Teddy wrung out his work clothes. My shade was up and the Frys' drapes were open. Their lamp was shut off but each time the TV screen flickered bright, I could see Charlie's head.

I didn't want to admit that I was luckier than Charlie. But Charlie's ma *was* in heaven, while mine was only in Hollywood. And mine was coming home as soon as she made her dream come true, but Charlie wouldn't get to see his ma until he was an old man and got called home. And if I was forgetting my ma in five years, Charlie probably wouldn't even remember his ma's face by the time he got to the Pearly Gates. He might even walk right past her without knowing it was her.

Maybe it was thinking about Charlie's dead ma that made me remember the old funeral song, because even with one ear pressed against my flat pillow, that's what I heard myself humming.

It was the song that the old lady who lived down the hall above the bar in Peoria taught me, because she didn't think it was right for a kid to be singing barroom songs. She taught me two of them, and when Ma came back because I puked on the old lady's quilt and cat, I sang them both for her. Ma didn't like them, though. She clamped her hands over the sides of her head like earmuffs and said, "Oh, those funeral songs give me the willies. Sing something else, Teaspoon."

I could hear Ma saying that, and almost stopped myself when the humming turned to soft singing. Almost like she could hear me. But I wasn't singing it for her anyway. I was singing it for Charlie. Even if he couldn't hear me. Just as I sang it a long time ago for the old jukebox man.

It was the night before we pulled out of Peoria, and the regulars from downstairs had a little party for us. We even got a going-away cake, chocolate with vanilla frosting. They bought Ma beers until she was tippy, and gave me so much soda pop that my belly got fat and achy (I didn't know how to burp on purpose then). All night long the regulars kept asking Ma why we had to go, and every time, she'd answer, "I told you. You sit too long in one place, and you grow mushrooms under your ass."

It was a fun party, but still I felt bad because I knew I'd never see those people again. Not Stella, who'd made the cake and who had hands spotted like a leopard and who called me Toots before and after I got the name Teaspoon. Rusty, who came straight from work every night, dirt still under his fingernails, and always bought two beers and one candy bar for me. Don, who was my ma's boyfriend from time to time, who once picked me up and gave me a piggyback ride around the pool table, and later taught me to play a little. But the one that caused me to feel the saddest at the thought of never seeing him again was the old jukebox man.

He hadn't come the Wednesday before we were leaving, and when I asked Clem who owned the bar if he was coming to our party, he said probably not, because he wasn't a regular. Just the jukebox man. "His wife died last week," he said. "That's why he didn't show up Wednesday. Doesn't matter, though. He comes more than he needs to, anyway."

But he did come. Not to scoop coins out of the jukebox, but to say his good-byes.

He went to Ma first and took off his hat, standing beside her stool until she stopped talking to Don and turned to look at him. His whole body made little nods as he wished her well in her move and in life, and the whole time he talked to her, his old eyes were peeking sideways down at me.

When Ma went back to her laughing and talking with the regulars, the old jukebox man asked me if I'd sing for him, one last time. I told him I would, and the folks at the bar who'd heard him ask started shouting out their favorites. But I didn't pay any attention to what they were yelling. Instead I watched the old man, who was walking over to the jukebox, slower than I'd ever saw him walk before, his back folded over like the heavy sad he was feeling was sitting right on his shoulders.

So I stopped, right there in the middle of the empty floor. And I started singing the best of those two funeral songs the old lady had taught me—"Amazing Grace"—because the jukebox man had a funeral.

I sang it *Acapolka*, because that song wasn't on the jukebox.

Closing my eyes so I could sing it good, because I wanted it to be like one of those parting gifts they give game show contestants who don't win, and I wanted the prize to be good.

I guess the people on the stools only wanted to hear barroom songs, because they didn't clap when I finished the song. They just sat there, a few of them wiping their eyes, until Ma lifted her glass and said, "What is this, a party or a funeral?" and they laughed and turned around to pin their elbows back on the bar.

But not the jukebox man.

He just stood there looking at me with watery eyes, his lips twitching like they didn't know if they wanted to turn up or down. Then he came to me and lifted me up, his arm holding me like the seat of a swing.

"Teaspoon," he said. "I hope the only blue you ever have in your life is the blue in your eyes. But if those sad times come—which they're bound to—you remember to keep a song in your heart. Making music when you're happy, it got the power to heal others. But making music when you're sad, it got the power to heal you."

He took one of my dusty feet and gave my toes a jiggle with hands like Mr. Morgan's, chocolate on top and vanilla on the bottom. "It don't matter if that hurt go all the way down to here. Music will reach down there, scoop it up, and leave them feeling light enough to tap again."

Then the old jukebox man itsy-bitsy-spidered two fingers up my leg and across my belly. Pausing over the place that thumped when I ran extra-fast or got scared, telling me that the music would lift the sad from there, too, then he itsy-bitsied to just under my chin. "And then the music stops here," he said, making a tickle on my neck, "melting that lump that's making your throat close up like a fist." Then he reached his fingers above my head, as high as his hand could reach, "Carrying that sad all the way to heaven so the good Lord—who got bigger and stronger arms than you—can hold it for you."

I didn't even know I still had that memory in me, but I guess I did. And remembering it made me look over at Charlie's house and feel twice as sad for him. Sitting in that old-smelling house with nothing to do but watch love stories with no happy endings, with no means to make music that could carry his sad up to Jesus.

I didn't call to Teddy to say I was going over to the Frys', I just wiped my eyes and went.

"Who is it, Charlie?" Mrs. Fry called when Charlie answered my knock.

"Teaspoon," he said.

"Teaspoon?" Mrs. Fry said, like she'd either forgotten who I was, or didn't hear.

Teddy said that watching TV in a dark room was bad for your eyes. Mrs. Fry was half blind already, so I guess she didn't think it mattered if she lost what little sight she had left—though she should have thought of Charlie, who had enough afflictions already, without her turning him into a four-eyes. I poked my head into the dark room. "Just me, Mrs. Fry. I came to say I'm sorry about being so naughty tonight. I didn't mean to act up like that. I've got afflictions, though. Like your Poochie. But I'm going to learn to do better because I got somebody to help me now. Anyway, I'm sorry."

Mrs. Fry stretched her neck out, like maybe I could hear her a bit better over the blaring TV if she leaned forward. "You make your peace with Teddy, too?"

"I did," I said.

"Good, because he's a good man. And he's doing right by you."

"I know that," I said.

I asked Charlie to step out on the porch, where it was dark and he couldn't see that I'd been crying, and I said my sorrys to him. "And you can play my ma's piano whenever you want, but you have to wash your hands first. With soap. Every time. Got it?" Charlie nodded fast and grinned like a chimp.

I started down the porch steps and turned when I felt Charlie practically breathing down my neck. "Geez, Charlie. I didn't mean right now. It's late and Teddy's gotta get to work early. I got my Sunshine meeting with Brenda in the morning, too."

When I got home, Teddy was still in the bathroom wringing out clothes. "There's some of Mrs. Fry's homemade bread on the table if you're hungry," he called. "There's some slices cut, and strawberry jelly in the refrigerator." I unwrapped the bread, which still smelled like new and was glossy from butter that had melted into the crust while it was still hot.

The next morning, I got up and scrubbed myself squeaky clean like Brenda. I put barrettes in my still-damp hair and buttoned a sweater over my dress to cover my elbows and stepped outside. And there he was. Charlie Fry. Waiting for me at the bottom of the steps so he could follow me to the Starlight like a duck who didn't know who his mama was.

CHAPTER NINE

Maybe, when you do good after doing bad, Jesus gives you a reward since you were sorry. That's what I thought, anyway, after I made my apologies to Teddy and Charlie and Mrs. Fry, and then showed up for my Sunshine Sisters meeting to find Johnny Jackson in the parking lot, leaning up against a dinged-up Perkins Construction truck wearing an employee shirt, smoking a cigarette and tapping the toe of his engineer boot with the heel of the other.

"Johnny!" I shouted as I jumped off my scooter and turned it over to Charlie. "What are you doing here? You working for Mr. Perkins now?"

Mr. Perkins was up on the back of the truck, which was long and flat like a stage, unhooking the belts that held stacks of wood the color of honey. Another guy, small as Teddy and with a beard that looked like it had dandruff, was helping. The little guy looked over at Mr. Perkins when I said that. And even though he had a cigarette stuck in his mouth, he said, "We'll see how much work we get out of that hood, huh, Glen?"

Mr. Perkins didn't grin. Instead, he nodded over toward a white pickup, where Johnny's friend Doug—the dopey-looking one I called Dumbo Doug (but not to his face) because he had ears big as Dumbo's—was rooting around in the back. "Probably more work than we'll get out of that moron. He can't even find his tool belt and he had it strapped on him two minutes ago."

Mr. Perkins jumped down when the wood was unhooked. "Crissakes," he said, glancing at his watch. "If she was in such a goddamn hurry to get this work done, then you'd think she'd be here on time to let us in." He spit on the cement, then added, "That's rich folk for you. Their time is always more important than yours. Someone gets here in ten minutes to open these doors, or we're pulling out."

"Oh," I said. "Brenda's probably letting you in because her and I got a Sunshine Sisters meeting this morning. But you don't have to worry about her not showing. She's very responsible." Dumbo Doug said something under his breath that only the little guy heard, and I could tell by the way the guy snickered that it wasn't something nice, either.

Figured. Dumbo Doug was a part of that little group of people who didn't like the Sweetheart of Mill Town, along with—sad to say—Johnny Jackson, and most of his friends. I knew this for a fact, because the day after Brenda got crowned, Johnny and his friends were working on Johnny's hot rod while I sat on the steps with Jennifer and Jolene looking at clothes in the Montgomery Ward catalog, and I heard Johnny say that Brenda Bloom was a stuck-up bitch, just like her ma. And Dumbo Doug said that a one-legged cat had more talent in its missing leg than Brenda Bloom had in her whole body.

When Brenda pulled into the Starlight parking lot ten more minutes later, she looked rattled. And as she hurried to the door, fumbling in her purse for the keys, she gave the Perkins crew the same look folks gave Poochie when they passed the Frys' yard. The bearded guy named Mel looked back at Brenda like he was Mr. Miller and she was a Taxi Stand Lady. Dumbo Doug didn't look at Brenda, though. He was too busy looking at the new car Mrs. Bloom had given Brenda for a graduation present. He whistled like that car was a lady, and said, "Holy shit. A brand-new Thunderbird. Rag roof. Thunderbird blue. Holy shit." Johnny didn't look at the car. Or at Brenda, for that matter.

Brenda was apologizing all over the place as she unlocked the door with a newly engaged hand—the ring not pretty and dainty like her, but big and clunky and old-lady-gaudy like Mrs. Gaylor—and Mr. Perkins said it was okay, even though a few seconds earlier it wasn't, and inside we went. Me and Brenda went back to the concession stand, even though we weren't going to make boxes or stock the candy, and the guys went to stand in front of the screen and listen to Mr. Perkins, who I think was delegating to them.

Brenda looked at Johnny plenty that morning. Not with her head turned to the front of the theater to stare, like I think I did, but glancing with short little looks from the corner of her eye. I was looking at him so I could figure out if the fluttering in my belly was love. And Brenda? I think she was just trying to figure out if he was going to hurt her.

CHAPTER TEN

Long as I could remember, Teddy never missed a day of work. But two weeks after Johnny started working at the Starlight, I came home to find Teddy wearing a bandage wrapped around part of his hand and running up half of his arm. His fingers were poking out, and they looked puffy and sore. "What happened to you, Teddy?" I asked.

"Oh, I just took a little spill at work and sprained my wrist," he said, wincing. "A couple of days off, and I'll be good as new." Teddy had his newspaper spread flat on the table and was holding it down with one elbow as he turned the page.

"Well, look here. An engagement picture of your Brenda and Leonard Gaylor," Teddy said, flattening the pages with his good hand. I hurried over to stand behind him, and sure enough, there they were. Leonard sitting and Brenda standing half behind him, her hand on his shoulder, that aggie-sized ring on her finger.

I never saw Leonard before, I'd just heard of him—I didn't go to his games, and he didn't come into my neighborhood—and he wasn't handsome at all like I'd imagined. He had one of those faces that looked like somebody pinched their fingers over his nose when he was a baby—while it was still squishy and soft like clay—and gave it a tug so hard that his upper lip got pulled forward right along with it, and neither boinged back into place after they let go. "He's ugly," I said.

"Teaspoon, you need to learn not to comment on people's looks," Teddy said.

"Why?" I said. "People comment on my looks all the time." Soon as I said it, though, I got it. "Oh, you mean if they're ugly."

Teddy cleared his throat. "Well, a man doesn't have to be handsome to be a good person."

If anybody should have been an expert on that, it was Teddy, so I listened up as he read the article out loud. It didn't say anything about Brenda I didn't know, but there was lots about Leonard. Mostly about how he won lots of awards.

"He's obviously a very accomplished, respectable young man," Teddy said when he finished reading. "He'll probably make a good husband for Brenda."

I was happy at the thought of having Teddy around for a couple of days, but Teddy sure wasn't happy about not being able to work.

That night, just to cheer Teddy up and help him forget about his throbbing wrist, me and Charlie put on a show for him and Mrs. Fry. Okay, maybe it wasn't perfect—it was what you'd call an *impromptoe* performance after all. And maybe that string of medleys wasn't planned, but necessary because we didn't know the rest of each song, but still we had a lot of fun. "When it rains it pours," Mrs. Fry said when she saw Teddy's wrist, and she gave his good arm a there-there pat.

Mrs. Fry was right on that count, too, because the next morning—Teddy's first day being stuck home—we got our first good soaking rain since school got out, and I woke up to a grumbling sky and a grumbling Teddy.

I always liked the sounds of summer storms, that thunder in the distance rumbling like a drumroll, and lightning clanging like marching band cymbals. "Wow, it's really coming down, huh, Teddy?" I called as I got out of bed and went to my window.

The sky was so dark it looked like night, even if it was seven o'clock in the morning. Charlie was standing at his bay window, his head tipped back watching the sheet of rain that ran down from the eaves. He gave me a slow wave.

"Hey, Teddy, is it true what Mrs. Fry says about how if you go out in the rain and get wet, you'll catch a cold?" I asked as I headed to the bathroom. "I don't know if I believe that, or else we'd get sick every time we took a bath. I don't care if it's true, anyway. I got a Sunshine meeting this morning and I'm not going to miss it."

Teddy didn't answer, probably because he didn't hear me over the storm, to say nothing of the racket he was making with pots and pans. "Mrs. Fry knows a lot of things, but she doesn't know everything, I don't think," I shouted, my voice echoing in the empty bathroom like I was singing. "She sure doesn't know how to cut hair, anyway. You see Charlie's head yesterday, Teddy? She's got it all gouged up again."

There was a crack of lightning so close that I swear, the hair on my arms stood up. I jumped off the toilet quick because Mrs. Fry said you weren't supposed to be around water when it was lightning. Even if she didn't know everything, I wasn't taking any chances.

When I got to the kitchen, water stretched clear from the doorway to the table, puddling on the floor. I looked up and sure enough, water was coming down from that brown, bulged stain on the ceiling that gave us grief last summer. "Whoa, Teddy. The roof's leaking again," I said, but he was already squatted down in front of a cupboard we hardly used, clanging around with his good hand. "Teaspoon, would you come here and get that big soup kettle way in the back?"

While I moved pans to tug it out, Teddy grumbled at himself for not replacing those boards that got wrecked in last summer's bad storm, and for slapping a tar patch over it instead, because now look at the mess he had on his hands after a winter of heavy snow.

"Well, Teddy, like Mrs. Fry says, a poor man has poor ways." I wasn't sure exactly what that meant, but I knew it was something she'd say at a time like this.

Teddy mopped up the mess, then propped the soup pot under

the leak, which was running like a faucet. I liked the sound of those water drops hitting the denty bottom of the pot, *plip, plop, plip, plop,* but Teddy sure didn't.

"Hey, Teddy," I said "You sure are cranky this morning. You worried about missing a couple days of work because you won't make as much money on payday? Especially now that you have that bad bill?"

"Bad bill?" Teddy asked.

"Yeah. You know. The one you were looking at when I came back from my first Sunshine meeting. You haven't been yourself since then, Teddy."

Teddy didn't say anything, so I just hummed a little.

"Hey, Teddy. Can you believe how good Charlie can play piano?" I said while Teddy rinsed off the mop in the sink. "He doesn't even need a sheet of music to play. Brenda said that's called playing by ear. Look at how good he could play 'How High the Moon' the first time he tried, and he's never even heard that song on the radio, just me singing it. Lots of people tell me I sing with heart. I didn't even know what that meant, until I heard Charlie play. Charlie plays with heart, doesn't he, Teddy?"

"Yes he does," Teddy said.

"Hey, did you like the little show we put on for you last night?" I asked, hoping to make Teddy smile, since I wasn't having much luck making him talk.

Teddy got the eggs out of the refrigerator so we could have breakfast. "I sure did," he said, answering in the same tone he used when he asked me if I brushed my teeth before bed.

"I think we sound like a real act, don't you? Charlie can't play fast songs as fast as they should be played, but he doesn't miss a note.

"Hey, Teddy. Did you hear me? I said, '... he *doesn't* miss a note,' instead of *don't.* Can you believe it? And I'll bet I haven't said *ain't* or *gonna* even once today. Well, maybe once. I sure am learning how to talk good from listening to Brenda, though, aren't I?

"Speaking of Brenda, she hasn't been able to get a hold of Les

Paul and Mary Ford's agent yet, but did I tell you who we did get booked?"   •

Teddy said I hadn't, so while he cooked our eggs, my mouth started leaking like a roof fixed by a poor man. "Louis Prima and Keely Smith! They're coming all the way from Las Vegas for a one-nighter. Can you believe it? Brenda said he's funny as can be on stage, jumping all over the place like a wild man and making folks laugh. Brenda saw him in New York back when he had an orchestra twenty-seven people big. Course, he's not bringing a band that size to the Starlight. But he's bringing Keely, and everybody loves her.

"And Mimi Hines is coming with Phil Ford. I never heard of them before, but Mrs. Bloom said that Mimi Hines is one of the most underrated singers there is today. I guess she's funny, too. Mrs. Bloom showed Miss Hines's eight-by-ten glossy at the big meeting we had with all the Sisters so we could tell them about the gala. Boy, did those girls go nuts when they heard we were going to be in the show! Some of them happy-nuts, like I went when I heard, but others, like Mindy Brewer, went scared-nuts."

Teddy set my plate on the table and told me to sit down, then he went to get the ketchup for his eggs.

"Mindy's a Sunshine Sister who isn't real pretty because her top teeth stick out like this," I said as I pulled out my chair, and I showed Teddy by poking my top teeth out and hanging them over my bottom lip. "Her hair used to be all snarly, too, but it's not like that anymore, now that she's learning how to be respectable. Anyway, Mindy and her Big Sister were sitting at the same table as Brenda and me. And when Mrs. Bloom held up Mimi Hines's eight-by-ten glossy, I leaned over and said in her ear, 'Wow, Mindy. You've got the same teeth as a famous lady.' Mimi's aren't as pokey-outie as Mindy's, but she's got some big choppers on her, for sure. Mindy put her hand over her mouth like she always does when she smiles, but when Mrs. Bloom set Mimi's picture back on the table, Mindy was still staring at it.

"I'm going to have to get one of those eight-by-ten glossies when I become a singing sensation," I said. "Brenda doesn't know how much they cost."

Teddy didn't eat but a few bites before he set his fork down and got up. He scraped the rest of his eggs and a triangle of toast into the garbage—even if there were kids starving in Africa—then he put his dirty plate in the sink and stood at the window.

"Is the rain going to stop soon, Teddy?" I asked as I licked yolk from my fork. "I've got a Sunshine Sisters meeting at ten o'clock."

"Sooner or later," Teddy said while he watched the sky.

"Boy, Teddy, there sure is a lot to do to make a gala. By the time we're set up, practically everybody in town will be helping. The city orchestra is going to play for the filler acts and some music while people are getting seated. Brenda has to find the local acts, have programs and posters printed up, figure out our costumes...all sorts of things. I try to keep track of it all so I can help Brenda better, but even with our to-do list, I forget. So mostly I let Brenda tell me what to do. She is my boss, after all, even if she is my Big Sister."

Teddy turned to me, the corners of his mouth curling up for the first time all morning. "You really like Brenda, don't you?" he said.

"I sure do, Teddy. She's about the nicest person I ever met. We got all these plans to be made and she's real busy because Mrs. Bloom delegates to her all the time because she's trying to get that drive-in theater up and running. Can you believe it, Teddy? A drive-in theater right here in Mill Town. Busy or not, through, Brenda never gets crabby or bullheaded like I can sometimes when you ask me to do something. And it doesn't matter how much I sing, or how much I chatter, her eyes never get twitchy at me. Not ever."

Teddy was sipping his coffee and trying to look like he was listening, even if he had that faraway look on his face again, like I was a game of Scrabble he couldn't concentrate on. I couldn't roll my eyes at him, being the respectable work in progress that I was, but I wanted to.

"And look at this, Teddy…" I pulled my sweater off one sleeve and bent my elbow to show him. "You know how these were all cracked and grubby looking? That wasn't even dirt, Teddy. Brenda and I were upstairs having our second meeting, and it can get hot as the blazes up there and I got all sweaty, so Brenda told me to take off my sweater. What choice did I have but to 'fess up to having an elbow affliction? After all, that's what she's supposed to be helping me with. My afflictions. Who would have thought it was just dry skin, huh? Brenda brought me a bottle of skin lotion to put on them."

I ran into my bedroom and came back with my bottle of Jergens. "See, Teddy?" I unscrewed the black cap and poured a dab on my hand, rubbing it into my elbows good. "I'm putting it on every morning and every night, and they not only look better, they don't feel tight and sore anymore, either. Now my elbows smell just like Brenda's hands." I stuck my elbow under Teddy's nose. "Here, take a whiff."

"Nice," Teddy said. "And Mrs. Bloom?"

"Oh, I doubt that a rich lady who looks like Marlene Dietrich would get scaly elbows, Teddy."

"No, I meant, do you like her, too?"

"Yeah," I said. I didn't tell him that Mrs. Bloom was one of those people Mrs. Fry would say ran hot and cold. But she was. Sometimes she was nothing but a bossy queen, ordering everybody around and acting like she was going to chop their heads off if they didn't move fast enough or do things right. And sometimes, that somebody was me. Like when I talked too much, or touched things I shouldn't. But other times, she could be real nice. I hurried to think of something nice she'd done or said. "She let me pick out a candy from the case once, and she says I'll be the best singer of all the Little Sisters."

Teddy took his cup from the counter and poured more coffee into it to make it hotter, then waited for it to cool—which always made me wonder why people didn't just drink it cooled off in the first place. But that was grown-ups for you. What they did didn't always make sense.

Teddy looked out the window again. "Looks like the rain's finally let up," he said.

And sure enough Charlie was at our door. "I had to wait so I wouldn't get wet and sick," he said when I let him in, like I didn't know that already.

"I got time to play a little before we have to go?" he asked, and I told him he had time for one song while I finished getting ready. Charlie held out his hands to show me they were clean. "You didn't wash them when it was lightning, did you, Charlie?" I asked. He shook his head, then sat down at the piano while I went to find my shoes. "Hey Charlie, you know the song 'Sisters'?" I yelled into the living room. Charlie called back that he didn't, so I told him I'd teach it to him once I learned it better, since I'd only heard it that one time while watching the movie from the catwalk. "Did I tell you that there's a dance teacher who lives over by the Starlight who's going to be our music director and *chorusographer*? His name is Jay. Not Mr. Jay. Just Jay. Brenda said he can dance as good as Fred Astaire. We're going to sing with real dance steps and feather fans, just like in the movie.

"Hey, Teddy," I yelled, extra-loud. "Did I tell you that the Starlight's getting a grand piano? The Blooms bought that empty building right next to the Starlight, the one that used to be a furniture store, and that's where they're going to keep it during regular movies. They're going to have a big warm-up room for dancers and musicians in there, and some dressing rooms." Charlie yelled back that Teddy was in the bathroom and he didn't think he'd heard me, so I went back to talking to Charlie. Yelling extra-loud when I shoved my head under my bed to look for my other shoe.

"That's the place that's got a ramp out back, in the parking lot, Charlie. The one I like scootering down." I finally spotted my other shoe and pulled it out. "I don't know why I have to wait until that piano comes before I get to hear Brenda sing, though, Charlie. I asked her why she can't just sing to the music that plays in her head, like I do, but she won't."

I didn't even know if Charlie was listening to me anymore, since he was pianoing now, but on the hunch that he was, I kept talking. "Hey, Charlie, isn't it nice that once Brenda learned that you come with me every day, she said you can come inside when you need to use the bathroom, or get thirsty? Course, don't go hogging too many soda pops, Charlie. That would be impolite."

I dug in my drawer looking for two matching socks. I never rolled my socks together even if Teddy said it was a job I should be doing, but I had good reasons not to. If they were rolled, I had to unroll them to see if they had holes in the toes. I found a pair without holes, even if they weren't exactly the same shade of blue, then sat on the floor to put them on.

"Hey, Charlie. Now that you can come inside, you'll get to see the grand piano when it comes. Well, Johnny would have let you come in and take a peek anyway. He's nice that way."

I was glad neither Teddy or Charlie could see me when I said Johnny's name. Especially Teddy, since the last time I said *Johnny* in front of him, he slipped his hand up under my bangs to check me for a fever because he said my face was flushed.

When Teddy got out of the bathroom, his face looked Jergens-smooth but for five little scraps of toilet paper stuck on where he'd nicked himself with the razor. Probably because he had to shave with his left hand. "Where you going, Teddy, all shaved and wearing your good shirt?" I asked.

"I have to run to the bank," Teddy said.

"Why? It's not Friday. They give you an advance since you won't be working on Friday?"

"Just business," Teddy said.

"Oh," I said, then I dipped into the bathroom to brush my hair. Teddy and Charlie and me left the house at the same time, so while I wiped the rain off my scooter's handlebars with the hem of my shirt, I whispered to Charlie we'd better cross the street like we were taking that side—at least until Teddy got out of sight—even if the cussing Taxi Stand Ladies wouldn't be out this early. So that's what we did. Stood in front of the Jackson house, me taking my sweet time tying my shoes to make it look good until Teddy turned the corner.

When we got to the Starlight, I turned my scooter over to Charlie and was about to step inside when Johnny called to me to wait so him and Doug could get out the door first. They were carrying the short row of Starlight seats that used to sit up front, on the side.

"Hey, what you doing with those?" I asked as they tilted the seats to get them through the door, Johnny cussing at Doug to tilt them more.

"They're going to the dump," Johnny said.

"Nooooooo!" I said. "Good seats like this?" I ran my hand over the red velvet cushions as Johnny glided them out and told me to watch my fingers. "Why are you taking them to the dump?"

"Because that's what the boss lady told us to do," Johnny said, and Doug added, "I'd like to tell her to shove them up her ass—these suckers are heavy!"

"I wish those seats could come to my house instead of the dump," I said as they carried them over to the Perkins truck.

"Now, what would you do with theater seats, Teaspoon?" Johnny asked with laugh.

"Have a piece of the Starlight magic at my house," I said.

I was about to step inside to see the hole the missing seats made when Johnny called to me, "The Blooms aren't in there, Teaspoon."

I headed back to the truck. "What do you mean they're not in there? Me and Brenda have a meeting."

"The old bag was snooping around the stage and fell on her

ass," Doug said, and I turned around. Doug laughed as he wiped his hand across his forehead, then pulled a pack of Marlboros out of his shirt pocket. "Hey, Jackson. You like the way Perkins hurried over there to kiss her owie . . . probably afraid she's going to sue his ass now.

"Damn hysterical if you ask me, her screaming over a little twist of the ankle like that."

Johnny jumped off the truck and grabbed Doug's cigarette, taking two quick puffs before handing it back. "Shut up, shit head," he said, giving a sideways glance at me.

Doug didn't stop, though. "And that Brenda, getting all rattle-assed waiting for the ambulance to come."

Charlie's face went white when he heard the word *ambulance.*

"I didn't hear no ambulance, did you?" I asked Charlie. "But maybe that was when it was storming bad." He didn't answer.

"Course, she *would* get rattled. She won't even know when to wipe her ass without her ma there to tell her."

"Man," I said. "First Teddy gets hurt, now Mrs. Bloom. I hope she's not hurt bad."

Mel poked his head out of the door just then and said, "The rest of these seats aren't gonna carry themselves out, dipsticks."

Doug tossed his cigarette down and they headed for the door just as Mr. Morgan was coming around the corner from the alley. Johnny started telling Mr. Morgan that the Blooms weren't around, and Mr. Morgan said he knew that, but Brenda had called and asked him to come in and lock up after they left for the day. Doug shook his head and spit on the sidewalk, then grumbled something to Johnny. Johnny didn't say nothing, though, except, "See ya, Teaspoon."

I caught Mr. Morgan before he followed Johnny and Doug inside and asked him if Mrs. Bloom was hurt real bad, but he just shrugged. "Brenda didn't say, an' I didn't ask. None of my business."

∗   ∗   ∗

Me and Charlie didn't have nothing to do but head back home, since Mr. Morgan said that he didn't think it would be a good idea to let us two in *again* without permission.

"Boy, Charlie," I said after I was done blabbing about Mrs. Bloom's ankle and how I didn't like that Doug, "wouldn't an Orange Crush taste good right about now? If Brenda was around, we could have gotten one, too, because I think today's my payday. It's been two weeks since I started my job, and I get paid every two weeks, just like Teddy. I don't know how much money I got coming, but I'm going to buy us each a Pez dispenser."

Charlie grinned.

"Wow, Charlie," I said as we moved down Bloom Avenue. "I'm not even having to slow way down so you can keep up. And you aren't even sweating real bad like usual. Your shirt's getting baggier, too."

Charlie looked down and shrugged. "Grandma G keeps asking me if I'm feeling sick, but Teddy told her it's probably from all the scootering I'm doing at the Starlight."

"Must be," I said. And then, "I think maybe we're *both* getting rid of some of our afflictions, Charlie. You notice how I'm being nicer, and not saying *ain't* and *gonna* as much now?"

"Yeah," Charlie said. "And you ain't humming so much anymore, either."

"Really?" I said. "Huh. I wasn't even trying to fix that one."

I looked over at Charlie, making ready to ask him if I still sang all the time like I used to, when he stopped, his face going marshmallow-white. "What's the matter?" I asked.

Charlie pointed down the street. There was a cop car parked at the corner, the Taxi Stand Ladies standing next to it.

"Come on," I said, "let's go see what's up."

Charlie looked like he needed to burp as he stood there, refusing to budge. "They taking them to jail?" he asked.

"Now, why would a cop take them to jail, Charlie? The Taxi Stand Ladies aren't crooks."

I scootered to the corner while Charlie stayed glued to the

sidewalk. I reached the cross-street just as Ralph's taxi did. I expected him to stop, but he just rolled by.

I wasn't afraid of high places, like Charlie, and I wasn't afraid of police officers, either. So I butted right in front of the Taxi Stand Ladies when I reached the blue-and-white car. "Oh, I know you!" I said, as I hung my hands on the rolled-down edge of his window. "Your name is Officer Tim. You came to our school after Mr. Morgan's little sister got hit by a car, a long time ago. You showed us how to make hand signals when we ride bikes."

"Is that right," the officer said, because he must have forgotten.

"Hey, do you have to use hand signals when you ride a scooter, even if you stay on the sidewalk?" I asked. Then, before he answered, I realized what I'd done. "Uh-oh. I just interrupted grown-ups again. Cripes, and I was doing so good, too." I looked up at Walking Doll. "Is *cripes* a cussword, because if it is..."

"Well, ladies," the officer said, like I wasn't talking. "I'd better shove off. So, like I said, you two don't get in the car with any cops who forgot to put on their uniforms, you should be okay." Then he winked and drove off.

"Goddamn people, anyway," The Kenosha Kid said. "Worrying about the dirt in other people's backyards so they don't have to look at the messes in their own."

I yelled to Charlie that the coast was clear and waved him toward us. Then I wrinkled my nose. "You guys don't even have a backyard, do you?"

Ralph's taxi crossed the intersection right after Charlie did, and he lifted his pointy finger off the steering wheel and pointed it at The Kenosha Kid. That Ralph, he sure didn't make any sense, the way most times he'd only let one of them ride even if the whole backseat was empty, yet when the taxi was almost full, he'd motion for both of them to squeeze in.

The Kenosha Kid groaned, even if she was smiling. "I wish that stupid bastard would discover soap and water," she said, talking either about Ralph or the guy in the backseat, I didn't know which.

"That guy isn't a Huxley, is he? There's a Sunshine Sister named Anne Huxley who needs to discover soap and water, too." The Kenosha Kid laughed and said no, then slipped into the taxi, smiling like it didn't even stink in there.

"Hey, how come you guys are out so early? I don't usually see you until late afternoon."

"Well," Walking Doll said, "there's a plumbers' convention going on in town," which I took to mean that they figured they'd better take their spins in Ralph's taxi while the getting was good, since as the day wore on those guys would probably be hogging the taxi. "Where were you two?" The Kenosha Kid asked.

"Over at the Starlight because I was supposed to work this morning," I said, which always went over better than me telling them I had a Sunshine Sisters meeting. Neither of them were thrilled when I first told them about the program, Walking Doll saying I didn't need "any snooty little bitch teaching me how to be," because I was perfect just how I was (even if I wasn't), and The Kenosha Kid saying that they'd ruin me. But they both lightened up when I told them that Brenda was paying me to help her, and, best of all, that the Blooms were making me a star in their gala. "But turns out, Mrs. Bloom fell and had to go to the emergency room and Brenda went with her, so no work today. We're just going to go home and play."

I was about to tug Charlie so we could take off, too, but Walking Doll stopped me. "Hang on a second, Teaspoon. I want to show you something." She waited for the taxi to pull away from the curb, then she took her clutch purse from where she had it tucked under her arm—probably because the mailbox was sitting in a pool of water bigger than the one that was on our kitchen floor—and she opened it.

"What do you got?" I asked as I leaned over to see what she was digging for.

"A locket," she said. She pulled it out by its silver chain and petted it for a second, like it was a kitten.

"Hey, it's shaped like a heart," I said.

Walking Doll worked her long red fingernails over the tiny clasp, and once she had the heart split apart, she handed it to me.

There was only one picture in the locket, on the right-hand side. "It's my ma," Walking Doll said. "She was nineteen, the same age as me. It was taken while she was expecting me. I cut her face out of a bigger picture, but I wish the picture would have been smaller so her hair showed."

"Well," I said. "It's not like somebody looking at it would think she was bald." I studied her face a bit. "She's real pretty. And I'm not just being well mannered, either. She is, even if she looks tired in this picture."

I held the locket so Charlie could see.

"She's got eyes like you. And her smile is the same."

"We had the same hair, too," Walking Doll said. "Well, before I dyed mine."

I squinted up at Walking Doll. "You dye your hair?"

She laughed. "Come on now. How could someone pale as me have blue-black hair like this?"

"Snow White did," I reminded her.

Walking Doll bent over and pulled her hair away from her part on both sides to show me a strip of pale brown hair.

"Huh," I said.

"We had the same feet, too," she told me.

"Where does she live?" I asked as Walking Doll took the locket from me and snapped it shut.

"Well, let's just say that she's keeping Charlie's ma company," she said, dropping the locket back into her purse. Walking Doll looked down the street at nothing.

"Why don't you wear it instead of keeping it in your purse?" I asked. "You afraid of losing it in Ralph's taxi?"

"Something like that," she said.

It seemed like I should say something else to her, but I didn't know what. So I just wrapped my arms around her waist and gave her a squeeze instead. Walking Doll spread her arms like a duck getting ready to fly, and she giggled. "What are you doing?"

"Giving you a hug."

Walking Doll looked like she didn't know if she should laugh or cry. "Well, see you," I told her, then off me and Charlie went, me wondering if my ma and I had the same feet.

I walked with Charlie over to his house to tell Mrs. Fry we were back, but when I opened the door, I could hear Teddy talking in the kitchen. "... I don't know. But what I *do* know is if that's the case, money will be the only bargaining tool I'll have. I had no idea there was a *lien* on that house, though." Teddy's voice sounded a thousand pounds heavier than him. "And a big one, at that," he said, which made me wonder if Teddy didn't need his eyes examined, because even a four-eyes could see how bad the front porch was tipping. "Twenty-five hundred dollars," he said.

"That mother of yours... I tried to tell her," Mrs. Fry said.

I held the door open and shoved Charlie inside.

"If I don't get that loan, I don't know what I'll do," Teddy's voice was low and quiet.

"I know how you worry, Teddy," Mrs. Fry answered. "I worry about the same things with Charlie. Did you talk to Mr. Miller? He's such a nice man. I think he'd try to find a way to help you out."

"Hello?" Teddy called when I shut the door, even though I shut it respectable-quiet. Mrs. Fry said she didn't hear anything—which of course, she wouldn't. Even if I'd given it a good slam.

Teddy appeared in the kitchen doorway. "It's the children," he called back to Mrs. Fry. He smiled at us, even though his forehead was wearing a worry wrinkle the size of the Grand Canyon. "You're back early."

"Yeah, I didn't have a Sunshine meeting this morning after all, because Mrs. Bloom fell off the new stage and hurt her ankle and had to go to the hospital." Teddy said that was too bad (because he was a better person than Dumbo Doug), then he thanked Mrs. Fry for the coffee and told her that he'd better go get something accomplished.

"You ask Mr. Miller about that loan again, Teddy," she called back, "and you take care of that wrist. Don't do too much."

"You went to the bank to get a loan, Teddy?" I asked, because if he had, then that would be the granddaddy *contradiction* of all times, because Teddy didn't buy anything on credit. After my loan from Jesus, I understood why. "You need a loan to fix that leaning porch and our bad roof, Teddy?"

Teddy looked away. "Yeah," he said.

"Too bad you have to fix the lean, because a few boards to fix the roof probably wouldn't cost that much. I've got a payday coming and I could give you some money to help buy the boards. As for the cost of fixing that lean, I guess you're on your own, Teddy."

Teddy kissed the top of my head without smiling. "You're a sweetie," he said.

CHAPTER ELEVEN

That night, while me and Charlie played *Live at the Starlight,* there was a knock at the door. "Can you get that, Teaspoon?" Teddy shouted. "I'm busy."

"Like I'm not!" I shouted back, then added a sorry, because that was the respectable thing to do when one of your afflictions let loose.

I opened the door and there he was, Johnny Jackson, standing at *my* door. "Special delivery for Teaspoon Marlene," he said. He motioned to the sidewalk where Doug and a row of three Starlight seats were waiting. "Where would you like them, miss?" he said.

"Teddy! Teddy!" I screamed, and he came running into the living room like maybe Lizzie Borden herself was at the door. He was holding a paring knife in his left hand and a little potato, gouged like Charlie's head, clamped in the swollen fingers of his right. "Look what Johnny brought me, Teddy. Straight from the Starlight Theater!"

"Mrs. Bloom was sending them to the dump...Teaspoon wanted them. I hope it's all right," Johnny said.

"We can put them right here in the living room, Teddy. There's room up against that wall opposite the piano. Then you and Mrs. Fry can sit in style for our shows."

Teddy nodded, so Johnny and Doug carried them in while Teddy moved the end tables, and me and Charlie went nuts.

"Enjoy, little star," Johnny said once the seats were in place.

Teddy followed Johnny outside like respectable grown-ups do when a visitor is about to leave, and I did, too. Teddy asked Johnny about the hot rod he was working on, and Johnny talked about "dropping the chassis," even though I couldn't imagine Johnny dropping anything, him having muscles like Popeye. Dumbo Doug crawled back in the truck and Jolene called from across the street, "Hey, Johnny? What are you doing over *there*?"

I looked back up at Johnny, handsome as James Dean. I still couldn't believe that he brought me those seats. "Well," Johnny told Teddy. "We have to get the rest of these to the dump before they close, then get the truck back to the shop. Have fun with the seats, Teaspoon," he said.

"*Johnny!*" Jolene yelled again, louder. Like maybe he didn't hear her the first time.

"Aren't you going to thank Johnny?" Teddy asked me. And it was funny—as much as I was in love with Johnny, I never got tongue-tied with him. Well, until that moment. I think because I was over-wowed at the thought of having a part of the Starlight magic in my very own living room. And at the thought that Johnny had brought it to me. That alone made a lump the size of Charlie's knee clog my throat, and I was afraid if I said a word, I'd start crying—I just shook my head yes and looked up at him.

I got the lump in my throat swallowed after Johnny had slammed the truck door. After all, I was a Sunshine Sister now, and I was well mannered. So feeling choked up or not, I stepped in front of Teddy and shouted so Johnny would hear me over the rumble of the engine. "Thank you, Johnny! That was about the nicest thing anyone could have done for me." Johnny leaned over so I could see his hand wave through Dumbo Doug's window.

Me and Charlie were sitting in the Starlight seats, me rubbing my hands over the soft red velvet armrests, when there was another knock at the door. There she was, Miss Tuckle, a casserole dish in her hands, her hair pinned up on the sides and lipstick on her plain-Jane lips. She had earrings and a necklace on, too, and her best Sunday school dress.

"Hello, Teaspoon," she said. "Mrs. Fry told me that Teddy hurt himself at work, so I thought I'd bring you two supper."

I was just about to tell her that Teddy was taking care of our supper when he stuck his head into the room and saw her. "April, come in," he said, grinning like Dopey dwarf.

And Miss Tuckle was just as "nice" the next day, too, bringing Teddy some oven mitts she made herself. All because when she'd taken the reheated casserole out of the oven the night before, she had to use two dishtowels that were damp and she'd burned two of her fingers.

The day after that, when I came home from the Starlight, there they were, Teddy and Miss Tuckle, walking down the sidewalk away from the house, Teddy's bandaged hand and his good one waving like a m-a-e-s-t-r-o, which is what Brenda said those orchestra directors can be called, while Miss Tuckle walked with her head cocked toward him. "She's up to something, Charlie," I said, and he asked me what. "Stealing Teddy from my Ma, the same way Betty Rains stole Mrs. Carlton's man, that's what."

Miss Tuckle could tell that I was mad at her, too, by the way I didn't sing, or smile, or even talk all the way through the next Sunday school class. (Okay. I might have hummed a little.) So when I got up after class, she grabbed my shoulder and gently kept me in my chair. When the last kid left the room and it was just Charlie and me, she said, "I'm not trying to take your mother's place, Teaspoon. Teddy and I are only friends, and he could use a friend right now."

I scrinched my eyes at her. "He's got me. I'm his friend."

"I know that, sweetie," she said. "But grown-ups need grown-up friends, too."

"Well, he's got Mrs. Fry. She's eighty-two years old. You can't get much more grown up than that, can you?" I said.

"Well, Mrs. Fry is a good friend to Teddy, it's true, but we need different friends for different things. You do and talk about different things with each of your friends, don't you?" She had me there on that one, because I'd never sing with the tone-deaf Jackson kids, or jump rope with slow-Moe Charlie.

I tilted my head and studied Miss Tuckle. "You swear that you and Teddy aren't doing the Juicy Jit..." I glanced up at Jesus, then stopped, just in case saying *Juicy Jitterbug* was swearing. I cleared my throat and started over. "You swear that you and Teddy are only friends, and not doing boyfriend-and-girlfriend stuff like kissing and whatnot?"

Miss Tuckle turned sunburn-pink. "I swear we're not," she said.

"Okay...hold that thought." I ran out of the Sunday school room, and sure enough, I found a stack of Bibles on a little table in the church entrance hall. Bibles, I think, that were for borrowing by the sinners who forgot theirs, so they could follow along as the good pastor read. I grabbed four or five of them and ran back downstairs. "Here, put your hand on these and look at Jesus, and *then* swear that you and Teddy aren't doing boyfriend-and-girlfriend stuff together. Then I might believe you."

Miss Tuckle looked uncomfortable, but she put her hand on that stack of Bibles and she swore it.

"I don't know, Charlie," I said as we walked home. "She *did* make a swear to God, yet you saw how giggly she got when Teddy gushed about her stupid casserole and her pie, didn't you? Her eyes got all googly looking. She's trying to wear her hair more like a glamour girl now, too. And did you get a whiff of her when she came over last time?" Charlie shook his head. "Well, lucky you, because she was wearing some stinky stuff that was so strong it made my throat burn."

I scootered a few more swipes with my foot, then said, "I sure hope Miss Tuckle wasn't being a fibber-face when she made that swear. If she was, she's going to have some explaining to do. To me, and to God. She's lying, and I won't ever talk to her again. And God, he just might condemn her to damnation forever."

"Where's damnation?"

"I don't know, Charlie, but it's got a cussword in it, so you can bet it's not anyplace nice."

The next week, Teddy invited Miss Tuckle over for dinner as his way of saying thank you for her bringing all of that food over while he was laid up with his wrist. The wrist he claimed was better so he could go back to work, even if he winced when he did little things like turned a doorknob.

Teddy made fried chicken that night, even if cooking chicken got a tad bloody in the pan, and when I said it smelled good, Teddy hit me with a bomb by telling me I was eating my dinner over at the Frys. "Why?" I asked.

"Well, Mrs. Fry is making spaghetti with meatballs for you and Charlie. She knows it's your favorite. It would be rude if you didn't have your supper there after she went through all that trouble."

"Well why aren't all four of us having supper there, then? It could have saved you all *this* trouble."

Teddy looked uncomfortable, like people look when their butt itches and they can't scratch it because they're in public. He stuttered a bit when he said, "Well, we each didn't know the other was making a big meal."

"Good thing I know you're too respectable to lie, Teddy," I said, "or I'd think you were just making all that up."

✳   ✳   ✳

"Something smells fishy," I told Charlie as we sat on his steps after our spaghetti. And that Charlie, who misses the boat so many times that if he really was in the water he'd have drowned by now, said, "No. Teddy was making fried chicken."

I rolled my eyes. "I don't mean that I *really* smell fish. I just meant that I think Mrs. Fry and Teddy planned this like sneaks, just to get me out of Teddy's hair so he could be alone with Miss Tuckle. Maybe even so they could do the Juicy Jitterbug."

"What's that?" Charlie asked.

"Something grown-ups do in their beds," I said, and Charlie said, "Oh. You mean that sex stuff."

"That sex stuff?"

"Yeah," Charlie said, "How big people make babies." Then he told a story so ridiculous I had to laugh. I'd seen a wee-er once. Jack Johnson's. He'd dropped his pants, right behind the shed, and said, "Look what I got." I wish I hadn't. It looked like a pinkie finger with no bones, flopped over two lumps of skin that had swallowed a couple of steelies. I took one look at that goofy-looking mess and told Jack that if I had a boy's wee-er, I'd hide it like cracked elbows.

"You're making that up. There's no way a guy could get that thing in a girl's pee-er," I told Charlie. "It wouldn't fit, for one. As floppy as it is, it would be like trying to stuff a wool sock into a baby shoe."

Even as I stated my case, though, I wondered. Maybe that was why the bed banged so loud, because a guy would have to work like crazy to make that thing go in there. I told Charlie my doubts and he said that wee-ers didn't stay little. They grew real big and stiff when men were going to "do it," which I took to mean the Juicy Jitterbug.

"How do you know that?" I asked Charlie.

"Cause our house was only one room, and I saw my ma and dad doing it more than once. My dad and some other ladies, too. When I was supposed to be sleeping."

I stayed quiet for a while, my head going back and forth, back and forth, thinking Charlie was all wet one minute, then thinking maybe he knew what he was talking about the next. After all, who would have thought that Charlie had the smarts to know how to play the piano, either? But that was Charlie for you. Full of surprises. And he did seem awful sure of himself on this one.

"No wonder Miss Tuckle never married or had a boyfriend before," I told Charlie as we sat, me watching my house. "She probably thought the whole thing sounded disgusting, too."

I narrowed my eyes until Charlie blurred. "Hey, wait a minute. Maybe that's why she has her sights set on Teddy. She's probably thinking that a guy as little as him has to have a little wee-er, too, which wouldn't make it quite as painful."

"Maybe," Charlie said.

I looked across the street, where Johnny was leaned under the hood of his new hot rod, which was nothing but a junky old car he was going to fix up. "Hey, Charlie. If you get married, do you *have* to let your husband do that to you, do you know?"

"I think so," Charlie said, and I said, "Man."

I sat there thinking for a minute, then I said, "Hey, Charlie. If that's how you make babies, and your dad was doing that with your ma and some other ladies all the time, then how come you're an only kid?"

Charlie shrugged. "I dunno. Maybe he was doing it wrong."

The night was warm, the wind still, and with the Jacksons inside probably having their supper, you could hear an occasional faint Miss Tuckle giggle through the screens. "Okay, that's it," I said to Charlie. "I'm going spying. You stay here. I'll be right back." Charlie looked disappointed, but the sorry fact was, Charlie wasn't as fast as me and I didn't plan on getting caught. "If Grandma G comes out and sees me gone, you just say I ran out to my shed to get something for us to play with, okay?"

"Is there something for us to play with in there?" Charlie asked.

"Course not, but how would she know that?"

It wasn't easy sitting still and quiet under the window because skeetos with the appetite of a Charlie were gnawing on me, and I had to rub them away instead of squashing them with a slap.

"Teddy," Miss Tuckle said after she got done giggling over something or other Teddy said (which couldn't have been funny, since Teddy's funny bone was undersized, like everything else on him). "I hope I didn't offend you with my offer earlier. And I hope you don't think I'm trying to buy your friendship. Though I have to admit, when I was younger, I *did* try to buy friends by giving them gifts and being overly helpful."

Teddy's voice sounded uncomfortable when he said, "I wasn't above that myself. Though I can't imagine you needing to buy anyone, April. You're kind. Sweet. A genuinely nice person."

I could almost hear Miss Tuckle blush.

"Well, anyway," she said, after a soft giggle, "I just want you to know that I'd be more than happy to lend you the money. You can't keep putting up with this emotional blackmail. That's no way to live."

"Oh, April, I couldn't take money from you."

"Wait. Hear me out. Okay?" April said, even though I knew she was wasting her time, because Teddy didn't do handouts.

"I make decent money, Teddy. And I've not really had anything to spend it on. I've lived in my tiny apartment since I left home, and I make all my own clothes. I've just never had much reason to indulge in the things a lot of other women indulge in. What I'm saying is that I have money in the bank doing nothing but collecting dust. You can't go on like this, afraid to let Teaspoon get the mail for fear there will be another one of those letters in the box, then having to fork out money you don't have for fear of the repercussions if you send nothing.

"I know we haven't known each other long, but I can tell a trustworthy person when I see one. And what good is money if you can't do something worthwhile with it? You need a loan, and with that lien on the house..."

Teddy must have made like he was going to say something because Miss Tuckle said, "Don't say anything just yet. Just think about it, okay? We could work out a payment plan with interest, if that would make you feel better. Teaspoon's future has to be more important than my uncomfortableness at offering this, and, more important than your pride in taking it."

I turned around and rested my back against the siding when Teddy changed the subject to something dull. *My security? The lean? My future? Blackmail?* What on earth were they talking about?

And then I got it. Before the roof started leaking, one day when Teddy came out to the mailbox, his foot hit a creak on the porch and he stopped and bounced in place on boards that were frayed like old ropes. Then he said, "I don't know how much longer this old porch is going to stay secure." He shook his head and carried his mail inside. Wasn't that just like Teddy, to worry about me running back and forth across an unstable porch. Like what? I was Charlie-fat and might roll right off it, or fall right through it?

And my future? Sure enough, Teddy was thinking about how one day after he got old and the Lord called him home, I'd inherit this place, just like he did. Teddy just didn't want to leave me the same run-down house his ma left him. That Teddy, what a worry-wart. He was only thirty-eight years old. Mrs. Fry was eighty-two and she was still kicking. That should have told him something. As for me seeing a bad black bill in the mail, what difference did it make what color the envelopes were or if I saw them or not? I always knew when a bad bill came anyway, because Teddy's eyebrows would bunch until payday.

I wanted to jump up right then and there and stick my face up to the screen and yell, *I'll use the back door, then, for crying out loud! And it won't matter what shape the house is in in a bajillion years from now anyway, because Ma will be back before then and we can fix it up with her movie-star money.* But I didn't do that, of course, or Teddy would have known my ears were snooping.

"I should go," April said. "Please think about my offer, Teddy."

I heard the couch spring squeak and knew they had gotten up, so I raced around the back of the house so it would look like I was just coming from the Frys.

"Hi," I said, maybe a bit too loud, because I startled Miss Tuckle, which would have been funny, had Teddy not put his arm on her back to steady her.

Teddy walked her to the car and I tagged behind them. I could tell Miss Tuckle thought my friendliness meant that I liked her like I did when she was only my Sunday school teacher. Little did she know that I was just hanging around so Teddy wouldn't forget he was somebody else's boyfriend and that Miss Tuckle and him were only friends and try kissing her, like men always did when they said good-bye to ladies in the movies.

Poor Miss Tuckle, all slumped and skinny and homely. I almost felt sorry for her as she slipped behind the steering wheel of her car and smiled up at Teddy, like she didn't know that he would never give up a pretty movie star for an old maid who made oven mitts.

Teddy was more quiet than usual the next day, like he was thinking, but he wasn't as fidgety, either. And when he decided to take a stroll because the evening was breezy and the sunset pretty, I went with him, just in case he decided to veer over to Miss Tuckle's place, which I'd learned from Mrs. Fry was right above the drugstore.

We went down Thornton Street, past Mr. Miller's house, and Miller came out of his garage and called, "Hi there, Big Guy," in that booming voice of his that always sounded like he was doing a TV commercial.

Miller headed right over to the sidewalk, so we had to stop. Then we had to wait while he lit a cigar—Cuban, he said. Ordered special for him by Pop. "Sorry I couldn't be more helpful to you the other day. But you get that lien squared away, and we'll do some business," he said. Teddy nodded without looking Mr. Miller in the eye.

"And while you're at it, maybe you should get yourself some cash for a car, too. I'd give you a good deal."

"Teddy's face got red, and started twitching right here," I told Charlie after Teddy and me got home, and I tapped my face right on the sharp bone under my ear to show Charlie where Teddy twitched. "And he didn't talk the whole way. I told him right out that what Mr. Miller said sure was idiotic, since if we could get the lean and the leaks fixed in the first place, we wouldn't even need a loan.

"I don't know, Charlie," I said. "Trying to figure out why big people fret so much is about as hard as trying to figure out why Poochie barks all the time. All that worrying, it's nothing but a big waste of time."

CHAPTER TWELVE

You'd think that since I'd seen Leonard's picture in the newspaper, I'd have recognized him right off the bat when he came into the Starlight. But I didn't. At least not at first.

He came through the exit door near the screen that Johnny and the guys had propped open with a brick so they could carry boards and tools in and out without having to turn the doorknob when their hands were full. With the sun bright behind him, Leonard didn't look like nothing but an exclamation mark standing in that doorway.

I was looking for a phone number Brenda had written on a piece of envelope that she was sure she'd left on the concession stand counter when he stepped inside. The guys glanced up and got back to work. Well, except for Johnny, who watched Leonard skip over the scraps of wood and tools on the floor like he was playing hopscotch.

In his fancy slacks and button-up shirt, I thought Leonard was a salesman. Even before he got close enough for me to see his pinched nose, though, you'd think I'd have recognized him by his hair. Platinum as a starlet's, the top flat, like a miniature lawn that just got mowed.

Leonard didn't ask the guys if Brenda was around. He waited until he reached the concession stand and he asked me. I pointed up toward the projector room. "She's up there. I'll show you where in a minute." I hurried and fanned through the papers again, thinking maybe I missed the corner of the envelope the number was on the first time, and wanting bad to find it because Brenda was not having a good day.

"Ah, here it is!" I said to Leonard. But Leonard was already up to the nosebleed seats.

When I got to the projector room, the phone number in my hand, the door was open, and so was the door to the meeting room. I could see Leonard and Brenda standing next to the long table. Brenda had a stack of papers in her hand. The edges were mismatched and messy and she was trying to straighten them by rapping the bottoms against the table. "I told you, Leonard. I can't see you this afternoon. There's an organizational meeting for the gala at four thirty and I'm in charge. Everything's a mess and I feel like I'm drowning in details."

I backed up a little, then dipped to the side of the room like a good Sunshine Sister who didn't interrupt big people when they were talking.

"What? Your mother twists her ankle a little and she can't do a thing now? I played the whole state tournament my senior year with a sprained ankle," Leonard said.

"It's not just her sprained ankle," Brenda said, "though she does have to stay off it and keep it elevated and iced for a while. She's working from home with her assistant, but most of the work concerns the drive-in. She wants it open as soon as possible since this place will be closed for some weeks. This means everything related to the Starlight is falling in my lap. The construction, chairing the committees for the gala, booking the acts, lining up ... well, everything."

I wanted to jump into the projector room and remind Brenda to delegate, *delegate,* but I was making progress with my afflictions and I didn't want to blow it, so I slipped up against the wall and listened, peeking now and then, even if that probably wasn't the respectable thing to do, either.

"Plus," Brenda continued, "Mother doesn't want me leaving while the workers are here."

Leonard peered down at the Perkins crew. "Why? What are they going to do, steal Jujubes?" He laughed like he'd made a funny, then he huffed, "I don't know why she clings so hard to this old relic. Or why she's erecting another theater. It's not like she needs the few bucks it'll generate. But I suppose she needs something to keep her busy."

"Leonard, please," Brenda said.

"My poor little overworked pet," Leonard said, in a voice every bit as creepy as the voice of a movie bad guy. "All the more reason to come play hooky with your big daddy for a while."

Leonard must have grabbed Brenda then, because I heard the papers swish, and her groan. "Leonard, I had those all in order." Brenda said this like she was saying it in fun, but she didn't sound like she was having any fun to me.

Leonard sighed. "Well, I can see you're going to be a drag today. Okay, then. I'll let you get back to your little party plans. I'll pick you up at five thirty."

"Five thirty?"

"Thad and Trish are having a cookout. We'll have a few beers... play a little tennis maybe. I told them we'd be there."

"But I don't know how long this meeting's going to last. We have a lot of ground to cover. Probably more than I even know."

Leonard's sigh sounded more like a grunt. "I would have thought you'd clear your plate for your fiancé, since I only get home about one weekend out of the month. But suit yourself. Call me if you can be on time. If not, you know where Thad lives."

Mrs. Fry never did say if it was okay for men to stomp when they walked, but it must be, because Leonard stomped like a giant across the projector room and headed down the stairs.

I was about to step into the projector room to give Brenda the phone number when she came barging out. "Leonard, wait!" Her voice echoed so that even the guys down by the half-made stage heard and looked up.

I could tell that Brenda was apologizing, the way she was holding out her hands like she was pleading, even if she was talking quiet and glancing down at the stage, then up to toward the nosebleed seats, like she was afraid we would hear her.

Leonard had his right hand in his pocket and the other straight at his side, but then his left hand came up like a stop sign for a bad dog, and Brenda stopped talking. She pinched the sides of her skirt and twisted the material with nervous fingers while Leonard said words I couldn't hear. Before he could turn to walk away, Brenda got on tiptoes and gave his cheek a quick kiss. She nearly jumped out of her skin when she turned and saw me watching.

I helped Brenda pick up the papers that had fallen in the meeting room. Four pages of information for each committee we'd have, with the tasks for each listed, along with a calendar and what Brenda called a "time line." We put the papers back in stacks, one stack for each page, one through five, then Brenda took one page off each pile, straightened them, and handed them to me so I could staple them together. While I waited for her to get me a new stack, I kept looking at that new ring on her finger. Boy, that diamond sure was a honker! So heavy that it kept slipping and leaning up against her pinkie, like it needed a rest from standing up by itself.

Good thing Brenda had me there to help her get ready for her meeting, because she was so busy on the phone that she didn't have time to do anything else. Things like wiping out the coffee cups with napkins in case they had any dust or baby spiders in them that might float up to the top when the coffee got poured. And running to check both bathrooms to make sure there was toilet paper in every stall (there was, because that was Mr. Morgan's job, and that man was on the ball). Important stuff like that, that could ruin a perfectly good meeting for fancy folk if they weren't done.

Brenda started each phone call with, "Mother thought you might be able to tell me how to reach Les Paul's agent...," always jotting more numbers on scrap paper and getting more and more agitated. Finally fifteen minutes before the meeting, she made her last call for the day. And afterward, she sat staring for a while, then crumpled up her notes and tossed them in the trash can and stared at nothing.

Boy, I don't care how lit the Starlight was, when you walked outside on a sunny day, that sun about blinded you. I squinted and blinked a few times, thinking it was just my eyes playing tricks on me when I saw nothing in front of me but white. That is, until my eyes adjusted and I saw the car, big as me and Teddy's living room, parked sideways, so close to the doorway that had I not waited for my eyes to get used to the light, I would have ran smack-dab into it.

"Isabella? *Isabella!*"

For just one second there, I thought it was my Ma, coming back in a movie-star car—but she would never call me by my given name. Nope. That crabby voice could only belong to one lady. Mrs. Bloom. "Don't shut that door!" Mrs. Bloom yelled. "Those idiotic construction workers must have locked it behind them, and I don't have my keys on me."

And there she was, stretched out in the backseat, her fat foot wrapped and propped on the seat, a lady wearing a nurse's hat and a lot of chins squeezed behind the steering wheel. Boy, Mrs. Bloom sure didn't look like a movie star that day. Her hair was flat in the back, and her eyes looked as pinched as Leonard's nose.

"Get me Brenda, please!" Mrs. Bloom said, all grouchy.

I opened the door and kept my knee against it, leaning in and yelling Brenda's name, loud as I could.

"*Go* inside and get her, for heaven's sake," Mrs. Bloom snapped.

I turned around. "You having a bad day, Mrs. Bloom? I think

you are. But like I learned from watching Teddy when his wrist was paining him, when grown-ups get hurt and can't work, even the ones who are good as Jesus get a little owly." I didn't say the other part. That I knew that meant that grabby ones like her were going to be even worse.

"Go!" she said.

I shut the door tight behind me so it wouldn't blow open and thump in the wind—something that always irritated the best of them, so it would probably double-irritate Mrs. Bloom—and so she wouldn't hear me yell again, which is exactly what I did. Three times. And finally Brenda appeared on the steps in the nosebleed section. "Your ma's here and wants to talk to you," I yelled.

Brenda came down the stairs. "She's got a nurse with her. I didn't know regular people could have a nurse. I thought they had to stay in hospitals or doctor's offices."

Brenda kind of smiled. "That's our maid. It's a maid's hat." I ran to get the card I'd made for Mrs. Bloom and met Brenda outside.

"Mother, what are you doing here?" Brenda asked, squinting into the car. "You look like you're in a lot of pain. Are you taking the pills the doctor gave you?"

"I can't take those things. I told you that. They knock me out for hours. And I have too much to do."

"Well, you should at least be home resting," Brenda said.

"Which is exactly where I would be, if you would have answered the phone. How can I rest when I'm worrying about how things are going here? I tried calling several times, but the line was busy, busy, busy."

"Yeah, that's because Brenda was busy, busy, busy," I said. Brenda used her hand to tell me to stay quiet, and Mrs. Bloom used her voice.

"Tell me you weren't visiting with Julie or Tina," Mrs. Bloom said. "Not with this much work to be done."

"I've not talked to them since I started working on the gala,"

Brenda said. I looked up at her to see if there was any huff in her face, since there wasn't in her voice. There wasn't.

"Has Glen been stopping by regularly as he promised?"

Brenda nodded, and while I didn't think she was lying, being the Sweetheart of Mill Town and all, I hadn't seen Mr. Perkins since the guys started working.

"And did you get ahold of Les Paul and Mary Ford's agent? We have to get them booked, Brenda. Mrs. Gaylor told me that it's all over town that they're our lead act. How, I don't know, since I never breathed their names to anyone. Did you?" Brenda shook her head, and I slipped farther behind Brenda, and grumbled about Susie Miller in my head, because I had a sneaking suspicion she was the big mouth who repeated that bit of info I leaked.

"Well?" Mrs. Bloom said.

"I'm on top of things, Mother," Brenda said.

"Don't play games with me, Brenda. I'm in too much pain to be patient. Either you've booked them or you haven't."

Brenda looked down. "They're booked," she said.

"Thank God," Mrs. Bloom said. She let out a big sigh. "That sure is a load off my mind."

"You booked them?" I shouted. "Wow, Brenda! I didn't know that!"

Brenda put her arm on my shoulder, "You have something for my mother, don't you, Teaspoon?" she said.

"Oh, yeah." I reached my arm through the window. "I made this for you at Sunday school, Mrs. Bloom. It's a get-better card."

Mrs. Bloom took it from my hand like she didn't know what it was, even though I'd just told her.

I think she liked the picture of the Starlight Theater I drew on the front, because she looked at it for a long time before she opened the folded page to see what I'd put inside. And when she read, *Get well Mrs. Bloom because we miss you at the Starlight and thanks for letting me be Brenda's Sunshine Sister so I can get respectable and sing in your show so I can get famous,* her eyes got blinky and teary.

"Why, thank you, Teaspoon," she said, using my nickname for the first time.

I suppose I should have felt good about making Mrs. Bloom happy, and I guess I did a bit. But mostly I felt bad. I didn't really mean it when I wrote that I missed her. I was just being well mannered like the code said I should be. I put my head down and wondered if being respectable made other people feel like fibber-faces, too.

Before Mrs. Bloom left, she apologized to Brenda, and to me. "I'm sorry for snipping. I should have known you'd come through, Brenda. You always do. And Teaspoon, well, thank you for the nice card."

CHAPTER THIRTEEN

By the last week of June, we had a string of days so hot and hair-frizzing humid that the grown-ups lost their zip. Poor Teddy couldn't even get three blocks down the street before his shirts lost their respectability, sweat spots blooming under his armpits and between his shoulder blades. And the Taxi Stand Ladies (who ordinarily liked summer best) stood humped over the mailbox by noon, blowing breath up into their faces from jutted-out lower lips, or pulling out the necklines of their dresses to puff on their balloons. They weren't taking all that many spins in Ralph's taxi, either, probably because even with the windows open to stir a breeze, the black seats were heated like griddles.

And when Charlie and I made our way into The Pop Shop to get refills for our Mickey and Minnie Pez dispensers, Pop had two fans rattling air on him but was still grouchy enough to tell Charlie and me to hurry because we were taking up store space.

Mr. Perkins was extra-grouchy during the bad heat streak, too. Every time he stopped at the Starlight he yelled at Johnny and Doug more than usual, calling them slackers, even though the stage was done but for a couple more coats of varnish, and they had the hallway leading to the furniture shop mostly done.

Yep, most all of the grown-ups were extra-grouchy during that bad heat streak, but of all of them, Mrs. Bloom was the grumpiest.

With her ankle still paining her, and the Starbright Drive-In open-ing July 1, she wasn't coming to the Starlight much, but she had the phone ringing off the hook harping at Brenda about this and that, until Brenda was wired tighter than my curls. Heat and wired like a curl or not, Brenda didn't get ornery. But I couldn't say the same for the Jackson kids.

Across the street, the boys fought like alley cats with the toy Spud Guns they'd bought with the money from their new lawn-mowing business. Cussing up a storm as they peeled the sides of potatoes and poked the plastic nozzles into the white meat to pull out a potato "bullet," then chasing each other to get a closer shot, because the bullets didn't go all that far and they hurt more up close. Aiming at their sisters' bare legs or each other's heads until the whole yard was filled with potato bullets and Jolene's and Jen-nifer's shrieks. Mrs. Jackson came out onto the steps now and then to beg them to play nice, but she didn't have the zip to yell hard, so they just kept on shooting and screaming.

Me and Charlie, though? We didn't lose our zip. And we didn't get ornery.

Well, I did once.

"You want to play marbles when you get back?" Joey yelled when I hurried down the steps on one of those hot-as-blazes mornings.

"She's not gonna come over," Jolene shouted to Joey, plenty loud so I could hear. "She's a snob now, just like Brenda Bloom. She thinks she's too good for us—even if her best friend now is a fat, dumb little boy."

It took everything I'd learned from being a Sunshine Sister to keep me from marching across the street to pound that smirk right off Jolene's freckled face. Instead I yelled, "You're just jealous because I'm going to sing at the Starlight Theater, and because your brother likes me better than he likes you." I knew this last part would get her goat the most, because she'd been extra-snippy with me ever since Johnny brought me those seats from the Starlight.

"Yeah, right," she said. "Brenda Bloom...my brother...they're just nice to you because they feel sorry for you. All because you don't have a mom."

"I have a ma," I screamed. "She's in Hollywood, and she'll be home as soon as—"

"Yeah, we know," Jolene said, her hands on her hips. "As soon as she gets to be a famous movie star." Jolene struck what she thought was a movie-star pose.

That was it! I glanced up and down the street, then back at my house and Charlie's to see if anybody I had to be good around was watching me. They weren't, so I did what no respectable girl should do. I headed across that street, my fists bunched.

"Fight! Fight!" Joey called and Jack and James came running into the front yard.

Jolene tossed *my* jump rope down and spread her legs. "Don't you even dare, Teaspoon!" she warned. But I dared all right. I grabbed a fistful of her sweaty hair and yanked it so hard she screamed. "Take it back!" I shouted, my hand twisting so that Jolene had to stay bent over if she wanted that wad of hair to stay on.

"Let go!" Jolene cried as she flopped her arms to try to get ahold of me.

"Take it back first!"

I didn't even notice that Jennifer had run into the house until I saw her come out, her braid in her mouth, Mrs. Jackson right behind her.

"Girls!" Mrs. Jackson yelled, hair so messy you'd think someone had been pulling hers, too. "Teaspoon, you go back on your side of the street, and you stay there."

"Yeah!" Jolene said, all brave now that her mommy was there to protect her.

"Well, you keep your fat lip on your side of the street, and I will!" I yelled as I crossed the road, even if Mrs. Jackson was standing right there.

I grabbed Charlie and my scooter and we headed to the

Starlight—even if it wasn't time for a Sunshine meeting—me grumbling the whole way about how I hated Jolene for making me get afflicted again.

I stopped grumbling when we got to the theater, though, because there was a delivery truck backed up to the ramp outside the old furniture store. Four guys were sweating up a storm as they rolled a crate the size of a car up the ramp. Brenda was watching from inside. "The grand piano!" I shouted. "It's gotta be, Charlie. Come on!"

I had to help tug Charlie up the ramp because the rollers on it kept wanting to push your feet backward if you didn't go fast. Finally one of the delivery guys reached down and yanked Charlie up. "You could have used the steps," he said, pointing to the ones next to the ramp.

The furniture store's warehouse room was nothing but a big mess, with a high ceiling and cement floor. There was a long wooden table in the back, some shelves lining both sides of the corner near it, scraps of wood, upholstering material, broken arms and legs from chairs and tables, and enough dust on the floor that the piano crate scraped like a shovel, dragging a path through it when the delivery men moved it to the center of the room.

It took about forever before that piano was unloaded and unpacked, but finally there it was in all its glory, the black wood so shiny Charlie and I could see our teeth.

"Wow, look in here, Charlie!" I said, as I leaned over and peeked under the lid Brenda propped open. "Did you ever think there was so much junk inside a piano?" Brenda told us what a lot of the inside parts were called, and struck a couple of keys so we could see how the hammers worked.

"Play it for us, Brenda! Play us a song and sing!" I pestered.

I don't know what I was expecting. Well, yes, I guess I did. Brenda Bloom was the Sweetheart of Mill Town. Pretty and talented enough to win the Miss America contest if she entered it. So I guess I was expecting her voice to be radio-singer good. A voice that made me get goose pimples on my arms and tingles in my stomach.

Brenda had to go into the theater to get one of the music books the Mill Town City Orchestra was going to use, because she couldn't play by ear. I was hopping in place while I waited for her to get back.

"What you going to play?" I asked, peering over her shoulder when she sat down and started paging through the book. "Oh, Irving Berlin...hmmm," I said. I didn't know most of those songs, but when I saw one called "They Say It's Wonderful," I said, "Play that one, Brenda. With a title like that, it's got to be good."

Brenda straightened her back and her skirt, then pulled her chin up like Teddy and started the song.

Oh man, did that grand piano sound pretty when she played the intro. So pretty it made my eyes want to sting. I glanced over at Charlie, and his eyes looked like they *were* stinging.

Brenda didn't fumble a note in that introduction, and her timing was perfect. But still...

And when her voice came in? Well, I wouldn't exactly say Brenda had a voice that would worry the ears off a rabbit, but it wasn't exactly one that would make them perk up and take notice, either. It was soft, kind of pretty, but like that soup you have to drink when you're pukey. The kind where you can scoop with your spoon all you want, and you're not going to find any meat or vegetables at the bottom of the bowl to fill you up.

I looked down at my arms, willing the little hairs to stand up like I thought they would when I heard her sing for the first time. But they were laying down asleep. Even when Brenda hit the chorus, which was usually the most magical part of a song, they still didn't wake up. But Brenda was good. *She had to be.* She'd had lessons in voice and music from the time she was four years old, and everybody in Mill Town said how talented she was. Well, except Dumbo Doug, but what did he know?

When Brenda finished the song, I clapped and elbowed Charlie to do the same. Brenda brushed off our applause. "I'm really not that good," she said. Brenda was right about that, but I wasn't about to agree with her. So I told her she sang real good, and then I asked Jesus to forgive me for fibbing again.

"You want to play a song, Charlie?" Brenda asked.

I thought Charlie was going to pee his pants right on the spot. He glanced up at Brenda, like he was trying to figure out if she was kidding. "Go ahead, Charlie," I said. "But wash your hands first."

While Charlie headed into the Starlight to use the restroom, I leaned over and whispered to Brenda. "His hands are always grubby because he's got a bit of a sweating problem. And a picking-scalp affliction."

Charlie got back in such record time that I had to check to make sure he'd really washed. He had, because his hands looked clean as bread dough and smelled like soap, but they were still a little damp, so I made him rub them on his shirt.

Brenda scooted over and patted the bench. Charlie sat down, his cheeks red like Christmas. "Go on, Charlie," I said.

Charlie looked up at me and said in a whisper, "I don't know what to play."

"Play something grand, like the piano," I told him.

I didn't know Charlie knew a real fancy song, but he sure did. One so grand that there were letters in the title, instead of just words.

Charlie was a little shaky at the start, I suppose because he hadn't played the song in so long, or because Brenda Bloom was watching, but after a few notes, he was moving like the wind. *That's* when the hair on my arms *and* the back of my neck woke up. Standing so straight that it was like they were on their tippy-toes to get a better look at Charlie's hands.

Brenda's mouth fell open, I think because she was expecting him to play a sloppy version of "Chopsticks." "Oh my," she said when he finished. "Who taught you to play like that, Charlie?"

Charlie shrugged, so I told Brenda that it was his dad. "Ain't that something, Brenda? Who would ever think that a crook could teach a kid to play like that."

"He taught you Canon in D?" she asked.

"No. Some guy that used to come by the house did."

"Oh, Charlie. What a gift you have. That was beautiful. Just beautiful." Charlie ducked his head and grinned.

"Now do one for me to sing, Charlie," I said. I looked at the ceiling and did a lot of hmmming before I figured out a song fancy enough for such a fine piano. "Oh, I know, Charlie. Let's do that classy Etta James song. 'At Last.'"

That piano sounded so fine that it was like I was singing the melody and it was doing the harmony. And while I sang, I felt chills on *my* skin. Brenda must have got them, too, because she started fanning her face. When the song ended, she put her hand over her heart and said, "I don't even know what to say. You children are blessed. Just blessed."

"And we got a gift, too? Both of us?"

"Yes. Yes."

Brenda asked us to do another one, and I told Charlie we should do something snappy now, so how about "Maybellene." We didn't have it down pat yet, but like I told Teddy, to Charlie's hands and my throat, that song worked like a tickle.

Charlie and me hardly got the song off the ground, though, when a voice boomed from the hall, "Brenda!"

Mrs. Bloom hopped in on her crutches, then stopped, her wrapped foot held up like the pink, plastic flamingo bird Mrs. Delaney had propped in her yard. "Brenda!" she shrieked again. "What on earth is the piano doing here? It wasn't supposed to be delivered until every bit of work was done in this building." She circled the grand with short hops. "My God, the dust circulating in this place...what were you thinking letting them unload it, much less unwrap it?

"Uriah!" she bellered. "Uriah, get in here!"

She looked back at Brenda. "I leave you in charge and can't

reach you, then come in to find the phone is ringing off the hook, people are waiting in the theater to talk to you, and no one knows where you are. Then I find you back here, letting children play on an expensive piece of equipment that shouldn't have even been unpacked. What's the matter with you, Brenda?"

Mrs. Bloom looked at Charlie, sitting on the bench, his head tucked turtle. "And you? What are you doing touching this piano? This is *not* a child's toy!"

Mrs. Bloom's mad was firing like a machine gun in a war movie. "And you...," she said to me. "Weren't you just here yesterday? Your meetings are to be twice a week tops, as it says in the handbook. We have businesses to run, and situations on our hands. We don't need to be tripping over kids while we're handling them." She pointed to the door by the ramp and told Charlie and me to leave. "Now!"

"Geesh," I said.

Charlie was out the door before me, running like Mrs. Bloom was hot on his heels—which she wasn't. Not only because she couldn't run, but because she was busy yapping at Mr. Morgan even if he wasn't in the room yet, telling him to find something, *anything,* to cover every inch of that piano.

My scooter was on the other side of the furniture ramp, so I called to Charlie to wait up while I got it. He didn't, though. He was halfway across the parking lot, heading for the alley. Running as fast as a skinny kid.

Johnny was outside cutting boards, the table saw squealing like bad opera, his bare back brown and shiny. He was reaching under the table to shut the saw off when Charlie whizzed past him. And before the saw stopped buzzing, I heard him shout, "Charlie, stop!"

Johnny dropped the board he had in his hand and ran to where the corner met the alley. That's when I saw Charlie lying on the cement, right in front of the nose end of the Perkins' dinged-up truck.

"Charlie!" I screamed. I dropped my scooter and ran.

"Jesus Christ, he came out of nowhere!" Dumbo Doug was shouting as he circled the front of the truck, his hands holding the top of his head.

Johnny ignored Dumbo Doug and got down on one knee at Charlie's side. Brenda must have heard the ruckus because she came flying across the parking lot, shouting, "My God! My God!"

"You okay there, little buddy?" Johnny was saying when me and Brenda reached them.

Charlie looked like a bird that just hit a window, too stunned to make a sound. He didn't cry, and he didn't answer. He just lay there. Still. His eyes round and staring.

"I'll call an ambulance!" Brenda said.

That's when Charlie got un-stunned. "Nooooooo!" he cried, his eyes suddenly gushing like a dog-chewed garden hose. "I don't like *ambolances*! No!" Charlie squirmed and wiggled to get up, but Johnny was holding him down at the shoulder.

"You drive him, Johnny," I said. "His ma went off to heaven in an ambulance. So you're not going to get him in one unless you clunk him over the head."

"We shouldn't be moving him," Brenda said, which was probably true, because now that Charlie was up all the way, he was bent in half, holding his hip and crying, "Ow, ow."

Johnny picked Charlie up like he was light as a pillow and looked at the still-running Perkins truck, the door hanging open and junk all over the bench seat. Dumbo Doug was right behind him, "I wasn't even going fast!"

"My car!" Brenda said.

Her Thunderbird was parked close to the furniture store, so Johnny ran Charlie to it, telling him over and over in a voice gentle as a lullaby, "You're gonna be okay, Charlie. You're gonna be fine."

Brenda handed Johnny the keys (probably because she was

shaking so bad she would have ran over ten kids if she drove), and he put Charlie into the car, scooting him to the middle of the seat and telling him to watch his feet so he didn't bump the shifter. Brenda's car only had a front seat, so Brenda took my hand and ran me to the passenger side. She climbed in and patted her lap.

Johnny was backing up when Mrs. Bloom hopped out the furniture store door and yelled, "What's going on? Brenda, where are you going?" The top was down on Brenda's convertible, so hearing her wasn't hard—but then we probably would have heard her if we'd been in an army tank, as loud as she was bellering. Brenda looked back with worry on her face.

"It's okay," I said. "Mel's heading over to her. He'll explain."

Johnny wove down the streets, using the horn to keep people from crossing. Not that I saw anybody. I couldn't see nothing but a Sunday school picture of Jesus on a rock, kids all around, one colored to look like Charlie—shirt and pants made fatter with a navy-blue crayon colored past the lines, brown speckles on his face, red spots on his head—so Mrs. Fry would know which one was him.

Johnny carried Charlie to the first desk he found, and the lady behind it got a wheelchair for Charlie to sit in, probably because she could see how heavy Charlie'd be, even to somebody with big muscles, as the naked top of Johnny attested to. She looked up at Johnny's bare chest like maybe he should put a shirt on. Or not.

"The names of his parents, please?" she asked, still looking at Johnny. Charlie was crying so hard that he couldn't have answered even if she'd asked him, so I tried to help. "I think his dad's name is Roy. Or maybe it's Ray. But it probably doesn't matter because he's in the clink, where he's going to stay until Charlie's a man. And his ma's in heaven, where she's going to stay for good." The nurse wrinkled her nose as she tipped her head to one side. Either because she thought that was a sad story or because the whole place stank like bleach, which was getting to me, too. "Are you his sister?" she asked me.

"No. I'm his...his friend," I said.

"Well, do you know if Charlie is his given name, or is it Charles? And do you know his birth date?"

That's when Johnny blew a gasket. "Look, unless you plan to send him a birthday gift and want to know how to fill out his card, who gives a shit? He got bumped by a truck and he obviously needs a doctor. Now get him one and save the questions for later."

"Sir," she said, "these are customary questions we need answered before the doctor can treat him." She looked at Charlie, who had his arms wrapped around his middle and was carrying on like, well...like he got hit by a truck...and she asked him the same questions.

"His birthday is December sixteenth," I said. "I don't know what year, but he's eight."

She smiled at me, took down what I said, then stopped smiling when she looked back at Johnny. "Insurance?" she asked.

Johnny slammed his fist down on the desk then, and the lady jumped. "Sir, settle down, please."

"Look lady, this kid was hit by a Perkins Construction truck in the parking lot of the Starlight Theater. So obviously, somebody's gonna pay this fucking bill. Now call him a doctor, or I will."

"I'll call security if you don't get a grip on your temper, young man," she said.

"Well if the security guard can do a goddamn X-ray, then call him!"

Just then Brenda reached the desk, her cheeks flushed, either from running from the parking lot or because she heard Johnny cussing bad. And the second the lady behind the desk saw her, everything about her changed. She sat up Big-Sunshine-Sister-straight and a smile popped on her face. "Miss Bloom," she said.

Johnny slapped his fingers against the edge of her desk, then backed up. "Amazing how money talks. And it doesn't even have to say a word."

∗ ∗ ∗

Charlie didn't want to go into the examining room without me, but they said I couldn't go, so it was probably a good thing that Charlie's hand was so sweaty with scared it slipped right out of mine as the nurse wheeled him away. "If he looks like he's going to puke, tell him to burp," I called. "And if that doesn't do the trick, sing something for him. Music makes him happy."

I hadn't cried in front of anyone but Teddy for ages, and I hadn't cried when Charlie got hit. But I started crying when I heard Charlie blubber my name from down the hall.

Brenda and Johnny reached out to lay a hand on my back at the same time, and I think their hands touched for a second, because I felt them in the same place and it made the hair on my arms stand up. Not like when good music played. But like when lightning hits so close somebody could get struck.

Johnny didn't sit. He paced by the window and grumbled about Dumbo Doug and the lady at the desk, then he asked me why Charlie was running like a bat out of hell in the first place. I was sitting next to Brenda on a chair with a plastic cushion that was sticking to the back of my legs like some kid pranked it with school paste. My fingers were making the *here comes the church, here comes the steeple* actions even though I wasn't making them do it.

"Cause Mrs. Bloom yelled at him for playing the new grand piano," I said. "I don't know why. He washed his hands first."

I didn't think about the fact that I was being a tattletale until Brenda piped up, "She wasn't upset with Charlie. She was upset with me, Teaspoon."

"Well, she hollered at Charlie. Me, too. Not that I cared so much. But Charlie did. He gets scared when people yell at him."

I looked up and Johnny was staring at Brenda. "Look, why don't you go back to the Starlight and deal with your distraught mommy. I'll see to it that Charlie and Teaspoon get home safely."

Brenda sighed and I took her hand and pulled it over to hold it on my lap. "I want Brenda to wait with us, Johnny."

We didn't have to wait too long, though.

The doctor came out and shook Brenda's hand, asked how things were going with the remodeling, then got down to business. "The boy's fine," he said. "He's got a good bruise on his hip and a small laceration on his buttock, but they're superficial wounds. A little ice and a couple days' rest, and he'll be good as new."

Brenda thanked him while the nurse brought us Charlie, who was walking slow, but walking. He had two suckers in his hand—one for him and one for me—so I unwrapped them both and gave Charlie the green one, because green was Charlie's favorite flavor.

"I'll walk back," Johnny said when we got outside.

"You don't have to do that," Brenda said.

"Ride with us, Johnny," I begged. "Charlie wants you to, don't you, Charlie?" Charlie nodded like Johnny was Superman and he didn't want him to fly away just yet in case another truck tried to run him over.

Brenda drove, and I got to sit on Johnny's lap. I didn't look at him, though, just in case my face was flushing. I didn't talk to him, either, because I suddenly felt shy. Not that Johnny minded. He didn't seem to be in the talking mood. Even when we got to the corner of Washington and Thornton and a carload of guys he knew shouted to him—one saying, "Hey, Jackson, how'd you get *that* ride?" Johnny didn't say nothing back. He just lifted his arm from the side of the door and flipped them the bird.

Brenda didn't know where me and Charlie lived, so I had to tell her which street to go down. We were going to drop Charlie home first, since her and Johnny were both heading back to the Starlight to finish working, and I had to go back there to get my scooter.

When Brenda pulled her car up between Charlie's house and mine, I looked at my dumpy house with the peeling paint and leaning porch like I was seeing it through the eyes of a Big Sister, and it made me feel like a flunky. "Teddy's going to get that lean fixed," I said to Brenda. Johnny glanced up at his house as he pulled Charlie out, and I wondered if he was embarrassed about his crummy house, too, even if it wasn't as crappy as mine and Charlie's. Not that Brenda was looking. She was looking straight ahead, her hands tight on the steering wheel.

Mrs. Fry came outside before Johnny and Charlie even got to the steps. She patted Charlie here and there while Johnny explained, like she wanted to make sure he was still in one piece, then pulled her hankie out of her apron and dabbed it over her face and her chest. We heard everything Johnny was saying, not only because the top of Brenda's car was down, but because Johnny was being loud, because he knew Mrs. Fry was hard of hearing. "The doctor said he's going to be fine, Mrs. Fry. And don't you worry about the bill. It will be taken care of."

Johnny gave Charlie a final pat, then came back to the car and got in. He didn't say a word, and neither did we.

Mrs. Bloom's car was gone when we got to the Starlight, and the guys were outside eating their lunch. Dumbo Doug was leaned up against the Perkins truck snapping at his sandwich like a Poochie, and Mel was crouched down, his boots made into a chair for his butt while he drank from a thermos. Dumbo Doug dropped his part-eaten sandwich in his lunch pail and hurried to find out how Charlie was. Dumbo Doug was still carrying on about how it wasn't his fault, but I didn't listen to him. Neither did Johnny, who was busy rooting around the Perkins truck for his lunch bucket.

I expected Brenda to run straight inside when we got back to the Starlight, but she didn't. She just stood there, feeling her fingers, like maybe they'd gone numb.

I started heading over to the ramp, where my scooter was propped.

"Teaspoon? Can you come here?" Brenda said.

"Hold on a sec," I said. I hurried to get my scooter and rode back to her. "Yeah?"

Brenda glanced over at the guys who were half watching while they ate.

"I don't want to be your Sunshine Sister anymore, Teaspoon," she said.

Brenda's words might as well have been a construction truck, because that's how hard they smacked me.

"You can stay in the show, of course. But I'm going to assign you a new Big Sister."

I started blinking hard. "Why, Brenda? What did I do wrong?"

Johnny, who had a pop bottle tipped up to his mouth, froze that bottle in midair, his eyes on us.

"Nothing. You didn't do anything wrong. I just don't want you tagging after me anymore, watching my every move. Mimicking me. You understand?" Brenda was talking loud for Brenda, and she was blinking hard, too.

"Why? I've gotten rid of most of my afflictions, haven't I? I'm not nearly as pesky as I used to be. Charlie said I'm not even humming much anymore. And I'll bet I haven't even said *ain't* or *gonna* in three weeks. Why don't you want me for your Little Sister anymore, Brenda? Why?" My eyes started making water.

She turned away. "Just because," she said. She dropped her arms to her side, and made like she was going to go into the theater.

I don't know why, but suddenly it was like my worst affliction had only been sleeping like a mean dog, and Brenda's raised voice had woken it up. Then there was nothing I could do to keep my mad on a leash.

"Well fine then! I don't want you to be my Big Sister anymore, anyway. You're more noodley than Jennifer Jackson, and Teddy, and Charlie all rolled in one. Always doing what you're told and never talking back, even when you should.

"You didn't say nothing to your ma when she yelled at Charlie. And you didn't say nothing to that ugly Leonard Gaylor when he wrecked your papers and got all huffy with you because you had to work. You just kept smiling and apologizing, even if the mad you were feeling was making you twitchy."

I could hear Dumbo Doug snicker and say in hushed voice, "Give it to her good, kid."

"And know what else, Brenda Bloom? Dumbo Doug was right. A three-legged cat *does* have more talent in his missing leg than you've got in your whole body. You didn't even make the hair stand up on my arms when you sang, because you even do *that* noodley! I don't care how many lessons you've had, you can't sing near as good as me. And you can't play near as good as Charlie, either! And know why? Because you don't sing and play with your heart. Just with that noodley part of you.

"So I don't even care if you don't want to be my Sunshine Sister anymore. And I don't want to be in your stupid show, either!"

The minute I said that last part, I had to take it back, because that was what Mrs. Fry would call cutting off your nose to spite your face. "Well, that part isn't true. I *do* want to be in the gala, and I'm gonna be. But I'm not going to look at you even once the whole time we're rehearsing."

I couldn't think of one more mean thing to say to her, yet my whole body was still tight like a fist, so I did the only thing I could think to do. I flipped Brenda Bloom the bird.

Mel started laughing, and so did Doug—even if he was probably a little miffed because I'd tattled on him and he'd heard me call him Dumbo Doug. I looked at them and scowled, then crossed my arms and waited for Brenda to start crying.

But Brenda didn't start crying. She started laughing instead. Laughing so hard that she wrapped her arms around herself and bent over like her belly might burst.

"Why are you laughing?" I said, my jaw getting all the tighter. "I wasn't making a joke. I meant what I said!" I looked over at Johnny and Mel and Dumbo Doug, "You guys know every word I said is true. Tell her! Tell her!"

Brenda did start crying, but it was over the top of her laughter. "Oh," she said, "they'd never tell me, Teaspoon. That's why I'm laughing. Because a little girl like you dared to speak the truth to my face, which is something no one else has ever had the guts to do."

Mad shoved Brenda's laugh all the way off her face, as she tipped her head toward the guys. "Certainly not those two-faced cowards."

I thought maybe Brenda was going to say more, but she didn't. Instead she hurried into the Starlight, leaving me standing there with the guys, who were looking everywhere but at each other.

I stood there for a minute, feeling drained like a sink that was clogged and just went down, then I dropped my scooter and headed after Brenda.

She was standing in the aisle, four or five rows in, crying the hard kind of tears that hurt your throat.

"Teaspoon?" Johnny's voice reached me before he did. But then there he was, standing behind me, his hand on my shoulder. "Come on. Let the spoiled rich girl have her tantrum alone."

I slipped out from under Johnny's hand and took a few steps forward. I was mad at Brenda for sure, but now that I'd made her cry, I felt bad. "Those things I said... I didn't really mean them. I made them up because I was mad. *Really.*"

Brenda turned and looked at me. "No. You meant them. So don't dishonor yourself by taking them back. Everything you said is true, and I'm glad you said them.

"All I really have going for me is that I'm a Bloom. And you know what that means? That means that I get acclaim when I don't deserve it, and special treatment when I don't want it. It means that I have to live up to everybody's expectations, just like my mother does. And it means having people be nice to my face, then stab me in the back when I turn around because they hate the perks I get for being a Bloom. And you're supposed to what? Admire me? Strive to be like me?" She shook her head while she looked up at the starless ceiling, then said, "What a joke."

Brenda didn't even take a breath while her eyes turned up to look at Johnny. "You," she said, "standing out there with that disparaging look on your face. To you—to everyone—I'm the girl who thinks she's special because she has it all. Well, here's the irony. I don't think I'm special, but obviously *you* do, if you think that because I'm rich I don't struggle with loneliness or fear or sadness at times, just like everybody else.

"The second you heard me tell Teaspoon I wasn't going to be her mentor anymore, you decided I was being a self-centered, spoiled bitch. One who had grown bored with her little pet. Just like you thought I was looking down my nose at you in the hospital, or when I drove into your neighborhood. It would never have dawned on you that maybe in telling Teaspoon what I did, I was just trying to be kind."

Brenda started crying harder then, choking on her words. "Kind, because every day I spend with her, I see her losing another little piece of who she is, and replacing it with who she thinks she should be. Well, maybe I can see that all I'm teaching her is to have shame. And maybe, just maybe, I don't want her waking up one day to realize that she's turned into nothing but a miserable imitation of an imitation.

"Go ahead. Smirk at that, too. You think you march to your own drum. But you know what, Johnny Jackson? You don't! I've seen you with Teaspoon and Charlie and I know that underneath that tough exterior is someone far softer and more decent than what you show everybody else. And do you know why you don't show that part of yourself to others? Because like me, you do what's expected. People just happen to have different expectations of you."

Brenda took off then, hurrying up the theater aisle and disappearing around the corner of the concession stand. And Johnny turned and headed toward the door, not stopping as he bent down to scoop up a tool—like that was the reason he'd stepped inside in the first place.

I found Brenda in the ladies' restroom, standing in a stall with the door open, blowing her nose into a wad of toilet paper.

"Brenda," I said. "Please don't cry. Yeah, I meant some of the things I said, but not all of them. Just don't cry, okay?"

Brenda bunched the end of the toilet paper wad and twisted it up one nostril.

She threw the paper in the toilet, sniffled, then came out of the stall, dabbing at her puffy eyes with the backs of her hands. She put her arms around me, pulling me to her and kissing the top of my head. "And I meant all the things I said, too, except for the part where I said I didn't want to be your Big Sister anymore. I do. I just don't want you turning into me."

I rested my face against Brenda's shirt, which was warm and smelled like soap. "Don't say that, Brenda. There's lots of good things about you. Sure, you're just a bit on the noodley side. Most days, anyway. But you weren't just now." I looked up. "Holy cow, Brenda. If I hadn't been hearing those words come out of your mouth with my own ears, I wouldn't have believed they came from you."

Brenda laughed, and her eyes got teary again. "Still," she said. "I think I have more to learn from you, than you from me."

"Well, maybe you could watch me and learn those things. But I wouldn't recommend you copying the afflicted parts."

Brenda and me decided that I should go home and check on Charlie. She gave me a handful of candy bars for Charlie, then she walked me to the door. "Oh," I added, because I just thought of it. "Brenda, you should talk to Jesus. He helped me with my cussing, so He'd probably give you a hand with your noodleyness, too."

Brenda opened the door, and there he was. Johnny Jackson. He had his hands in his pockets, his shoulder was leaned against the side of the Starlight. He looked up when the door opened, and his face read like a sorry card.

He didn't tell Brenda that he wanted to talk to her. He didn't need to. Brenda gave my shoulder a pat and said she'd see me in the morning for our regular meeting. Then she backed up from the doorway and let Johnny inside.

CHAPTER FOURTEEN

Lots of things changed after Dumbo Doug ran Charlie over. For starters, Charlie couldn't follow me like a duck to the Starlight anymore, because Mrs. Fry was afraid he'd get run over again. So after a couple of days of lying on the couch, ouching and walking penguin-slow when he had to get up to pee, he went back to his old Humpty-Dumpty ways. Planting his butt on their steps when I left for a meeting.

I told Teddy that Charlie might as well get sent to the clink like his dad if all he had to do while I was at my meetings was to stay a prisoner to those steps. So Teddy went over and talked to Mrs. Fry about letting Charlie come over to our house and play the piano when we were gone. "You sure you wouldn't mind?" Mrs. Fry asked, her face nothing but a wad of old wrinkles. "I do feel bad for the boy. I know this isn't much of a life for a him."

"Of course I wouldn't mind," Teddy said. "As long as he's careful to close the door tight behind him when he leaves."

"And washes his hands first," I added.

So that's what Charlie did. Three times a week. And it didn't matter if I was gone for one hour or four, when I got back, there he'd be, playing like I'd only been gone five minutes.

* * *

Things changed for me and Brenda after that, too. When others were around, we were as respectable as we had to be, and stuck to acceptable topics for Sunshine Sisters. But when we were alone, we were, well...more like ourselves you'd have to say. I talked too much, and sang or hummed when we weren't talking, and I asked too many questions. And Brenda, she started talking louder, and when I sang, sometimes she sang along, doing the melody when I asked her to so I could practice my harmony. Brenda was definitely happier. Giving me lots of quick hugs and popping kisses on my cheek when she thought I was funny.

Yep, lots of things changed after Dumbo Doug ran over Charlie. Not just for Charlie and Brenda and me, but for Brenda and Johnny, too.

A couple of days after Brenda yelled at Johnny and the guys, me and Brenda were standing on the new stage looking it over to figure out how we could decorate it for the big night. Johnny, who was down below digging in a toolbox, hopped right up on stage with us and said, "How about a big moon suspended against the back wall? I could make it for you."

"Hey, that's a good idea," I said. "You could paint the moon silver, then we could add glitter to it so it's all sparkly. It would probably take a mess of glitter, but wouldn't that look swell?"

That very night, about two hours after the Perkins crew left, Brenda and I were sitting under a dome, having a soda pop and taking a rest before Brenda drove me home. Brenda had her knees propped on the seat in front of her, her pony-tailer on her wrist like a bracelet and her hair hanging waterfall over the back of her seat, when the door by the stage opened. Brenda startled and jumped to her feet—probably because she thought it was her ma, who would yell at her for being a slacker—but it wasn't Mrs. Bloom. It was Johnny Jackson. The regular Johnny, not the Perkins Johnny, wearing a white T-shirt and jeans instead of green Perkins clothes, his hair combed shiny in place. "Hey, what's he doing here?"

"I don't know," Brenda said.

"I'll go find out," I said, my insides happy as I skipped down the Starlight steps, Johnny grinning at me.

"I wanted to let Brenda know that Glen said it was okay if I use the shop after hours, and to find out what size she wants the moon," Johnny said while looking up the rows of seats to where Brenda was standing, her hair messy and bright on her shoulders under the lights.

I hopped up the stairs behind Johnny. I didn't expect him to stop while he was still about six steps from Brenda, so when he did, I ran into his back. Johnny laughed a little as he fumbled his arm behind him to catch me. With his arm around my middle, he lifted me crossways like a sack of potatoes and gave me a little shake before he set me down.

"Hi," he said to Brenda in a quiet, but not noodley, way. Brenda clasped her hands together and swayed a little from side to side as she said hi back.

Brenda asked me if I'd pour Johnny a drink, too, and then she invited him to sit down. Side by side as they were, they looked like a couple at Bugsy's Car Hop, so I slid my feet against the carpet to their seats and asked Johnny what kind of soda pop he wanted, then play-roller-skated over to the concession stand to get his Coca-Cola. "Take a candy for yourself if you want to, Teaspoon," Brenda called after me.

After I got his drink and a box of Jujubes for me, I sat down on the other side of Johnny and shared my Jujubes with him. First I was thinking about the moon Johnny was going to make, then I started humming a little of "How High the Moon." "Hey, Johnny," I said between verses, "how high *is* the moon, anyway?"

"Oh, about three hundred thousand miles away," he said. "Something like that."

"Huh, imagine that," I said, as I poured the last two Jujubes into my hand and told Johnny to pick one. He took the red one, so I popped the yellow one into my mouth and hummed as I chewed it gone. Johnny and Brenda weren't doing much but laughing, so I went over to the other dome to sing a little "When You Wish Upon a Star" like I had a microphone. I spun in lazy circles as I sang, stopping after the second verse so I could ask Brenda if we could turn the stars on.

"Sure. Why not. Be right back," Brenda said. Johnny went with her.

The minute those stars lit, I lost my lazy and ran up one aisle and down the other, my arms spread wide and my head tipped back so I could watch them twinkle over me as I sang.

I expected Johnny and Brenda to come right back to sit under the stars, too, but three songs later, when they still weren't back, I went looking for them.

I got up to the projection room, stopped to peek at the stars out the windows with no glass, then peeked in the light switch room. They weren't in there, so I headed up the ladder steps because the attic door was open, which meant Brenda was probably showing Johnny the catwalk.

I could hear Johnny and Brenda talking as I went up, and I heard my name, so I stopped and got spy-quiet.

"Teaspoon's crush on you is so adorable," Brenda said, like a ratfink.

"She's a terrific kid," Johnny said, and my insides sparkled and I didn't feel mad at Brenda for being a tattletale anymore. "My old man walked out on me when I was five, too. I guess that's why I have a soft spot for her."

What?

"My stepdad doesn't treat me any different than his own kids, but, well, when you have a parent who agitates the gravel on you like that, it makes you wonder what you did that was so bad they didn't want to stick around."

Holy cats! I didn't know that Mr. Jackson was Johnny's stepdad. But how could I, with Johnny having that lightbulb shape to his head just like his ma and the rest of the Jackson kids? Even if

Johnny's was a hundred-watt, while most of the rest were twenty-five-watt bulbs, at best, they still looked like a set.

"It probably feels the same when you have a parent die when you're a kid, huh?" Johnny said. "Because leaving is leaving."

"Or maybe you can't miss what you've never had," Brenda said. "I don't know."

"Do you remember him?" Johnny asked.

"Sometimes I think I remember him singing to me once, but Mother said she'd never heard him sing. Who knows. I guess we all remember things as we want to remember them."

Johnny gave a soft laugh. "Man, I don't believe that I'm having these kind of conversations with Brenda Bloom."

"I don't believe I'm having them, period," Brenda said.

They were quiet for a good minute, so I got super-still. I didn't hear more than a soft giggle from Brenda.

"I don't hear her down there anymore," Brenda said. "Maybe we should get back."

"Oh, she's probably getting more candy or pouring herself some more soda pop. Teaspoon's pretty independent," Johnny said.

"I think she just likes to work the fountain, because she doesn't drink half of what she pours. Either that, or she forgets she's poured it." They both laughed, but I didn't. The way Brenda said it, it almost sounded like she was calling me afflicted.

Yep. A lot of things changed after Dumbo Doug ran Charlie over. Mostly, Brenda. And I wasn't the only one who noticed.

CHAPTER FIFTEEN

Brenda and me were at the Starlight, about two weeks after Charlie got hit. It was a Saturday. Mrs. Bloom had delegated the job of cleaning the warehouse part of the furniture store to Mr. Morgan. Like Brenda said, Mrs. Bloom was *obsessed* with the thought of dust ruining the new grand, even though Mr. Morgan had wrapped it like a mummy in old blankets and sheets of plastic. "And don't stir up the dirt while you're cleaning," Mrs. Bloom ordered, though how he was going to clean that place without making dust fly was beyond me.

Mr. Morgan wasn't real happy about having to come in and clean after he'd asked to have the weekend off since his ma and dad were coming to Mill Town for a visit and the Starlight was closed anyway. So Brenda told him she'd come in and help so it could get done faster. I said I'd help, too.

Brenda looked like Cinderella before the animals got her respectable, dressed in blue pedal pushers with a stain on the leg (I didn't even know Brenda could get a stain!), a short sleeveless blouse that, to tell the truth, was ugly enough to have come from a Jackson sack, and a scarf tied Aunt-Jemima on her head. Even with the ramp door open, we were sneezing like nuts from the dirt we weren't supposed to stir.

Brenda and Mr. Morgan said I was a good helper, but I don't

think I was because every time I picked up a tool, I'd ask them if it was a bargaining tool, because I remembered Teddy saying something about needing one a while back, and as far as I knew he still hadn't gotten one. Then Brenda or Mr. Morgan would have to tell me all over again that it was an upholstering or carpentry tool. Then maybe I'd pick up one of those books that Brenda said was a *ledger* and page through it, looking for a new fancy word I might have to read out loud, or want to toss in a Scrabble game, even though all those books seemed to have in them was numbers. And while I was working, I'd sing a little of this song or that, and now and then Mr. Morgan would join in.

I was holding up a metal something-or-other and asking Brenda if it was an upholstering tool, too, when Brenda went stiff. I turned, thinking I'd see Mrs. Bloom standing there on her crutches, scowling at the dirt swirling from Mr. Morgan's broom. Instead, it was Leonard picking his way across the room, watching his white shoes like he might step on one of those land mines like in *Bridge Over the River Kwai*.

"Leonard, what are you doing here? You didn't tell me you were coming home this weekend." Brenda dabbed at her sweaty, dusty face with the backs of her hands, like a cat trying to clean herself. All she did, though, was make smears.

"You'd have known if you'd picked up your phone last night."

"I'm sorry. I didn't hear it." Brenda grabbed a coffee can filled with rusty nails and tossed it in the garbage can. "I was exhausted, so I went to bed early."

Leonard looked around the room. "No doubt you were, if this is the sort of work you've been doing. Isn't that what you've got *him* for?" Leonard said, poking his thumb toward Mr. Morgan.

I didn't want to listen to Leonard because I didn't even like the sound of his voice, so I tried to ignore him like Mr. Morgan was doing. It didn't work so well, though. Not when he got up close to Brenda and started growling at her, asking her what the deal was . . . why she'd acted so different on the phone all week.

"Maybe because I was trying to figure out why you were calling every night, when ordinarily you only call once a week."

"What? A guy has to have a reason to call the girl he's going to marry?"

Brenda didn't say anything. She just went back to her work, using one hand like a broom and the other like a dustpan to get the upholstering tacks off the workbench.

"You didn't answer my question. What's going on?"

"I did answer. I fell asleep early because I was tired," Brenda repeated.

Leonard grabbed Brenda's arm then, and the stray nails she had in her fist pinged against the cement floor. He grabbed her tight enough that her skin went pale around his fingers. The whites of Mr. Morgan's eyes turned to half-moons as he glanced over at Leonard without moving his head or slowing his broom. "Go wash your face and hands. You've got some explaining to do," Leonard said.

"You're hurting her arm," I snapped. Mr. Morgan stiffened.

Leonard looked over at me, the skin around his pinchy nose wrinkling. "Who does this kid think she is, anyway?" he said.

"Teaspoon. Brenda's Sunshine Sister," I reminded him.

"Well, mind your own business, Tablespoon. Or whatever your name is," Leonard said.

Brenda told me to keep working, and she followed Leonard out of the room and down the new hallway

As soon as they left, I looked at Mr. Morgan. He was wiping his sweaty face with a grubby-looking handkerchief. "You hot?" I asked. "I'll go get us a soda pop."

"You mind your own business, Teaspoon," Mr. Morgan warned.

"I know. I'm just going to the concession stand," I said, even if that was a lie as big as the grand.

The Starlight was dark, but for the little lights glowing from the ends of each aisle seat and a smudge of light showing through the empty projection windows. I hurried to set two paper cups under the spouts of the fountain, just to make it look good. Then I headed up the stairs, glancing back twice, hoping my dusty shoes weren't tracking, because what kind of a spy leaves footprints?

I figured no one would see me if I stayed outside the projection room door on my hands and knees and peeked around the corner. After all, who would think to look on the floor across a dark room for a pair of snooping eyes and ears?

"What in the hell's going on here, Brenda? And don't tell me nothing, because I know better. You've been acting odd all week." Leonard had Brenda up against the wall, his hands braced on both sides of her like clink bars, his legs spread.

"Maybe I should ask you the same," Brenda said, her voice shaky, but not noodley. "I heard you got pretty cozy with Pattie Melbourne at Thad's cookout."

"What the hell are you talking about? And why are you trying to turn this around? We're talking about you here, and the way you didn't have time to talk to me all week."

"So you hurried home to check up on me, even though you know how busy I've been?"

"Thad told me you had some trash in your car."

"I don't know what you're talking about," Brenda said. She pressed her hands flat against the wall.

"Of course you do. Trish said she thought it might have been that scum that works here."

"Scum?" Brenda said. "I didn't have any *scum* in my car. But Johnny Jackson went with me to bring Teaspoon's little friend to the hospital after he got hit out in our parking lot. I was too shook up to drive."

Leonard didn't look very strong, wax-bean-skinny that he was, but he must have been because Brenda let out a yelp when he grabbed her wrist. "That kid got hit two weeks ago, Brenda. They saw you last night. And Thad said he heard your Thunderbird was up on River Road."

"Let me go, Leonard," Brenda said.

"Let you go?" Leonard's voice got higher as he mocked her, then he laughed. "You're mine, Brenda. And I think you'd be wise to re-member that."

And then, though I don't know why, because it certainly wasn't one of those romantic times that make a lady's eyes go dreamy, Leonard leaned down and kissed Brenda, movie-star-hard.

"Hmmmm," he said. "My little girl smells dirty."

"Leonard, please," Brenda said. "Don't kiss me when you're angry."

Leonard grabbed Brenda's other wrist then, and she let out an-other yelp. He held her arms wide, then kissed her again. And I swear I heard the back of her head hit the wall.

That's when my affliction flared up.

I didn't bother getting to my feet. I just scampered across the projector room on my hands and knees, crawling fast as a baby with rabies. And before either of them registered that I was in the room, I yanked Leonard's pant leg up and dug my teeth into his ankle.

Leonard let out a yelp, then his heel came off the floor—I sup-pose when he twisted around to see what was suddenly paining him—but still I didn't let go.

"Ow, ow," he shouted. "What in the hell?" Leonard started cussing, but I just bit down all the harder, my head jerking along with his leg when he tried to get me to let go.

"Leonard!" Brenda shouted, "Careful! You're going to hurt her!"

"I'm going to hurt *her*?" Leonard screamed between curses, swatting at my head until I had to let go.

I scrambled to my feet, my chest still thumping with mad. Leonard was rubbing his ankle, and I was rubbing off my tongue with the bottom of my shirt cause, respectable or not, Leonard Gaylor was the kind to have cooties.

Leonard glared down at me for a second, then glared at Brenda. He was shaking mad. He ran his hands through his bristly hair, then pointed a finger at Brenda. "Don't go making me look like a fool. I staked my claim on you a long time ago. Nobody with any worth wants to buy a used car, Brenda. And I've put more than a few miles on you."

He took a deep breath. "I'll be by at eight to pick you up. Have yourself cleaned up by then."

As I headed home that day, I wished Charlie was still able to wait for me outside the Starlight, because I wanted somebody to spout my mean thoughts about Leonard to. But a couple days later, when I came home from an early-evening "all Sunshine Sisters" meeting, so the *Mill Town Monitor* could take our picture and talk to us about being Sisters and the gala, I realized that it was better if Charlie couldn't tag along to my meetings anymore, because Charlie made a better spy than he did a listener.

Well, sort of.

"What do you mean, Teddy and Miss Tuckle kissed like Eskimos?" I asked.

"You know," Charlie said, getting up, and leaning his face over to make his nose spar with mine like the Jackson boys did with their cardboard swords, only not as hard. "Like that."

"When did they do that?" I asked.

"When he walked her out to her car because she was gonna leave. They were standing by it, real close, talking. Then they did that."

"Then what happened?"

"He opened the car door and she left."

"They're supposed to be just friends. She swore it," I said, wondering if an Eskimo kiss meant the same thing as a lip kiss. "Did they talk like just friends while she was here?"

"I dunno," Charlie said. "I was playing. And they left."

"Where'd they go?"

"I dunno."

I plunked my hand down over Charlie's, so he had to stop playing. "Charlie, listen up. The next time she shows up here while I'm gone, you keep your eyes sharp and your ears peeled, got it? You're going to be my spy from now on, and I want you to tell me everything that goes on here when I'm gone."

Teddy sure was proud when he got his next *Mill Town Monitor*. "Look at that. My little Teaspoon, right in the center front," he said.

While Teddy was cutting the article out of the paper so he could tape it to the fridge, I told him, "You know that part where the reporter man wrote that I said I liked the Sunshine Sisters program because it teaches me how to behave so I won't get in so much trouble in school anymore? And where I said that Mrs. Bloom was real nice to let us be in the gala because it makes us feel special? Well, the words he said were supposed to be a *quote*—that's what Brenda said it's called when they print the exact words you said— but that wasn't exactly what I said. I said that Mrs. Bloom is real nice to let us be stars in the gala, because it will help us not feel so bad about having afflictions. Like Mindy Brewer, who is shy about her big teeth, but is going to smile on stage without holding her hand over her mouth now, because Mimi Hines has big teeth and she doesn't cover hers."

I think Mrs. Bloom was happy about what I said, too, because she wasn't crabby with me when she came in while me and Brenda were having our next meeting. She was crabby at Brenda, though.

"Mrs. Gaylor said that Leonard seemed very upset last Saturday afternoon when he came in and saw you working like a common laborer—as he should have been. I delegated that work to Uriah, not you.

"She also said that you were cool to Leonard on the phone last week...when he finally managed to reach you."

"I've been very busy, Mother."

Mrs. Bloom sighed. "Of course you've been busy, dear. But men don't understand when a woman gets busy. You'll need to learn how to juggle your social obligations and your duties to your husband, if you want to keep him happy."

"Leonard should marry a clown then," I said.

Mrs. Bloom's head snapped around. "What did you say?"

"I said that Leonard should marry a clown. If he wants to be made happy and see somebody juggle, then he should just marry a clown."

"Isabella!" Mrs. Bloom said, and Brenda turned away, her hand going over her mouth like she had bucked teeth and didn't want us seeing them when she smiled.

Mrs. Bloom looked at Brenda. "I can see you've been neglecting your Sunshine Sister mentoring duties as well," she said.

CHAPTER SIXTEEN

If there was one thing I could count on (besides the Jackson kids being annoying), it was that if I was at the Starlight, Charlie was at my house playing Ma's piano. And yep, that's where he was when I got home from having a meeting with Brenda and the guy who was going to be our music director and our chorusographer, Jay.

"Where's Teddy?" I asked when I got inside. "I want to tell him about our routine. Jay showed me all the steps, Charlie. And I did real good. So I might want to be a dancer *and* a singer. Anyway, I want to tell Teddy that." I glanced out the screen door while I asked, so I could wave at Johnny, who was walking over to our side of the street to talk to Brenda.

"He's over at my place," Charlie said. "With Grandma G and Miss Tuckle. They been over there a long time. Ever since Teddy got home."

I glanced up at the clock. "He's been home for, what now, almost two hours?"

"I guess so," Charlie said. "I think something's going on."

"What do you mean?"

Charlie stopped plucking at the piano keys and looked up.

"Well," he said. "I was home having supper when Teddy came over. He had something in his hand, and..."

"What?"

"Mail."

"Oh, doesn't that figure, Charlie. Teddy never did take that loan from Miss Tuckle, the best I can tell, because the porch is still leaning. Probably because he got his head on straight and remembered that he doesn't like loans. Or else he figured out that walking on a rotting porch wasn't going to kill me. He slapped some more tar on the leaky roof and said it would have to do, and relaxed a bit after he gave up on getting that loan from Miller. But now, shucks, another bad bill and he'll be worrying all over again."

"Anyway," Charlie said. "He came over and he looked like he needed to burp. So Grandma G made him sit down and she got him coffee. She asked him what was wrong, and he looked at me. Then Grandma G looked at me. And then she told me to hurry and finish my supper."

"Then what happened?"

"Then Miss Tuckle came, and she saw that Teddy was upset, too."

Boy, getting anything out of Charlie was like pulling teeth. "And?" I said.

"Well, then Grandma G told me to hurry up and finish my supper all over again. And when I got done, she told me to come here and play piano and be a good boy. So that's what I did."

I peeked out the screen, and sure enough, Miss Tuckle's car was parked up the street, three cars in front of the now empty spot where Brenda's car had been. "Come on, Charlie," I said. "Let's go over to your place and find out what's going on."

I don't think Charlie wanted to go. I think he wanted to play *Live at the Starlight* instead, but he followed anyway.

The three of them were still at the kitchen table when we got there. Teddy had his head down, his hands spinning his coffee cup. Mrs. Fry looked like her dog just died—well, if she had a *nice* dog.

A small groan came out of Teddy when he saw me, and Miss Tuckle swiveled in her chair. She gave me her best Sunday school smile. "Teaspoon, Charlie...how would you two like to go with me to..."

Teddy stopped her. "It's okay, April," he said. He got up slow, like he was full of bruises from getting smacked.

"What's going on, Teddy?"

His hand fluttered like a leaf against my back as he led me out of the kitchen. Charlie started following and Miss Tuckle said, "You stay here Charlie." Me and Teddy reached the front door and I turned around. Miss Tuckle and Mrs. Fry and Charlie were watching from the middle of the living room. Charlie looked as scared as I felt, but Miss Tuckle and Mrs. Fry just looked sad.

Teddy didn't say a word as we crossed our yard. He just climbed the steps, then stood holding the door for me. "Come on inside and sit down, Teaspoon," Teddy said.

But I didn't budge. I'd seen enough movies to know what it meant when everybody gawks at one person with a sad, worried look, then takes them aside and tells them to sit down.

My legs went stiff and icicle-cold. "Teddy? Did my ma die?"

Teddy hurried to me and put his arm around me. "No. No, Teaspoon. Your ma's fine. Come inside. Come on."

Once inside, Teddy tried to get me to sit on the couch, but I wanted to sit on the Starlight seats instead.

Teddy turned to me, his knees butted against my leg. He took my hand and set it on the red armrest, putting his hand over mine. It felt cold, even though the day was oven-baking warm.

"I don't know how to say this so it won't be quite such a shock to you, so I guess I'm just going to have to say it.

"Teaspoon, I heard from your ma. She's coming here at the end of next month."

Funny how it went. I'd been waiting to hear those words for half of my life, yet when Teddy said them, they were like raindrops that had fallen on dust. And all those words did was sit there, beaded on my skin.

I don't know long it took before they soaked in, but suddenly they did. And tingles started rushing up my legs, filling my whole self with happy. I leapt out of the Starlight chair and tossed my arms above my head, yelling and hopping in circles. "My ma's coming home! My ma's coming home!

"Wow, Teddy. Can you believe it? She's coming home! Next month? That's August then, right?"

"Yes, August...but late in the month. She didn't give an exact date."

"Wow Teddy, I can't believe it." I looked up. "Thank you, God and Good Jesus!"

Teddy had his elbows on his knees, his fingers clasped, his thumbs pushed together. He glanced up at me and smiled without unbunching his lips.

I carried on until I got winded, then I gave Teddy a big squish. I'd planned to make it a quick one because I had more cheering to do, but Teddy wrapped his arms around me and didn't let go until I told him to. He had tears in his eyes when he finally did. And not happy ones, either.

"What's the matter, Teddy? This is what you and me been waiting for since she left. Ma's coming home! We're going to be a family again. Not just Teaspoon and Teddy, but Teaspoon and Teddy and Catty."

"Honey," he said. "Your ma didn't say *why* she was coming back. I think you need to remember that."

"Why would she have to say it, Teddy? We *know* why she's coming back. Because she found her dream. And because she misses us like we miss her."

I clamped my hands to the sides of my head. "Boy, Teddy. Doesn't it figure? I've been checking the movie posters outside the Starlight practically since she left, but...oh, wait...the Starlight's been closed for a while now, so who knows how many movie posters I've missed. Doesn't matter, though. What matters is that Ma's coming back to us!"

Teddy blew out again and looked at me. "Teaspoon, I don't want you getting your hopes up too high. Maybe she's just stopping in to say a quick hello, or—"

"Teddy!" I said. "Have you gone crackers? Course she's not stop-ping in just to say hi. She's never stopped by to say hi once in all this time."

Teddy tried to say something else, but I didn't have time to sit and listen to that naysayer. I had to tell everyone my belly-busting good news!

"Did you hear the good news?" I asked Charlie as I pumped my foot against the sidewalk. "My ma's coming home. We're going to be a family again."

Charlie was jogging alongside me, his breath thumping with every step he ran. He looked over at me, his eyes getting wide. "So your ma's not taking you away then?" Charlie asked.

I put the skids on my scooter. "Where'd you get a crazy notion like that from?"

"Well, after you and Teddy left, Grandma G said to Miss Tuckle, 'He's scared to death of what that woman might have up her sleeve. It would kill Teddy if she took that little girl away.' Then Miss Tuckle asked Grandma G if your ma would really do some-thing like that...take you away after all this time, even if she didn't have a home to bring you to. And Grandma G said, 'There's no telling what that woman will do.'"

"Mrs. Fry said *that*? What's the matter with her anyway? First she forgets my ma even exists and tries to find Teddy a new girlfriend, then when she's reminded of her, she forgets she even liked her."

"Well, Teddy did look worried. Even before Grandma G said those things."

"Yeah, I know. But he was afraid of giving me a shock. I think he thought I might faint or something. Somebody should tell Teddy that that's just in the movies, like foggy in-love eyes."

"I don't want you to go away," Charlie said, in a voice that sounded like he was crying, even if he wasn't.

"My ma's not taking me anywhere, Charlie. Now come on, let's pick up the pace. I want to tell the Taxi Stand Ladies and Brenda she's coming home."

It just figured that when we got to the corner, the only person standing there was Mrs. Jackson, mailing a letter. She was no Taxi Stand Lady, but I told her my good news anyway. "That's wonderful, Teaspoon," she said. And she smiled when she said it, like she was happy for me. Like I wasn't the same kid who beat her daughters to a pulp every so often.

I was happy when I saw Brenda's car back in the Starlight parking lot. I dropped my scooter and ran to the door, but when I yanked on it, it wouldn't open. Charlie even helped me tug in case it was just jammed. Still it didn't budge. "Maybe it's locked," Charlie said.

"Brenda doesn't lock the door when she's inside and expecting someone, because you can't hear a knock through this heavy door unless you're standing right next to it. I thought some man and lady were coming by to audition for one of our filler acts. But hmm, maybe that's tomorrow. Either way, her car's here, so she should be."

We tried the door in the alley but that wouldn't open, either, so we had to give up.

I was so excited that I couldn't pay attention to anything but my happy thoughts as we headed back. I just kept scootering while I talked, telling Charlie as much about my ma as I could remember. And Charlie kept on trotting beside me, watching his feet and saying only an *oh* now and then—I think because he was tired from running. And then he wasn't alongside of me. I stopped and turned, and there was Charlie, halfway down the block, looking this way and that.

"Teaspoon? Where are we?" he called.

I looked up at the street sign, then scootered back to him. "Holy cow, Charlie. We're all the way over on the end of Thornton Street. How could that be? I could find my way home from the Starlight with my eyes closed."

Charlie was still panting, even though he wasn't running anymore. He sniffed the air and looked up. "Audrey's Calf," he read.

I handed Charlie my scooter and hurried to the big glass windows to peer inside. "Charlie, this is it! Audrey's Café! The place where I met Teddy for the first time. I remember the counter, and the jukebox that was right beside it." I backed up and looked in both directions, and sure enough, there was the GREYHOUND BUS sign farther down the street. "Yep, that's the bus depot I remember! Did you come into town at the same place?"

Charlie shrugged, then said, "Probably."

"I was throwing a hissy fit because I was hungry, so Ma brought me here." I leaned close to the glass and peered inside. "Yep, I remember those seats. Green. Teddy was sitting right over there in the corner, having coffee and apple pie. I remember that.

"Teddy said that Ma looked like a brunette version of Greta Garbo, standing next to the window—right here, Charlie. Right on the other side of this glass—a spotlight of sun coming through the window to light up the red in her hair. And he said that even with my nose and eyes running like Niagara Falls, he thought I was the cutest little thing he'd ever seen, with a head full of Shirley Temple curls, only dark, and a nose like a button. That's what he said. He bought us each a hamburger and fries, then took us back to his place."

I dug in my pocket. It was empty, but for three pennies. "Too bad we spent my payday on soda pop and Pez, or we could have bought a plate of fries to share. It would have been like a celebration party, held in an anniversary place." Charlie was disappointed, even if it wouldn't have been like an anniversary party for him.

"Are we lost, Teaspoon?" Charlie asked, but I was only half listening when I straddled my scooter and looked up and down the street.

"No, I kinda know where we are. I was just watching somebody. Look, Charlie. Doesn't that lady way down the street look like Walking Doll? She's got the same bird-black hair and dancer legs like her, anyway."

Charlie looked down the street where I was pointing. "Yeah," he said. "But Walking Doll don't wear hats."

"Or her hair in one of those French twists. I think only fancy ladies do that. Plus, far as I know, Walking Doll and The Kenosha Kid never leave their corner except to take a spin with Ralph. She doesn't wear those Mrs. Bloom suits, either. Still, that lady does look like her and walk like her, doesn't she? Let's catch up to her and get a look from the front. If it's her, she'll borrow us money for fries."

I gave Charlie my scooter and I ran, because I knew we'd make better time that way.

We got a block away and I was more sure than ever that the lady was Walking Doll. "Hey, Walking Doll!" I shouted.

The lady turned her head and looked back so fast that I couldn't get a good look at her face. Especially with that little veil coming down from her hat to hang over her eyes.

"Can't be her," I said as she reached the crosswalk and trotted across the road. "Walking Doll wouldn't ignore us like that." Further proof came when a Lincoln Continental came along, swerving to the wrong side of the street, right where the lady was walking, and she got in. She didn't even have her door closed before the car did one of those U-turns and zipped back down the street in the same direction it had come from.

"Was that Mr. Miller's car?" Charlie asked.

"I don't know," I told Charlie. "With the sun setting and the sky all orangey and pink, nothing looks the right color. It was a Lincoln Continental, though. If that *was* his car, and *was* Walking Doll, then that would sure be a shocker, because Walking Doll hates Mr. Miller."

"Sure did look like her, though," Charlie said.

"Yep," I said. "But it's like I told you plenty of times, Charlie. You can't always believe your eyes."

CHAPTER SEVENTEEN

The next evening, I got to tell Brenda about my ma coming home.

We were having a night meeting with all the girls, plus moms, so Brenda could tell them what was expected of them as far as rehearsals and costumes went.

The whole theater was packed when I got there, and I had to look hard to spot Brenda. She was standing next to her friends Tina and Julie.

"Brenda!" I said when I found her. "I've got to talk to you. You aren't going to believe this one!"

The Starlight was filled with so much talking that a girl could hardly hear herself think. So I grabbed Brenda's hand and dragged her to the second concession stand, heading for the little room behind it, where the phone was. "Teaspoon," Brenda said with a laugh. "I have to start the meeting. Mother's already heading for the stage."

"This will only take a second. Promise!" I shut the door behind us. "Guess who's coming by the end of next month? In time for the gala, even. Go on, guess!"

Brenda laughed. "Teaspoon," she said, like I was tickling her. "How on earth am I supposed to guess?"

"Try!"

"Um...the Andrews Sisters?"

"Brenda!" I said, laughing a little myself. "Stop that. Guess for real."

I couldn't wait for Brenda to make the right guess, so I shouted it out. "My ma! Can you believe it? She's coming back to me and Teddy!"

Brenda's smile softened like her eyes. "Ohhhh, Teaspoon," she said. And she grabbed me and lifted me right off the ground and twirled me in a circle.

"It's a dream-come-true summer," I told her when she put me down. "My ma's going to be so proud when she sees me on stage, Brenda. She loves the Starlight as much as I do."

"Awww, honey," Brenda said. "Of course she'll be proud." She pulled me to her again, her hand soft against the side of my head, her fingers tangled in my curls. She smelled like lilacs and love.

Brenda was still hugging me when there was a rap on the door and Miss Gaylor, Leonard's sister, older than Leonard by a year, poked her head in and looked down at us with a nose every bit as pinched as her brother's. "Your mother is waiting. She sent me to find you. Everyone's here and seated."

But everyone wasn't already there and seated. Because as I found a seat and Brenda headed up to the steps to the stage, the door next to it opened and in walked Teddy, his clothes looking spiffy, even if there was no spiff on his face.

I jumped up and crisscrossed my arms above my head, then ran down the aisle to meet him when he still didn't see me. "What are you doing here, Teddy?" I asked.

And he said, "Well, I have to know about rehearsals and those costumes, don't I?"

I led Teddy to a seat next to mine, and I was glad he was there so he could tell me later what Brenda and Mrs. Bloom and Jay said, because I couldn't hear a thing but the music playing inside me because Ma was coming home. And outside of me, too, I guess, because Teddy had to nudge me a few times and make the *shhh* sign.

After our meeting, I dragged Teddy to meet Brenda because he hadn't met her yet, and they shared compliments the way me and Charlie shared penny candy. And while Brenda introduced Teddy to Mrs. Bloom, I ran off to tell Mindy about my ma coming home, even if she probably didn't know that my ma was gone.

And on the way home, while Teddy pushed my scooter down the dark streets and I ran ahead, racing from one streetlight beam to the next, singing a verse or a chorus of all my favorite songs, while the crowds in my mind cheered like crazy, sad-sack Teddy shuffled behind me like a tired roadie.

Teddy didn't lose that sad-sacked, worrywart face no matter how many days passed. And each time I saw it, I was reminded of the only story Teddy ever told me about when he was a kid. How once an old geezer blew into Mill Town on a hot-air balloon, right where the feed mill on the edge of town is now, but back when it was just a field. Teddy didn't see that part, but he saw him leave.

Teddy was about six years old, and even though his ma was tugging on his jacket because everyone else was gone, Teddy wouldn't budge. He said, "It was one of those times you want to freeze in your eyes forever. I knew when that balloon was gone, I'd never see it again, so I wasn't about to leave until all I could see was its memory. It was the first and only time I refused to listen to my ma, and even if she'd whipped me—which she didn't—it would have been worth every blister."

That's what Teddy told me. And I thought of that story every time I saw him watching me out of the corner of his eye, like I was something he wanted to freeze in his eyes.

Miss Tuckle looked like a sad-sack, too. At Sunday school she didn't talk except to help Charlie and a couple others pronounce some Bibley words and to ask us the questions at the end of the lesson. It made me feel kind of sorry for her, because like I told Charlie, Teddy was her Moby-Dick. Her last chance to save herself from being a flunky.

CHAPTER EIGHTEEN

In some ways, I was sorry that Teddy told me about my ma coming when he did, because it was like getting excited about Christmas while the leaves were still on the trees. I tried to just think about the gala so time would go faster, but that didn't work so well. Not with everything at the Starlight one big mess, with people coming and going and everybody yakking at once.

I at least tried to be a good helper to Brenda, and keep her set straight on things the best I could. Like when Mrs. Bloom would limp into the Starlight and ask Brenda if she'd gotten this done, or that done, or a committee member asked the same, and Brenda said yes. I'd give her hand a tug then and say, "No, Brenda, remember? You were going to call her after you met with Jay, but then the director lady came in." Or, "You couldn't reach him, remember, Brenda?" And Brenda would blink at me with stretched eyes, like she couldn't believe she'd gotten mixed up enough to think that she'd done something she hadn't.

But who could blame her, with that to-do list growing longer every day instead of shorter? Just looking at it was enough to make a girl take up biting her fingernails, which is exactly what Brenda started doing. A few times, she tried to cut in when her ma was talking about how exciting our acts were and stuff, to tell her that there was a problem they *really* needed to talk about, but Mrs.

Bloom just snapped at her, "I don't want to hear about problems, Brenda. I want to hear about solutions." And Brenda would shut her yap. I asked Brenda what the problem was more than once, thinking I could help her find the solution, but she told me I was doing enough work already.

Considering how much work there was to do, you'd have thought Brenda wouldn't have wanted to give me a week's vacation from work and Sunshine meetings. But she did. "You've earned it, Teaspoon," she said. "Plus, once rehearsals begin, you'll have to be here almost every evening for six weeks straight. Your mother is coming home, and I know you're excited. This will give you time to concentrate on her homecoming."

I argued with Brenda at first, reminding her that she needed my help more than ever now. "Plus," I said, "I need the bucks. Trust me, Brenda. I don't make enough to pay for my shoes and costume, and Mrs. Fry is going to be stuffing me in her old-lady shoes and sewing me a crooked dress."

"Don't worry about it, Teaspoon," she said. "You have some overtime coming. Enough to cover your costume."

"Really? You mean time and a half, like Teddy gets when he works on Saturdays?"

"Yep."

"Hot dog!"

Brenda assured me that she would get things done while I was on vacation, but I was worried because there was still so much that needed to be done. Like the moons. Not just one moon, like we first planned, but three of them, each painted silver and sprinkled with glitter. One a sliver, one a half-moon, and one a full moon. The sliver was going to hang at the beginning of the show, while a local act, Mrs. Derby, sang "Love Is a Many Splendored Thing" (which Brenda and I agreed was a poor song choice, her having a voice like Ethel Merman). That sliver moon would hang there while Beulah and Morris Farthing danced like Fred and Ginger to a tune the Mill Town orchestra played, and while the wonderful

Mimi Hines and Phil Ford did their performance. Then Johnny would bring that moon up with a pulley during intermission and drop the half-moon for Louie Prima's rip-roaring, leg-slapping routine. Then, right before us Sunshine Sisters came on, Johnny would pull up the half-moon and drop the full one, so it would be in place for us and the ace act of Les Paul and Mary Ford.

That night after our meeting—my first evening of vacation—Brenda tossed my scooter into her trunk and insisted on driving me home because it was close to dark and she was afraid I'd get splat like a Charlie. Just as we pulled up in front of my house, Johnny climbed into his car and backed it out on the street, and when I got out of the Thunderbird, so did Brenda. She got into Johnny's car.

"Hey, where you guys going?" I shouted from the sidewalk. Brenda glanced at me and didn't say anything, probably because she couldn't hear me over the blaring radio. Her and Johnny leaned toward each other, like maybe they were talking over what I might have asked, so I shouted my question again. Then Johnny leaned over so I could see him around Brenda, and he shouted back, "We're going over to Perkins to work on those moons for the stage." I sure was happy to hear that, because it meant that our stage decorations would get done.

They worked on those moons until late that night, and the next, and the...well, they worked like dogs every night after that. Which had me wondering, why didn't Brenda just delegate the job of making the moons to Johnny instead of helping herself? But that was Brenda for you. She was just too softhearted for her own good.

One night when they went to work on the moons, I waited for Brenda to come back for her car because I wanted to ask her why Jay was making the Big and Little Sisters walk off the stage at the end of our number divided up, Little Sisters to the right and Big

Sisters to the left, when I thought we should walk out in Sister-pairs. I told Jay this, but he only tapped his pencil-thin mustache until I finished my bellyaching, then said, "Ah...no." And when I started to argue, he said, "Subject closed, Pip Squeak," and walked away like he was dancing.

I had to wait until long after Teddy was sawing logs before I heard Johnny's car come down the street. Time I spent trying *not* to think about whether Ma really looked like Glinda or sang like Teresa Brewer.

When I heard Johnny's car, I got out of bed and peeked out my window. The Frys' house was dark so at least I didn't have their TV blinking Morse code in my eyes, and could see the Jacksons' driveway good.

I didn't slip on my shoes, and I didn't turn on the lights because I didn't want to wake Teddy. I just walked lady-like quiet to the front door and opened it slowly, then stood looking through the rusty screen, waiting for Brenda to get out of Johnny's car and come across the street. They must have been talking moon-making because it was taking forever.

I had to squint good to see if there was really somebody moving around the side of the Jackson house where the streetlight couldn't reach, but then I saw them, Jack and Joey—or maybe James—creeping across the front lawn snake-belly-style, then jumping up fast and yelling, "Boo!" against the passenger-side window.

Brenda screamed bloody murder, and Johnny's door flew open. Jack and Joey ran like jackrabbits back around the house, while Johnny shouted threats at them.

I stepped on the porch as Johnny and Brenda headed over to my side of the street, Johnny's arm around Brenda's waist, probably because she was still shaking from being spooked.

"Boy, Johnny," I said when they got to Brenda's car. "Your brothers sure do have a lot of afflictions."

"Teaspoon!" Brenda said, like I'd scared her all over again. "What are you doing up at this hour?"

The cement steps were rough against my bare feet, and the grass damp and chilly as I hurried to Brenda's car. "I wanted to talk to you about how Jay's making us come on and get off the stage. I don't know why we can't come out in pairs." Then I hurried to Brenda, took her arm and moved her farther into the street. "We could walk out like this. Then each pair could do a twirl, like this, so the Big Sisters would be behind us when the song starts. Then maybe twirl again before we walked off."

"How about we talk about it at rehearsal tomorrow night?" Brenda said, looking up and down the street like she was expecting company she didn't want, even if the streets were empty, with not even a Taxi Stand Lady in sight.

"Oh, and would you tell Jay to stop calling me Pip Squeak, too? I hate that nickname, and no matter how many times I tell him to stop it, he keeps saying it. He keeps it up and I'm going to kick him in the shins. Just see if I don't. Then he's going to hate me and probably not let me stand center-stage.

"Hey, Johnny, did Brenda tell you that her and me are going to be center-stage? That's where the best singers get to stand because everybody looks in the middle most. That's what Jay said. And this is what we have to do when the orchestra starts our song." And I put my hands up over my face, like they were a blue fan, and hummed the intro, then pulled them down to start the song.

"Teaspoon?" Brenda said, while smiling.

I stopped my demonstration, even if I was to the good place where we do something special with our fans. "What?"

"Tomorrow, okay?"

"Okay. Anyway, Johnny. It's going to be a swell gala. You're coming, aren't you? I get free tickets, so I'll give you one."

Johnny put his arm around Brenda and gave her a little tug toward him, while he laughed and said, "It's a deal, Teaspoon." Brenda smiled.

"Okay," I said. "Night then." I opened the screen door to go inside, then turned around. Johnny and Brenda were standing face-to-face talking quietly, Brenda's hand on Johnny's arm. "Oh, and one more thing. Could somebody besides me yell at Rebecca Lang to stop sticking her top teeth out when Mindy's singing? It's mean, and it makes Mindy feel afflicted all over again. Jay doesn't see her because Ivy's Little Sister, Betsy Franks, who has a head the size of a melon, is probably blocking Rebecca. But boy, if somebody doesn't make her stop it, I'm going to be kicking her in the shin, too."

Johnny put his head down, but I heard him laugh. "Enough thinking for one night, Teaspoon. Go to bed." Brenda was laughing, too. But just then, a car too fancy to belong in me and Johnny's neighborhood came down the street. Brenda must have thought that car was going to smack her, because she jumped out of the way and hurried to her car, leaving Johnny standing there alone. "We'll talk about it tomorrow, Teaspoon. I need to get home," she said as she unlocked her door, her head down. Then she got in her car before me or Johnny could even say good night.

I looked at Johnny standing in the street, his hands in his pockets, as Brenda gave a quick wave and sped for home. Johnny's head was down so I couldn't see his face, but something about him looked sad just the same. "Well, good night, Johnny," I said, and he said, " 'Night, Teaspoon," then walked back to his side of the street.

It wasn't easy to shut off my thoughts. I thought about how many days until Ma came home, and I thought about the gala. Then right before I dozed off, I had one of those hey-wait-a-second thoughts that made me lie awake wondering why, if Brenda thought that car was going to smack them, she didn't yank Johnny off the street with her. She already had ahold of his arm.

CHAPTER NINETEEN

As the days passed, I got as jumpy and owly as Poochie, snapping at anybody who looked at me twice. "What's the matter, Teaspoon?" Teddy asked me as we sat down to a late-Sunday-morning breakfast.

"People are getting on my nerves," I said.

"What people?" Teddy asked.

"That Jay for one. The guy who's teaching us our song and dance. It doesn't matter how many times I tell him not to call me Pip Squeak, he does it anyway. And then there's those Jackson kids. They're so dumb! Last night when Brenda brought me home, Jolene kept waving and saying, 'Hi Brenda! Hi!' like they were best friends or something. Then when I was waving to Johnny as they drove off, Jolene yelled, 'He's *our* brother, not yours, Teaspoon.'

"And I said, 'So? He brought *me* Starlight seats, not you! And Brenda's *my* Big Sister, not yours.'"

I made a point of not looking at Teddy's face when I repeated what I said, because I knew his eyebrows would do a double dip over that one.

"So what did that idiot Jolene say then? She said, 'So what? Brenda's *our* brother's girlfriend.' Now, how stupid is *that*, Teddy? I yelled back, telling her it was stupid, too. I reminded her that Brenda is engaged to Leonard Gaylor—whether I like him or not—

so she couldn't be Johnny's girlfriend. Johnny's getting paid to make the moons and Brenda's helping him because she's soft-hearted. That's all.

"So then that dumb Jolene said, 'Oh yeah? Then how come Jack and Joey saw them kissing when they snuck up on Johnny's car? And how come he took her up on River Road if they're just friends, when everybody knows that's where the big kids go to neck?'"

"Those Jacksons, Teddy. They're nothing but liars and gossips. I wish I never had to look at them again."

Teddy poured me some orange juice and set a plate of French toast down in front of me. I was going to comment on the fact that Teddy had changed breakfast up a bit, but I couldn't stop belly-aching long enough to tell him how much I liked French toast.

"And then there's those Sunshine Sisters who don't know their right from their left foot for nothing! No wonder when Mrs. Bloom hobbles in to listen and watch, she keeps yelling, 'Synchro-nize your steps, girls!' And there's one Big Sister who sounds like a dog who got hit by a car. I'm not kidding you, Teddy. And no mat-ter how many times Jay tells her to tone it down—which means *shut up because you sing like a wounded dog*—she keeps bellering. She's going to ruin our whole song!"

I tore off a piece of French toast, dipped it in the Aunt Jemima, and stuffed it into my mouth, ignoring the dribble of syrup slip-ping down my chin.

"I'll tell you, Teddy. About the only people that aren't getting on my nerves right now is you and Charlie. Probably because you both know when to shut your yaps."

"I'm assuming Brenda is included on your list of people who aren't getting on your nerves?" Teddy asked.

"I hate to say it, Teddy, but no, she's not. The more rattled she gets, the more noodley she acts. That Leonard came to the Starlight the night before last, and he was nothing but nasty. I didn't hear what he said because it was too noisy with our music going, but his face sure did look crabby. And when Brenda tried walking away because Jay was calling her back to the stage, he stuck his face right up against hers and snapped something. I'll bet anything he got spit on her face when he was doing it, too." Then I stuck my face up to Teddy's, Leonard-close, and I shouted, "Am I getting spit on your face up this close, Teddy?" He told me I was.

"Yeah, that's what I thought." I sat back down as Poochie started barking at God knew what.

"I asked Brenda what Leonard was so crabby about when she was driving me home, but she didn't say. Must have been about wanting to take her on a date, because Johnny was waiting for Brenda when we got back here, but she had to tell Johnny she couldn't work on anything because she had to get home. She didn't tell him why, but by last night Johnny knew, because Dumbo Doug told him he saw Brenda and Leonard at the Starbright Drive-In. Johnny doesn't like Leonard. I know because I asked him. And know what I think, Teddy? I think that Johnny told Brenda to tell Leonard to take a flying leap, because when Johnny came across the street last night, he looked as owly as I've been feeling. And the first thing out of his mouth to Brenda—even before he said hi to me or picked me up to give me a little play-shake—he said to Brenda, 'You didn't tell him, did you?' And Brenda said, 'It's not that simple, Johnny.' Then Johnny just did one of those about-faces and headed back home. Brenda called after him, 'I have to get through the gala first, Johnny.' Who knows if Johnny heard her, though, because he had already jumped on his new motorcycle—well, it's not new, but new to him—and started it up, and you know how noisy that thing is."

Teddy sat down and watched me scoot the last square of French toast through my puddle of syrup. He said something, but by this time Poochie had been barking and snarling for a good five minutes. Finally I said, "That dang dog. I can't take it no more!" I got up and stomped through the kitchen and out the back door.

Charlie was on his knees weeding Mrs. Fry's flower bed, which explained why Poochie was barking. But I didn't care why he was barking. I shot right across the yard screaming at the top of my lungs. "You want me to slug you, you stupid, mangy, afflicted, yapping mutt? Because I will if you don't stop barking!" I pointed to his doghouse. "You get your butt in there and shut up, Poochie. *Now!*"

I could hear Teddy yelling behind me to get back, and see Mrs. Fry rapping on her window. But I just kept right on yelling until he tucked his tail between his legs and skittered into his doghouse, going so fast that some of the dog hair dangling from his doorway tore loose and floated off.

Afterward, Teddy made me go in the house, where he sat me down on the couch. I pushed his arm away and sucked the snot back up my nose.

"Teaspoon. I don't think your mood has much of anything to do with any of these things. I think you're just anxious about your ma coming."

"It's taking forever, Teddy," I said, my voice cracking.

"I know, I know. I probably should have waited before I told you, but I wanted you to have time to adjust to the idea."

Teddy pulled me so close to him that I could smell his armpits, which weren't very respectable at the moment. "You're nervous about seeing your ma again, aren't you?"

When he said that, I started bawling harder.

"Do you know why?"

His bony chest was hard against my ear as I shook my head.

Teddy didn't say another word. He just kept his arm around me as I cried, his hand rubbing my curls down.

It must have been a crying kind of day, because when I got to the Starlight, more crying was what I found.

I went through the whole theater looking for Brenda but didn't see her. So I headed up to the lit meeting room. It was empty, but the door to the catwalk was open. I figured Mr. Morgan was up there doing some work or other, so I headed up, thinking he could tell me where Brenda was.

But it wasn't Mr. Morgan on the catwalk. It was Brenda. Sitting at the end of one petal, her arms wrapped around her legs, her face resting on her knees. "Brenda?" I called. "What are you doing up here?"

Even in the dim light, I could see that she was crying. Still, she smiled at me. "I come up here from time to time. I have since I was little. I don't know why. I guess I just like the solitude."

"Solitude?"

"The quietness. Being alone."

I sat down beside her. "Oh. Can I be alone with you?" I asked.

"Sure," she said.

"You sad, Brenda?"

She swallowed hard. "Yes."

"Why?"

Brenda shrugged and turned away, like she wanted to cry in *solitude* some more.

"You worried about the gala? Because if you are, you shouldn't be. Teddy told me this morning that people always get rattled when a big event is coming, worrying about every little detail, but that in the end, everything comes together. It'll come together, Brenda."

Brenda kept her face turned away and nodded.

"Last week when I was on vacation, I made Charlie go over 'Sisters' so many times that even he got sick of the song. And Charlie never gets sick of a song. I just want everything to be perfect, so I can make my ma proud. That's all. You worried about not making your ma proud, too?"

"Yes," she whispered, her face still turned away. "At least today. Other times, I don't care anymore."

"And I heard Johnny get mad at you, Brenda. You feeling bad about that, too?"

Brenda didn't answer me, but she didn't have to, because her eyes started leaking lots then.

"Charlie's sensitive like you are, too," I told her. "But just for the record, Johnny was just trying to be a good friend. He just happens to be a tad on the hotheaded side."

Brenda got busy mopping her face. "Hey, Brenda," I said. "You know how after the gala's over and you start showing regular movies again? Sometimes can I come up here to watch? You know, just for old times' sake? I miss not doing that." Then I pointed out the petal where I always used to lie, and which hole I used to look down.

"Sure you can," Brenda said. Then she rubbed the skin under her eyes and tilted her wrist toward the little bit of light there was. "I suppose we'd best get downstairs. There's a few who always come early."

CHAPTER TWENTY

Three weeks of days came and went, and I can't really tell you much of anything about those days because they were nothing but a busy blur, with everyone around me having nerves stretched tight as a fat man's belt. Until finally it was the middle of August.

I was sitting on my porch steps waiting for Ma in case she decided to come a couple of weeks early when Mrs. Fry came out with Poochie's food and water. She looked over at me and said good morning, told me Charlie would be out as soon as he cleaned the oatmeal off his shirt, then she said, "Teaspoon, a watched pot never boils."

I suppose I looked confused because she explained what that meant. And by the time Charlie came outside, his shirt polka-dotted with wet spots, I'd thought of the perfect way to keep busy until Ma came. Me and Charlie would make a show for Ma.

Charlie thought that was a good idea. "What songs does she like?"

"Anything except funeral songs," I told him. So we spent the whole rest of the morning testing out songs for our program.

We were right in the middle of "Shake, Rattle, and Roll," because best I could recall, snappy songs were Ma's favorites (though I wasn't sure how snappy this one was going to be since Charlie kept playing it slow-Moe), when I looked up and saw the time.

"Holy cats, Charlie," I said. "I've got to get to the Starlight! Mrs. Campbell and her daughter are coming to fit the Little Sisters for our dresses today.

"Brenda tried warning me about how I'd have to stand still while they tugged on our half-made dresses and put stickpins here and there, but I told her I know all about that, and as long as they have good eyes, I'll be fine. Oh, and we're getting our shoes today, too. I hope they make clickity noises when we walk. Gotta go, Charlie. You keep working on speeding up that song until I get back, okay?"

When I got to the Starlight, the Campbells were on the stage, two racks of bright sea-blue dresses beside them. Mrs. Campbell was pulling stickpins from a pretend tomato on her wrist and poking them along the hem of Alice Limpkins's dress while Alice spun ever so slowly on an overturned crate. Mrs. Campbell's daughter, Miss Campbell—both of them with faces as round as the Campbell Soup kids, so remembering their names was easy—was busy dropping one of the blue dresses over another Sunshine Sister's head, but I couldn't see who because her face was covered.

I slipped into the shorter line, behind Mindy.

"See that dress that's hanging in the front...right there on this rack?" Mindy said. "I heard that girl up there telling her friend that that's what our dresses are going to look like when they're all done. Only they'll stick out more because we're going to wear something under them to make them do that."

The Little Sisters dresses weren't going to look exactly like the ones Rosemary Clooney and Vera-Ellen wore. Ours had lace from the waist up, like theirs, but the sleeves were short little ones like the brims of baseball caps, not tight ones that went down past the elbow. And instead of a lace sash that hung down the front, kind of on the side, ours were going to get tied in the back, like a baby's. Ours were shorter, too.

"Where's our gloves?" I asked Mindy.

"They're not done yet. Mrs. Campbell got a McCall's pattern to make them with so they could be the same blue as our dresses. But it takes a long time to sew so many gloves."

Rebecca heard us talking and said, "My ma offered to sew some, and so did Alice's mom."

They were going to blab about those gloves forever, but I was done listening. Especially when I noticed that everybody was holding shoe boxes but me.

"Brenda handed them out," Mindy told me. "She was over by that table there." She pointed to the table that had been set up below the stage. There weren't any boxes left on the table, though. And no Brenda. "See?" Mindy said, opening her lid to show me a pair of shoes, shiny and white as pearls, with a skinny strap and a white button that was just for looks. "I think they're patent leather," Mindy said, even though I thought patent leathers had to be black.

I told Mindy to save my spot, then I went to find my new shoes.

Brenda wasn't in the theater, nor upstairs. She wasn't in the furniture store part, either. I didn't know where to look next, so I decided to head back to the stage and get in line in case any other girl was tardier than me and didn't care if my place was saved or not. But first I had to pee.

I barely got through the restroom door when I heard somebody puking. Smelled it, too. And whoo! I was just about to turn around to go find a grown-up to make the sick kid go home before she gave us all the pukes when I recognized the shoes in the stall. Flats, as Brenda called them, with a little string bow tied by the rounded toe. Her favorite pair for regular days.

I bent over to talk under the door. "Brenda? That you in there puking?"

A ribbon of toilet paper slipped to the floor, then disappeared. "Just a minute, Teaspoon," Brenda said, her voice hoarse. She coughed, then blew and flushed.

"Man, Brenda. You don't look so good," I told her when the stall door opened. "You don't smell so good, either."

Brenda went to the sink and used her hands like a cup. She rinsed out her mouth, then splashed water on her face. She yanked the cloth towel and dabbed her face with the clean part. She still didn't look so good, though, with her face popcorn-pale, but for two patches of red blotching her cheeks.

"I'm okay," she said, as she dabbed at her eyes; puffy on the outside, cherry-red on the inside.

"You pick up a stomach bug?" I asked. "If you did you should have some ginger ale and broth. That's what Teddy always gives me when I get that bug."

Brenda shook her head. "I just get like this when something big is going on. Before my first recital, I threw up on and off for a week straight."

"Man," I said. "Glad that doesn't happen to me. I just get butterflies. Happy ones."

"You have to go?" Brenda asked, looking at my legs that were crossed at the ankles.

"Yeah."

"Okay, I'll see you in a bit."

"Hey, Brenda," I called, my voice echoing. "You have my new shoes?"

"I do. You get in line for your fitting and I'll bring them to you."

Boy, that bathroom echoed good when you talked loud, so I sang a little bit of "Sisters," smiling as I did, because I was remembering how Jay told the Little Sisters that they should take a lesson from "Pip Squeak here" and work harder on the song and steps. And how after he said that, he leaned down and said in my ear, "You sing like a dream, Pip Squeak."

I ran through the whole song, my toes tapping against the floor tiles, before I remembered that I was supposed to be in line so I could get my new shoes. I left the bathroom without washing since no one was looking, then raced out and up the aisle to squeeze my way between Mindy and Rebecca. "Hey, no butting in line," Rebecca said, giving me a shove. But then Brenda handed me my shoe box and told Rebecca, "No shoving." Rebecca really wanted to deck me then, because she was still afflicted in that way, but she didn't.

The whole fitting thing took forever and a day, so it was a good thing I had my new patent leathers to keep me busy. Boy, they sure were pretty, glossy as piano ivories, the little heels making tippity-taps every bit as noisy as a lady's high heels.

"You're going to make scuffs," Rebecca told me as I tapped make-it-up-yourself steps while standing in place.

"I am not. Johnny Jackson himself told me that they put so many coats of varnish on this stage that it would take a dinosaur's toenails to scratch it."

"I'm not talking about the stage, stupid," she said. "I'm talking about your shoes."

Mindy turned around and glared at Rebecca. "You'd better not talk to Teaspoon that way, or I'll scuff your *face*!"

I grinned at Mindy as I worked my legs like a drummer's sticks. "Wow, Mindy," I said. "I think you just lost another one of your afflictions."

"See you at rehearsal tonight," Brenda said as she walked me to the door, carrying the empty shoe box that had my name written on the lid in marker. "Maybe you should put your shoes in here before you go outside." I told her that I couldn't scooter while carrying a box, so I'd just wear them home and leave the box at the Starlight.

"I'm glad you're feeling better, Brenda," I said, then out the door I went, my new shoes clicking and gleaming in the sun like they were made of magic.

CHAPTER TWENTY-ONE

It was August twenty-seventh, and I was zipping back from the Starlight, where I'd gone in the afternoon just to see if Brenda was around because I had nothing to do while Charlie did some work for Mrs. Fry. Brenda wasn't, so I scootered around Bloom Avenue for a while, watching my patent leather paw at the sidewalk, then headed for home.

Both of the Taxi Stand Ladies were on the corner when I got to Washington Avenue, watching me come down the street, which I was sure meant they were admiring my new shoes. But when I got to the corner, I could see they were watching my face instead. "Teaspoon?" Walking Doll said with a bit of a smile on her red-apple lips. "I think your ma is here."

I stopped, my whole head going blank like a TV station that just went off the air.

"Short? Pretty? Auburn hair?" The Kenosha Kid asked.

I couldn't breathe to answer her. I couldn't even nod my head. All I could do was stare down the street where Charlie was waiting, waving his arms like nuts.

Charlie darted toward my house once he knew I'd seen him, and Walking Doll said in a teary voice, "Go on. Go see your ma."

I let my scooter fall against the sidewalk and I started running. Crying and laughing at the same time.

Teddy was waiting on the second step when I got there.

I stopped. "Teddy? Is it her?"

He nodded, then came down the steps and put his arm around my shoulder to lead me into the house. Charlie held the door open for us.

Once I got through the door, it was like my new shoes had Bazooka stuck to the heels, and I couldn't budge. I looked on the couch. On Teddy's chair. On the Starlight seats. But I didn't see Ma. So I looked at Teddy to make sure it wasn't just hope I'd been listening to when I asked if it was her.

I heard a lady's voice come from the kitchen. "Teaspoon? That you?"

"Ma?" I called back.

And then there she was. Standing in our living room, like she'd never left it. Shorter than I remembered, her hair spilled to her shoulders in Greta Garbo waves. She was dressed in pink and mint green, and prettier than six Glindas put together. I looked at her eyes, her smile, and I remembered her face like I'd never forgotten it.

CHAPTER TWENTY-TWO

"*Oh my God!*" Ma shouted. "Look at how much she's grown!" I think she was talking to Teddy, but I wasn't sure because I was the one she was looking at. "Come here and give your ma a hug!" she said.

I ran to her and wrapped my arms around her waist, my face pressing tight against her balloons. I breathed the smell of her in so hard that my nostrils clamped shut, like they wanted to make sure they never let go of her smell again. "Ma…Ma…" That's all I could say. Just "Ma."

Ma pushed me an arm's-length away and spun me in circles while she gasped. "Look at you…just look at you! You're a living doll!"

She gasped again and shook her head. "Isn't she a little doll, Teddy? She has my bone structure, don't you think?"

Teddy had his head tipped to the side and his eyes were watery. He nodded, then said, "Charlie, how about you and me take a little walk and let these girls visit." He put his hand on the back of Charlie's gouged head and they walked out the door.

Ma took my hands, squeezing them and giving them a little shake. She leaned over so her face was in front of mine. "Did you miss me?" she asked, her voice high and hopeful.

"Course I did, Ma. You were gone for a long, long time. Five years."

"Five?" she said. She straightened, cocked her eyes up and off to the left, her mouth moving silently, like she was counting behind her teeth. "Oh my God, I think you're right," she said. "I'm sorry, baby."

Ma grabbed her purse from the end table and took it to the couch. "Come sit with your ma and tell me everything," she said.

I ran to the Starlight seats. "Do you remember these, Ma?"

Ma's pretty eyebrows, arched like rainbows, dipped some. "No, I don't remember those being there," she said.

"They weren't. They're seats from the Starlight Theater. We just got them. Want to sit over here?"

"In a bit, honey. Right now I'm looking for something."

Ma started digging in her purse, and I wondered if she was going to take something out for me. Maybe a stick of gum, or a little toy. She pulled out a cigarette and put it between her lips, then kept digging, so I leaned over to watch her hand. I saw her scoop up something gold and shiny. Maybe a new barrette that I could wear to the gala so people could see my eyes. But it was only a cigarette lighter.

Ma lit her cigarette than looked around the living room. "I suppose Teddy threw out all of the ashtrays. Get me that coffee cup over there, Teaspoon, will ya?" She was pointing to the one sitting next to Teddy's chair.

Ma watched me as she smoked, her lips going from banana-shaped smiles to circles that blew doughnuts of smoke above our heads. "Remember how you used to like those?" she said. "You'd jump like a puppy reaching for a stick, so you could poke your finger in the hole." Ma laughed. "What a cutie you were. And still are."

I smiled.

"Teddy told me you're a part of some girls' program or other, and that you're gonna be in some kind of a show in a couple of weeks?"

"In seven days," I said. "At the Starlight. Can you believe it, Ma?"

"The movie theater?" she said, looking confused.

"It's a live theater now, too. I thought it was a dream come true, making my debut at the age of ten, and at the Starlight Theater to boot. But now that you're home and get to come, well..."

My voice cracked on the last part of that sentence, and Ma tapped me under the chin with a curled hand. "Don't go getting all teary on me now, Teaspoon. This is supposed to be a happy day, and I want to see my baby girl smile, not cry."

"I'm not going to cry, Ma," I said, breathing in hard. "Jay, that's the guy who is our chorusographer—"

"Chor-e-ographer," Ma said, laughing. "It's *choreographer*."

"Oh. Anyway, Jay is teaching us dance steps for our big number. It's really going to be good. We come on right before Les Paul and Mary Ford. Can you believe it? I can't! And Jay's putting me and Brenda Bloom herself smack-dab in the first row, right in the middle. That's the best spot, isn't it, Ma?"

She nodded, then said, "Gloria Bloom's daughter?"

"Yeah," I said. "She's my Big Sister. My mentor. Anyway, we're dead-center. Well, except for when we do this little dance part and walk around in a big circle. But I come right back to dead-center when we're done. Our number was my idea, too. Want to see me do the song?"

I jumped off of the couch to sing. "Pretend my right hand is my fan, okay?" I held my fan hand over my face while I la-laed the beginning of the intro, nodding my head once to the right, then the left, then *sashaying* in a circle around an imaginary Brenda. Then I started singing, "Sisters. Sisters..." I sang it to the part where the Big Sisters sang, "Never had to have a chaperone, no sir," and the Little Sisters sang, "I'm here to keep my eyes on her." Then I stopped because I didn't want Ma to see the whole dance—especially the parts I liked best, where we dipped on one leg with a bounce, then kicked a foot to the side to sway and sashay some more.

"Just like that!" I said. "Jay said he's never seen a kid with lungs like mine. He said what I got is *projection*. And he said that with my voice, my looks, and my *charisma*, I got star quality. Imagine that, Ma. Star quality. Me! And he should know, because he was in some shows in New York City."

Ma smiled and said, "Of course you got star quality. You're my daughter, aren't you?"

"The whole show is going to be great, Ma. You're going to love it!" I hurried through the names of the stars, our acts, the songs, our dresses, the fans, everything. Putting it all in one long sentence, so that by the time I finished telling her about the moons, I had to pause to take a breath, because big lungs or not, I didn't have any more air left in me.

"Huh," Ma said, "I'm surprised the Blooms are doing the big-band thing. That era's come and gone. But I don't suppose word of that has reached Mill Town yet, so folks around here will probably eat it up.

"Teaspoon?" Ma said when I got quiet and stood still, staring at her. "Why you looking at me like that?"

"Ma?" I said slowly. "Did you find your dream?"

"Huh?" she asked.

"The dream you went to find. Of becoming a star on the silver screen. Did you find it?" I almost felt like I was going to get Brenda's pukes in those few seconds it took Ma to take a suck on her cigarette and blow the smoke out so she could answer me.

"Well," she said, the word trailing a smoke ring. "Come sit down and I'll tell you the whole story of how I became the star of *Attack of the Atomic Lake Lizard,* my first film. And the sequel, *Revenge of the Atomic Lake Lizard.*"

I let out a whoop. "I knew it! I just knew you'd do it, Ma!" I jumped into the air and came down on my butt, right beside my movie-star mama!

"It took a while," Ma said. "I didn't have enough money to get all the way out to California. Story of my life, a day late and a dollar short. So I was held over in Denver for a few months, playing a piano bar and stashing every dime I made. And I needed it, too, because a month after I got there, that damn wreck of Teddy's broke down and I needed another car."

Ma grabbed Teddy's cup and put out her half-finished cigarette, then tucked one leg up under her other. "I worked my ass off, doing some bartending during the day, working the piano bar nights, but damn it, I did it. I got myself out to Hollywood, and after a lot of trying, I auditioned for the lead role in this movie. And you know what got me the role?" she asked.

"Your acting ability and star quality?" I asked.

"Well, besides those things," Ma said, smiling. "This!" And she stood up, faced me, put her hands out like she was going to sashay, and then she screamed. Screamed so high and so loud that if my hair wasn't already curly, it would have been by the time she got done.

Ma laughed and fell onto the couch. "The director said I was the best screamer he ever worked with. I told him that's because I've had a lot of things to scream over in my life."

She giggled herself silly, then moaned a happy sigh. "I got the movie poster in that mess of a car of mine, somewhere."

"Let's go get it!" I said.

Ma sank back against the cushion, her hair opening like a fan. "Not now, Teaspoon. Your ma is bushed. I drove over five hundred miles today. I need a nap." She yawned, then turned her head lazily toward me. "God, it's good to see you again," she said.

"It's good to have you home, Ma," I said, as I fought back tears because she wanted to see me happy.

Ma reached her arm around my head, the warmth of her skin soaking right through my curls. She closed her eyes. "Teaspoon?" she said, her voice going sleepy. "Did Teddy find somebody else?"

"Somebody else? What do you mean?"

"Does he have another girl in his life?"

"Oh. You mean besides me?"

"A girlfriend," Ma said.

"Course not, Ma. *You're* his girlfriend. He's got a new lady friend, Miss Tuckle, but she's only his Sunday school friend. Like Charlie is my friend. Mrs. Fry, it turned out, was a Benedict Arnold and tried to make Miss Tuckle and Teddy be more than friends. Miss Tuckle swore on a stack of Bibles that they weren't, though, so it didn't work."

"Sunday school friend," Ma said, her voice sounding far away, like she was already halfway to dreamland.

Ma didn't let go of me after she dozed off, so I snuggled my head against the dip between her shoulder and the top of her balloon, and wrapped my arm around her waist, and listened to her breath rise and fall.

I never was the kind who could sit in a hug for long before my feet wanted to get moving again, but I stayed right there, pressed up against Ma, sitting still so I wouldn't wake her. Twice or three times, I lifted the bottom half of my legs so I could look at my new patent leathers, but other than that, I didn't squirm.

Outside a rain had begun. Not a storm. Just one of those kind of rains that feel like lazy. The window behind the couch was open, so I could hear the drops and feel the cool they brought. I closed my eyes, thinking about how I hoped Ma would let me take that movie poster to the Starlight so I could show it to Brenda and the Taxi Stand Ladies along the way. And how I was going to stand on my sidewalk and hold it up so the Jackson kids could see it while I stuck my tongue out at them.

Only when I felt a small swish of air push against my skin as a thin blanket came down over us did I realize that I'd dozed off just like Ma. I looked up and there was Teddy, standing by the couch, looking down on us, his face sad, though I didn't know why.

I untangled myself from Ma, slowly so I wouldn't wake her, then got up and followed Teddy into the kitchen.

"Did Ma tell you, Teddy?" I asked, probably with too much projection, because Ma stirred and groaned a little.

"Tell me what?" Teddy asked, as he filled a kettle with cold water.

I backed my butt to the counter, and used my hands to hoist me up so Teddy could hear me when I made my voice get Brenda-singing-soft. "That she found her dream."

"Your mother and I didn't really have time to talk, Teaspoon. She was only here about ten minutes before you got home."

"Oh," I said, almost glad, because that meant I could tell Teddy the good news myself. "Well, she did it, Teddy. She went looking for her dream, and she found it. She's a movie star now, just like I always knew she'd be. A lead role, and a sequel. We always knew she'd do it, Teddy, didn't we?"

Teddy got his paring knife out and got busy peeling dusty potato skins into long loops. He didn't look up. Probably because he had a sharp knife in his hands. I watched for a bit, then said, "Boy, Teddy. I would have thought you'd be happier, having Ma back. But you look more worrywartish than ever."

"There's a lot of things we don't know yet, Teaspoon. Things only time will tell."

I didn't know what things Teddy was talking about, and I didn't want to know. I slid off the counter instead of jumping, so my new shoes wouldn't click and wake Ma, and I told Teddy that I was going down to the corner so I could get my scooter.

Teddy looked down at me. "Charlie and I already brought it home. It's in the front."

"Then I'm going to go get Charlie. Him and me made a show for Ma. Soon as she's up and we've had supper, we'll perform it for her to celebrate her homecoming. Tell her that if she wakes up before I get back."

It was still raining some when I got outside so I ran fast so I wouldn't get wet. Not that I cared, but I knew Mrs. Fry would!

Mrs. Fry was cooking, too, and Charlie was sitting on the couch staring at a turned-off television set, doing nothing. I was going to get braggy about my ma being home, but when I looked at Charlie I decided that would be mean, since his ma couldn't come back. I figured it was okay to talk about her movie, though, because as far as I knew Charlie was never waiting for his ma to become a movie star. "Guess what, Charlie? My ma was in a movie. Two of them. The leading lady."

"A real movie?" Charlie said.

"Well, what other kind is there?" I asked.

Charlie shrugged. "Does it have monsters in it?"

"Yep," I said.

Charlie went back to staring at the black TV screen.

"How come you don't have it turned on, Charlie?" I asked.

"Cause Grandma G says it has to stay unplugged when it's storming."

I glanced through the worn-thin curtains. "It's not storming. Just raining." Charlie shrugged, and I shook my head. "I suppose because it's *storming* you can't go outside now, either."

"You got that right," Charlie said.

"Well, I'm going to hurry down to the corner and see the Taxi Stand Ladies. I won't see Brenda tonight, so I might scooter down to the Starlight, too. I wish you could come, Charlie."

"Me, too," he said.

I headed to the door. "Hey, Charlie. Where'd you and Teddy go on your walk?"

"To get ice cream," Charlie said, his eyes still staring at the TV.

"At the drugstore?"

"Yeah."

"Was Miss Tuckle there?"

"No."

"Good," I said, because even if her and Teddy were only friends, something about it wouldn't have seemed right if they'd gotten together to be friends on the very day Teddy's girlfriend came back.

"We had our ice cream first, then we went upstairs to where she lives."

I raced back to the couch so fast that my patent leathers worked like ice skates on the bare floor.

"Geez, Charlie," I said as I fell down beside him. "You're supposed to be my spy. Why didn't you head right over and tell me as soon as you guys got back?"

"Because Teddy said we had to give you and your ma time to visit. Plus, it was already raining by then."

I shook my head. "Well, what happened? Did Teddy say anything about my ma?"

"Just that she was here."

"How'd he say it?"

Charlie shrugged. "Just regular-like, I guess. Why you asking, Teaspoon? Miss Tuckle already sweared on a stack of Bibles that she wasn't Teddy's girlfriend."

"Yeah, I know. And although I don't think she'd lie to God, He's the only one who'd know for sure. Plus, that isn't the only reason I'm asking. I'm asking so I can find out if Teddy is happy Ma's home, because he isn't exactly acting like it. Did he sound happy when he said it?"

"No." Charlie's eyeballs hurried to the upper corner, like their conversation was hanging up there. Forever later, he said, "I think he just sounded worried."

"Did Miss Tuckle say anything to him?"

"No. She just put her hand on Teddy's arm, then she showed me how to work her phonograph so I could listen to music. Then she asked Teddy if he wanted coffee."

"Let me guess...they went into the kitchen, and you couldn't hear them with the record player on."

"Yeah."

"Boy. If you weren't my friend, I'd fire you as my spy." I shook my head and sighed. "See you later, Charlie. Come over after supper so we can put on our production for Ma."

"Okay. If it's done raining by then."

I pulled open the door and looked back at Charlie. "Did Miss Tuckle or Teddy say anything as you guys were leaving?"

"Just *thank you* and *you're welcome*."

I was just about to close the door behind me because I thought that was it, but then Slow-Moe Charlie said, "Oh...then Miss Tuckle said to Teddy, 'My offer still stands. Just know that.' "

I shoved the door back open and drilled Charlie like a dentist, but turned out, they were only talking about our leaning porch and her offer to give Teddy a loan. And didn't that just figure.

When I got to the corner, only The Kenosha Kid was there. "Teaspoon!" she shouted as I got close. "Was it your ma?"

"It sure was!" I told her about Ma's movie, how pretty she was, how glad she was to see me, and how we fell asleep on the couch together. "I wish Walking Doll was here so I could tell her, too, but you can fill her in, okay? I want to tell Brenda that Ma's home, and get back before she wakes up. Tell Walking Doll I'll bring the movie poster as soon as I get my hands on it."

"You can tell her yourself. That's her coming now."

"Where?" I asked, checking out the sidewalk, both coming and going.

"In that green car right there," she said.

Sure enough, there was a car at the corner, and Walking Doll was sitting behind the steering wheel. "What's she doing in that car?" I asked, waving.

"She got it from Miller's car lot. Just now."

Walking Doll made a left turn and disappeared behind The Pop Shop.

"How'd she do that? She doesn't even have a job!"

The Kenosha Kid didn't say anything. She was too busy watching Walking Doll hop-run across the street toward us, shaking her new car keys like jingle bells.

"Hey, where'd you get money to buy a car? Even Teddy doesn't have enough money for that, and he's got a job."

Walking Doll laughed. "Let's just say that it was compensation collected on behalf of my ma."

"Well, ain't that something. All Teddy's ma left him with was bills and a leaky, leaning house."

"Well, Teaspoon! *Was* that your Ma?" Walking Doll asked as she hopped up on the curb.

"It sure was," I told her. "The Kenosha Kid can catch you up. I've got to get over to the Starlight to tell Brenda that my ma's home, too, but I got to hurry. Teddy's making supper, and afterward me and Charlie are going to put on a live performance for Ma. Nice car, Walking Doll!"

"Have fun, kid!" they called, and off I went.

When I got to the Starlight, I zipped down the alley. The parking lot was empty, except for Brenda's Thunderbird and the Perkins Charlie-thumping truck, which I decided meant Johnny brought over the moons. They had to be done, because him and Brenda hadn't gone to work on them at night for days now.

I propped my scooter and slipped inside. Even though the day was gray and hazy, the raindrops so small they looked like fuzz, it still took a bit for my eyes to adjust to the darkness of the theater.

I heard Johnny before I saw him. "That's bullshit, Brenda, and you know it!" Wow, was his voice booming with projection, even though he was up by the concession stand, instead of under one of the domes where a person could get some good amplification. "You were going to kiss him off three weeks ago."

Johnny was mad at Brenda for *not* kissing that creep Leonard? Had he gone berserk?

"You don't understand, Johnny." Brenda was crying. "I just can't create that kind of upheaval right now. After the gala, Johnny. I told you. Give me until then," Brenda said, loud enough that I heard every word.

I couldn't see Brenda, but I had seen her cry enough times to know that she probably had one arm wrapped around her waist while the other dabbed under her eyes.

I didn't know what to do, or what to think. Turning and going back outside would have been the respectable thing, I guess, but I wanted to know what was going on, because this wasn't exactly making sense. So I just stood at the door, my hand on the knob.

"You're not going to, either, are you?" Johnny shouted. "Despite everything, you're going to marry that fucker anyway." Johnny grunted, then said in a voice more sad than mad, "I was a fool to think you'd do anything else. Now I don't know who to feel sad-dest for. You, I think."

Whoa!

It got quiet for a second, so I slipped back out the door. I didn't want Johnny to catch me being an ear-peeker, plus I had some fig-uring out to do. First Johnny was yelling at Brenda for not kissing Leonard, then he was upset because she wasn't breaking up with him. Something wasn't adding up here.

In the movies, they always kiss somebody when they're saying good-bye. Maybe *that's* what Johnny meant. He was telling Brenda to kiss Leonard good-bye, even though, if I was Brenda, I'd go for a handshake instead.

I grabbed my scooter, planning to be a good Sunshine Sister and wait my turn to talk to Brenda, maybe scooter around the parking lot while I did, when the door shoved open and Johnny came out. I don't think he saw me standing there or he would have given me a sack-of-potatoes shake. But he just got in the Perkins truck and took off, his tires smoking behind him.

I went inside. Brenda wasn't at the concession stand anymore. I figured she was probably in the restroom blowing her nose. But I was wrong. She was in the bathroom throwing up and crying hard at the same time.

I put my hands on the door and leaned my face up to it. "Brenda?" I said.

Brenda made a few gulping noises, like she was trying to stop puking and crying. "Teaspoon?" she said when she'd stopped enough to be able to speak.

"It's me. I just came to tell you something quick. I have to show you something, too."

"Can it wait, Teaspoon?"

"Yeah. I guess so. You okay, Brenda?"

"I will be," she said. "We'll talk later, okay?"

"Okay."

I got to the bathroom door, then stopped and turned back to the stall. "Brenda?" I asked.

"Yes, Teaspoon?"

"I heard Johnny yell at you. I didn't mean to ear-peek, but I did. Anyway, I just want you to know that Johnny gets a little hot under the collar sometimes. Like I said, all the Jacksons are like that. Well, except for Jennifer. But Johnny's not mean. He was just trying to be a good friend."

CHAPTER TWENTY-THREE

When I reached my block, Ma's car was gone, and suddenly I felt scared enough to puke, too. I pumped my leg like the dickens, then dropped my scooter in the grass and raced into the house. "Ma? Ma!" I called.

I checked every room, and didn't stop yelling until I saw her suitcase opened on Teddy's bed, clothes dripped over the side, the pink-and-green outfit she'd been wearing lying empty on the floor.

"Teaspoon?" Teddy called from the living room. "Where are you?"

"In your room," I called back.

"I could hear you shouting all the way over at the Frys'," Teddy said when he stepped into his room. "What's the matter?"

"I saw Ma's car gone," I said, blinking away tears there was no reason to cry anymore.

Teddy sat down on the bed. He had an envelope thick enough to be holding every bad bill in all of Mill Town sticking out of his shirt pocket, but he didn't have a gouge between his eyebrow. "She went over to The Dusty Rose to see if any of the old gang are still around."

"Whew, Teddy. I thought she was gone for a minute there." I could feel a gouge digging between *my* eyebrows then. "Did you tell her I was coming right back?"

"I gave her your message, yes," Teddy said.

"You think she'll come back by showtime? Me and Charlie were going to give our performance tonight."

"I think that will have to wait until tomorrow night," Teddy said.

"Did she dig her movie poster out of her car before she left?"

"I don't think so. She can do that tomorrow, too. You come have your supper now, okay?"

I stood over the pans still on the stove. A pot of boiled potatoes, an empty fry pan with brown goo stuck to the bottom, and a little kettle swimming with sauerkraut and chunks of browned sausage. "Geez, Teddy," I called, because he was still in his room. "Why'd you make sausage and kraut? Ma doesn't even like sauerkraut, remember?"

"Well, you do," Teddy said, "so eat up."

Charlie was in the front yard on his knees when I got back outside, a stack of weeds with dirty roots sitting on the damp grass alongside a half-eaten chocolate cupcake. "We probably have to wait until tomorrow before we can put on Ma's show," I told him.

"That's okay. Grandma G says I have to weed tonight anyway. Every time it rains a little, I got to stay inside. Then when it stops, I gotta weed. I'm starting to hate rain, Teaspoon."

"Don't blame you, Charlie." I eyed his cupcake. "Grandma G made cupcakes, huh? There any left?"

"Yeah, there's more. But Grandma G didn't make them. Miss Tuckle did."

"I didn't see Miss Tuckle's car."

"I think she parked around the corner."

"Weird. Not like any other cars were hogging up the street. She still here?"

"No," Charlie said. "She just brought over the cupcakes, and visited a little with Grandma G and Teddy, then she left."

Charlie picked up his cupcake and peeled back more paper so he could stuff the rest into his mouth.

I went inside and grabbed a cupcake from the table. Fast, so Mrs. Fry wouldn't turn from the stove and see me. Not that she'd mind, it's just that she'd start talking to me and I'd have to repeat my answers back to her about fifty times.

I was barely down the steps when the Jackson girls came outside, jump ropes in their hands. I watched them as I licked the chocolate frosting off my cupcake. I hadn't played with the Jacksons since their ma chased me home. And although I didn't miss playing with them, or even fighting with them, I sure did miss jumping rope.

I looked down at Charlie, who was leaned over on all fours, one hand pawing at the dirt like a dog trying to remember where he buried his bone. I knew a good friend would help Charlie weed, but I was wearing my gala shoes and I didn't want to get them grubby. "Hey, can I come jump rope?" I yelled across the street.

Jennifer cupped her hand and whispered something to Jolene, then Jolene said, "Okay, but no fighting. Our ma's right in the living room."

I told Charlie to yell when he was done working, then headed across the street. "My ma's at The Dusty Rose," I told the Jackson girls as I hurried to their side of the street.

Jolene held out the plastic handle of my old jump rope, but I was busy peeling the liner from my cupcake. "What did you say about your ma?" she asked.

I gulped the last clump of chocolate cake down and stuffed the empty liner into my pocket. "I said my ma's at The Dusty Rose."

"For real?" Jolene said.

"Yep. She came back just today. She found her dream of becoming an actress, so she came home."

"Is she really an actress?" Jennifer asked.

Jolene looked at Jennifer. "You dummy. She's probably not even home, much less an actress."

Man oh man, I thought. We hadn't even twirled the rope once and already the Jacksons were picking a fight. "Yes she is. Her car was in front of my house all day, if you didn't notice."

"That old brown Hudson?" Jolene said.

"I don't know what kind of car it is, but yeah, it's brown. And it's not old, either. Just dirty, from driving so many miles. It's a long way from Hollywood to here, in case you didn't know."

Jolene wrinkled her nose. "Is she really an actress?"

"She sure is. She starred in two movies. *Attack of the Atomic Lake Lizard* and *Revenge of the Atomic Lake Lizard*. When she gets home, or in the morning if it's too late tonight, she's going to get the movie poster out of her car, and I'll prove it to you."

"Did she bring you those new shoes?" Jennifer asked.

I looked down at my patent leathers, which were pinching my heels. I wanted to fib and say yes, but I had that promise to Jesus not to tell fibs anymore (a promise I was starting to regret), so I didn't.

"Then why you wearing them now, if they're your shoes for the gala?"

"Because I want to."

"You're going to ruin them," Jolene said, her voice every bit as bossy as Susie's or Rebecca's.

"No I won't. I stopped tap dancing in them."

We were jumping Double Dutch when Dumbo Doug's car pulled up to the curb, Johnny in the passenger seat. My feet got tangled when I saw him, and Jolene called out, "I'm next!"

Johnny rolled down his window and yelled to Jolene to run up to his room and get his wallet. Jolene sighed and tossed down her end of the rope. I watched the car while she was gone, waiting to see what my stomach would do.

"I can't find it!" Jolene screamed from an upstairs window.

"On my dresser!" Johnny yelled back.

Jolene disappeared again, coming back two seconds later. "It is not!"

"Want me to go help her look, Johnny?" Jennifer asked.

Johnny slipped out of the car. "I'll get it," he said.

The last time Charlie and me were in The Pop Shop, Pop was busy trying to find the cigars Mr. Miller ordered, so I flipped through a couple of movie magazines. I found one of James Dean, in living color. He was wearing blue jeans and a brown, short-sleeved button-up shirt. There was one little V cut in each sleeve, like somebody with bad eyes like Mrs. Fry was holding the sewing shears, and his shirt was unbuttoned almost to his belly, like maybe somebody forgot to sew on the buttons while they were at it. His hair was messy and poking up on his head, and his eyes were squintier than usual, like maybe the smoke from his cigarette was getting in them. I had never seen James Dean look so dreamy. And now here was Johnny, wearing a shirt almost exactly like James Dean's, only blue, without the V's, and with a couple more buttons fastened. He looked every bit as dreamy as James in it, too.

On his way back to Doug's car, Johnny picked me up and tipped me sideways, sack-of-potatoes-style, and gave me a little shimmy. He smelled like beer and Old Spice. "See ya," he said as he set me down. And I'm not kidding, it was like he had shook every bit of worry I had about Brenda, or Ma, or Teddy, right out of me, leaving nothing in me but happy giggles.

By the time Jolene came back outside, my ankles were hurting so bad I couldn't jump rope anymore. Charlie was just getting off his knees anyway, picking up the bundle of pulled weeds so he could carry them into the backyard and toss them in the thick brush behind Poochie's doghouse. "I gotta go," I said to the Jackson girls. "Ma will be home soon. I'll show you the poster as soon as I get it."

"You'd better, or we're not gonna believe you," Jolene called behind me, as I hobbled across the street without bending my knees or my feet.

✳   ✳   ✳

I took off my gala shoes and paired them together in my bedroom, then pulled off my socks to find two puffy blisters the size of quarters on my heels. Teddy fixed them up with medicine and Band-Aids. I was just putting my socks back on when Charlie came to the door. He went straight to the piano, but I told him we had to make Ma an invitation first. So I got out my crayon tin and folded a piece of school paper. Charlie drew a star on the paper, because he drew better stars than me, then I printed, *Teaspoon and Charlie* inside it in my best handwriting. And on the inside, I wrote, *Appearing live in our living room, 7:00 Sunday night.* Then we practiced until Charlie had to go home because it was getting dark.

I was back on my knees on the couch, watching cars go by and hoping the next one would be Ma's, when Teddy suggested we finish our Scrabble game. I don't think he really wanted to play, but maybe he was thinking about how watched pots never boil.

Me and Teddy kept the Scrabble board over on the little metal table near the pantry so we wouldn't bump it and mess up the letters when we moved around the kitchen. I dragged two chairs to the table and went to my room to turn the radio on—about the only way I could stay entertained when playing with Teddy, who always took so long to make a word that Charlie and Mrs. Fry could have run a ten-mile relay race and walked back before he had a word laid down.

I sang a little of "Begin the Bageen," with the radio when I turned it on, while I shuffled tiles around, hoping a word would show up.

"Hey, Teddy? What's a *bageen*, anyway?"

"A dance," Teddy said. "Kind of like a slow rumba."

"How do you spell it?" I asked, crossing my fingers because I had a *B* tile, and they were worth three points.

Teddy spelled it, and what could I say but "Shucks" because I didn't have an *E* or a *G*.

I couldn't find a word to make so I tossed my tiles back in and picked new ones. Then it was Slow-Moe Teddy's turn.

"Hey, Teddy," I said as he looked at his tiles, then back at the board, and back at his tiles again. "This feels like old times, doesn't it? You and me at home playing a board game, while Ma's at The Dusty Rose?"

"I guess it does," Teddy said, his head down studying his letters. "But we used to play Chinese checkers back then. Until I lost too many of the marbles."

A snappier song came on then, so I picked up the two windowsill shelf thingies that we weren't using and tapped them together to the beat of the song. "Hey, Teddy, what are these things called, anyway?" I asked, as I held them out.

"I don't really know," Teddy said. And boy was I sorry I asked, because then Teddy started reading the inside of the box to see if it told.

"Geez, Teddy," I said. "I didn't want to know *that* bad."

Teddy, that lucky, put down the word *quick*. Twenty points! So I set down the only word I had the letters to make: *gluck*.

Teddy's eyebrows bunched even more than they already were. "Gluck?" he said. "I don't think that's a word, Teaspoon."

"Sure it is," I said, even though I wasn't sure. So of course Teddy had to get out the *Webster's* to prove me wrong. Good thing "Davy Crockett" came on the radio then, so I had something good to tap and sing to while Teddy flipped pages. "Sorry, but *gluck*'s not a word," he finally said. "You'll have to try a new one."

I glanced up at the clock.

"She'll be back eventually, Teaspoon. But probably not while you're still awake."

"I don't want to play no more, Teddy," I said. Then I went to sit by the window, while Teddy put the chairs back and shut the radio off. I sat there until he told me I needed to go to bed because I had Sunday school in the morning.

∗　∗　∗

I lay awake for a long time that night, listening to the wind rustling the leaves of the tree between my house and Charlie's, humming songs that sounded like harmony to that rustling, then stopping every time a car came down the street. Waiting to see if it stopped.

And finally one did. One filled with loud music and shouting. I leapt out of the bed and looked out the window.

The noise was coming from Dumbo Doug's car, parked in front of the Jacksons' house, right under the streetlight. Boy, drunk people sure did talk funny, their words stretched out like hot taffy. "Johnnnnnnnnnnnny," a girl's voice said when the back door opened. "Don't goooooooooo."

Johnny shut the door behind him and a girl with dark hair like mine, only straighter, leaned out the window, her arms holding the outside of the door like she might spill out onto the street if she didn't hang on to something.

Johnny didn't say anything to her, he just backed up a bit, his body slow and staggery, a beer bottle dangling from his hand.

"The other direction, Jackson," Dumbo Doug said when Johnny took a couple of steps into the street. Dumbo Doug had a girl with him who I couldn't see, but who I could hear.

Johnny was circling the front of the car when that idiot Dumbo Doug let the car move forward enough to bump his hip. "Doug!" the dark-haired girl screamed. Johnny dropped the beer bottle he was holding and cussed loud.

The Jacksons' front door opened and Mrs. Jackson stepped out in her robe. "Johnny?" she called. "What's going on out there? You're going to wake up the whole neighborhood!" She was harping loud enough to wake up the whole neighborhood herself, but I suppose she had to yell if she wanted to be heard over all that racket.

Mrs. Jackson poked her head back in the door, and out came Mr. Jackson. "They're going to wake up the whole neighborhood," Mrs. Jackson harped as she followed Mr. Jackson to the street.

"Doug, you get yourself home. And in one piece, too. Go!" she said. Mr. Jackson tucked Johnny's arm over his shoulder and helped him into the house, Mrs. Jackson harping behind them, "You boys and your good times!"

But my oat-sowing Johnny didn't look like he was having a good time to me.

I didn't mean to doze off, but I did. A soft thud and the jiggle of my doorknob woke me.

"Don't go in there, Catty. Let her sleep," I heard Teddy say. His voice sounded so far away that I thought it might be coming from a dream.

"I wanna see my baby girl," Ma said.

"Tomorrow. Let her sleep. I put clean sheets on my bed. Go lay down, Catty. It's late."

Ma giggled, and not too softly. "Your bed? Oh, maybe you *are* happy I'm back after all." I heard two thumps, like shoes hitting the floor.

"Remember the good times we used to have, Teddy?" Ma said, her voice movie-star flirty. Ma's voice dropped to almost a whisper. "It's been a long time."

"Longer for me than you, I'm sure," Teddy said. And then he told Ma to go get some sleep.

I propped up on my smooth elbows and blinked the sleep from my eyes.

Ma sounded like she was auditioning for a Shirley Temple part when she said, "Go get some sleep? Aren't you coming with me, Teddy?"

"The blankets on the couch are for me, Catty."

"Well, fine then. I'll just go where I'm wanted." I flung one leg over the side of my bed to help Ma because I thought she was turning my doorknob in the wrong direction, when Teddy said, "Catty, please. It's almost two thirty. Tomorrow. When you're sober."

Ma got crabby then. "You telling me what I can and can't do with my own kid? She's *mine*, Teddy. I can do what I want with her."

The door burst open then, and Ma came in, filling my room with the smell of beer and perfume. "Mama's home," she called. "Wake up!"

I suppose Ma could see my smile in the bit of streetlight that glowed through my filmy curtains, because she smiled back at me. She dropped on my bed, pinning my leg. I yelped, so Ma shimmied her butt so I could pull myself free. "Sorry, honey," she said. "But I just couldn't let the day go by without saying good night to my little girl. You have a happy day, Teaspoon?"

"The happiest," I told her. "That is, until September third, when the gala comes and you get to see it. And Teddy, and Charlie, and..."

Teddy appeared in the doorway then, his hand on the knob. "There, Catty. You've said good night. Now I'll help you to your bed."

Ma ignored him. "Scoot over, Teaspoon," she said. Then she stretched out beside me on my skinny twin bed. "And you scoot out, Teddy," Ma said. "We're gonna have ourselves a little girl talk."

"Yeah," I said. "Girl talk."

"Teaspoon's got Sunday school in the morning, Catty. Don't keep her up too long."

"Go!" Ma shouted with a laugh, as she snuggled close to me. Then Ma told me about her fun time at The Dusty Rose, and how she met up with "old friends and new," and all the nice things they said about her. I listened, but not so much to what she was saying, but to the sound of her voice, rising and falling like a melody.

I don't know who fell asleep first, and by morning, I didn't remember much of anything Ma said. What I remembered, though, was the feel of her cheek up against the side of my head, and waking up with the wall cool against my back.

CHAPTER TWENTY-FOUR

In the morning, after Sunday school, Charlie came home with me. "She still sleeping?" I yelled when I got inside.

"Not anymore," Ma called from my room.

Charlie followed the smell of baking cake like it was coming from the Pied Piper's flute, while I poked my head into my room. "Hi, Ma."

Ma stretched out on the bed, her arms reaching above her head, her wrinkled blouse rising above her belly. "So you had to go to Sunday school," she said with a sleepy laugh. "What's that Teddy trying to do, corrupt you?"

"No. He's trying to help me get rid of my afflictions," I said. "Listen to this one," I said, reciting the only Bible verse I remembered. Miss Tuckle had made us memorize at least one, so I'd made it into a jingle. I sang it for Ma...

> *If ye have faith as a grain of mustard seed,*
> *ye shall say unto this mountain, Remove hence to yonder place;*
> *and it shall remove; and nothing shall be impossible to you.*

"Jesus," Ma said.

"That's right, Ma! Jesus said that! It's from Matthew. I don't know what all of it means, because it's said in Bibley words, but I know what it mostly means. That if you believe you can do something, then you can. Though I don't know about moving a mountain."

Ma yawned. "Sweetie? How about you leave me alone for a bit until I wake up enough to clear the cobwebs from my head."

"Okay. See you soon," I said.

I went into the kitchen where Teddy was mixing up some chocolate frosting.

"Hey, Teddy. Did you know that Ma knows some of the Bible? I didn't." I looked over at Charlie, who was peeking into the hole on the top of the cocoa can. "Don't even think of taking a lick, Charlie. That stuff doesn't taste good until it's mixed with sugar."

Ma shuffled into the kitchen while me and Charlie were having some cake, the frosting slipping off the top like Teddy warned would happen because the cake was still warm. But who cared. It tasted just as good.

Ma leaned over and gave my cheek a kiss. Then she circled the table and gave Teddy one, too, which made me happy. She stuck her finger in the frosting on Teddy's plate and licked it as she eyed Charlie with sleepy eyes. "Charlie, right?" she asked. Charlie nodded. Then she leaned down and kissed his cheek, too. "Morning, Charlie."

Charlie looked up at Ma, his mouth making a shy, frosting smile.

"Did you save any scrambled eggs from breakfast for Ma?" I asked Teddy.

Before he could answer, Ma said, "Just coffee for me. My head is killing me, and my stomach isn't feeling much better." Her bare feet made swishing sounds on the linoleum as she made her way to the bathroom.

Teddy got up to get her coffee, and I got up to get her the invitation me and Charlie made for our *Live at the Starlight* performance.

"What's this?" Ma asked after she sat down. Boy, even with her hair a snarly poof and her lipstick gone, Ma looked movie-star pretty. Which reminded me...

"Ma, don't forget to get your movie-star poster out, okay? The Jackson kids don't believe you're a star now, so I want to show it to them. Me and Charlie want to see it, too."

"When my head stops thumping, okay?" she said. She stirred some milk into her coffee and took a sip. Then she picked up our invitation, reading it out loud.

"You put together a show just for me?" she said, all happy.

"We sure did, Ma."

"But you're making me wait until tonight," she said with a pout.

"You don't have to wait if you don't want to. Me and Charlie could do it right after we finish our cake."

"Well, I've got to take a bath and get rid of this headache. But after that. How would that be?" I grinned at Charlie.

Before Ma got in the tub, me and Charlie helped her carry some of her bags into the house so she could get some clean clothes. After we carried in the second armload, Teddy dried his dishwater hands and came out to help. "How much of this are you bringing in?" he asked.

I rolled my eyes. "Boy, Teddy, what a dumb question. All of it, of course."

Me and Charlie and Teddy did most of the hauling, while Ma dug through junk in her trunk for her movie poster.

My heart was beating like a bass drum when she found it, rolled like a pirate's spy glass. "Here you go. Be careful with it, though. It's the only copy I've got."

I slipped the rubber band off one end, and there it was, a red-and-black poster, as real as Charlie's grasp on my arm. The scary creature had blood dripping out of his squinty eyes and a fat sharky mouth. More blood dripped from rips in its skin, which looked scaly as bad elbows. A trail of blood left by his long tail was smeared across the page.

The monster was carrying a lady that anyone could see was Ma over his shoulder, even if half of her was upside down. Okay, maybe her butt and balloons were a little bigger in the picture than in real life, her legs a little longer, but there was no mistaking her face that was turned so we could see it, her mouth opened in a scream.

"*Attack of the Atomic Lake Lizard,*" I read out loud. "*One Hundred Feet of Scaly Death!*"

"Is that a real monster?" Charlie asked.

I rolled my eyes. "There's no such thing as real monsters, Charlie. Even in the movies. Right, Ma?"

I could feel Jolene and James spying on us from across the street, so I held the poster up, pointing it in their direction. "It's my ma's movie poster! Come see!"

James ran around the back of their house to get his brothers, and they all came running to the front yard, cardboard swords in their hands.

Jolene read the poster out loud. And when she got to the part that said, *Starring Mack Filbin and Catty Marlene,* I felt so proud I could have cried.

"Cool. Blood," James said.

Jennifer chewed on her braid, looking at the poster from the corner of her eye, like she didn't want the lake lizard to know she was looking at him. "Did the monster kill you in the end?" she asked.

"Who cares about that," Jack said. "Did he rip off your dress when he attacked you?"

Jolene elbowed Jack. "I'm telling Ma you talked dirty."

The Jacksons asked a bajillion questions, talking right over each other and shoving each other out of the way so they could stand closest to Ma.

Ma took the poster from me and scooted her butt on the hood of her car, holding it up like she was playing Show and Tell as she answered every question they had. Charlie was butted up to me so that our bare arms were touching. I could feel his sweat smearing on me, so I gave him a little shove and told him to move over. A few seconds later, though, Charlie was stuck up against me all over again. I suppose because he was scared. Either of the monster on the poster, or of the Jackson kids—not that there was a whole lot of difference.

"Is that real blood?" Jennifer asked while Jolene stared up at Ma with her big yap hanging open.

Ma laughed. "This poster is just a drawing."

"Did you use real blood in the movie, though?" James asked.

I rolled my eyes. "Now, where would they get gallons of real blood from, James?"

"The hospital. They have blood there."

Ma laughed. "The movie was in black and white, so we used chocolate syrup."

"What about the monster?" Joey asked.

"Oh, that's Stan. Poor guy worked up such a sweat inside that rubber suit that he had a rash the whole week we were filming."

I think the Jackson boys were disappointed, finding out there were no real monsters or blood in the movie, and that Ma didn't get naked. But their eyes perked right up when Ma told them how she played a lady named Eleanor Wilkinson, and how the government tested some atomic bombs in the lake where her family had a summer home and that atomic stuff fell into the water and made a lizard grow big and deadly mean. How he went on a killing rampage, and the leading man, Mack Filbin, who played a scientist (and her boyfriend by the end), had to save her by finding a way to kill the lizard.

"He chased you all over Kingdom Come, didn't he, Ma?" I asked.

"Yep." She lifted her leg, bare in her shorts, and pointed to a scar on her thigh. "I got that when the monster was chasing me and I fell, cutting it on the lid of a tin can someone left near the water," she said. "It hurt so bad I cried. Course, that was perfect for the movie, so they left that part in."

"Wow," James said.

Ma jumped off the car, handing me the poster. Then suddenly she wasn't Catty Marlene anymore. She was Eleanor Wilkinson.

She raced along our house, breathing hard and looking back in a panic, like she thought she was being chased—and she was, by us—then into the Frys' backyard. Poochie went nuts, of course, and Ma crouched down behind a bush, peeking out at him and screaming like he was the monster—which in a way, he was.

Boy, Ma was some actress! When she got down and stuck her legs out from the side of the bush and made them jump and twitch farther and farther into the open, you could have sworn that monster was yanking her out. She kicked and screamed as she tried to get loose. Screamed so loud that Mrs. Fry came running.

Ma fell back on the grass, her head landing right in Mrs. Fry's flower patch, laughing like crazy, while we applauded her performance and laughed right along with her. "Wow, that was cool!" Jack yelled over Poochie's barks. I leaned over and yelled at Poochie to shut up, and he backed up a little, even if he was still yapping.

"Land sakes," Mrs. Fry said, "I thought Poochie was killing somebody out here!"

Ma sat up, and Mrs. Fry hobbled over to her flower bed, lifting a crushed stem from the ground and frowning when the purple flower top flopped sideways like its neck was broken. "You kids get out of this yard now," she said, looking at Ma like she was one of us. "And Charlie, these weeds are growing up again, so you'd best get busy."

Charlie looked at me. "It didn't even rain," he said with a shrug.

So Charlie stayed home to work while Ma signed napkins with autographs, one for each Jackson kid, and after they left, I helped Ma unpack.

Teddy had cleaned out three drawers for Ma to use (or maybe they were already empty, since he didn't have anybody giving him hand-me-downs), so Ma had to figure out which things she wanted in there, since all her stuff couldn't have fit in ten dresser drawers.

Ma sure had some pretty things! I took a hat, shaped like a swimming cap, with a clump of fake flowers on the side, and slipped it on my head while I dug through her jewelry case. I untangled some necklaces, grabbing at a string of pearls. I didn't think I grabbed that hard, but that necklace snapped right in half. I gasped, but Ma only laughed. "Those are popper beads," she said. She took the necklace from me and showed me how the little knobby end on one bead fit into the tiny hole in the bead of the other. "See?" She popped off a couple more and said, "It's so you can make the necklace any length you want."

"Cool," I said as she handed it back to me so I could play with it some more. But I didn't. I slipped it long over my head, then started digging in the big suitcase Ma was rummaging through. "This is for your balloons, isn't it?" I said, as I pulled out a balloon holder. "They have these in Montgomery Ward catalogs. Did you order this from Montgomery Ward?"

"What did you call them? Balloons?" Ma laughed so hard she almost fell on the bed. She took the white contraption from me, and put it on over her dress, shaking her balloons. "They're called breasts, Teaspoon. And this is a brassiere. A bullet bra. And no, I didn't get it from Montgomery Ward. It came straight from Frederick's of Hollywood." She tossed the *brassiere* on the bed and I picked it up to examine it. The *cups,* as Ma called them, were shaped more like a dunce hat than a bullet, with stitching that spiraled to a pencil-lead point.

I looked up at Ma and decided that this was what Mrs. Carlton meant by *feminine influence.* Having someone to teach you about breasts and bullet bras and popper beads.

While Ma made piles of folded shirts and skirts and hung long plastic bags she said were for garments, I matched up her shoes like they were socks. I put on a pointy pair that had skinny heels so high that I had to ballerina-walk to reach Ma so I could show her how they made me almost as tall as her. "Hey," she said, like she'd suddenly thought of something. "Do the Jacksons have a telephone?"

"Yes," I said, as I clomped in circles around her. "Why?"

"Well, then I don't have to keep running to find a pay phone so I can check in with my agent." Ma told me to keep pairing shoes and she ran across the street to talk to Mrs. Jackson about using her phone. She was back by the time I had the last shoe lined up with its match, then headed for her bath.

"I hope you don't mind Charlie playing your piano, Ma," I said later, while we were setting up for our performance. "I tried to save your piano pristine for you. But Charlie's the only one I let play it. And he always washes first." The second I said that, Charlie shot up and hurried into the bathroom, while I got out our bag of props.

While Ma waited, she ran her finger over the top of the piano and looked at Teddy. "You were such a sweetie, buying this for me so I could improve enough to play in public," she said. "I'm surprised you didn't sell it."

"Why would he do that?" I asked as I pulled the flat black box out of our prop bag. "Remember these, Ma?" I said, taking out one elbow-length glove.

Ma took the glove, turning it over in her hand. "These were mine?"

"Yeah. Can I use them for our show?"

"You can keep them," she said. "I've got more gloves than I know what to do with." And that was the truth, because I'd put those in pairs, too.

I took Ma's hand and sat her down in the middle Starlight seat. Then I led Teddy over to sit beside her. Ma goody-goody clapped her hands like she couldn't wait for the show to begin, so I yelled for Charlie to hurry.

I slung Teddy's old tie around my neck, making it into a quick bow so I would look like Randolph Carter, the emcee at the Starlight. Then, while Charlie took his seat at the piano, I welcomed Ma and Teddy to *Live at the Starlight.*

While Charlie played an intro to our first number, I scuttled around him to crouch behind the piano seat so I could rip the tie from my neck and put on Ma's gloves, because our first number was going to be classy.

Ma put two fingers in her mouth and whistled loud when I returned to the stage, stopping just for a second to kick over a scatter rug so my patent leathers would make good clippy noises on the linoleum as I sashayed.

Ma whistled again after we finished "Ain't She Cute." Teddy just clapped. Probably because he didn't know how to whistle.

We were just about to break into an oldie but goodie, "Kiss of Fire," the song Georgia Gibbs used to sing—just to help nudge Teddy into remembering how him and Ma used to kiss—when the screen door bounced with knocks. Teddy cranked his head around and gave me a hold-on-a-second finger.

But I told Charlie to keep playing. And I kept singing. Because like Jay reminded us every practice, if we gawked and stopped singing every time someone in the audience got up, one song could take two hours.

"We heard music and thought we'd come over to see what was going on," Mrs. Fry all but yelled (which was a testament to my claim that she was half deaf). Miss Tuckle was right behind her.

"Well, we're glad you did," Teddy said, speaking for all of us, even if I wasn't glad.

I gave Charlie the *cut* sign, then tapped my patent leather. I was thinking about how they had the nerve, talking right through our number like they were a bunch of afflicted Sunshine Sisters at a first meeting.

"Mrs. Fry!" Ma said, and she gave her a friendly hug. Mrs. Fry gave Ma's back a quick pat, her wrinkly Benedict Arnold face not even smiling as it hung over Ma's shoulder.

"Sorry for barging in like this," Miss Tuckle told Teddy in a regular-volumed voice that she knew Mrs. Fry couldn't hear.

Teddy introduced Miss Tuckle to Ma. Poor Miss Tuckle. Even with a little curl in her hair, she was looks-afflicted when you compared her with my movie-star ma. A fact that made me happy, because I knew that even if Teddy had begun thinking Miss Tuckle didn't look so bad while Ma was gone, he had to be reminded of the truth now when he saw them standing side by side.

Teddy led Mrs. Fry and Miss Tuckle to the empty seats on both sides of Ma, saying he'd stand. Miss Tuckle cranked her head up and smiled at Teddy, so the last thing I was about to do was sing some romantic song about kissing! I told Charlie to do "Shake, Rattle, and Roll" instead.

Boy, Ma sure did like that number! She started Teddy and Mrs. Fry clapping. Then she got up and danced, right on our linoleum stage. "Pick up the tempo, Charlie," Ma said, snapping her fingers in time until Charlie got his fingers working at the same pace as her snaps. Then Ma started singing with me. Shouting a few *go, go, goes* into the chorus for good measure. Ma didn't sound anything like Teresa Brewer. She sounded better!

And when we closed off the show with the Penguins' "Earth Angel," Ma took over the whole chorus and told me to do the *ooos* and *ahhhhs* in the background. We sounded like a real act!

When our program was over, Ma took my hand. Then she took Charlie's hand and slid him off the piano seat. She had us make a line, lift our hands together, then drop them as we bent at the waist to take a bow.

"Oh, that was fun!" Ma said, her face flushed and her voice breathy when we stood back up straight.

Teddy yelled, "Bravo! Bravo!"

"That was wonderful," Miss Tuckle said. "And it's easy to see where Teaspoon gets her talent." Ma made her hand do that oh-please-I-don't-deserve-your-praise wave, but she was grinning.

I was picking up the props, and Charlie was picking at the piano keys again, when Mrs. Fry stood up. She smoothed the front of her housedress and leaned closer to Miss Tuckle, talking half-deaf loud. "She couldn't let that child be the center of attention even once, now could she."

Miss Tuckle's face went pink.

CHAPTER TWENTY-FIVE

After the big show, Ma stretched out on the couch for what she said would be a "little" nap. But she didn't wake up until suppertime. And after she ate, she took her makeup and hair case into the bathroom.

"Where you going, Ma?" I called through the door. With the water running, she must not have heard me, so Teddy answered from where he sat at the table doing a crossword puzzle. "To The Dusty Rose, I'd imagine," he said.

Ma came out about half an hour later with her hair sprayed in stiff waves. She was wearing a pretty pencil skirt and a flimsy sweater she called "a knit" that clinged tight over her bullet bra. A thick belt held her knit in place.

"What are you looking so pouty about?" she asked me as she slipped into some pretty pumps.

"I want you to stay home with us," I said.

Ma laughed and gave me a hug. "Tell you what. You can come with me. I've told everybody there about my pretty baby girl, and I didn't have even one picture to show them."

I looked over at Teddy, and Ma giggled. "What are you looking at *him* for? I'm your ma. And if I say you can go, you can go."

Teddy looked up, a *not*-so-Jesus-gentle look on his face. "I wouldn't exactly say that The Dusty Rose is an appropriate place to bring a ten-year-old child," he said.

"It's okay, Teddy," I told him. "When me and Ma lived in Peoria, I was only four and five, and we went downstairs to the bar every night."

Ma went over to Teddy and nestled her nose against the side of his neck. "You could come with us to make sure your girls stay safe, you know."

Teddy scrunched his shoulder up and leaned his head against it so that there was no room for Ma's face. She looked hurt as she backed away.

Teddy set his pencil down. "Teaspoon, could you leave your Ma and I alone for a minute?"

"Yeah, go in your room and pick out the prettiest dress you have," Ma said, giving my butt a playful slap. I hurried to do as Ma told me, shutting my door behind me.

My closet didn't have one thing pretty in it, since the best dress I had was lying crumpled in my hamper, mustard stains down the front. So I found my second-best dress. A pink-and-blue plaid that had a skirt full enough that you could hardly tell the hem was crooked. I flung myself and the dress on the bed, then pulled off my dirty socks to see if my blisters were healed enough to wear my patent leathers. Like I heard Mrs. Bloom say, the right accessories could save any outfit.

That's when I heard Ma shout, "What's *that* supposed to mean? *Then waltz out of her life again for another five years?*"

"Catty, lower your voice. Please," Teddy said. "Teaspoon will hear."

But I wasn't going to hear nothing, because I flicked on my radio and cranked the sound to ten.

The Dusty Rose was a supper club, which I figured meant it would be nicer than the bar we used to live above. And it was. It had stools with backs on them, not just those metal ones with red seats that wobbled like they were going to tip over when you spinned on them. And folks didn't have to eat their burgers or fish fry at the bar, their elbows crowded, because they had round tables with plastic tablecloths scattered through the whole place, a short red candle in bubbly glass on each.

The place was filled with people when we got there, half at the bar and half at the tables. Cigarette smoke and the smell of fried food hung above the bar and tables like umbrellas.

"Speak of the devil," a guy with ears like Dumbo Doug's at the corner of the bar yelled, lifting his glass like he was giving Ma a toast. The guys sitting on both sides of him, and the big one standing behind them, called out a few hoots.

Star quality. That's what Jay called it when someone had the ability to light up a stage just by walking across it. Ma wasn't on a stage, and she wasn't screaming like a starlet, but still most every head in The Dusty Rose turned to look at her as she *sashayed* behind the line of stools to get to the guys who were calling her.

"And who's this pretty little thing?" the guy with the big ears asked when we reached the corner of the horseshoe bar.

Ma pulled me in front of her, her hands hooking together like popper beads. "This is my baby girl. Teaspoon," she said.

The guys laughed at my name, so Ma started explaining how I got it. I stopped her, though. "I want to tell it!" I said, and she let me.

"She got her big lungs from her mama, though," Ma said when they were done laughing. As I watched Ma talk to the guys, turning her attention from one to the next, I thought about how that brassiere she had on should be renamed an "arrow bra."

"You gonna treat us to a song later, little lady?" a guy big as Paul Bunyan asked.

"She might if you're good, but how can she sing when her throat is as dry as dust, just like her Mama's?" Paul—it turned out, his name *was* Paul—ordered Ma a brandy old-fashion sweet, like she asked for, and me a root beer.

"What you got there?" he asked, looking down at the rolled poster I'd brought along because Ma said maybe I'd like showing it around. I was holding it in front of me like wedding flowers.

"It's my ma's movie poster," I said. "Want to see it?"

They did, so I stepped back to the empty table behind us and unrolled it, spreading it flat as I could, while they crowded around. Oooh, did those guys stink like beer!

"Is that really you, Catty?" one of the guys behind me asked.

"Course it's Catty," the Paul Bunyan guy said. "Don't you recognize her?" In one swoosh he picked Ma up and tossed her over his shoulder, then turned to the guys so that he was standing at the same angle as the lake monster. He gave Ma's behind a swat. "Now can you tell it's her?"

"Hey, put me down," Ma screamed. She laughed and beat at his back, but not hard, more like she was just acting.

Everybody chuckled like crazy. Well, except for some older ladies eating at a nearby table, and a few of the ladies at the bar.

I was trying to spot the piano Ma used to play as I rolled the poster back up, when my hand felt a gob of grease stuck on the back. I took a napkin from the table and wiped it off, then hurried the poster over to a lamp hanging from a chain. Sure enough, that grease had soaked through, making a gray splotch that covered Ma's whole face. I rolled it quick and put the rubber band back on, then ran it out to the car.

Being at The Dusty Rose was a lot different than I remembered it being at the bar in Peoria. I wasn't sure why. Maybe it was because I was too big to run in circles going nowhere, just for the sake of running. Or maybe it was because they didn't have a pool table so I couldn't roll the white ball into pockets, and there was no jukebox to sing to while Ma drank and smoked and laughed at the bar. Whatever the reason, it wasn't the same.

I circled the room, staying close to the walls so I wouldn't be in the way of the waitresses carrying trays of food on their shoulders, running my hand across the folds in the thick red-plaid curtains when I came to a window. Curtains that didn't quite reach the sill, so on my second lap around I counted the flies that were lying belly-up on the sills. There was thirty-one of them total.

My ankles were pinching in my patent leathers, and I didn't want new blisters, so I went over to stand by Ma.

"You want another soda pop?" Ma asked. "A bag of chips?" My supper was still napping in my stomach, so I shook my head. But Paul got me a bag of potato chips anyway. And a Baby Ruth candy bar to go with it.

"There's a piano back in the corner," I told Ma. "Maybe we could do a number together."

Ma turned around. "What, Teaspoon?" I repeated it. Louder this time, because the folks at the bar were all talking at once. "Hey, you cheap bastard," Ma yelled to the guy behind the bar. "You get that piano tuned *yet*?"

"Now, why would I have bothered after you left?" he said. "You should know that the music just went out of our world after that."

"Smart-ass," Ma said, and some of the guys laughed.

"How come you don't have a jubox?" I asked.

"Folks like to hear each other talk when they eat."

Ma looked at me and she shrugged, making her mouth frown like a sad clown's.

I think Ma didn't remember that I could sing *Acapolka,* and I didn't remind her. Not after I looked down the bar at everybody talking loud at once—like they were all singing a different song, in different keys.

I wandered off again, stopping to watch the water falling in the land of sky-blue waters on the Hamm's beer clock, then studying the bubbles in a candleholder, until a lady Mrs.-Fry-old, who stunk like beer and smoke and old, stopped to tell me to be careful so I didn't light my "pretty curls" on fire. She touched my hair with yellowed fingers, and I hurried back to the empty stool next to Ma.

The Paul Bunyan guy got up to "drain" something (I think he meant his wee-er) and Ma's attention floated over to the lady and man who had been hidden by mountain-big Paul. "Oh, Betty," she said. "This is my little girl."

Ma tugged me off my stool and pulled me to stand close to her crossed legs. "Say hi to Betty and Dale, Teaspoon," she said.

Betty Rains. The one Mrs. Delaney pointed out to Mrs. Perkins after Betty left The Pop Shop. The one who stole Mrs. Carlton's husband. I'd have recognized her anywhere. She was wearing a blouse that showed a long crack between her balloons—*breasts*—and glittery wings on her glasses. The guy had his head turned toward Betty, but when Ma introduced me, he turned around. If that was Mr. Carlton, he looked a whole lot different than when I saw him at our Christmas program last year. His hair was different. Darker, and combed into a do that I think was suppose to be a Duck's Ass, though it looked more like the bottom of a duck that had either been sitting too long or had gotten it kicked in a fight.

While Betty Rains oooed and ahhhed over me, saying Ma wasn't kidding when she said I was a real beauty, I looked at the man. "You're Mr. Carlton, aren't you?"

He nodded.

"I thought so. Your wife was my schoolteacher. She's a real nice lady. Pretty, too, even with her lips painted out of the lines. She could have made me a flunky, but she didn't. I told her she should sing on more days than Sunday, because singing makes you feel happier, and that I figured she could use some happy since you ran off with—"

Ma grabbed my arm and swung me back to my stool. She changed the subject fast. I suppose because she didn't have anything to add to the conversation, seeing that she didn't know Mrs. Carlton.

The Paul-Bunyan-big guy came back, and Betty Rains said, "My turn." She was wobbly when she got up, so she stood still for a minute, hanging on to Mr. Carlton's shoulder. She smiled at me when she noticed I was staring at her, so I asked, "Miss Rains? How old were you when you filled out?" She smiled, her head tilting. "Aw, precious, don't you worry. You'll fill out soon enough."

"Oh," I said as I stared at her legs, which, if they were tree trunks, Charlie could have climbed without snapping them, "I'm not in any hurry. I was just wondering."

After Betty Rains zigzagged to the bathrooms, I didn't have anyone to talk to, so I just leaned against Ma's back and listened to her words hum through the side of my head.

I didn't even know I fell asleep until Ma did her movie-audition scream, horror-movie loud, and her friend with big ears caught me midair. "Whoa, little lady," he said as I shook with startle. "You were ready to take a nosedive there." He set me back upright on my stool.

"Oh, honey, did Mama scare you?" Ma laughed and cuddled me.

I wiped the bit of spit oozing out of the side of my mouth and blinked. "Can we go home now?" My eyes were already wanting to float shut again, and I couldn't stop them.

"Aw, my baby's tired," Ma said. "We'll leave in a minute, Teaspoon."

But we didn't leave in a minute. So after I almost fell off the stool the second time, I got up and wandered across the room, past the empty tables, some of them cleaned off, some not, and I went to the dark corner where the piano sat. One of the ivories was busted off and I dipped my finger in the ridge where it used to be. Then I stretched out on the bench, using my arm for a pillow.

The lights were turned on bright and they stung my eyes when Ma woke me up at closing time. "Come on, baby. We've gotta go home now." Ma's voice was all slushy.

She drove weavy down the streets, singing a bit of this song and that, microphone-loud. I had my head leaned against the door, half sleeping. That is until Ma hit a curb going around a corner and made a bump—which made me glad that there wasn't any Charlies on the street this time of night.

"You sure were cute, showing off my poster to everyone like you did."

I squinted my sleepy eyes at Ma, who was trying to look at the street and the cigarette she was lighting at the same time. "Nobody believed that you were going to become a star, Ma. But I believed it. Every day I believed it."

Ma reached over and patted my bare leg, dropping a speck of orange ash down to sting my skin. But just for a split second. "Awwwwww," she said. "I appreciate that, Teaspoon."

"I'm going to make my dream come true one day, too, Ma. Just like you did. One day, everybody's going to have an album by Isabella Marlene in their collection. And radios all over the country are going to play me. You just wait and see."

"Of course you will. You're cut from the same cloth as me. And people like us, we don't let anyone or anything keep us from getting what we want."

"Yeah. It's like an affliction we both have. But maybe a good one, huh?"

"Shit!" Ma yelled as she swished her hand across her lap. I saw her cigarette move like a shooting star to the floorboard. Ma lifted her foot so I could pick it up, then she tossed it out the window.

I was waking up, but I think Ma was getting more sleepy. She yawned as we pulled onto Washington Avenue, and quieted so all I could hear was the air whomping in through her cracked window. I looked outside at the empty streets as quiet as us, and started humming a little bit of "How High the Moon." Soon Ma was singing the words. So I turned my humming into singing, because tired or not, it was a good opportunity to practice my harmony.

We were finishing the last verse as we swayed up the front steps, then we turned, like the porch was our stage, and took a bow. We were giggling. So loud Ma had to shush me before she opened the door.

Teddy wasn't on the couch, and the kitchen light was on. Ma steered me to my room then helped me spill into my bed. Dress, shoes, and all.

CHAPTER TWENTY-SIX

Me and Charlie were on our way to The Pop Shop with the last of my payday, our almost empty Pez dispensers in our pockets, me riding my scooter as Charlie played Kick the Rock by himself. Charlie was moving slow-Moe chasing that rock, but with me still tired from my late night at The Dusty Rose, I wasn't exactly breaking any speed records, either.

"I got up because I had a bellyache last night," Charlie told me. "I was in the bathroom and I could hear your ma and Teddy fighting. Cause the window was open and there wasn't even a wind. I could see them, too. In your kitchen. Before I sat down, anyway."

"They were fighting? I didn't hear them fighting."

"They were, though. Teddy was mad because your ma took you to a bar. He wasn't yelling. But talking real crabby."

My scooter slowed even more. "Was Ma talking crabby, too?"

"I dunno. I don't think so, cause she was kind of laughing. Yet her words were crabby ones.

"She said you were her kid, and she could take you anywhere she wanted." Charlie stopped, and I turned around to see what the holdup was, thinking maybe he was busy putting another row of Pez under Mickey Mouse's head because I swear, that kid couldn't walk and take out a Pez at the same time. But he wasn't. He was just standing there, his fat arms curved like half-moons over his puffy sides. "Teaspoon? Is your ma gonna take you anywhere she wants?" Even his mouth looked like a half-moon. One turned upside down.

"Charlie, I told you a hundred times already. My Ma isn't taking me anyplace. She's back in Mill Town now, and she's here for good."

"I don't think so," Charlie said.

"You're just talking worrywarty now."

"Well, your ma told Teddy that he wasn't exactly making her feel welcome. And that maybe she should just move on."

"Oh man. That's what I've been afraid of, Charlie. I don't know what's wrong with Teddy, but he's not treating Ma like a girlfriend. They aren't doing the Juicy Jitterbug. I don't think that's a good sign, do you, Charlie? What did Teddy say when she said maybe she should just move on?"

"I don't know. I had to flush the toilet then. I didn't hear."

"Geez, Charlie. What did you go and do that for?"

"Because Grandma G gets upset if I don't flush."

"I meant *then*, Charlie. Why did you have to do it *then*?"

"Because I was done." Charlie shrugged. "I heard Teddy say one more thing, though. After the toilet stopped making noise, I heard him say, 'It's not that I didn't believe in your dream. It's that I didn't believe in you.'"

I didn't know what that was supposed to mean and neither did Charlie. There was nothing left to do but scooter and find something good to sing.

The Pop Shop was busy when we got there. Me and Charlie kept getting butted out of the way every time someone needed to get around the candy section to grab a paper or magazine, or what have you, because that's the rule when grown-ups want something and so do you and your paths are going to crisscross: Grown-ups get to go first.

About the third time we had to move, Pop got cranky and told us to hurry and get our candy and get out. I rolled my eyes. "Let's forget the penny candy today, Charlie, and each get one big candy. It's quicker." Charlie picked out a box of Boston Baked Beans, and I decided on a box of Winstons because I wanted to pretend I was blowing smoke rings.

While I was digging my last payday out of my pocket, a lady at the counter asked Pop if she could buy two tickets for the big show at the Starlight. My ears perked up and I leaned over so I could see around the guy in front of me. "You're selling tickets for the gala here, Pop?"

"Been selling them for a while now," he said. "Not like I had any choice. Bloom owns this building. It's a royal pain in the ass."

Pop handed the lady two tickets and took her money. She looked at them for a second, then said, "Hmmm. Maybe you'd better give me two more. For my sister and her husband." Pop's forehead wrinkled as he counted out two more tickets.

"Hey lady," I said, as I ditched ahead in line to reach her. "I'm going to be in that show! I'm singing and dancing with the Sunshine Sisters! We're singing 'Sisters,' and wearing dresses just like Rosemary Clooney and…"

The top of Pop's head turned red as Charlie's Boston Baked Beans—like it always did when he got mad. "Get back in line, kid, or I'll throw your scrawny butt out of here!"

I glared at Pop, thief of the Taxi Stand Ladies' money that he was, and my affliction got the best of me. "I wasn't trying to weasel my way father up in the line, I just wanted to tell her—"

"Are you talking back to me?" Pop said. "You even think of doing that, and you'll be putting those candies down where you got them and booted out of here until you learn how to be seen and not heard."

All it took was for Charlie to hear Pop raise his voice and he was darting out the door. Good thing I was quick and yanked those Boston Baked Beans out of his hand as he went, or he would have been sitting in the clink next to his dad. I slammed both of our candy boxes on the counter and headed out after him. "Charlie!" I called, as he ran across the road. "Stop! You want to get smacked by a truck again? Pop didn't mean he was kicking us out *this time*. Only that if... well, never mind. It doesn't matter now." (Well, except to my sweet tooth.)

"Hey, I know. Let's go over to the drugstore and have an ice cream. I don't know how much they cost, but I know I've got enough for at least one sundae. We can ask for two spoons if we have to share."

"I didn't ask if I could go there," Charlie said.

I sighed. "Geez, Charlie. We'll say that Pop's place was extra-busy, and it won't even be a lie. And anyway, it's your fault that we didn't get any candy since you ran out. You can ride my scooter so we make better time."

I talked about the gala the whole way there, telling Charlie about how the Big Sisters were getting fitted today, which meant that the theater would be locked because the older girls would have to get naked to try their dresses on. I added the last part because if I learned anything from hanging around with the Jackson boys, or in taverns, it was that guys perked up and listened if you said the words *naked* and *girls* in the same sentence. Which I figured was about the only way I was going to keep Charlie's attention, because I think he was getting tired of all my gala talk.

"And did I tell you that they're going to have some food there, too? Pinwheel sandwiches, I heard, for one. And a great big white sheet cake, flowers the same blue as our dresses."

I told Charlie about the food part for the same reason I said "naked." To make double-sure he'd stay listening, so I could keep talking. If I didn't, I knew I'd go back to wondering why Teddy wasn't making Ma feel welcome, even though we'd waited five long years for her to come back.

"Hey, Charlie. You think they'll let me bring my scooter in?" I looked up and down the street, trying to see if there were any potential thieves lurking around.

"Look at that boy down there. In front of the dime store. Does he look a bit shady to you?" I figured Charlie would be the better judge, him being the son of a jailbird.

Charlie didn't answer. He just tugged on my shirt, using his cuss finger to point into the drugstore because he had a Pez pinched between his thumb and pointy finger. "Look," he finally got out. "It's Teddy and Miss Tuckle."

"Hold this." I handed Charlie the handlebar of my scooter and stuck my face up to the glass.

I pulled away from the window and picked up my scooter. "Come on, Charlie," I said through gritted teeth.

I marched right into the drugstore and stomped across the black-and-white-checkered floor until I reached the booth where they were sitting. On the same side. Even though they had a whole empty seat right across from them.

They each had a strawberry sundae, and Miss Tuckle was scraping the bottom of her stubby dish, where the red juice was puddled. "Right or wrong, Teddy, what choice do you have? One day she'll under—"

Teddy saw me first. "Teaspoon," he said, his face going that shocked kind of pale. Miss Tuckle looked up and stopped talking, her head pulling back like I'd taken a swing at her, even though I hadn't. Even though I wanted to.

"Busted!" I said.

"Teaspoon," Teddy said. "What are you and Charlie doing way over here?"

"Never mind that," I said. "What are *you* doing here? You said you were running errands."

Teddy gave Miss Tuckle a quick glance, then he pointed to the empty side of their booth. "I did run errands. Sit down. We'll get you two some ice cream."

"I don't want to sit down," I told Teddy. Then I looked at Miss Tuckle. "You said you were only friends. You swore it on a stack of Bibles. Yet you're sitting all cozy."

Teddy slipped out of the booth. He glanced over at the chubby redhead at the counter, then leaned over to me. "Teaspoon, let's go outside for a minute."

"No!" I yelled. "She lied! And you two are as bad as Mr. Carlton and Betty Rains! No wonder Ma doesn't feel welcome."

Teddy grabbed my arm with one hand, and the scooter with the other. "Come on, let's go outside," he said, like we were cowboys about to have a showdown.

I dug my heels into the floor so that when Teddy tugged, the only way he could move me was to slide me. "You told me yourself that we shouldn't do things we wouldn't want our Sunday school teacher finding out about. Well then, seems to me that a Sunday school teacher shouldn't do things she wouldn't want her students finding out about, either!"

Teddy's face was red. "Sorry," he called to the redhead. She didn't look sorry to be overhearing my hissy fit, though. Not any more than Mrs. Delaney and Mrs. Perkins looked sorry when they stood in the butcher shop and tried to look like they weren't ear-peeking when the old butcher's wife talked about people. Being as afflictedly mean as I felt at the moment, I lifted my free hand and pointed at Teddy, who was yanking me something fierce. "He's supposed to be my ma's boyfriend!" I yelled. Then I pointed back to Miss Tuckle. "And *she's* a Sunday school teacher, and she lied on a stack of Bibles, but you can bet they're doing the Ju—!" Teddy clamped his hand over my mouth.

Charlie was standing near the door, his head turtle-tucked. "Come here, Charlie," Miss Tuckle said behind me.

I jerked my face free from Teddy's hand. "Don't do it, Charlie! Stay away from that sinner!"

Teddy tried calming me down after we got on the sidewalk, but there was no stopping me. "How could you be a cheater to Ma, Teddy? You did the Juicy Jitterbug with her. Lots of times. And that means you're her boyfriend!"

"Teaspoon. Let's go home. We'll talk there."

"No!" I screamed. "*You* go home."

"Teaspoon, I understand you're upset, but stop making a scene. We'll go home and talk. Quietly and calmly."

"If Ma leaves because of you, Teddy, I'll never forgive you. Never!"

He told me to stay right where I was, then he took one backward step and leaned into the drugstore to ask Miss Tuckle to see that Charlie got home safely. While he was concentrating on that, I yanked my scooter out of his hand and took off.

I didn't turn my head around when he called after me, but I turned my arm around, my scooter wobbling a bit when I let go of the handlebar. And then I did something I *never* thought I'd do to Teddy. I flipped him the big cuss.

It's not like I didn't see the splotch of blue to my left when I got to the four-corners with only two stop signs. I did. But I couldn't risk stopping and waiting for the car to pass unless I wanted Teddy's hand coming down on my shoulder like the claws of a crabby parrot. So I bumped down the curb and darted across the street.

There was the screech of car tires, then a loud honk. But I just hopped over the next curb, scootering until I heard someone shout, "What's the matter with you, kid? I could have killed you!" I turned to see Mr. Miller standing behind the open door of his Lincoln, and Teddy running past him, his legs and arms pumping like a steam engine. "Crissakes, Big Guy. You can't control one goddamn thing in your life, can you?" Mad at Teddy that I was, after Miller said that, I was wishing Teddy was the finger-flipping type himself.

When I reached the next four-corners, I didn't have any choice but to stop or get splattered. Sure enough, Teddy's hand grabbed me, parrot-clenching mad.

He was huffing, his face sweaty and red as the top of Pop's head. "I ought to tip you over my knee and spank you a good one, right here," he said.

"Go ahead and try!" I said, "I'd just kick you. Hard, too!" I knew Teddy wouldn't really spank me. Especially while we were standing on the street, him being respectable and all. Still, I felt a little hurt that he'd even think about doing it.

Teddy took a few gulps of air, but he didn't burp. He just steered me around, his hand gripping a wad of my shirt because I complained that his hand was hurting my shoulder. Even though it wasn't.

Ma was still napping on the couch when we got home, so I went into my room, shutting the door quietly, even though I wanted to slam it.

It took a while before I heard Teddy move away from my door, but finally he did. I was glad, too. I didn't want to talk to that cheater-face. All I wanted was a little *solitude*. And that made me wish I had a catwalk to sit and cry on like Brenda had.

Having nowhere else to find solitude, I crawled into my closet and sat down under the crooked hems of my dresses, closing the closet door behind me to almost shut.

There was the rumble-whooshing of water filling the tub, and Teddy's footsteps as he went here and there, probably scooping up dirty work clothes.

The tub was still running when Ma woke and called out, "Teddy? Teaspoon?"

Ma opened my bedroom door and called my name. I was halfway to standing, my mouth ready to call back to her, when I heard her yell to Teddy in the living room.

"Where's Teaspoon?" Ma asked.

"She's not in there?" Teddy asked.

"No."

Even in Teddy's footsteps, there was the sound of worry. So I sat back down, crossing my arms and thinking, *Good!*

Teddy came into my room. His footsteps stopped, then moved across my floor. Maybe checking the window. "She must have slipped out the front door when I was in the bathroom." He sighed. "Maybe it's just as well, Catty. I've been waiting for the chance to talk to you alone...when you're sober."

Ma made a huff sound.

"Why are you here, Catty?" Teddy asked.

"What kind of question is that?" Ma asked, her voice rising kite-high, a little laugh the tail of her sentence.

"It's a fair one," Teddy said. "One I think you have an obligation to answer. For my sake, and for Teaspoon's."

Suddenly I wished I *had* snuck out the front door.

"I came back to see my baby. Isn't that obvious?"

"After five long years, you suddenly had this overwhelming urge to see your daughter? You expect me to believe that?"

"Well, I wanted to see her plenty of times, but I couldn't just pick up on a dime and drive across the country."

"Interesting choice of words," Teddy said. Like they were playing Scrabble or something.

"What are you getting at, Teddy?"

"The truth. Why you're here. What you want. Did your supply of adoration run out, Catty? Or was it your supply of money?"

"I can't believe you're talking to me like this. What's wrong with you? You were so sweet once."

"Maybe I took your advice, Catty. Aren't you the one who was always telling me that I needed to grow some balls?"

"Stop it, Teddy. You're being cruel. I don't like you like this."

"*I'm* being cruel?" Teddy said, and this time he laughed. "You walk out on that kid—and me, for that matter—and stay gone for five long years, then you waltz back into our lives and you expect everything to be as it once was? You're leading her to believe you're here for good, Catty. She believes in you."

"Teddy...," Ma said, her voice choked with hurt. "You used to believe in me, too."

"No," Teddy said. "I used to love you. I never believed in you."

"Teddy...," Ma said, like she might cry.

"I wonder sometimes, Catty, how you can even look at yourself in the mirror. Maybe the stage makeup helps."

My insides started shaking, like there were sobs in there trying to get out. I made my hands into earmuffs, but I could still hear them.

"Why'd you send me money to help me get the rest of the way to California then, if you didn't believe in me?"

"For the same reason I sent it to you when you wrote and begged for it because you got kicked out of your apartment in Denver. And the same reason I sent another bundle to California after that so-called Hollywood director who was putting you up—you know, just as a friend—threw you out. I may not be the brightest guy, Catty, but I can read between the lines."

"Okay, okay. I may have made some mistakes with you, and with Teaspoon. But we've all made mistakes. Isn't that what you told me, Teddy? But no matter what mistakes I've made, you can't accuse me of not loving my baby girl. You know I love her."

"You love everybody, Catty. The drunk at the bar, the stranger on the street, your boyfriend, your daughter. You love them all. And you love them all equally. But that's not what I was talking about."

Ma started crying then. Big choking Brenda-puking sobs. I stood up, wanting Teddy, somebody, to hug her and make her tears stop. Instead Teddy just said, "And you're supposed to be an actress," like he'd never even seen her movie poster.

"Listen, Catty. Let's cut this drama. Level with me. How much do you want?"

"How dare you question my motives, you son of a bitch," Ma screamed. I heard the thump of something against a wall. Probably a shoe.

That's when I shoved the closet door open with both hands and yanked open my bedroom door. "Stop fighting!" I yelled. "Just stop it!"

Teddy's shoulders and head yanked back. "Teaspoon," he said. He sighed out his mad and fell back into his chair, his elbows pinned to his knees as he ran his hands through his still-sweaty hair. "I didn't know you were here. I'm so sorry."

I ignored Teddy and ran to Ma. "Tell him you're not leaving, Ma. Tell him you've found your dream and you came back to be his girlfriend and my ma. Please, Ma, tell him! Tell him you love us best!"

Ma put her hand on her waist, right above her butt. She rubbed her forehead where her bangs were sticking and she looked down at Teddy, her eyes shining hard like Mrs. Bloom's jewels. Then she took my hands and led me to the couch.

"Listen, sweetie," she said. I was crying already. "You remember how we talked about needing to chase our dreams?"

"Yeah, but you found yours," I reminded her. "You got a poster to prove it."

"Honey," she said, leaning her face close to mine. Her breath smelled like Dentyne. "Dreams aren't just a one-shot deal...or they shouldn't be. I wanted to be a piano bar singer, and I became one. I wanted to star in a movie, and I starred in two. But Teaspoon, what I've got under my belt is two low-budget B movies. What I want is to become another Greta Garbo. Grace Kelly. I'm twenty-seven years old, honey. I'm passing for twenty-two now, but I can't do that forever. And I can't stay in Mill Town forever, Teaspoon. Just until my agent finds me another, better part. You understand?"

I lowered my head so Ma wouldn't have to see my tears.

"Oh, honey. Don't cry. I love you with all I've got, but I've never been one to let mushrooms grow under my ass. You know that."

I threw my arms around her neck. "Don't leave me again, Ma. Please." I could feel tears dripping down my cheeks and wetting Ma's shirt beneath my chin.

Even with strands of Ma's hair covering my face like coppery netting hanging from a hat, I could see Teddy fall against the back of his chair, his arms dropping into his lap, his eyes going up like he was looking for something. Maybe a brown bulge in the ceiling. Or maybe Jesus.

Suddenly Ma's whole body perked, and she pulled me away

from her so we could see each other's faces. "You can go with me!" she said.

Teddy sat straight up, stiff as a pencil, then he groaned. "Oh, Catty, no..."

Ma stopped him. "No, what? Don't take my baby with me? Leave her behind and break her heart again? You're my ex-boyfriend, Teddy. Nothing more. And this isn't for you to decide. If Teaspoon wants to come with me, then she'll come with me."

"So you're asking her to make this decision?" Teddy said, blinking at Ma with you've-got-to-be-kidding eyes.

"Why not?" Ma said. "Teaspoon's old enough to decide who she wants to live with."

"Catty...no child should have to decide something like this."

"What? You afraid she'll choose me over you? Like you chose that frumpy, whatever-her-name-is over me?"

Ma's fingers worked like a comb to push the curls out of my eyes. "We can chase our dreams together," she said, her voice turning as excited as rock 'n' roll. "I can sign you up with my agent. You can do commercials...audition for parts. Where's Hollywood going to find a prettier, more talented little girl than my Teaspoon?"

"My God," Teddy said, standing up. "Catty, this is absurd."

"Absurd? Why? You don't think Teaspoon has the talent to make it in Hollywood?"

"You know that's not what I meant," Teddy said.

"Then what's absurd? Going after your dreams?" Ma snapped. "Well, I suppose to someone whose dream was to become an electrician—and you couldn't even make that one happen—it *would* seem absurd. But to folks like me and Teaspoon, who have bigger dreams—"

"This isn't about dreams, Catty!" Teddy was shouting now, and he didn't sound like Teddy at all. "It's about being a responsible, respectable parent. There's nothing wrong with you chasing your dreams, but to abandon a small child...walk away and not look back for five years…living out of your car half the time…you can't take a child off to that kind of life because of a sudden whim. Have you lost your mind?"

"A whim?" Ma gave me a quick glance, then turned back to Teddy. "Why do you think I came back here, Teddy, if not to ask my little girl if she wants to go with her mama? What possible reason do you think I had in coming?"

Teddy looked at me, sucked his bottom lip into his mouth, then he turned away.

Ma turned back to me, playing with one of my curls. "And Teaspoon understands there's sacrifices to be made when you're chasing your dream."

"Oh, you've taught her well about sacrifices, Catty. Me, too, for that matter. But this has to be about what is best for her," Teddy said.

Ma bent my head back so she could look straight into my eyes, then waited. Like she had just asked me which I wanted, a soda pop or a candy bar.

"Catty," Teddy said, his voice cracking. "Her gala is in five days. She's worked so hard for this. Don't do this to her now."

Ma put her hand over her balloons. "Oh, I wouldn't take her before her big debut. I've worked the stage, Teddy. I know that the show must go on."

The candy and chips I'd eaten at the tavern were swirling sick in my stomach. "I'll give it some thought," I said, tapping my heart. Because what else could I say?

"Okay," Ma said with a little pout. She kissed my cheek, then got up and slipped into Teddy's room to get her makeup case.

Teddy kept his hands in his pockets when he looked up at me. "Doesn't rehearsal start an extra hour early tonight?" he said. "If you don't feel up to going, I could go talk to Brenda."

"Teddy. I can't miss tonight. It's our last practice before dress rehearsal. And we haven't practiced in two days."

Teddy gave his head one nod, then stared at me, like he was deciding if he wanted to say more or not, while I watched him, freezing him in my eyes.

Teddy gave me a hug before I left, like he'd forgotten he was mad at me for flipping him off, embarrassing Miss Tuckle, and scootering in front of Mr. Miller's car. I wanted to forget my mad about him being a cheater and hug him, too, but instead I kept my arms tight to my side. It was his fault that we couldn't be Teaspoon and Teddy and Catty. And because of it, now I had to decide if I was going to say good-bye to the only ma I'd ever have, or, to him. And I didn't know if I was going to be able to do either.

CHAPTER TWENTY-SEVEN

Charlie was sitting Humpty-Dumpty when I got outside. I didn't know if he heard the fight or not, because even if he was trying to ear-spy, I'm not sure he would have had much success with their screen open and the television blaring another love story gone wrong. Either way, I didn't want to even think about what was just said, much less talk about it. I was too mixed up inside.

Across the street, Dumbo Doug's car was out front of the Jacksons' house, and the whole Jackson family was on the lawn, even Mr. Jackson. They were standing in a semicircle around Johnny, who had a big duffel bag sitting in the grass by his feet.

"I think he's going away," Charlie said when he saw me staring.

Jolene was wiping her eyes, and Jennifer went to lean up against Johnny's side, chewing on her braid. I turned away because I couldn't look, and got on my scooter. "See ya, Charlie," I said, not looking at him. And not looking when Johnny called my name.

I got about four blocks down, almost to the Starlight, when Dumbo Doug's car pulled up to the curb. "For crissakes, Johnny," I heard Doug say as his car stopped, the nose pointing in the same direction I was going in.

"Teaspoon, wait up!" Johnny called, as he jogged across the street.

I stopped my scooter, but I didn't look at him.

"I'm going down south with Doug to work on the crew Perkins set up there. I'll make bigger bucks, and, well, I just need to get away for a while. I couldn't leave without saying good-bye to my favorite girl, though. And telling you that I'm sorry I'll have to miss your show. You break a leg though, okay?"

I stared straight ahead and didn't say a word.

"You take good care of yourself. And enjoy your ma being back. When I write to my family, I'll stick a note in there for Jolene to give to you."

Fat chance of her doing that, I thought, but I didn't say it out loud.

Johnny picked me up, potato-sack-style, like always, and he gave me a shake. But it didn't shake the sad out of me. It only stirred it up more. "Take good care of your Big Sister, too, okay?" He set me down, gave my head a rub, then ran back to Dumbo Doug's car, leaning over and pressing the horn as they pulled away.

CHAPTER TWENTY-EIGHT

We were standing on stage, holding our blue feather fans, stubby, dumb versions of the Big Sisters' fans, which were exactly like Rosemary Clooney's and Vera-Ellen's. "Ours don't even have pleats in them so we can open and close them like the Big Sisters' can. What a gyp," I told Mindy.

"Girls, girls!" Jay shouted, his hands making short, fast claps. "How could you forget almost everything you learned in two days?"

And sure enough, it seemed like most had. At least the other Little Sisters. They kept flubbing up the lyrics, and stepping right when they should have stepped left. Jay turned so his back was to us. "Right! Left!" he said, holding up his hand to show them the difference, then doing the same with his legs. Not that it helped. When the number ended—even after the fourth time—some of the Little Sisters went right (even though only the Big Sisters were supposed to exit right), and some went left, so that our line parted like the Red Sea. "I told you we should exit with our Big Sisters, Jay," I said.

Jay ignored that, but he didn't ignore me. "And Pip Squeak," he said, right about the time I was harping at the girl next to me to follow me if she was too afflicted to know right from left. "You're singing like a dream, honey, but spark it up a bit, will you? Get some bounce back in your step. You're dead-center so all eyes will be on you. Smile. Perk. Got it?"

"Well, their eyes aren't on me now, Big Squeak," I said. Some of the Big Sisters, respectable as they were, giggled. Well, except for Brenda, who hadn't smiled once since rehearsal started, just like me. Jay didn't get after her, though, even if she was dead-center behind me. Probably because she was the half boss. Or maybe because he thought she was feeling sick, which is how she looked.

"You still puking lots?" I asked Brenda when I found her in the restroom line after Jay told us to "take five," and "visit the little girls' room" if we had to.

"Don't you worry about me, Teaspoon. I'm fine."

"You sure?" I asked, my eyes taking in the droopy waist of her dress.

"I'm sure. But I'm not sure about you. You look down today, Teaspoon. Is everything okay?" What could I say, with Little Sisters running all over the place, and everybody talking until you couldn't think straight. And me not wanting to talk about the choice I had to make anyway, because just saying it out loud would make it more real. So I kept my head down, just in case Teddy was right when he said that eyes are the windows to our souls, because I didn't want Brenda seeing my soul being darker blue than my eyes.

"You said on Saturday that you had something to show me. Did you bring it along?"

Brenda was talking about the movie poster. I shook my head.

"Teaspoon? You sure you didn't bring it? You're not just being politely quiet, are you? Because no matter how nervous I am, or how I feel, I still want you to share things with me."

"Okay," I said.

"Bring it tomorrow. I want to see what you were so excited about." Brenda forced her lips to stretch into a smile.

"Speaking of showing something…" Mrs. Bloom said, appearing out of nowhere and not even apologizing for butting in on our conversation. "Why didn't you tell me that the programs came in this week? My God, they're gorgeous."

Mrs. Bloom held a program up, and feeling frumpy or not, I got up on my tiptoes and peeked over her arm. "Let me see! Let me see!"

Mrs. Bloom bent down and showed me the glossy, greeting-card-fancy cover. I ran my finger over the moon at the top, then over *How High the Moon,* the letters bumping under my skin. "Wow, huh?" I said. "Does it list our act inside?"

"It sure does," Mrs. Bloom said as she opened it, pointing with a fingernail every bit as glossy as the paper. "Right there. Right before Les Paul and Mary Ford."

Brenda suddenly looked pukey. "Mother . . . we have to talk."

Mrs. Bloom shook her head. "No time for talking," she said.

"Mother, please. We have a major problem here."

Mrs. Bloom looked at Brenda, her head cocked, her lips stretched. "Then fix it," she said. She plucked the program out of my hand and went off to show it to Leonard's mother.

Even if having to decide who to live with was an appropriate topic for Sunshine Sisters to discuss—which it probably wasn't—I didn't want to talk about it. Brenda didn't really want to talk, either, so we drove in silence until she pulled up in front of my house. I was fumbling for the door handle in the dark when Brenda said, "Oh, wait. Your tickets. I got good ones for your family, too. Center seats, three rows in. I'm afraid the rest of your guests will have to sit a ways back, though."

Brenda might have been talking to me, but she was looking over at the Jacksons' like she was trying to see if Johnny was home—which of course he wasn't, even though his hot rod was in the driveway. She opened her purse and pulled out a flattened roll of blue tickets. Something fell out with it, crashing like a baby rattle to the floor.

I reached down and picked up a drugstore pill bottle. A full one. I held it and tried to be a quick peeker, but Brenda grabbed it from me and plopped it back in her purse. "Eighteen, right? For your family, the Frys, the Jacksons, Mr. Morgan, and two of your former teachers. And two more friends. Anybody else?"

"Brenda. That medicine. You said you weren't sick."

"I'm not," she said, her voice going happy-high. "Those are my mother's pills. For pain."

"Why do you got them, then?"

"I brought them along for her. I knew she'd be on her feet all day. Okay...eighteen tickets, right?"

"I only need seventeen now," I said.

Brenda's hand came over to rest on my arm. "Teaspoon...your mother...she's not gone, is she?"

"It's not my ma's ticket I don't need anymore," I said. "It's Johnny's."

"So he's decided he's not coming to the gala? Oh Teaspoon. I'll talk to him. I'll let him know how important this is to you."

"He was supposed to change our stage moons, too," I said.

"I'll talk to him. I promise."

"No you won't. Because he's not here. He went down south to work."

When Brenda didn't say anything by the time it seemed she should have, I looked over at her. She was staring out the window, her eyes so glittery they must have had tears in them. "Are you sure?" she asked slowly.

"Yes. He told me good-bye."

"When?"

"Right before rehearsal."

She propped her elbow on the window and rested her cheek against her hand. Her cheeks were skinnier now. Flat enough so that her dimple didn't hardly make a dent anymore when she wasn't smiling. And I couldn't tell if it was shadows from the street-light or what, but her eyes were dark as wet pavement underneath.

"Brenda?" I asked, trying hard not to cry. "You don't have some bad disease, do you? One of those that could make you the late Brenda Bloom?"

"Late?" Brenda said. She turned to me. "Of course I don't. Why would you ask such a thing?"

"Because you look sick. And you act sick, too. And you have medicine in your purse."

"It's just nerves, Teaspoon. That's all. I get like this. And, well, the gala is four days away and there's still so much to do."

"Whatever happened to our to-do list, anyway?"

"Don't you worry about that. Just concentrate on how this is your dream come true. And about how wonderful it is that your mother is here to watch your debut."

I changed my roll of tickets to my left hand so my right would be free to work the door handle, because all I wanted to do was crawl in my bed and pull the covers up over my head.

"Teaspoon?" Brenda said right after the door clicked open, but before I pushed it wide enough to get out.

"Yeah?"

"You're very special to me. I want you to know that."

"I do know that," I said.

"And I want you to always remember that your Big Sister loved you, just the way you were. Remember, too, that you don't ever need to change for anybody. Promise me you'll remember those things, okay?"

"Okay," I said. "I love you just the way you are, too, Brenda."

Teddy was sitting on his chair working a crossword puzzle when I got inside. He looked up and asked me if I was okay. I said no.

Teddy leaned over and set his puzzle down by his coffee cup. "You want to talk about it, Teaspoon?"

I shook my head, and I didn't tell him why not. And he didn't ask. But if I had told him, I would have told him that I didn't want to talk about nothing, because for tonight anyway, everything I was hearing sounded like a good-bye.

CHAPTER TWENTY-NINE

In the morning, Charlie was at the piano sitting on his hands like he'd once sat on his legs on the catwalk. I suppose he'd been told not to play until Ma and I woke up. Poor Charlie had missed a lot of daytime piano playing time since Ma pulled into town, because she slept late and took naps in the afternoons.

"What are you doing here so early?" I asked Charlie as I shuffled through on my way to the bathroom, an old shirt and high-water pants slung over my arm.

"Teddy took the day off, and Miss Tuckle took him and Grandma G someplace. That's why," he said.

"Where'd they go?"

"I dunno. They just waited for the mail, then they left. What time does your ma wake up?"

"Not anytime soon, Charlie," I said.

When I got out of the bathroom, I checked to make sure Ma was still sleeping, then I poured me and Charlie some orange juice. "Come on, Charlie," I said. We sat on his steps, which were bigger and better for sitting than mine. Two Humpty Dumpties with nothing better to do than drink juice.

"Charlie," I said. "Do you think I'd be good in commercials?"

The corner of Charlie's mouth bunched his cheek even more than usual. "What kind of commercials?" he asked.

"What difference does it make? Here, watch. I'll do the Crest commercial for you."

I set down my juice glass, then hurried around the corner of the house. "Are you watching, Charlie?" I called.

Charlie didn't answer, so I yelled the question again. Then there he was, standing at the corner of the house looking at me. "Okay. Now I am," he said.

I shoved Charlie back and told him to go wait on the steps, while I got into character. "Ready?" I called.

"Wait," he said, even though how long could it take him to walk a few steps and sit his butt back down?

When Charlie was ready, I made myself get happy inside, thinking that if I did, I'd look happy on the outside—since that's how I believed it worked. Then I ran into the yard shouting, "Daddy! Daddy! I only had one cavity!"

I didn't know quite what to do next. *Pretend* the old lady who was supposed to ask me how many cavities again asked again (probably because she was Mrs. Fry deaf), or *make myself* into the old lady?

I decided that if I did her part, too—since playing an old lady would be harder than playing a girl in a headband—it would show Charlie my acting skills at their finest. So I squatted down and looked over where the girl-me should be and asked the question. Then I got up fast, put on my wide-as-the-sky smile, lifted my pointy finger, and said to her, "One! Just one!"

I stopped because I didn't know the dad's lines, and waited for Charlie to give his review. He didn't, though. He just took the last gulp of his juice, then looked at the little shreds of ripped-up oranges clinging to the walls of his glass, like he was deciding if it was worth it to rub them out with his finger or not. "Charlie!" I said. "What do you think? Did I look just like the girl in the commercial?" I asked hopefully, because I knew that if I pulled it off, then that would mean I really *was* ready for Hollywood, in case I went with Ma.

"Well," Charlie said, poking his finger into his glass. "Not really. She has longer hair than you..."

I rolled my eyes. "You're a hopeless case, Charlie Fry," I said. "A hopeless case."

I sat back down, my baby-bottom-smooth elbows resting on my knees, looking down at my patent leathers, which were a far cry from baby-butt-smooth.

"You sad because school's starting soon, too, Teaspoon?"

"I haven't had time to give school a thought, Charlie. I got too much on my mind. But when I do, yeah, I'll be sad about that, too."

We were still sitting when Miss Tuckle's car pulled up to the curb, right behind Ma's Hudson. Teddy, being the gentleman he was, was driving, and he got out of the car and opened the door for Miss Tuckle and Mrs. Fry. Teddy had a store bag, but nobody else had anything. Well, except Mrs. Fry, who was carrying her big purse over her arm, and a thick white envelope in her hand. The kind of envelope that has something inside that needs to be kept in a safe place.

I watched the three of them coming up the walk. Acting all proud of themselves, and staring at Charlie—which was all right by me.

"Where were you guys?" I asked when we stood up so they could get up the steps.

"Just helping Mrs. Fry take care of some business," Miss Tuckle said.

"I didn't ask you," I said.

As soon as those words got out of my mouth, I knew what was coming. I owed Miss Tuckle one apology already—or so Teddy would think—for calling her a sinner and giving the red-haired lady at the drugstore some gossip. And although Teddy hadn't said a word about it since—probably because he was afraid that if he played the bad guy, I'd decide to ride off into the sunset with Ma—I knew that being a smart-mouth two days in a row was pushing it.

But Teddy didn't say a word. Not after Miss Tuckle gave him a forgive-her-for-she-knows-not-what-she-does half smile, which only riled up my afflictions more. All three of them just walked into the house, and Charlie and I moved back closer together.

After some time, I said, "If Teddy, Miss Tuckle, and your great-grandma hadn't come home, at least we could have watched a little TV."

"Yeah," Charlie said. "Or if your ma wasn't sleeping, we could go play *Live at the Starlight.*"

"You know how to play Scrabble, Charlie?"

"No," he said. "But if you really want to play, maybe you could teach me."

"Never mind, Charlie." I didn't bother to explain that I wasn't asking because *I* wanted to play Scrabble with him. I was asking because I wanted to know if Teddy would have someone to play with if I left with Ma.

I sighed. "Stinks, don't it, Charlie, when you can't figure out where you want to be?" Charlie nodded.

CHAPTER THIRTY

I don't know how long it was before Teddy came outside all chipper, like nothing happened in the last two days. "I have an idea," he said. "Teaspoon, you have some gala tickets to hand out, don't you?"

"Yeah," I said.

"Well, Miss Tuckle just offered us the use of her car. How about if the three of us go deliver those now?"

"Most of them are going to the Jacksons," I said. "And we don't have to drive there."

"Yes, but weren't you going to give one to Mr. Morgan and Miss Simon and Mrs. Carlton?"

"I can give Mr. Morgan his ticket at dress rehearsal tonight—not that he needs one. He's the usher so he'll be there anyway. But I asked Brenda if he could sit in a seat and watch during our 'Sisters' performance if he had a ticket, and she said yes. As for Mrs. Carlton and Miss Simon, I don't even know where they live."

"Well, with school starting next week, the teachers are likely to be at the school. I think they always go in a week or two early for meetings and to set up the classrooms."

"Charlie and me could walk there," I said, still feeling grouchy.

"But it would be nice for us to drive there, wouldn't it? Sort of like a pre-celebration."

"A pre-celebration?"

"Yes," Teddy said. "Important events call for preparation. That's what makes them feel special when they finally arrive. Like when you put up your tree before Christmas, and bake cookies. This is a big event for you, Teaspoon. One that should feel as big as Christmas, with nothing to think about but the happy day that's coming. So I think it calls for a little getting-ready-for-the-big-event care, don't you?" When I didn't answer right away, Teddy said softly, "I want to make this time extra-special for you, okay? I'm so very proud of you."

My throat got tight so I went inside to put my sweater away, and to put my hair back in barrettes. It seemed to me Ma should be a part of my pre-celebration, too, but she was sound asleep, her arm flung over her eyes.

Charlie got all nervous walking into the school, even if it was as empty as a church on weekdays. Teddy put his hand on his shoulder and gave him a smile.

We found Miss Simon and Mrs. Carlton in the same classroom and they both looked up, surprised to see us there. "To what do we owe the honor of this visit?" Mrs. Carlton asked.

I held out the two tickets. "Mrs. Carlton. Miss Simon. I'd be honored if you'd attend my debut performance at the Starlight Theater. Saturday, September third, at...well, the time and everything is right there on the ticket. Come early if you want refreshments, because they're serving punch and pinwheel sandwiches and a big sheet cake."

I knew I sounded real respectable, even if I had to *improvise* a little toward the end because I forgot some of the speech I'd rehearsed in the car—which is what Jay said you call it when you rehearse well, but then something goes haywire and you have to make things work anyway—and my old teachers must have thought I sounded respectable, too, because they told me how proud they were of me and that they were honored and "touched" that I thought to personally invite them. Miss Simon even brought up my interview in the *Mill Town Monitor*. She was so proud of me that I didn't want to tell her what I'd really said, in case that wasn't as respectable. "And did you notice, Mrs. Carlton, that I didn't say even one *ain't* or *gonna* in the interview, or here? I think that affliction is cured for the most part."

She had noticed, and so had Miss Simon. They told me that they'd see me on the third. "And," Miss Simon added, "Charlie, I'll see you in my classroom next week."

"Oh wow, he's going to be in your room this year?" I asked. She nodded. "Wow, Charlie. You're one lucky duck. Miss Simon is real nice. Nothing like that Mr. Garrison, who thumps the top of your head with his ruler if you're not listening."

We said our good-byes and were halfway home before it dawned on me that I'd forgotten to tell Mrs. Carlton that I had feminine influence again.

CHAPTER THIRTY-ONE

I don't know exactly what happened, but after we handed out those tickets, it was like everything turned as upside down as a pineapple cake. With the sad, mixed-up feelings I was having over knowing I had to pick who I wanted to live with getting flipped to the bottom, and the fun, good-as-candy gala stuff sitting on top.

That night at our dress rehearsal, Brenda was happier than I'd seen her in weeks. Laughing at this and that, chitchatting with Tina and the rest of her friends. And popping my cheek with a kiss every time she passed by.

We were in our dressing room (really the big warehouse room, because the real dressing rooms were going to be used by the big acts), changing into our fancy *White Christmas* dresses, when Mrs. Bloom came in to ask Brenda, "Who's doing the stage makeup? Where are they?"

We were going to wear makeup on stage? Hot dog!

Brenda blinked at her ma, like she didn't know, either, so I piped up, "Two ladies who do the best makeup in town, that's who! But they couldn't be here tonight. Which is just as well, Mrs. Bloom, because I happen to know firsthand that when you put makeup on a kid, they get it all over their clothes." She thought about it a second, then said, "I suppose," and hurried off to harp at somebody else about something else.

"Don't worry about the makeup ladies," I told Brenda. "I wasn't being a fibber-face when I told your Ma that. I didn't ask them yet, because I didn't know I should. But they'll do it. You can bet on it."

Brenda helped me dress like a Big Sister was supposed to. We stood in front of the big mirror that covered most of one wall, me in my undershirt and big mesh slip, socks bunched around my ankles, and arms up and ready. Brenda was already dressed, and looking prettier than Rosemary Clooney and Vera-Ellen put together. She tossed my blue dress above my head and it floated down over me like a parachute, then tied my bow in the back and fixed my barrette that had been knocked cockamamie.

Boy, that tulle and lace was scratchy as dry elbows, but still, our dresses sure were pretty. "Where's my fan?" I asked Brenda, and she pointed to where Mrs. Gaylor was digging in a big box while Big and Little Sisters waited in a line every bit as crooked as a Mrs. Fry hem.

The second I had my fan, I ran back to the mirror. Wow, I sure did look professional when I waved my fan, little as it was. I held it up in front of my face, then lowered it. Stage-smiling as I broke into the first verse of "Sisters," my head and feet moving just how they were supposed to on each note, which was a good thing since I *was* going to be dead-center.

"You're so dumb, Teaspoon," Rebecca said, giving me a shove. "And your shoes are scuffed. You'd better clean them up before the program."

"It's a gala, stupid. Not a *program*."

But just like Mrs. Bloom's harping didn't knock Brenda's good mood out of her, I didn't let Rebecca shove me out of mine, either. This was another of my pre-celebrations and I was having the time of my life, like Teddy said I should—scuffed patent leathers and a decision that made my whole body hurt just to think about it or not.

For the next two hours, we sat in the front row and watched the show until it was our time to perform. Boy, that Beulah and Morris Farthing really *did* look like Fred and Ginger as they twirled and fancy-stepped to "Cherry Pink and Apple Blossom White," played by the Mill Town City Orchestra. Even Mrs. Derby wasn't all that bad, though I still thought she should sing "There's No Business Like Show Business" with that Ethelly voice of hers.

I could hardly believe my eyes when it was our turn and almost every Little Sister got their right and left straight. Even Jay was happy with us, calling out "Brilliant!" and "Bravo!"

I was so excited that I chattered all the way through taking off my gala dress, and I didn't stop once all the way home. Brenda didn't say much—not that I gave her a chance—she just drove, wearing the kind of smile you usually wear when you're doing nothing but sitting in the sun, listening to some good tunes.

"You're feeling better, aren't you, Brenda?" I asked. "Is that because it's almost over?"

"Yes," she said, her voice slow and dreamy as she glanced out the front window and up, like I'd just asked her if she could see Jesus in the clouds.

When I got inside, Teddy and Charlie were sitting at the table, a chocolate cake in the middle and four glasses bubbling with just-poured Orange Crush beside four plates. Then Ma came out of the bathroom, and man, if *that* wasn't a shocker! "Ma," I said. "I thought you'd be at The Dusty Rose by now, so I didn't even look for your car when I got home. I thought that was the reason you didn't want to go to dress rehearsal with me tonight."

"Teaspoon," Ma said, with a not-mad scolding voice. "I told you I didn't want to go because I want to wait and see the real thing."

Teddy pulled out a chair for me, like I was some kind of princess or something. Then Ma held up her glass and told the rest of us to do the same. They gave me three *hip, hip, hoorays.*

While we waited for Charlie to have seconds, Teddy disappeared into his room and came back with the bag I'd seen him with the day before. "What do you have there, Teddy?" I asked, grabbing the top of the bag and giving it a tug so I could see what was inside. "Clothes?"

"Just a little something so we all look respectable on your big night," Teddy said.

He pulled out a fine new shirt for Charlie. A dark blue one that fit around his tubby middle, but wasn't long like a dress. He'd bought a pair of light brown trousers, too, but we didn't get to see those right then because Mrs. Fry was busy hemming them—which meant that Charlie might be wearing light brown pedal pushers to the gala. Charlie sure was proud when Ma held the shirt up against him and said that he looked as handsome as Humphrey Bogart in navy.

"What did you get me?" I asked, clapping my hands.

"Well," Teddy said. "You have your outfit, so, well, here…" Teddy pulled out a pair of white anklets trimmed with blue lace.

"Holy cow, Teddy. How'd you know about lacy anklets?"

"Well, I had a little help picking them out," Teddy said, and I turned to Ma and smiled.

I thought that was it, but no. Teddy took out a little black box with FILLERS FINE JEWELRY stamped in gold letters on the lid, and handed it to me.

I was still staring at the box when Ma squealed, "Hurry, open it up so we can see!"

I pulled off the lid, and inside there was a short silver chain curled up on a bed of cotton. Ma plucked it from the box. "Oh, it's a charm bracelet," she said. "They're all the rage, Teaspoon." She held it up to show me the little silver star dangling from it.

"A star for my little star," Teddy said. "Look on the back."

I flipped the star around while Ma held it, and there it was—September 3, 1955—the date of my debut! "Every big event you have, we'll get you another charm to mark the special day," Teddy said, while I laughed and blinked tears and Ma told me to keep my arm still so she could clasp it to my wrist.

I flipped my wrist this way and that, watching the little star flip and glow. Then I wrapped my arm around Teddy's neck, holding my arm out so I could still see my bracelet, and gave him a one-armed squeeze.

Teddy even had something in that bag for Ma to wear to the gala. A nice pair of clip-on earrings that she liked so much she gave him a kiss. I glanced at Charlie when she did this, and I could tell that he was thinking the same thing as me. Only somebody in love would buy fancy clip-on earrings. And only someone in love would kiss them for doing it, too. I decided, right then and there, that maybe that big spat they had the other night was just that. Nothing but a spat. After all, Teddy and me had those all the time, but we still loved each other. I probably didn't even have to decide now!

After that kiss, Teddy disappeared into his bedroom and came back with a man's dark blue suit hanging in a plastic bag. "And this is so I can go to your gala in style, too." he said. "I was due for a new one after fifteen years, don't you think?"

"Wow, Teddy!" I said. "What did you do, rob Mrs. Bloom's safe?" Everybody laughed. Well, except Charlie, who apparently didn't know I was kidding.

When our little party was over, Charlie headed home with a piece of cake for Mrs. Fry and an extra for him for later. Ma headed to The Dusty Rose, but not before telling Teddy thank you all over again, and Teddy looking her right in the face with frosting-soft eyes and saying, "Thank *you*," though I don't know why since Ma didn't get him anything.

"Teddy, can you help me get my bracelet off now?" I asked. "I want it saved pristine for the gala." It took Teddy a while to undo the little clasp, but when he did, I put the bracelet back in its box and put the box on my dresser right next to Ma's movie poster.

Both Taxi Stand Ladies were on the corner when I pulled up on my scooter, and they laughed like crazy when I asked them to be our makeup ladies. "You can't be serious, Teaspoon," The Kenosha Kid said.

"Course I am. Brenda said that stage makeup has to be thick and bright so we won't look like ghosts on the stage. There isn't a lady in town who knows how to put on makeup like that, except you two. I swear, even on the sunniest days, I can be down a whole block and see your makeup like I was standing right beside you."

"Did you…um…tell Mrs. Bloom that you were asking us?" The Kenosha Kid asked.

"No. She didn't ask."

They exchanged giggles. "Is Miller's kid a Little Sister?" Walking Doll asked.

"No. Even though she's afflicted enough to be. But she's coming to the show with her family. She said it was only to see Les Paul and Mary Ford, but I think she wishes she were a little sister."

"We'll do it," Walking Doll said, and The Kenosha Kid gave her one of those suspicioned looks.

When I got home, Teddy had the house all spiffy-clean and he was in the bathroom washing out a few things. I poured myself a glass of water, clear up to the rim because I was that thirsty, and a plop of it landed on the toe of my shoe. Thinking that water might ruin the shine, I wiped it off with the dishrag and sighed, because under that wet there wasn't nothing but black scuffs. "Hey Teddy? You know how to get black marks off patent leather?"

"No, Teaspoon. Maybe your ma does. You can ask her in the morning."

Didn't that just figure. Give Teddy a cow-bloody pair of pants and he knew how to get them clean enough to wear to church. But give him a pair of scuffed patent leathers, and he was worthless. I set down my butter knife and went to my room to dig through the empty coffee can I kept my old school crayons in.

I suppose I should have figured that a white crayon couldn't get out black scuffs, considering that the white crayon itself was full of them, but I had to try something. It didn't work. So I went back into the kitchen to get an S.O.S pad from under the sink. I figured if it could clean brown sausage crud out from a pan, then for sure it could get a few black marks off patent leather.

I scrubbed until my shoes were bubbled with blue soap, but when I wiped them with the corner of yesterday's dirty shirt, I found that it hadn't taken off the scuffs at all. It sure had taken off the shine, though.

Near tears, I went into Teddy's room where Ma's stuff was strung all over, messy as my room, and started digging around, hoping I'd find something in a tube or a can that would take scuffs off shoes as easy as Jergens took scales off elbows.

I didn't find any cleaner, but I did find a bottle of silver nail polish in Ma's little makeup case. *Perfect!*

The nail polish didn't hide the black scuffs, but it did give them a nice glow after I dabbed it on thick enough. I paired them up on the little table by my window where the sun was shining so I could see what they'd look like under stage lights. So maybe my shoes would have a few little dents and dings on the toes, but it wasn't like anybody even five rows back, much less in the nosebleed seats, would see that. What they'd see would be my shoes sparkling silver like a moon.

CHAPTER THIRTY-TWO

When gala eve came, I was spinning like a top, and made Charlie play "Sisters" so many times that he got grumpy. "You said it was the last time, three times ago," he whined.

"So what!" I screamed. "Do it one more time. Do it, Charlie!"

Teddy came into the living room then and thanked Charlie for his patience, and told him to go home and get a good night's rest. Then Teddy took me aside and sat me down on the couch—even if I wanted to sit on the Starlight seats instead—and he said we were just going to sit quietly for a while.

"You're just overexcited, Teaspoon," he said. "It happens."

"But Teddy," I said. "I just wanted to do the song one more time so I know I won't forget the words or the steps. I might, you know, and I'm dead-center."

"You won't forget," Teddy said. "You know that song and those steps like the back of your hand. Why, I think you could even do them in your sleep." He rubbed the top of my arm with his thumb. "Just breathe, like a slow song," Teddy said. And I started humming one, just to remind myself how slow a slow song is.

"Teddy?" I said, when my legs finally stopped jumping and hung still over the seat of the couch.

"Yes?"

"The day after tomorrow, do I still have to say if I'm staying here or going with Ma, even if you two are done being mad?"

I could feel Teddy get stiff. "Don't think of that now. Just think of how everything is going to go just fine tomorrow night. One thing at a time, Teaspoon."

"But Teddy…"

"Shhhhhhh," he said.

I must have fallen asleep on the couch, and he must have carried me into my room, because when I woke up, I'd been sleeping in my clothes. I got out of bed and went to my dresser, tipping the clock toward the window so the streetlight could help me see the time. It was three o'clock. Too early to wake up, yet I wasn't tired anymore.

I went to the window and pressed my cheek to the glass so I could see if Ma's car was in front of our house. I could see a brown fender, so I knew she was home. At the Jacksons' house, every window was black, and I wondered if Johnny would come home by the time I turned sixteen in case I still wanted him to be my boyfriend. Then I looked straight ahead, at the Frys' bay window. I got the daylights scared out of me because there he was, Charlie Fry, looking like a ghost as a passing car's lights lit his face.

It wasn't like Charlie to be up in the middle of the night, so as soon as I got my breath back, I pointed toward our front yards, even though I knew it was a long shot that Charlie would figure out that that meant "meet me there." Then I ditched out of my room on bare feet.

Poochie's head was flopped out of his doghouse, and it lifted when I closed our door, even if I barely shut it. His eyes glowed like the devil's as he watched me go down the back steps. "Don't you even dare," I whispered, hoping Teddy was right when he said that dogs can hear lots better than people. Maybe they could, because Poochie put his head back down as I zipped between our houses.

I went right to the bay window, the ground so cold I had to keep my feet dancing, and I looked up for Charlie.

"I'm right here," Charlie said. He was standing in the grass, wearing pajamas that looked Mrs.-Fry-old, rolled at the ankles.

"Geez, Charlie. You're going to give me a heart attack yet."

"Well, you pointed for me to come out," he reminded me.

"You're sharpening up, Charlie."

Charlie's front steps were colder than the ground. "Grandma G said you get piles if you sit on cold cement," he said.

"What's piles?"

"That's what I was asking you," Charlie said.

I told him I didn't know, and that I had other things on my mind.

"Charlie," I said. "My ma isn't staying in Mill Town."

"I already know that," Charlie said.

I cocked my head to look at him. "You do?"

"Yeah. I heard Grandma G and Miss Tuckle talking about it."

"They talked about it in front of you?"

"No. I was in the bathtub. Miss Tuckle must have asked where I was, because Grandma G said, 'Oh, he won't hear us. You can't hear a thing from in there.'

"And Grandma G said, 'Can you believe it, April? That she'd make that poor child decide?' She said Teddy was *livered*, and that she didn't know what he'd do if you got caught up in all the promises your ma was making. Then Grandma G said that Teddy's scared she'll take you, then drop you off God knows where when she gets tired of dragging a kid along."

"She wouldn't do that!" I said.

Charlie shrugged. "She dropped you off here, didn't she?"

Something dropped in my stomach when Charlie said that. Something as big and hard as a scooter.

We sat there, me not saying anything. Just shivering. Then Charlie said, "Miss Tuckle told Grandma G not to worry, though, because she was going to help Teddy see that that didn't happen. Then they just talked about your leaned porch and stuff, so I started washing so I could get out of the tub. I was already wrinkled."

Charlie and I sat awhile longer, quietly, me staring at nothing, just thinking.

"Charlie?"

"Yeah?"

If your ma wasn't dead, and your dad wasn't in the clink, and you had to choose which one to live with because you could only live with one, who would you choose?"

"You," he said, stopping me right in my tracks.

I blinked because my eyes were watering, then I said, "You're a good friend, Charlie Fry," and I gave him a hug.

Charlie went back inside because he was yawning big enough to swallow his head, but I wasn't ready, even if I was shivering. I looked over at the Jacksons' house, which was dark and quiet for a change, and I thought of Johnny leaving, and Ma, when she left, and the folks back in Peoria...I thought of how most people leave, even when you love them and want them to stay. And as I headed back to my house, I thought about how if I went with Ma, I was going to be leaving Teddy thinking the same thing.

I went inside through the back door, standing still in the kitchen. I looked over at the metal table next to the pantry where Teddy and my last Scrabble board sat. We'd started that game so many days ago I couldn't remember whose turn it would be next. I flipped my letters around and plucked three *U*'s off my windowsill thing and exchanged them for letters worth something. Then I took *gluck* off the board and spelled something else, my fingers wide awake, even if the rest of me felt like it was sleeping.

CHAPTER THIRTY-THREE

I slept so late that even Ma was awake, having a cigarette and coffee at the kitchen table, squinting because the sun was spilling bright over the tablecloth. Teddy was leaning over her shoulder saying something, but he stopped talking when I came into the room. I glanced up at the clock, scared for a minute that I was late.

"You have plenty of time. It's not even noon yet," Teddy said, giving me one of those let's-stay-calm smiles.

"But I'm going early. At three o'clock—Brenda said I could. Even if I'm not working today, I know she'll need my help. The doors open at six for the refreshments, then the show starts at seven."

"Just sit down and relax, Teaspoon," Teddy said, even though he wasn't sitting. Ma was, but she went from sitting to standing, puffing smoke rings that blew apart before they hardly left her lips, and chewing on her fingernails like *she* had a gala coming up.

Teddy made me eat some eggs and toast, even if I didn't want any. Then Ma made me a bubble bath and told me to soak in it. I could hear her in the kitchen while I soaked. I suppose it was like what I heard Mrs. Jackson say before one of our Christmas programs when Jolene had to read part of the Nativity story—having your kid on stage was harder on the moms than the kids.

Ma did my hair so that my curls were tight and pretty, not bunched and frazzled, and she put my white barrettes in so folks could see my eyes. She helped me pick out my nicest dress, too, even though I told her it didn't matter because I had my dress for the show, because she said I had to look nice when I got there, too.

"What did you do to your shoes?" she asked me while clasping my charm bracelet, right before I headed out the door.

"Fixed them up so the scuffs wouldn't show so much," I said.

Ma was about to say something—probably compliment me for making them so stage-sparkly—but Teddy jumped in and said I'd better hurry along.

I was on the porch when the door opened and Ma called, "Wait!" I stopped and she opened the screen. She didn't say anything, and she didn't step all the way outside. She just stared at me, her lips doing that quivering thing lips do when you're trying not to cry. "What is it, Ma?" I asked.

Teddy came up behind her, and Ma shook her head. "I just wanted to take another look at you before you headed off for your big debut. That's all."

"Okay, but I don't want to be late, so could you look quick?" I spun in a circle, even if I was wearing an old dress, so she could see all of me.

Ma was smiling and crying when I got done with my spin. "Do you know how proud I am of you?" she asked. "Teddy's done a fine job raising you these past years. You're . . ." She stopped and took a deep breath.

"Respectable?" I asked hopefully, when Ma couldn't seem to find the words she was looking for.

Ma laughed, tears glossing her eyelashes. "Yes," she said.

I grinned. "Good. Because I've been working hard on that one," I said, then I jumped down the steps and grabbed my scooter.

The Starlight was beehive-busy when I got there. Helpers and people I'd never seen before were running from one side of the theater to the other, and everybody was shouting to each other. I spotted

Mrs. Bloom. She was standing back by the concession stands with two men in white jackets, yelling at the delivery guy who was carrying two big pots of flowers into the theater. "No, no. All flowers are to be left in the foyer!"

I figured wherever Mrs. Bloom was bellyaching, Brenda couldn't be far off, so I headed toward her. When Mrs. Bloom saw me, she called me to her. "Hurry," she snapped, even though I was whizzing up the aisle fast enough to win a race at the end-of-the-school-year picnic. "Show these gentlemen to the conference room," she said, nodding to the guys in white jackets when I got closer. "Bring down as many tables as you'll need," she told them.

I led the way, but when we got to the nosebleed seats, and I was sure Mrs. Bloom wouldn't hear me, I turned around. I looked at their white jackets. "You guys aren't doctors, are you?"

"No," one of them said. "Caterers."

"Good," I said. "Or Charlie would have had a cow."

While the guys folded table legs and argued about how many they could carry down at once, I went to the projector room windows to look out, thinking it would be easier to spot Brenda from up high. And I was right. She was on the stage talking to Jay, who was all gussied up like he was an usher or something.

I zipped out of there fast, knowing that if I got behind the guys as they lugged tables down, I'd have to find her all over again.

When I got to the stage, she was trying to make Jay's bow tie stay in place because it seemed to want to spin like a pinwheel.

I don't know what kind of mood Brenda was in, but it was a strange one. One I'd never seen before, and couldn't have described to Charlie if I'd tried. "Hi, Brenda," I said, as I stepped onto the stage, which was gleaming like it had been saved pristine for tonight. "I came a little early to give you a hand. I know I'm off the clock—I'm just being a nice Little Sister. I already helped your ma some."

"Then you can help by holding this," she said, handing me her purse, then twisting Jay's bow tie one last time. When she finished, she looked out on the theater, above the heads of the people hurrying like ants. "At this point, Teaspoon, there's nothing left to be done." She started walking away, moving floaty like that white dandelion fluff when you blow it.

I followed her. "There must be something we should be doing, by the looks of things," I said. "It's a real mess here."

Brenda kept walking. "Hey, Brenda," I said, looking up at the new curtain that was rolled far above my head. "Did Johnny bring the moons before he left?" Just saying his name made me miss him all over again.

Brenda turned. "Mel dropped them off," she said.

"Is he going to run the pulley to change them between acts, then?" I asked.

"Maybe. Or someone else will."

Suddenly Brenda stopped, looking down at herself. "My purse," she said.

"Here." I handed it back to her and Brenda opened it quick, swishing her hand around inside, like maybe she was afraid she'd lost her wallet. But it wasn't her wallet she pulled out and squeezed in her hand as she sighed with relief. It was that bottle of medicine for pain. She tucked it back in her purse. "I should lock this in the safe so I don't have to keep track of it," she said.

Some Little Sisters had showed up by the time we locked Brenda's purse away. A few started running up and down the aisles, and some were hovering around the tables in the back where the guys in the white jackets were shaking out tablecloths and setting out silver platters.

"Brenda!" Mrs. Bloom shouted from over near the dome lights. She had Anne Huxley and Melissa Jakes by the arms. "We can't have the Little Sisters running all over getting in the way. Why are they here before their Big Sisters anyway? They were supposed to come together." Mrs. Bloom blew out some mad, then took a big breath. "Herd them up and take them in the back. Start dressing them at five. Is makeup here yet?"

I figured Mrs. Bloom meant the ladies who were doing makeup, not the makeup itself, since she'd brought a big box of the stuff to the Starlight in the first place, so I piped up, "They're coming at five."

Mrs. Bloom handed Brenda Anne and Melissa's wrists and said, "I've given Uriah orders to see that the volunteers delegated to assist our main acts are in place by five, too. Check and make sure they're outside the dressing room doors then, Brenda, since you'll be down that way. I'm going home to have my hair done and to dress. I'll trust you to keep things in control here."

"See my new bracelet, Brenda?" I said as we headed down the hall, five Little Sisters skipping behind us, chattering about how scared they were. "It's a charm one." I twirled the chain around so she could see the engraved star. "Teddy said it's so I can remember every big singing event I have in my career."

Brenda stopped, her eyebrows bunching like Teddy's did when he got worried. She told the other Little Sisters to go inside the dressing room and not touch anything, then she took both my hands in hers and squatted down beside me. "Teaspoon," she said. "When you look back on this night, remember the good things, okay? That you were a star on the stage of the Starlight Theater, and that you shined. Remember it as a happy day, okay? For you, for Teddy, your Ma, Charlie..."

"And you, too?"

Brenda's eyes got watery, but she was smiling as she squeezed my hands, giving them a little shake each time she said *Yes. Yes.* "You remember that it was a very good night for me, too."

The Little Sisters—me included—ran around the dressing room even if we weren't supposed to. At least until Miss Gaylor stepped in the room and told us to knock it off in so many words. When the Big Sisters got there, Brenda handed them each an identical little blue box with a thank-you card taped to the bottom, while Mindy hopped beside me because she'd seen Mimi Hines in the hallway. Tina's and Julie's gifts came in a striped box, and after they opened them, they gave Brenda a hug. "It was so nice of you to write us such sweet notes and give us such extravagant gifts," Tina said, waving the little gift card, a thin gold chain dangling from her hand.

"It's just a little something to say thank you for being Big Sisters," Brenda said. "And for tolerating me the past couple of months. Mother bought the same necklaces for all the Big Sisters, but I wanted to give my best friends something special."

"Oh, Brenda. Thank you," Tina said as she dangled a necklace—a necklace with a sapphire stone that I'd seen on Brenda before—in front of her face like she was trying to hypnotize herself. And Julie, who was holding jewelry that I'd seen on Brenda, too, agreed. "It's okay, Brenda. We know you've had your plate full with the gala. Maybe after today, things can get back to normal again and we'll see more of each other."

When the girls scurried off, I said to Brenda. "Did you bring me a special present from home, too?"

Brenda put her hand on the side of my face. "I thought of it, Teaspoon. And I looked. But you know what? I have nothing of any real worth to give you. You already have the most valuable thing a person could have. You have hope."

"Maybe so," I said, "but I kind of like that necklace you have on."

"I can't believe I saw her," Mindy said the second Brenda was called away, still hopping and looking at me like I'd been listening to her the whole time.

"Who?" I asked.

"Mimi Hines!"

"Did you talk to her?" I asked.

"No. I was too scared."

I looked at the clock above Mindy's head and saw that it would be five o'clock in ten minutes. I grabbed Mindy's arm. "Come on, Mindy. I need to go meet the ladies who are doing our makeup, because they won't know where to go. We'll knock on Miss Hines's door so you can say hi to her." I told her I would talk first.

"Right there. That's where I saw her," Mindy said, pointing to the door with the MIMI HINES nameplate on it. The person assigned to being Mimi's helper wasn't at the door, so I knocked.

"Teaspoon!" Mindy's giggle was filled with scared.

Mimi herself answered the door dressed in a dark green robe— which reminded me that I'd have to get a nice robe when I got famous. Her head was piled high with brown curls, and a long fat one hung down over her shoulder. She looked real pretty. "Miss Hines," I said. "This here is Mindy Brewer. She's a big fan of yours. Maybe you could give her your autograph...or a necklace, or something." I shoved Mindy into her, then took off.

The Starlight had calmed down some by the time I got out to the main lobby, and everybody in it was dressed fancy as movie stars. Especially Mrs. Bloom.

She was over by the doors, right where I was headed, wearing a long black dress with a big brooch tucked between her balloons. She had a mink stole wrapped around her shoulders and folded inside her elbows. A fancy hat sat on top of her French twist. Some women I didn't know were standing near her, fussing.

"Oh, where did you get such lovely opera pumps, Gloria?" one of the ladies asked.

Mrs. Bloom stretched her leg and set the tip of her pointy shoe on the carpet so the ladies could see it under her full skirt. "They're from France. Gunmetal-gray. I didn't know what I'd think of this color, but I do rather love it."

"Yes, very smart," a lady in a fur wrapped around her shoulders said, and Mrs. Bloom replied with, "Why thank you, Helen, and your stole is breathtaking." Helen moved her shoulders side-to-side as she thanked her, making the fur on her stole ripple so that it looked as real as Poochie stirring from a nap. "I'm surprised to see so many women in Borgana and rhinestones," Helen said, "but I suppose…"

The women nodded and hushed.

I was leaned up against the door, my hands on the glass, popping it open now and then to peer down the street, when I heard Mrs. Bloom say, "Excuse me." Just like that, she was behind me. "Isabella, get your hands off the glass. You're making prints. And what are you doing out here in the first place? You should be dressing."

"I know. But I'm waiting for the ladies who are going to do our makeup. They won't know where to go."

I didn't see Mr. Morgan, but Mrs. Bloom did. "Uriah, come here," she snapped. Then she told him to wait for "the makeup girls" and to show them back. "And you go get dressed," she told me. Then she hurried off to trade compliments with more of her friends, I suppose.

"Who am I waitin' for, Teaspoon?" Mr. Morgan asked.

"The Taxi Stand Ladies. You know. Those two ladies who hang around across from The Pop Shop, where you stand if you need a lift in Ralph's taxi. The fancy ones. They're doing our makeup."

Mr. Morgan's eyes got huge. "Mrs. Bloom hired *those two*?"

"Nope," I said. "I did. I chose good, didn't I?"

Mr. Morgan nodded his head slowly, his mouth grinning wide. "Oh, yeahhhhh," he said.

I thanked Mr. Morgan and was ready to run off when the door opened. In walked Leonard Gaylor, tuxedo-spruced and carrying a bunch of red roses. I gave him a glare, and he walked past me. Fast. Probably because he was afraid I'd attack his ankles again.

"Leonard!" Mrs. Bloom called, tossing her head back. As I hurried past her, I could hear her telling a new group of women what a "patient dear" Leonard was while Brenda was busy putting the gala together. "...and then to bring flowers," she said. "How sweet of you." It was enough to make me want to bite Mrs. Bloom right above her gunmetal opera pumps!

The hallway leading to the dressing room was so crowded that I had to squeeze my way through. I got in between the side-by-side doors that had LES PAUL and MARY FORD on them when some man stepped on my foot. Hard. And while I was hopping in place and checking to make sure my shoes didn't get scuffs over the shine, I heard Mr. Carter, the emcee, say to someone, "I don't understand. They certainly should be here by now, you'd think. I'll talk to Mrs. Bloom."

The whole room was sparking like lightning when I got back to our dressing room and found Brenda. The Big Sisters were dressed and huddled in front of the mirrors, checking their hems to make sure their slips weren't showing, or pushing bobby pins in the parts of their hair that wanted to poke out. Most of the Little Sisters were twirling in their skirts, fanning their faces and each other's.

Brenda was pulling my dress over my head, being careful not to wreck my hair, when the Taxi Stand Ladies came in. I had to wait for the dress to drop so I could make sure it was them. Walking Doll had on the same suit Charlie and me had seen on Thornton Street, proving it *had* been her. She wasn't wearing her mole, but she was wearing her locket. The Kenosha Kid was dressed in a suit, too—even though I thought they both should have had on their silkies, which were fancier. Their legs were even in nylons, and their hair was twisted on their heads, Mrs.-Bloom-style.

They stood in the doorway at first, and Mrs. Gaylor hurried to them. Probably because she thought they were mothers of Little Sisters, and it was the rule, for tonight anyway, no mas could be in our dressing room, just Sisters. "They're our makeup ladies, Mrs. Gaylor," I shouted over the noise.

Mrs. Gaylor led the Taxi Stand Ladies to two chairs alongside the table where she'd handed out fans. I watched them and waved fast. Tina and Julie were watching them, too. Leaning close to whisper in each other's ears.

Brenda was patting my hair into place, since I told her not to brush it or it would just get poufy. "Brenda...the two at the table," Tina said. "Julie and I just figured out where we've seen them before. My God, Brenda. Do you know who they are?"

"Our makeup ladies," I said.

"Brenda," Tina said, her face tipped down, like she didn't want anybody to even read her lips. "They're the whores that hang on the corner of Fifth and Washington. The ones our mothers are trying to have run out of town. Remember them? My God!"

Whores? The Taxi Stand Ladies didn't have any babies!

Brenda just jiggled my barrette a little to make sure it was tight, then she told me to go get my makeup on.

Mindy had her makeup put on first, and when she was done, she found me in line. "She gave me her autograph, Teaspoon. On one of those glossies. She wrote on it, too. *For Mindy Brewer, my pretty little fan. Best Wishes, Mimi Hines.* Brenda put it in a safe place for me." Mindy was smiling, and she wasn't even covering her mouth, which was a good thing or she would have smeared her Taxi Stand Lady lips.

I sang "Sisters" to myself as I waited in Walking Doll's line, twirling when the dance steps required it. When the room stopped spinning, I saw Tina whispering in Mrs. Gaylor's ear. And Mrs. Gaylor's hand going over what little balloons she had, just like Mrs. Fry did when she got a worry or a scare, only Mrs. Gaylor didn't have a hankie.

Before you knew it, most of the Big Sisters were gawking at the Taxi Stand Ladies and standing back like they were scared of them. But not the Little Sisters, who beamed as Walking Doll and The Kenosha Kid painted their faces and told them how beautiful they were. Even if some weren't.

"You excited?" Walking Doll asked me as she rubbed red in circles over my cheeks.

"You bet," I said. "It's my debut. And my ma's coming. You can meet her, since I didn't get a chance to bring her to the taxi stand yet. She's going to wear a dress from a *boutique*."

Walking Doll sure was happy for me. So happy that she popped a kiss on my forehead. "Don't scratch or rub your face now," she said as she pulled the bib thing she'd strung around my neck off and rubbed a spit-licked thumb over my forehead.

I hurried to check myself in the mirror. Whoo-ee! I was wearing Taxi Stand Lady makeup, and Teddy couldn't even make me scrub it off.

CHAPTER THIRTY-FOUR

Brenda said if we were quiet, we could keep the door open so we could hear the whole show until our spot. I got Poochie-growly, though, when those girls wouldn't shut up and Mrs. Gaylor closed the door before the orchestra even finished tuning their instruments. "It's just a bunch of noise. What's there to listen to anyway, Teaspoon?" Rebecca said.

But it wasn't just noise. All messy sounding or not, it was the beginning of the biggest day of my life, and I wanted to hear every single sound it had in it so my ears could remember it forever.

I ran to the door and laid my ear against it, pausing once to yell "Shut up!" to the Sisters, who were still gabbing and racing around, their noise drowning out almost every sound the orchestra made, but the drums and horns when they got loud. I clamped my hands over my mouth so I wouldn't squeal out loud when the orchestra started the song Benny Goodman did, "Sing, Sing, Sing," even though Louis Prima was the one who wrote it, like Jay said.

When I couldn't take it no more, I searched out Brenda, who was standing off by herself, as sleep-dreamy looking as a just-fed baby. "Can't I please sit outside the door? It's my debut night, Brenda, and I can't hear nothing with all the racket going on in here."

Brenda opened the door for me. "Hey, how come...," some Little Sister called to Brenda before the door shut behind me.

I leaned against the wall, my hands clasped behind me, bumping in time to the music as I pictured my movie-star ma out there with Teddy and Charlie and the rest of the crowd, seated, after eating pinwheel sandwiches, sipping punch, and mingling with all the respectable townsfolk, waiting for me to light the stage of the Starlight Theater.

"Hey, Pip Squeak," Jay called as he came rushing down the hall. "Get Brenda." Boy, even when he was only walking fast, Jay looked like he was tap dancing.

I stuck my head in and called for Brenda, and when she came out, he told her she had to get to the stage because Mr. Carter was ready to introduce her and her mother. "We've got to stay on time. Five minutes for your mother's welcome message, and then the intro to our first act."

I was just about to follow Jay and Brenda, figuring I could watch from the side of the stage, when Mrs. Gaylor poked her head out of the room and peered down the hall. "You stay put, Teaspoon," she said, "or you'll come inside." I crossed my arms over my scratchy dress and promised not to move.

I couldn't hear every word Mrs. Bloom said, but she was welcoming everybody to the "new" Starlight Theater, and talking about the exciting show in store for them. She sure did brag Brenda up something fierce, saying how Brenda was responsible for the spectacle they were about to see. While the crowd was still clapping, she shouted into the mike, "From me and my wonderful daughter... enjoy the show!"

I didn't make plans to head down to the stage. It just sort of happened. I was listening to the music, and my feet danced me all the way down there all on their own.

There were about a dozen people standing in the dark area just off to the side, most with clipboards, whispering that Les Paul and Mary Ford were going to pull a "no-show." They were worried, but I wasn't. Paul and Ford were professionals. They'd come. So while they fussed and Mrs. Derby wailed like Ethel, I ditched between the worrywarts and stood on my tiptoes trying to spot Brenda on the other side of the stage.

"Hey, Pip Squeak, get back with the other girls. You're in the way," Jay said as Beulah and Morris Farthing headed out from the other side, then posed like mannequins behind the red curtain while Mr. Carter announced them. I didn't budge though, because I knew that if I was going to be a singer, I'd need to learn a few extra dance steps.

The curtain went up and the whole theater filled with "Cherry Pink and Apple Blossom White." It sure was magical, the way the Farthings glided across that stage like Fred and Ginger, Beulah's dark pink skirt, light as butterfly wings, floating in big circles around her legs. The crowd liked the Farthings a lot more than Mrs. Derby, which wasn't exactly a shocker.

"I said get back to your dressing room, Pip Squeak," Jay snapped, crabbier this time, because he was trying to clear a path for Mimi Hines and Phil Ford.

"Brenda said I didn't have to stay in there," I told Jay, which wasn't exactly a lie. He didn't squeak back at me, though, because he was too busy smiling at Mimi Hines, waiting for the curtain to drop and Mr. Carter to have his next blab so the stagehands could move the grand behind the curtain for their act.

When the piano and Mimi and Phil were in place, Jay cued Mr. Carter and the red curtain lifted.

I couldn't keep from clapping when the crowd saw Mimi Hines, dressed in elbow-length gloves and a white dress that sparkled every bit as much as the sliver moon that hung above her, while Phil Ford played on our baby grand.

That Mimi. She sure was a stitch, talking like a chipmunk and being funny as all get-out. When she slipped into her first number, though, her voice sounded radio-beautiful. I slid over and peeked out from the edge of the curtain, because I wanted to see if Ma and Teddy and Charlie were enjoying the performance as much as me. But with the stage lights so bright, and no lights in the auditorium but the dim ones at the edge of the aisle seats, I couldn't see nothing but dark shadows. And I could barely see those. I knew they were there, though. Teddy dressed in his new suit, Charlie not looking like Humphrey Bogart but still looking nice. And Ma, prettier than any lady in the seats or on stage, people gawking at her and whispering, *Isn't that Catty Marlene, the star of* Attack of the Atomic Lake Lizard *movies?* even though they were supposed to be doing nothing but clapping because Mimi Hines and Phil Ford had put on a show so good that those twenty-five minutes felt like two.

The second Mr. Carter announced that there would be a twenty-minute intermission and the lights brightened some, I slipped out from behind the edge of the curtain. There were so many people already on their feet—because they had to pee, or stretch, I suppose—that I couldn't even see the folks in the first few rows. So I headed down the steps.

Maybe it was the slick black bottoms of my shoes. Or maybe Johnny had used one too many coats of varnish. Whatever it was, when I hit the second to the last step, I went hurling like a piece of potato shot from a Spud Gun. Right into a small group of people standing and talking. A lady yelped as my head rammed into her butt, almost knocking her over, right before I hit the floor.

I landed on my knees, which hurt, and the lady's clutch purse landed on the floor beside me. "Sorry," I said as I scooped it up and scrambled to my feet.

She yanked her purse from my hand, and when I looked up, I was looking at Mrs. Miller. Susie was beside her, that snooty smirk on her face.

"You," Mr. Miller said. "Don't you ever watch where you're going?"

"She doesn't," Susie said. "And she hums and sings all the time, too."

That's when a hand came down on my shoulder. "Oh, don't be too hard on her. I think we've all had the experience of running into someone we didn't see was standing there, don't you?"

I turned and saw Walking Doll, who was looking hard at Mr. Miller.

Mr. Miller got so flustered you would have thought he was the one who'd just gotten head-butted.

"You okay, Teaspoon?" she asked, without looking at me. I told her I was, and she patted me on the shoulder. "Hello, Frank," she said, her tongue coming out to lick her bottom lip, like maybe she thought she had Kool-Aid on it. "I don't believe I've had the pleasure of meeting your lovely wife just yet." Walking Doll held out her hand to Mrs. Miller. "Since the cat seems to have caught Frank's tongue, I'll introduce myself. Dolly," she said. "Dolly Walker."

Dolly Walker? That sounded like a stage name to me.

"Your husband gave me a car dirt-cheap. But then I could expect such generosity from him. He and my mother were quite close back in their day, weren't you, Frank?"

I didn't have time to sit around while they chitchatted about olden days, so I interrupted. I told Mrs. Miller again that I was sorry I ran into her, then I dodged around the slowpokes clogging the aisle.

And there was Teddy, Charlie on one side of him, Mrs. Fry next to Charlie, but an empty seat where Ma should be. I squeezed my way between the feet and chairs of the people who must not have had to pee. "Hey, Teddy, wasn't that a great first half? And if you liked that, wait until the rest of the show. It's going to be even better! Where's Ma?" I asked, gawking at the backs of ladies heading toward the back of the Starlight.

"She'll be along," Teddy said.

"She go to the restroom?"

"I got to go to the bathroom," Charlie said.

"I'm going to go find Ma," I said. "Come on, Charlie. We can walk together."

Teddy grabbed Charlie's arm and said something to the side of his scabby head before letting go. "We don't have time, Teddy," I said.

I weaved Charlie up the aisle. "In that line," I told him, giving him a shove when we got in the back of the theater where the lines were strung long, especially the women's.

I ran up and down the ladies' line, looking for Ma, and Brenda. I didn't see either of them, but I did see Jennifer and Jolene. "How you liking the show so far?" I asked.

"Good. Except you could have gotten us seats some closer. Everybody looks like ants from where we're sitting."

"Yeah, sorry about that... have you guys seen my ma?" I asked Jolene.

"Your ma ain't here, Teaspoon," Jolene said.

"What are you talking about? Course she's here."

"No she ain't," Jolene said. "She went someplace with Mr. Favors after you left, and when they got back, she came over to use the phone. She called some guy named Paul and asked him to bring her to the airport in Milwaukee. And she gave James and Jack each a quarter for helping her get her suitcases outside on the lawn so she'd be ready when that guy came. She said she didn't have much time before her flight."

"You're lying," I said, blinking my eyes hard because tears would smear my makeup.

"Am not. Am I, Jennifer?" Jennifer shook her head. "Go ask our ma if you don't believe us."

But I didn't go find Mrs. Jackson. Instead, I went to the boys' line and asked Charlie if it was true. "I ain't supposed to say," Charlie said. Which *did* say.

All around me, people were watching the line and their watches, and talking about how exciting it was to have a live theater in Mill Town, but I just stood there, my breaths hurting my chest.

"I have to find Brenda," I said, more to myself than to Charlie. And I didn't care that the ladies' line was long. I barged right in front of everyone and slammed open the restroom door. "Brenda?" I called. "Brenda!" The bathroom got quiet, so I knew I'd have heard her if she called back to me. But she didn't.

CHAPTER THIRTY-FIVE

I didn't know where to go, or where to look. But the lights were dimming slowly, and people were hurrying back to their seats.

I went back to our dressing room, hoping Brenda would be there. She wasn't, but she had been, Mrs. Gaylor said.

"You're pairing up with Joyce Ellis," she told me. "Brenda isn't feeling well enough to go on. And Betsy, Joyce's Little Sister, got stage fright so her father took her home."

I could only stand there, trying not to smear my makeup. "I don't even know who Joyce is."

Mrs. Gaylor clapped her hands to get the girls to listen up. "Big Sisters, head out. You'll be going—quietly—behind the stage to line up."

"That's Joyce," Mrs. Gaylor said as the girls filed out of the room, pointing to a girl tall as Miss Tuckle. "Quietly," she repeated to the Big Sisters.

"When do *we* go?" Rebecca yelled, and Mrs. Gaylor made the *shhh* sign because the door was still open.

"But Mrs. Gaylor, me and Brenda are pairs. We're going to be dead-center."

"Teaspoon," she said, her jaw going Mrs.-Carlton-twitchy. "It's Brenda's instructions..." Then, like she just recalled another order she'd been given, she told all the Sisters to be sure and come right back to the dressing room when our number was over. She picked up a sheet that had all of our names written in circles stuck together like beads on a necklace, showing the order we were supposed to line up in.

For weeks I'd been dreaming about this night. Playing it over and over in my head until it became like a TV rerun of a musical. I knew how every line, every look, and every song would go. Only now the leading lady was missing, and her stand-in was about to step out of the picture, too. And it just couldn't be!

"Teaspoon, get back here," Mrs. Gaylor shouted as I flew out the door.

Mr. Carter's voice sounded far away, even though he was using a microphone to introduce Louis Prima and Keely Smith, and I was running down the hall toward him, not away from him.

I was squeezing between the suits and dresses crowded on the side of the stage, not even looking up to see who was inside them, just looking for Brenda, when Jay caught my arm. "Pip Squeak..."

Jay didn't have a chance to say another word to me, though, because Mrs. Bloom came rushing to us. "I just heard. Brenda's not going on? Where is she?"

"I don't know," Jay said. "I saw her about fifteen minutes ago. She told me she was sick, and to pair Teaspoon with Joyce."

Mrs. Bloom pressed her fingertips against her temples. "My God, what's going on here? We have a light out and apparently no Uriah...Brenda says she's not going on and has obviously crawled off by herself to nurse her nerves. This is spiraling into a disaster. A complete disaster!"

It was Mrs. Bloom saying Brenda had crawled off to be alone—to find some solitude—that made me suddenly think of where she might be. "The catwalk!" I said.

Jay caught my arm. "Teaspoon, where are you going? You have to line up." But I didn't want to listen to Jay. Or anybody for that matter. I only wanted to find Brenda. I shook Jay's arm away and took off.

I zoomed up the aisle, past a crowd of eleven hundred and fifty faces—minus one—that were facing the stage, their eyes scrinched from laughing as Keely Smith gave Louis Prima a hard time in their act. Clear up through the nosebleed seats and into the projector room.

The door to the catwalk was open a crack, just as I thought it would be. I yanked it wide with my gala-gloved hand, and was just about to go up when Mrs. Bloom appeared, her upper lip damp from climbing the stairs so fast. "Hurry," she said to me. "See if she's up there."

The minute my head cleared the top of the stairs, before my feet did, I saw a smudge of blue on the metal flower center. In the dim light, I couldn't see much more than Brenda's gala dress bunched as she sat, her back against the railing, her arms, pale as moonlight, wrapped around her legs.

I turned and peered down the ladder steps where Mrs. Bloom waited, her head tipped up. I didn't want to be a ratfink, but I nodded anyway. What was I supposed to do? If anybody could force Brenda on that stage, nerves and all, it was her bossy ma. And I had to go on. I just had to.

I headed down the stem to where Brenda sat, her shoes beside her on the catwalk, one tipped on its side. "What are you doing up here?" Brenda asked, her voice so sharp that I stopped. "Go downstairs with the other girls or you'll miss your song."

"It's *our* song, Brenda. 'Sisters.'" I took another step forward. *"We stick together through all kinds of weather.* Remember?" It was hard to think of the lyrics, though, with Louis's trumpet wailing out "Until Sunrise" downstairs.

"No, Teaspoon. I can't go on." Brenda didn't sound pukey. Just upset. "You go down and line up to do the number with Joyce."

Tears started blurring my eyes. "No," I said, shaking my head.

"Brenda?" Mrs. Bloom called out, her head peeking above the catwalk floor. Brenda groaned, her hands moving to hold the sides of her head.

It didn't look right, Mrs. Bloom stepping up on the catwalk, her long, fancy skirt bunched in her arms.

"Brenda!" Mrs. Bloom said after she brushed her skirt down and kicked off her shoes, probably because her gunmetal heels were sinking down between the holes. "What on earth are you doing up here? We have chaos brewing downstairs. Randolph just got word to me that Paul and Ford aren't here, and I called the motel. They never even checked in..."

"They're not coming," Brenda said, her voice flat as bad singing.

Mrs. Bloom stopped, even though she was only partway down the stem. "What do you mean, they're not coming?"

"They were never coming, Mother."

"That's insane. Of course they're coming." Mrs. Bloom laughed like *she* was insane. "You told me they were booked."

Brenda's voice shook as she tried to explain. "Yes. But booked elsewhere."

I could feel my neck stretch out, like my head was trying to get closer to what Brenda was saying.

It was Mrs. Bloom's turn to clutch her head. "You mean you knew this all along and you let me bill them? Not giving one thought to the humiliation we'd suffer for advertising them falsely? Brenda, how could you—"

"I couldn't correct you when you first misunderstood. Not with you in so much pain, and so anxious already. But I tried to tell you after that. Many times. And every time I'd start telling you, you'd just say, 'I don't want to hear about problems. I want to hear about solutions.' Well, I didn't have any."

"But...but...," Mrs. Bloom stuttered, rushing forward. I followed her, but slowly. "There's a vast difference between 'problems' and our big draw not coming. My God, Brenda. What were you thinking? I'll be the laughingstock of Mill Town. And so will you. I trusted you to do this gala right, Brenda. I trusted you..."

I don't know if Mrs. Bloom heard Brenda, she was so busy fussing. Plus the crowd downstairs was busting their bellies over Louis Prima. But I heard her. She said, "But you shouldn't have."

Brenda wasn't crying. Not that I could see her face well, but there were no tears in her voice, only sadness, when she said, "I'm sorry I let you down, Mother."

"*I'm sorry?*" Mrs. Bloom said as she clutched the metal railing. "As if *I'm sorry* is going to fix this debacle?"

Brenda uttered a few more sorrys, her head down so that they were muffled, while Mrs. Bloom uttered a few more *my Gods* and *what are we going to dos* and turned in tight circles. Downstairs, the crowd called Prima and Smith back for one more number, and Brenda lifted her head. "Go, Teaspoon. Or you're going to miss your debut. You hear me? Go!" But I couldn't go. I could only stand there and cry.

"Damn it, Teaspoon. Don't wait for me. I can't go down there. Do you understand? I'm sorry, but I can't."

"I'm not going, Brenda. Not unless you come with me."

It was like time itself was standing suspended, as it's called, just like the catwalk. Downstairs the crowd cheered and whistled over Prima and Smith's encore song, and then, after Mr. Carter drummed up a bit more applause for them, he started the Sunshine Sisters' intro.

Brenda groaned, then said, "I've let you both down. I'm so, so very sorry."

Brenda had been leaning against one of the black poles that served as a railing for the catwalk. But after her last sorry, she stood up. Slowly. She turned around and grabbed the long pole that went from the railing up to the tent-like middle of the ceiling. Then she lifted her long blue skirt, pretty as the sky, and stepped up on the bottom rail, her bare foot curling around it, her arms locked around the pole.

"Brenda!" Mrs. Bloom snapped when she looked up and saw what Brenda was doing. Brenda pulled her other foot up on the railing. "What on earth are you doing?" I couldn't move. My head couldn't think.

Mrs. Bloom took a step, her gloved arms coming out. "Get down from there. Brenda, get down!"

And Brenda screamed, "Don't come any closer. You hear me? Not one step closer. Either of you." Mrs. Bloom's arms were out now, her hands shaking.

I looked at the polka dots of light shining up through the thin as paper Starlight sky. "Brenda. You're scaring me. Get down. You could fall. It's a forty-five-foot drop."

But of course Brenda knew that.

Mrs. Bloom was probably thinking the same thing, because every bit of mad she had in her turned to shock and scared. "Brenda, don't be foolish. Get down. We'll make up an excuse... offer to reimburse them... anything. It'll be okay. Just get down. It's just a program."

"But it's everything to you, Mother. And I'm sorry. Sorry I couldn't be the perfect daughter you wanted me to be. And Teaspoon, I'm so sorry I couldn't have been a better Big Sister to you."

"My God," Mrs. Bloom said, worry as big as the Starlight sky in her voice. "Brenda. Come on. Get down. This is crazy. You can't do something like this over a *show*."

Brenda's golden waves swished against her back as she shook her head, then leaned it against the pole. She must have been shaking, too, because her skirt was fluttering even though she wasn't moving. "No. It isn't just about the show. And you can't make *this one* right, Mother. Neither can I."

"What do you mean? Brenda, what are you talking about? Just come—"

"I'm pregnant," Brenda whispered.

Brenda had her back to us, so she couldn't see her ma. But I could. I saw her hand come up to cover her mouth, then flutter back down, then go up again. She pulled her shoulders back up and said, "It'll be okay. You aren't the first engaged girl to find herself in this predicament. You and Leonard will marry immediately and we'll say you eloped... we'll pick a date the wedding supposedly happened... we'll say we were keeping it hush-hush until after the gala. You can have the baby in Madison and we'll not announce it here for a couple of months. People do that when this happens. Some will suspect, but they'll be too polite to say anything. It will all be okay."

"No!" Brenda shouted. "No it *won't* be okay. I'm not going to marry Leonard. I don't love him. And he wouldn't marry me anyway, because the baby isn't his."

Mrs. Bloom let out a gasp and cry and a yell all rolled into one. And when Brenda heard that, she lifted her foot again and stepped right up onto the top railing. Teetering, like a Charlie on ladder-steep steps.

I could feel pinch spots on the insides of my hands where my fingernails were digging in. I took a couple of steps forward and Mrs. Bloom snapped at me to stay back. But I couldn't. Because Brenda had put her free arm out, and her feet were scooting her sideways, farther from the pole, while the Sunshine Sisters sang below.

"Brenda! Don't jump. Please!" I screamed. "My ma left me today, Brenda. She's gone. Don't you leave me, too, Brenda. Please. *Please!* Don't you leave me, too!"

And that's when Brenda fell.

Not frontward, through the paper ceiling. But backward, onto the metal catwalk.

Mrs. Bloom rushed forward and fell right down to her knees next to Brenda, even if the metal diamond shapes hurt a person's knees when you did that. She stared down at Brenda for a while, her whole body shaking, then she wrapped her arms around Brenda and started sobbing.

I don't know how long Mr. Morgan was standing on the catwalk stairs before I felt someone there and turned around.

In his black tuxedo, he was invisible in the dim light, but for his white shirt that looked like a bib over his chest, and the white stage light box he was holding. He set the box down and walked to me quiet as a whisper. The Blooms still had their arms wrapped around each other, crying and rocking, when Mr. Morgan picked me up to carry me down the stairs, whispering, "Shhhh, shhhhh," into my curls.

He set me down in the projection room, and I went to the glass-less windows like a sleepwalker. Just in time to see the Sunshine Sisters leaving the stage—Little Sisters to the right, Big Sisters to the left, exactly like they were supposed to.

CHAPTER THIRTY-SIX

I fell asleep sitting on the couch next to Teddy that night. In the morning, I got out of bed and changed into play clothes, hanging my gala dress up to keep it pristine. I was just stepping out of my bedroom when Charlie came in, saying that Teddy was over at his house talking to Mrs. Fry and Miss Tuckle. They'd talked about the gala first, just like I guessed they did, then, Charlie said, Teddy gave Miss Tuckle a wad of money, saying it took a lot less than he thought it would.

It didn't make any sense at first, because Teddy didn't have money to give anybody. But after Charlie said a bit more, I figured it out. Teddy *had* taken that loan from Miss Tuckle to fix the roof and the lean. Teddy knew the price of boards, but he must have found somebody willing to do the work for less than he expected, so he gave her back what he didn't need. Like I told Charlie, it was the only thing that made sense.

I guess after Teddy gave Miss Tuckle the leftover money—minus two hundred, that he said he'd explain later—Mrs. Fry said that it was a "sin" what some people were willing to do for money. What could I do but shake my head and tell Charlie that his great-grandma was losing it, because what sin could there be in being a carpenter? Jesus was one Himself.

* * *

When Teddy came home, he told Charlie that Mrs. Fry wanted him home to help her with some work. Then while he took out the bread and eggs for our breakfast, he told me again, just like he had after we got back from the gala, how sorry he was that Ma left without saying good-bye to me. This time, though, he asked me if I was hurt because she didn't wait to hear if I wanted to go with her.

In the years I'd been with Teddy, he never once asked me not to cry. And he didn't ask then. But still, something in his eyes told me he was hoping I wouldn't. So I didn't tell him that when I found out she was gone, it felt like I got hit by a truck, and my heart was still hurting like it was bruised. Instead, what I told him was that if Jolene was telling the truth—that she'd heard Ma tell Paul on the phone that she had to leave immediately because her agent got her an audition for a part in Rock Hudson's new picture—then I couldn't blame her at all for leaving when and how she did.

Even sitting there at the table, Ma gone twenty-four hours already, I could still smell her. Maybe some of her perfume was still in the air. Or maybe it was my nose holding on to her smell, just like I asked it to do. Whichever it was, knowing that I'd remember her smell and how she looked and how she sounded this time gave me some comfort because, no matter how long it took before Ma came through Mill Town again, I'd remember her just as she was.

While four yellow slices of French toast cooked on the griddle, Teddy went to the pantry to get the syrup. But he didn't come right back. And when I looked, he was standing at the metal table, staring down at the words I'd spelled out on the Scrabble board. Teddy nodded and wiped his eye, still staring down at the tiles I'd put down where the word *gluck* (that wasn't a word at all) used to sit: *im staying with you teddy.*

"I know that's more than one word, Teddy, so it can't count," I said. "But how many points is that worth?"

And Teddy told me, "All of them."

✳   ✳   ✳

He was so choked up his words were zigzagging as he asked me to go sit on the Starlight seats because he wanted to show me something. He shut off the French toast and went to his room, then came back with stapled papers and handed them to me. I couldn't make any sense out of what they said because those papers had more Bibley words in them than the Bible itself, so I asked Teddy to just explain them.

Teddy looked down at the floor and bit his lip. Then he told me how Ma wanted to make sure everything would be okay back here while she was in Hollywood, so she signed those papers, making Teddy my legal dad. He told me that the papers didn't mean Ma wasn't my parent anymore, because I'd always carry her in my heart, but that from then on, forever, he would be my dad.

Teddy asked me if I understood, and I said I did. It meant that I wouldn't have to be a fibber-face and tell my new teacher he was my uncle, or make her twitchy by telling her that he was the boyfriend my ma left me with. It meant that if I ever got smacked by a truck, I'd know what to say when a nurse lady asked me my dad's name. Past that, I told Teddy, I couldn't see what difference it made, since he'd been my dad for the last five years anyway.

But it made a difference to Teddy.

CHAPTER THIRTY-SEVEN

You'd think that after Teddy lost his girlfriend for the second time, he'd have had to force himself to perk up before leaving the house again. But he didn't. His shoulders stayed back and his chin stayed up all on their own, whether he was inside or out. Charlie said Teddy even looked like he grew some. I didn't know about that, but what I did know is that Teddy had lost his noodleyness. Three days after the gala, the Jackson boys attested to the fact that I was right.

I had scootered down the corner to see if the Taxi Stand Ladies were there *yet*, so I could thank them properly for being our makeup ladies, and tell them about my new teacher, who seemed real nice. But the corner was empty for the seventh day in a row. Charlie was busy helping Mrs. Fry pack away some old junk, so I went over to the Jacksons, even if I knew that Jolene and Jennifer had gone shopping with their ma. And then Jack and James told me what Teddy had done.

Turned out, the night of the gala, after Teddy poured me into bed, the Jackson boys were in their yard playing flashlight Hide-and-Scare when a big Lincoln pulled up to the corner where Walking Doll was standing, and Mr. Miller got out, shouting cusswords at her. Joey was hiding in their neighbors' yard, and he went back to get his brothers, telling them, "Fight! Fight!"

The Jackson boys crouched down alongside The Pop Shop to watch. "We went like soldiers on a maneuver, up against the backs of the houses, until we got to The Pop Shop to watch," James told me, and Joey nodded.

"Boy, was Miller pissed," Jack said. "He was shouting at her, saying, 'What in the hell do you think you were trying to pull, you blackmailing little bitch? You got your car and that's all you're getting. You threaten me again, or you even think about opening your mouth, and the only thing you'll be getting is a knife in your back.'"

"You're making this up," I told them, even if something inside me was saying they weren't.

"Oh, yeah? Oh, yeah? Ask Teddy if you don't believe us!" Jack said. "He must have heard that whore scream, because he shot out of your house like a bullet and raced down to the corner."

"It's true!" James roared. "We saw the whole thing!"

Jack pushed James out of the way. "Miller slugged her while Teddy was running, and when Teddy got to the corner, Miller said, 'Stay out of this, Big Guy.'"

And then I knew they couldn't be making it up, because they didn't know what Mr. Miller called Teddy.

"...and then, Teddy, he grabbed Miller's arm, and Miller shook him off like a flea. He tried to give Teddy a punch, but Teddy ducked." Jack started laughing then, and so did his brothers. "Then Teddy...he...he...popped up and busted Miller's nuts with his knee." Jack doubled over laughing, so Joey continued.

"Yeah," Joey said. "And did that big bastard hit the deck hard!"

All of them were yukking it up good by then. Acting the whole scene out like they were the Three Stooges.

"Walking Doll. Was she okay?" I asked as Jack rocked side-to-side on the grass, fake-groaning and holding his wee-er.

"Well," Jack said as he was getting to his feet, "she couldn't have been hurt that bad, because she was screaming like a banshee. Cussing Miller out while he lay there groaning, saying that he might as well have killed her mother with his bare hands, because so much of her died the day him and his friends raped her that she was good as dead anyway."

The Jackson boys must have figured out that I didn't know what *rape* meant, because Jack told me that it's when a guy *makes* a girl do the Juicy Jitterbug, even when she doesn't want to. Which made my stomach feel like it had the flu.

"Miller was getting on his feet by then," Jack said, laughing less now. "Staggering, though, because the wind was still knocked out of him. And he said to Teddy, 'What you got to be so self-righteous about, you little prick? Who picked us up after the game...after that drunk son of a bitch drove us into the snowbank? Huh? Seems to me it was *you*, Big Guy, who took us the rest of the way to the cabin, even though you knew damn well what we were up to, because we asked you if you wanted in on the action.'"

"What did Teddy say to that?" I asked, hoping Jack would say that Teddy knee-socked Miller in his wee-er again for being a liar.

"He didn't say nothing we could hear. It was over then. Miller gave the whore one last warning, then he got in his car and drove away. Then Teddy sat down on the curb with that bawling whore. He even put his arm around her."

"Yeah," James added, "probably because he wanted to Juicy Jitterbug with her. But Teddy must've not had any money on him, because he walked back home, that whore with him, and he went inside. She waited in your yard until Teddy came out with some money."

I didn't know what he'd be paying for in advance, so I asked. The boys yukked it up good then, calling me stupid because I didn't know that guys paid the Taxi Stand Ladies to do the Juicy Jitterbug with them.

I didn't wait around to hear anything else they had to say. I just headed home, leaving the Jackson boys laughing behind me.

* * *

I never said a word to Teddy about what the Jacksons told me. Probably for the same reasons I didn't tell him when Jack told me that he was nothing but a shit shoveler back when he worked for the Soo Line.

And Teddy never said a word to me about where the heart-shaped locket—just like Walking Doll's, only gold—came from when he handed it to me a couple of weeks after the gala, saying only that maybe I'd want to put Ma's picture in it when I got one.

I wanted to ask Teddy, lots of times, if he knew where the Taxi Stand Ladies had gone, but I couldn't let myself do it. So I asked Pop. And all he said was, "Probably to do business elsewhere." Boy, did that make me happy, because I knew exactly what kind of business they went off to do. They went off to open a bakery! And every time I passed the mailbox after that, I thought of Walking Doll baking one loaf of memory after another, and The Kenosha Kid selling it behind the counter, making sure to give every customer that came through the door their proper change.

CHAPTER THIRTY-EIGHT

I missed the Taxi Stand Ladies after they left. The same way I missed Brenda during the two months she was gone.

Brenda sent me a letter, though, clear from Europe, saying that her and her ma were on a little vacation. She told me she was sorry I had to see such a thing on the catwalk. And sorry that she caused me to miss our big Sunshine Sisters number. She explained that sometimes, when people find themselves in a *predicament* they don't know how to get out of, they lose faith in themselves and they start thinking that the world would be better off without them. She talked about making mistakes, and how we all make them. How that doesn't make us bad, but it sure can make us sorry. Then she said that she figured out that most of the ones we make are the result of not being honest with ourselves about who we are, how we feel, and what we want in the first place. Then she thanked me for teaching her about those things, and for teaching her about hope.

It sure was a shocker, learning that Mrs. Bloom was poor as me and Teddy before she met the late Mr. Bloom. She never fibbed to him about where she came from, but maybe she should have, because he never let her forget it. Brenda said that's why her ma worked so hard to get respected. So that when Brenda got married, her husband could never throw it in her face that she came to him with nothing, and that she was nothing without him.

But Brenda wasn't thinking about getting married anymore. Instead, she was thinking about how she wanted to be a teacher. Not teaching kids how to be respectable, but teaching them reading and math, and things like that. She said Mrs. Bloom was going to hire managers for both of the theaters, and watch the baby while it was little, so Brenda could drive every day to Milwaukee to go to school.

When the Blooms got back to Mill Town, they didn't go anyplace for a while. Brenda said that was because it was hard to show your face when you knew people were gossiping about you. So I told them both what Teddy did back when he was nothing but a shit shoveler for the Soo Line, after Ma left and our neighbors were talking about him. How Teddy would pull his shoulders back, lift his chin up, and out the door he'd go, keeping them perked and not letting them drop until he closed the door behind him at night and then, on the side, I showed Brenda what *I* used to do to them behind my back, just so she'd have a couple of options.

Whether it was because of the smarts I passed along to them from me and Teddy or not, the Blooms started going places again. And yep, people stared at them. And yep, people said Miller-mean things about them behind their backs—especially the Gaylors—but they went out anyway. And they kept going out until the gossip wound down like a clock somebody forgot to wind.

When Brenda's baby came, she named him Daniel, which she told me meant "God is my judge." I told her that was a real nice name, but that maybe she should have looked for a name that meant "Jesus is my judge." You know, just in case the little guy ended up having a few afflictions, as I knew he would the second Brenda lowered him into my propped-with-a-pillow arms and I saw his little lightbulb-shaped noggin.

I had to give Jolene Jackson my plastic purse in trade for an address where I could reach Johnny. In my letter, I told him that I thought he should know that Brenda had a baby with a lightbulb-shaped head, because I knew that he'd never want a kid of his to wonder what he did that was so bad that his dad didn't want to stick around.

Two weeks later, while I was walking water out to Poochie, Dumbo Doug's car pulled up in front of the Jacksons, and Johnny got out. I dropped the pitcher and darted across the street. "Johnny!" I yelled.

He picked me up and gave me a potato-sack shake. He still looked like James Dean—which made me feel both happy and sad. Happy because Johnny was still the same. But sad, too, because James Dean was dead, and I was reminded of how I cried for two days when I heard.

"I knew you'd come back, Johnny," I said.

Johnny asked how I was, and he asked about Brenda and Daniel. Then he asked me where my little friend was.

"You mean Charlie?" I asked, and Johnny nodded.

"Oh, Charlie's not my friend," I told him. "He's my brother."

And I wasn't even telling a fib. Because as it turned out, the day that Teddy and Miss Tuckle and Mrs. Fry went off together and Teddy came back with our pre-gala celebration gifts, they'd gone to see the good judge Miss Tuckle knew at the courthouse. And Mrs. Fry, she took papers she got from her daughter stamped legal, giving Mrs. Fry *custody* of Charlie, just as Charlie's dad had given it to her before he went to the clink. That same day, Mrs. Fry had a will drawn up, saying that after she was called Home, Teddy would have *custody* of Charlie.

Mrs. Fry, she died in her sleep two days before Christmas. Teddy's the one who found her, after Charlie showed up at our place hungry because it was after ten o'clock and she still hadn't gotten up to make breakfast.

Teddy and Miss Tuckle and Charlie cried at her funeral. But I waited to cry later, because I was singing a funeral song for her.

"Amazing Grace." A cappella. And I wanted to sing it good, because it was Mrs. Fry's parting gift.

After the funeral, Teddy brought me and Charlie home and sat us down in the Starlight seats, and he got out Charlie's papers. The same ones he had for me. He handed them to Charlie, and I told him not to bother, because if I couldn't read them, then for sure Charlie wasn't going to be able to. So while Teddy was thinking up how to explain them, I just jumped in and told Charlie that from now on, he was going to have two dads, just like Jesus. His clink-dad, who he'd see when he got to be a man, and Teddy, the dad he'd see every day.

Charlie didn't say anything after I told him. But he didn't have to. I could tell from his face that he felt just like I did when Johnny brought me the seats from the Starlight Theater. Like he'd just been given something magical.

CHAPTER THIRTY-NINE

Teddy and me are walking toward home, the neighborhood so quiet that I can hear the clicks from my shoes as we glide out from under one streetlight beam into another.

I'm the one who bugged Teddy to go for the walk, even though we have Ma's Hudson to ride in if we need to go somewhere in particular. Teddy asked Charlie if he wanted to come along, too, but Charlie said he wanted to stay home and play piano instead. Just like we'd rehearsed.

Me and Charlie and Miss Tuckle choreographed the whole thing. I'm keeping Teddy gone for one hour so that Miss Tuckle can reheat the dinner she brought over, and Charlie can hang the decorations we made. All because we're going to have a celebration. From now on, Teddy's not going to be shoveling anything anymore. He's going to be a foreman at The Hanging Hoof. The boss man of the guys in his department. He's going to make more money, too, which is a good thing, because man can that Charlie eat!

"You've been awfully quiet tonight," Teddy says when we're still a few blocks from home.

"I was just thinking about everything that happened over the last few months," I said.

Teddy nods. "A lot has changed, hasn't it?"

"Sure has, Teddy."

I see a rock on the sidewalk, sitting in its own shadow, and I give it a little kick. I think about how hungry I am. Then I think about how I hope Miss Tuckle has the food done when we get back. And the next thing you know, I'm thinking about the sharp bump I felt on my gums this morning. So I stop. "I'm getting a new tooth, Teddy. See?" I turn toward the light and pull my top lip up. I use my tongue to point it out for him.

"Oh yeah," Teddy says. "That's a canine tooth."

I know what canines are, so I say to Teddy, "To bite Poochie with?" Teddy laughs, so I add, "I'm only kidding, Teddy. Poochie's not being so afflictedly mean anymore. Just like me. He even let me give him a pat on the head yesterday, even though he ducked the first couple times I tried."

We take a few more steps, then I say, "Hey, Teddy. Remember when you yanked my first tooth?"

Teddy smiles. "You carried it in your cheek for three days. I felt so bad."

"I know," I say. "You said that you should have known better. That there's some things in life that just hurt too much when you're forced to let go of them before you're ready. So I asked you what things, because I was scared you were going to try yanking something else out of my head."

Teddy laughs softly.

I give the rock another little kick. "I remember what your answer was, too," I said. "You said, 'Things like hope...love...childhood.' Remember that?"

"Yes," Teddy says.

"When do you think I'm going to lose those things, Teddy?"

"Probably never, Teaspoon. Probably never."

I start humming as I kick the rock a little father. I don't realize that I've gotten so far ahead of Teddy until I look back. I step under a streetlight beam and pretend it's my stage light, singing a bit of "How High the Moon" while I wait for Teddy to catch up.

Teddy smiles wider and brings up the gala. He tells me all over again how he never had a prouder moment in his life than he had that night. And that everybody, Miss Simon and Mrs. Carlton, Mr. Morgan—everybody—felt the same. He says, "You'd just learned that your ma had left, not even saying good-bye or asking if you were going with her...you'd missed your Sunshine Sisters performance...and you'd just witnessed such an awful scene on the catwalk. Yet..."

And then I'm remembering it, too—just like I have, probably one time for every star in the Starlight Theater—as I kick the rock again and run ahead after it.

CHAPTER FORTY

After the Sunshine Sisters left the stage, I uncurled my hands, which were stiff like frozen, and put them on the sill. I looked at the empty stage, the little star on my bracelet falling limp against my arm.

Mr. Carter was supposed to be giving Les Paul and Mary Ford a big intro, but instead he hurried off the stage to stand half hidden behind the edge of the curtain. Probably talking to somebody about what he should say or do next.

That's when Mr. Morgan put his hand over mine. Chocolate on the outside, vanilla underneath. For a minute, it was the old juke-box man's hand instead. I knew that the day had come when I had more blue in my life than the blue in my eyes. I remembered what he told me all over again. Remembered it until I could feel his fingers itsy-bitsying up my leg, and up over my heart, to tap over my throat. The place that felt clogged up and closed like a fist, with tears I didn't want to cry.

Below me, heads were gawking this way and that, or tipped toward their neighbors, whispering, or checking their watches. Suddenly I knew what I had to do.

I raced down the steps faster than I ever had, not slowing down until I got to row four.

Mrs. Fry and Charlie were sitting together, Miss Tuckle sitting in the seat where Teddy should be, the space reserved for Ma, empty. "Teaspoon," Miss Tuckle said. "What happened? Where were you? Teddy went to find you." And Mrs. Fry said, microphone-loud, "Is the show over?"

"Not yet, Mrs. Fry," I said, ignoring Miss Tuckle's questions. Not because I was still upset with her, but because there wasn't time. I grabbed Charlie's arm and said, "Come on, Charlie. I need your help."

"Where we going?" Charlie asked, looking nervous, like maybe I was going to drag him someplace high.

I yanked him to his feet. "Never mind that, Charlie. Move your butt, not your mouth. Mrs. Fry, can I use your hankie?" She didn't hear me, so Miss Tuckle asked, since she was closer to Mrs. Fry's ear. Mrs. Fry took her hankie out of her sweater sleeve and handed it over. "Quick, Miss Tuckle. Clean off my face if it's a mess, will you?" I hung on to Charlie tight so he wouldn't make like a banana and split while Miss Tuckle wrapped the embroidered hankie around her pointy finger, licked it, and gave my face a few quick swabs. "Thanks," I said. Then I heave-hoed Charlie down the aisle, over feet and around knees, and dragged him up the stage steps.

Things sure were a mess on the side of the stage where the audience couldn't see, with Jay and Mr. Carter, the gala helpers, and even the Mill Town orchestra director, huddled together trying to figure out what to do because they had eleven hundred and forty-nine people restless in their red velvet seats.

"Well, someone has to say something!" Jay squawked, like the big squeak he was.

"Well, I'm not comfortable saying anything," Mr. Carter said. "I wish someone would find Mrs. Bloom."

I dragged Charlie with me into the middle of their circle and looked up past Mr. Carter's big belly. "Mrs. Bloom has got to pull a no-show," I said. "Put us on, Mr. Carter. Me and my friend here can do 'How High the Moon.' We've been practicing it all summer. And while we aren't Les Paul and Mary Ford, we do the song real good. Put us on."

Mr. Carter leaned over his belly and glanced at me, then turned away like I was nothing but a buzzing housefly. So I turned to Jay. "Big Squeak, you know I can sing. You said so yourself. And Charlie here, even Brenda said he has a real gift. Not that it would matter much, even if we didn't have as much talent as a three-legged cat in a tap-dance contest, because who's going to throw rotten tomatoes at a couple of kids? It's like Mrs. Bloom said, kids always steal the show."

Jay looked like he was going to yell at me to get back to the dressing room. But then he paused.

"We don't have anything else, Big Squeak. Admit it. We've got to improvise."

Jay looked at Mr. Carter, and Mr. Carter started shaking his head. "Oh no...oh no...I'm not..."

"Pip Squeak's right. We have nothing else," he said. "Get out there, Phil, and tell them there was a mix-up and Ford and Paul can't be here. Apologize profusely, then announce the kids."

The orchestra director's head peeked over Jay's shoulder. "What key do you do it in, kid?" he asked. Charlie shrugged, so the director grabbed him and dragged him to the grand piano that was sitting behind the red curtain. Charlie played a couple of notes, then they hurried back offstage. The director made a beeline for the orchestra pit, and Charlie made a beeline for me.

Mr. Carter was still shaking his head, so Jay piped up, "Oh, for crying out loud." He grabbed the microphone and stand.

"Use Isabella Marlene!" I called to him as he pulled the red curtain open to head out. "That's my stage name. And it's Charlie Fry on the grand."

While Jay made apologies and tossed in a few jokes for good measure, Charlie stuck his hand in mine. "My stomach don't feel so good, Teaspoon," he said.

"Make yourself burp," I told him. And while Charlie swallowed and belched, I reminded him that it wouldn't be any different than playing *Live at the Starlight* at home. "Just keep your eyes on the piano keys, and play with your heart like you always do, Charlie."

"Teaspoon!"

I turned and there was Teddy in his new suit, weaseling his way through the crowd as easily as I could, being small and all. "Are you okay, Teaspoon? What happened?"

"Not now, Teddy," I said, "Listen. Me and Charlie are getting our intro."

"So without further ado, put your hands together and welcome a little lady who's bound to knock your socks off. Miss Isabella Marlene, with her pianist, Mr. Charlie Fry."

I was just about to head out when I noticed that the half-moon was still hanging, even if it should have been changed up an act ago. "Hey, Teddy," I called. "Tell Jay to drop the full moon." Then I squeezed Charlie's hand, gave him a grin, and said, "Let's go have our debut, Charlie."

I don't know why the crowd laughed while they clapped, when I tugged Charlie across the stage and set him down at the piano—maybe it was Charlie's high-water pants—but they did.

I got Charlie settled, then went to take my place, center-stage. I blinked against the stage lights, bright even with the center one out. And as I waited for the applause to die down, I looked up at the Starlight ceiling, blinking and twinkling, and I said in my head, and in my heart, *This is for you, Brenda. And for you, too, Ma.*

I paused a minute, took a big breath, lifted my shoulders up and perked my smile like you have to do when you're center-stage, and then I shouted, "Hit it, Charlie!"

That Charlie, he came in right on cue, and he didn't miss a note, even if he was playing a little on the slow side.

And sure enough, as I sang that first line, I felt the music going right down through me. Lifting that sad up and making my feet light enough to tap-dance. Well, if I *could* tap-dance, that is. So I just swayed to the music, my hands up, palms facing the crowd, sashaying a little this way, then that way, as I sang.

That music rose, going up over my heart to that place where you put your thoughts when you want to do the right thing, and opening my throat so that my voice rang out like church bells. By the middle of that first verse, you can bet it had carried every bit of that sad up to heaven so Jesus could hold it for me, leaving me with nothing to hold but those notes.

I sang the first verse, then turned my head quickly and shouted, "Pick up the tempo, Charlie!" snapping my fingers into the microphone so he'd know how fast he needed to go. There were a few chuckles, but that kid, he picked the beat up to perfect, like a little trouper. And then, man, we were cookin'!

Like magic, the orchestra joined in on the second verse. Boy, did me and Charlie sound professional with all those instruments behind us, the drummer's thumps and swishes making it easy for Charlie to keep time.

And that wasn't all! While Charlie was banging out the solo part with everything he had, Mimi Hines and Phil Ford came out on stage from the left, and Louis Prima and Keely Smith came out from the right. They stood beside me, but father back, and when I started singing the last verse, they joined in with harmony so good that even the angels had to be dancing.

By the end of the second chorus, that whole stage was filled up with every act we had in the show. The Sunshine Sisters in the back (probably because they didn't know the song, so who'd want them up front), and Mrs. Derby (who did know the song, but was singing Ethel-loud and not very splendored, so who'd want her up front, either), and the Farthings who danced across the stage, doing the jitterbug, I think, though not the Juicy kind.

I had my arms spread wide and my head back, the center-stage light shining bright in my eyes, as my voice climbed with the *ah, ah, ahs* for the big finish.

At the end of the last note, Mimi Hines reached for one of my hands, and Keely Smith reached for the other. But I shook their hands away and gave them the wait-a-second finger. Then, while the crowd roared, calling me back, I weaseled through the people on the stage, all the way back to the grand piano. I grabbed Charlie's hand.

Oh boy, was that something. Me and Charlie walking to center stage at the Starlight Theater while the crowd went nuts. Our hands clasped above our heads, while the rest of the acts did the same with their neighbors. A few camera flashes winked right along with the Starlight's stars before I said, "Okay, Charlie. Take a bow. Now!" And down we dipped as the crowd got to their feet.

ACKNOWLEDGMENTS

I'm grateful to have once again been given the chance to work with my editor, the exceptionally talented and committed Kerri Buckley, who lovingly guided this book through its many incarnations and served as the liaison between me and the rest of the fabulous Random House team: Nita Taublib, Jane von Mehren, Dennis Ambrose, Lynn Andreozzi, Paolo Pepe, Diane Hobbing, Laura Jorstad, and Katie Rudkin. And of course, to my amazing agent, Catherine Fowler, who is a joy to work with.

I am also indebted to the individuals who lent me their expertise in the areas of theater and music so that *How High the Moon* would be as authentic as possible: Erik O. Olson, Larry Kirchgaesner, Scott Fritsche, Roi Evans, Jason Paul Collum, and Brian Walker. Thanks also to Dixon, Debbi, Nadine, and Lynn at doyouremember.com, and to Karl Grube, who toured me through the Weill Center in Sheboygan, Wisconsin, the magical theater where I first met Teaspoon.

My appreciation, also, to my family and friends who lent me encouragement, support, and ideas: Kerry Kring, Shannon Kring, Jerry Ducommun, Lynn Kring, Sariah Daine, Sylvia Wollemann, Chris Pimental, Sugar Blue, Gayla Collins, Shelby Ehemann, and, most especially, Brenda Larson, my "feminine influence," who gave me the seed that grew this story and who passed away before it bloomed. I miss you, my wise, witty friend. Take good care of my little angels.

Last but not least, I'd like to thank the many individual readers, book clubs, and booksellers who share their love for my work with me, and with potential readers. Your enthusiasm and encouragement inspires me.

ABOUT THE AUTHOR

Sandra Kring lives in Wisconsin. Her debut novel, *Carry Me Home*, was a Book Sense Notable Pick and a 2005 Midwest Booksellers' Choice Award nominee. *The Book of Bright Ideas* was named to the New York Public Library's Books for the Teen Age list in 2007. Visit her on the Web at www.sandrakring.com.